SUMMER AT HOLLYHOCK HOUSE

Published by Sapere Books.

11 Bank Chambers, Hornsey, London, N8 7NN,
United Kingdom

saperebooks.com

ISBN: 978-1-912546-53-4

Chapter 1

'Happy birthday!'

Faith smiled dutifully as Joanna thrust a tastefully-wrapped parcel into her hands. 'Thank you.'

'Sorry we're late.' Joanna gestured at Eddie, who was shaking hands with Rob and muttering something about traffic. 'We got caught in the most awful tailback.'

Faith nodded, not really listening, as Rob's best friend's fiancée continued to explain the diversion they had taken in exhaustive detail. 'It was more of a long-cut than a short-cut,' she laughed, and Faith trilled along like she had never heard anything so funny.

'You're just in time for cake.' Rob ushered them into the flat. At the table — a white, plasticky identikit IKEA model with an implausible name, Shlaghaarten perhaps — Rob's friends Kate and Oliver were deep in discussion with his sister Sophia and her new boyfriend, who Faith thought was called Kev but it could have been Keith. 'We book on January 1 every year,' Kate was saying, 'that way we have something to look forward to.'

Rob disappeared into the kitchen and Faith half hoped he would stay there. She wasn't sure she could cope with another conversation about holiday destinations or property prices and the merits of new-builds versus project houses. 'But then you have to put up with workmen invading your space for an indefinite period,' Rob had sighed and Faith had disloyally thought that a house full of wisecracking labourers would brighten her day up quite considerably.

'I don't like new-builds,' she had grumbled.

'Faith grew up in a village,' Rob had explained to Keith or Kev or maybe it was Ken, rolling his eyes. 'She doesn't feel at home unless there's a rackety wind gusting through the place. Every day when I come home from work she's got all the windows open, and I have to go round shutting them.'

'Actually my parent's house isn't draughty,' she had corrected. It was stuffy and airless.

Suffocating, like this place.

Rob turned off the lights in the living room and came through holding a cake ablaze with pastel-coloured candles, illuminated like a miniature bonfire.

'Make a wish!' he urged as she blew them out.

I wish I could stop being so ungrateful, Faith thought, and then she thought she probably wished nothing of the sort, she just wished she was anywhere but here.

'How's the wedding planning going?' she asked Joanna as Rob cut the cake.

Joanna frowned. 'We've hit a glitch with the flowers.' She launched into a long and tedious explanation. 'We'll end up with nothing but a bunch of cactuses at this rate.'

'Cacti,' Faith said. 'Succulents.' They were succulent too, crazy and often phallic water-filled shapes with spines sticking out in all directions, refusing to allow all but the brave access to their beautifully soft, malleable interior.

Joanna didn't seem interested in discussing the mild onomatopoeia of succulence, so Faith turned her attention back to the cake.

'You next.' Joanna nudged her meaningfully.

Faith watched Rob fussing with the plates. He had some vanilla icing on his thumb, and he wiped it fastidiously on a paper napkin, carefully removing every trace. Rob's forehead beneath his sandy fringe was furrowed and his pale blue eyes were framed with equally pale sandy lashes. He was kind and considerate and pragmatic and they plodded along together quite easily, sharing few common interests but a comforting , routine-based rapport. She knew that after everybody had gone Rob would painstakingly plough through the piles of washing up before settling down on the sofa next to her to watch a movie of his choice and falling asleep twenty minutes in. *Netflix and no chill*, she thought wryly.

'We're saving for a house,' she said. 'No money for a wedding at the moment.'

Did she want to marry Rob?

Faith didn't want to think about it.

'Now then,' Rob announced, and Faith could tell by the way his left leg was tapping furiously against the floor that he was nervous about something. 'There's just one more thing.'

He dug around in his pocket again. Faith gulped.

Time seemed to slow down. The flickering light from the candles blurred together into a wavy haze of orange and yellow, tiny sparks shooting from the top, fireflies dancing on a summer's evening. Everything froze momentarily, other than the flames and Faith's heart, which was sinking into the pit of her churning stomach. There were a couple of gasps from the table, the sounds distorted and muted, then everything resumed at a normal tempo and he was walking over to her, his blue eyes unusually animated.

She stood up and he dropped down to one knee, proffering a small box which he opened to reveal a white-gold ring with a single, sparkling diamond set in the centre.

'Faith,' he said dramatically, 'will you marry me?'

No, she thought immediately.

Joanna was clutching Eddie's hand. Ken/Kev/Keith had put his arm around Sophia and Kate and Oliver were both beaming.

The room was still, everything poised, everybody waiting for her to say yes, everybody frozen in time again. No, not frozen, warped.

This is wrong, she thought. *It's all wrong.*

'We haven't talked about this,' she began.

'Just say yes,' Joanna urged.

Rob was still standing uselessly in front of her and Faith reached out and took the box from him. She studied the ring intently, wondering what on earth she could say, and eventually settled for: 'It's beautiful. Thank you.'

'Um, you're welcome?'

'Let's talk later.' She closed the box and handed it back to him.

'Well, it's getting late.' Oliver scrambled to his feet and Kate stood up with him. 'We should probably go...'

Through another chaotic, stop-start blur, Faith bid farewell to their friends and watched them, one after another, hastily collect their things and leave. Eddie was still talking about traffic and Faith practically shoved him out of the door. 'So glad you could make it. No, don't worry about being late in the slightest. These things happen. Good luck with the next fitting —' this to Joanna — 'and we'll see you all soon...'

She closed the door behind them and put her head against it.

'Are we going to talk about this?' Rob demanded from behind her.

'I'm just going to the loo.'

She locked the door firmly and sat down on the floor. She blinked a couple of times, watching the black and white tiles swimming in front of her eyes. Rob loved the tiles in the bathroom, the monochrome decor had been one of his favourite things about the flat when they'd come to view it just six months earlier.

It was their second home in a year, the first place they'd moved into together had been a little two-up, two-down on the outskirts of the commuter town in which they lived, and Rob had happily rammed it full to bursting with over-large IKEA furniture.

Funhaltert. Buzzkillen.

She'd thought if they moved somewhere a bit more central she might feel less terribly lonely. Rob had reluctantly agreed to move to the flat above one of the office buildings in the town centre. It didn't even have a garden, the most final of final insults, but at least he had got rid of some of the offending furniture.

But Faith still felt hopelessly stifled, hanging her head out of the bedroom window at night and wishing they hadn't moved after all because the flat didn't even have a balcony and she was starting to wonder what had been so wrong with the house and why she'd felt so unhappy there.

It wasn't the house, though. Or the flat. It wasn't the town, it wasn't the commute, it wasn't even the job. Well, it was, but the only reason she was living here and commuting and trying to get promoted at work was —

It was Rob.

She wasn't in love with him. She liked him, and they got along well enough, but she could already see their relationship was slowly heading into the realm of brother and sister.

And if she wasn't in love with him after three years, she was never going to be in love with him.

Oh god, she thought, *how am I going to tell him?*

She stood up and looked at herself in the mirror. Did she look twenty-six? She didn't feel it. She still felt about seventeen, and Rob was forever telling her she acted it. Given all that had happened back then she wasn't entirely sure she wasn't in some kind of arrested development, frozen in time herself, forever suspended in a world that insisted it would keep on turning.

Rob took it badly. Faith was a little surprised, because when she started to think about it the warning signs were plentiful. The fact they never really went out anymore, barring the odd ghastly dinner party with his mates. Always his, because he didn't like the friends she grew up with or the girls with whom she used to ride track bikes. The fact they barely had sex and worse, that she didn't actually mind. The way he was always going on at her about money, and had decided for both of them that it was time to save for a deposit without considering that she might not be so keen to put down roots here. The way he nagged her, chiding her for riding her bike on busy roads and for wandering around with her head in the clouds as if she were a naughty child. The way she reverted, inevitably, to type and found herself digging in as stubbornly as a teenager.

'We're not right for each other. You and me. Can't you see it?'

'No.' He looked utterly pathetic and she felt a sudden stab of wild irritation with him.

'We don't like any of the same things,' she snapped. 'We don't *want* the same things —'

'I just want to be with you,' Rob protested.

No, you don't, she thought. *But it's easier just to stay where we are and as you're always telling me, 'anything for a quiet life'. I don't want a quiet life. I want a noisy, rowdy one. I had one, once.*

'I think I should go back to my parents' house for a few days,' she said eventually.

'Just for a few days. You're sure? Just a few days?'

Faith was silent.

'I'm tired.' Of course he was tired, it was past ten pm. 'Let's go to bed.'

'I'll be in in a bit,' she said, but she knew she wouldn't.

Once Rob had gone to bed she reached for her phone and checked it automatically, before scrolling mindlessly through Facebook.

Her eyes fell on a few photographs Minel had uploaded, and Faith sent her a quick text saying she would be around for a few days and did she want to meet for a drink?

Then she texted Sara the same thing.

Faith had met Minel and Sara when she moved to Westchester — the village Rob had scorned — as a teenager. Somehow their friendship had survived the happenings of the year before Faith turned eighteen that had seen her withdraw from everything she once held dear. Minel, otherwise engaged at teacher training college and wrapped up with her now-husband Paul, had been too distracted to notice Faith's absence and Sara had been equally preoccupied with work. They in turn had just assumed Faith had too much on her plate with exams and leaving for university to probe too much into the reasons why they saw so little of her.

Despite her initial fears Faith had managed to keep in touch with Minel and Sara after she moved away, and salvage something of their closeness. But she couldn't say the same of the third of her former best friends, the one who had once been the closest of them all and the one from whom she had salvaged absolutely nothing.

She hadn't seen or heard from Rik since she left Westchester.

Which was proof, Faith thought through the familiar creeping sadness that had nothing to do with the man whose proposal she had just turned down, that the first cut really is the deepest.

Her phone bleeped. Minel had texted back.

I can't wait! Got something to ask you. S says she can't wait either. Let us know when you're here! Xx

Faith was suddenly desperate to see her friends again, needing some of Minel's comforting wisdom and Sara's down-to-earth wisecracks. She already knew that Minel would be concerned and understanding and try and fix everything for her, and Sara would tell her to look on the bright side, at least she could go out on the pull again.

Faith set off early, in her battered Land Rover that seemed to infuriate Rob so much. 'Why don't you just buy a Ford Fiesta?' he demanded repeatedly but Faith couldn't bear to part with the car, which she had worked so hard to acquire just before she left for university. It was about the only connection she had to her once-idyllic teenage years that didn't come with a hefty wrench to the heart, and she hung onto it in the vain hope she may one day find herself in need of a car that could churn through mud and pull trailers full of gardening equipment, although she conceded that was increasingly unlikely.

The ancient car certainly wasn't the easiest drive on the motorway, rattling in protest if she tried to push it over 50mph. Faith turned the radio up to drown out the noise. A singer was warbling about his teenage girlfriend, wondering where she was now. She switched the radio off and scowled.

Her parents still lived in the same house she had grown up in and it was both comforting and oppressive. Jeff and Judith had been at pains to emphasise that she was welcome home at any time and while their family dynamic had continued to fluctuate, the walls of her bedroom had stayed resolutely the same. It was still covered in the wood chipped wallpaper she had painted a cheery yellow after that final wonderful, awful summer, in need of a project to distract herself.

Her mother was sitting at the kitchen table drinking a cup of tea when Faith walked in, and she looked up and pursed her lips in a tight, disapproving version of what passed for a smile. Judith — always Judith, never Jude or Judy — Coombes was impeccably turned-out, a stark contrast to Faith who had never really shed her teenage habit of dressing for adventure, not aesthetic, and who frequently forgot to brush her black curls. Judith's once-dark hair was now tinted a discreet ash blonde and hung in a heat-straightened, shining curtain that stopped at her well-defined jaw.

'Hi Mum.' Faith headed straight to the kettle and switched it on. 'Where's Dad?'

'Still asleep,' Judith said. 'He had a late one with his golf buddies.' For a second a flicker of something approaching sadness drifted across her face, then just as quickly it was gone. 'It's lovely to finally see you.' Faith felt a twinge of guilt at the hint of accusation in her mother's tone. 'Are you staying long?'

'Maybe.'

Faith busied herself making tea as her mother watched silently, and then sat down at the table. She knew her mother wholeheartedly approved of Rob, considering him a stabilising influence on her somewhat wayward daughter. Being unmarried at twenty-six made nobody wayward in Faith's book, but her mother had always thought her a complete tearaway and pushed her strongly in the direction of anything she thought might help 'calm her down'.

Rob certainly had. He'd practically sent her to sleep, draining her energy away like a squishy, aged sofa.

'Why hasn't Rob come too?'

Faith took a sip of tea. 'We're taking some time apart.' She blew on her tea meditatively. 'Splitting up,' she confessed. 'We've split up.'

'Oh Faith.' Her mother's face softened.

What would it be like, Faith thought, if she could just confide in her mother the way her friends all seemed to be able to talk to theirs? If she could have rung Judith and said, 'Mum, I feel like a forty-six year old woman trapped inside the body of somebody twenty years younger' and if Judith could have just listened, without judging or telling her to 'pull herself together' or going off into a long lecture about the plight of others the world over and how Faith should be grateful for the fact she had a roof over her head and somebody with whom to share it.

If she could have said to her, 'I feel like I'm trudging through life robotically and nothing seems to have worked out the way I thought it would. The respectable job, the sensible boyfriend, the stability I've embraced have only made me feel more lost than ever before, and I increasingly don't even recognise myself. I don't know who I am anymore.'

And if her mother could have said to her, 'Well think about it Faith, when did things change?' And she would say, 'I know exactly when it all changed, it changed one sunny morning in September after I had come home two weeks earlier forever altered and found you sitting at this kitchen table in the exact same spot you are now and you told me —' *and that's why I can't talk to her*, Faith thought, *because it all comes back to that, and I still can't take myself, or her, back there.*

'I'm sorry to hear that,' Judith said when Faith didn't elaborate further. 'I thought you and Rob were very well suited.'

'So did he,' Faith sighed. 'He proposed.' Her mother didn't look quite surprised enough. 'Did he come and talk to Dad?'

'He did,' Judith confirmed.

It was the sort of old-fashioned thing Rob would do. Come and ask her father for her hand in marriage. In a way it was sweet, but Faith had always been quite adamant that she wasn't anybody's property, least of all her father's. She had thought Rob must have known that.

'Your father told him we'd be delighted to welcome him into our family,' Judith said.

'That's very sweet of you,' Faith said, thinking what Judith had really meant was 'hand her over'. 'I'm not sure I feel the same way.'

'I was hoping you'd come home so we could start planning,' Judith admitted and Faith felt another stab of guilt and annoyance.

She wasn't entirely sure she wanted to get married at all, but definitely not to Rob. She'd always thought if she did get married, it would be kind of cool to just take off and do it on a whim someday, admittedly with the person she wanted to spend the rest of her life with. She was probably too old for Gretna Green now, but once upon a time she might have considered eloping romantic and a bit crazy.

The problem was, there was only really one person she'd ever met who would have thought that way of tying the knot was fitting and she hadn't seen *him* since they were Gretna Green age.

'Not this time,' Faith said to Judith ruefully.

'Are you going to move back here?'

The ultimate insult, bouncing back home to Mummy and Daddy with all her worldy goods, which didn't amount to much, crammed into the open back of the Land Rover. She'd have to pay her share of the rent until the lease on the flat was up and she couldn't afford two sets on her salary on top of the monstrous price of a train ticket.

And if she used her savings, which Rob had been hoping would eventually become a deposit, that would be the end of any prospect of her retraining. She still remembered Rob's outrage when he'd found some of her prospectuses for horticultural colleges and waved them at her as accusingly as if he'd walked in on her shagging somebody else on the IKEA *Caffeinegulpen* coffee table. He had not supported her increasing desire for a career change, and made it clear living with a penniless, permanently exhausted garden design student didn't sound like an enticing prospect.

'Maybe just for a bit,' Faith said, hoping she didn't sound too ungrateful, 'if you don't mind. We can talk about it later. I'm going to meet Minel at Hollyhock House.' She wondered what Minel wanted to ask her. She had texted suggesting she come to Hollyhocks for lunch and although Faith had been surprised not to be invited to Paul and Minel's own house instead, she wasn't going to turn down the opportunity to nosy round Hollyhocks again. She hadn't been back there often.

Not often, since one sunlit, enchanted morning.

'Will you be back for dinner?'

'I'll let you know. But Mum, please don't worry. I can sort myself out. You don't have to change any of your plans for me.'

'It's not a problem, Faith,' Judith smiled kindly. 'This is your home.'

No it isn't, Faith thought, but she managed not to say it.

Chapter 2

Hollyhock House sat in a slight valley, well away from the quiet, pothole-laden country lane that saw, at most, eight vehicles per day during 'rush hour'. Just before the most concealed of entrances was a hump-backed bridge that presided loftily over an impetuously babbling stream making its excitable way across the border between Hollyhocks and its immediate neighbours.

It was proof, Faith thought as she steered the wheezing Land Rover around the familiar curves and bends, swerving to avoid the worst of the potholes and failing to notice several new ones, that the richer a person was, the harder their house was to find. The first time she had come to Hollyhocks she had spent what felt like hours cycling along this tree-lined lane, bouncing backwards and forwards over the bridge, disturbing its resident and very irate heron. Up and down she'd ridden, squinting for a sign amongst the lush green verges which had been liberally scattered with frothy heads of cow parsley, crowding together like parties of fairies in their milky white dresses.

The tiny sign itself was now almost invisible behind a rambunctious clematis Montana tangling seductively with a wisteria which had in turn long obliterated the delicate white arch once erected to support its rapacious tendrils. The lettering, ornate and all but impossible to read, was more sun-bleached than ever, in fact it seemed to have faded into nothingness.

The gravel drive was even more cratered than the lane she, Minel and Rik had fatuously entitled 'the big road'. She crawled past the familiar copse to the right and the lowering cherry laurel hedge to the left, wincing as she saw how out of control the toxic plant had become. It wasn't as if one needed additional privacy out here, she mused. Hollyhocks was so set back you'd need a helicopter and binoculars if you wanted to peep inside.

Faith pulled up at the end of the gravel drive. She admired her friends' childhood home for a moment, as it basked in the late afternoon sunshine. Mournful recognition seemed to be creeping up from the ground, separated from her skin only by a pair of battered Converse. Faith pressed her feet against the rubber soles, hoping they would ward it off. Hollyhocks might be ready to welcome back one of its lost children but she wasn't sure she could bear to open her heart in return.

It was another hallmark of rich people's homes, she thought to distract herself, that you couldn't even tell what they looked like close up. The pale golden walls and low roof poked out enticingly from variegated ivy, fragrant jasmine, showy Virginia creeper and rambling roses, interspersed with the jaunty spikes of hollyhocks and foxgloves.

To the side, behind the jumble of kitchen backing on to the conservatory and steps down to the utility room, the lawns were more formal and sweeping, although now liberally flecked with dandelions. At the end, glimmering azure, lay the swimming pool that had been put in, irritatingly, after Faith had moved away. Paul had parked some of his work vehicles next to it, near to the greenhouse and vegetable patch and the crumbling stone wall in front of the hay barn.

And behind the house, through the low arch in another stone wall, was the cottage Minel and Rik had shared. Rik had told her that when he and Minel's parents first moved here they had no idea of the existence of the little building, as it was completely obscured by ivy, brambles and climbing weeds. It was only one day when Minel and Rik's father Ravi had decided to take a pair of secateurs to the mess of green that he had discovered the cottage underneath.

Once upon a time it must have been used by the farm hands, when the land surrounding it had been cultivated, but nobody had farmed here for generations and the copse had run wild. Helena and Ravi had sold off the remaining pasture to the neighbours, who turned it into a tennis court.

'Faith!' She looked up at the sound of Minel's voice and beamed as her friend came spilling out of the door, followed by a wildly barking ball of sandy-coloured fluff.

'Hello,' Faith said, bending down to stroke the yapping puppy, feeling a wrench of recognition. 'No need to question this one's lineage.'

Minel laughed. 'Tackle to the core.'

Tackle had been the neighbours' dog, an ill-mannered wire-haired terrier cross. A creature of instinct, he was feared far and wide for his savage nature and monstrous libido and would attack or hump just about anything that moved.

Ignored by his legal owners, Tackle adopted Rik, spending more time at Hollyhocks than his own home. The rest of the time he wandered far and wide, slowly but surely impregnating every bitch in the village.

Faith and Rik used to rub their hands together with glee whenever a gleaming 4x4 stormed up the long and not-at-all potholed track to next door, knowing it would contain a yelling Westchester resident and a heavily pregnant dog.

As a result, ferocious wire-haired puppies sprang up all over the village and given that Tackle's wandering genes passed down from generation to generation as a blueprint and he had an equally undesirable habit of siring mainly males, the unstoppable cycle continued.

Was Tackle still around? Faith thought hopefully. It had been nine years, but he had only been young, three or four at the most, when she had known him.

'I think even the foxes around here are half wire-haired,' Minel sighed, scooping up the still-yapping puppy. 'I don't know what possessed me, taking this little one on.'

Faith did and she scanned her friend eagerly, desperate for any sign of a swelling in the belly, a fullness in her breasts or some sort of glow. Minel, catching her looking, shook her head.

'Come on in and have a cup of tea,' Minel urged, leading Faith into the long, heavily-beamed kitchen. She gestured to her friend to sit at one end of the scrubbed wooden table and shoved a pile of chintzy-looking magazines with titles like *House Beautiful* and *Your Vintage Home* out of the way.

'So, what do you want to ask me?' Faith said as Minel poured boiling water into two cream-and-blue striped mugs with heavy cracks down the enamel handles. 'How come you're living here at the moment? Where are your folks?'

'They're off on a cruise all summer,' Minel said. 'It's their thirty-fifth wedding anniversary next year and they're celebrating it in style already.'

'Good for them,' Faith said.

'Anyway that's what I wanted to talk to you about. We want to give them something really special, something that I know they've always wanted.' Minel's eyes were shining. 'So I've talked to Paul and he's agreed to take the summer off to build them a summerhouse.'

'Why don't you just buy one from the garden centre?' Faith asked.

Minel looked horrified. 'I'm not talking some glorified wooden shed,' she said. 'A proper one. Bricks — or rather, stone — and mortar. Wired and plumbed, a little refuge where they can store their swimming gear and have a cup of tea and sit and watch the world go by.'

And an expensive one, Faith thought, although money wasn't something her friend had ever had to worry about, and she supposed Paul would take care of all the labouring.

'We're going to put it at the top of the swimming pool,' Minel said.

A solitary bumblebee buzzed loftily past and disappeared out of the open front door.

'Really?' Faith frowned. 'But that would mean uprooting the rockery and filling the pond and —'

'And that's why I need you,' Minel interrupted. 'I need somebody to redo the garden.'

Faith opened her mouth to protest and Minel held up her hand. 'I know what you're going to say, but I don't want to hire any old gardener. I want *you*. You know this place better than pretty much anyone. In fact, I'm sure you and Rik were responsible for the pond in the first place.'

Faith nodded, hoping she hadn't flinched.

'So I want you to be the one to redesign it. My parents love the garden, Faith, they love how much of it came from your ideas and suggestions. They wouldn't let anybody else loose on it.'

Faith wouldn't want to let anybody else loose on Hollyhocks either, but the thought of coming here to take on such a mammoth task was as overwhelming as it was enticing.

'I'm not qualified. I'd have no idea where to start and I'm really out of touch.'

Minel shrugged. 'You'll do an amazing job.'

That straightforward confidence, Faith thought wistfully, could have just as easily come from Rik. Minel and her brother had always been so very different, separated in age by just two years but worlds apart in every other sense.

They looked nothing alike, Minel with her olive skin, delicately pretty face and hazel eyes took after their English mother and Rik's darker colouring and bolder features came straight from their Indian father. Their personalities were just as contrasting, Minel so gentle, sensible and down-to-earth compared to her hyper, reckless younger brother. Once upon a time Faith had thought Rik's wilder nature the most exciting of his many appealing qualities, until she had found herself shattered to pieces by it.

Faith herself had always occupied something of the middle ground between the two. Over time she had noticed more and more reminders of Rik's personality in Minel and occasionally even momentary flashes of physical resemblance that made her stomach jump and her heart beat a little faster.

Maybe I'm just projecting, she thought, because she's all of him I have left and she reminds me of who I thought he was, before he showed his true colours.

She felt a soft nudge at her ankles and reached down then abruptly removed her hand, wincing, as Tackle's grandson buried his needle-like teeth firmly in the base of her thumb.

'And I have a job.'

'Don't you get holiday?'

Faith wondered why she was still protesting. She already knew there was no way she could say no. The prospect of swapping her stuffy, air-conditioned office for a summer with her oldest friends landscaping Hollyhocks was utterly irresistible, even if it would mean she had to face some all-singing, all-dancing demons.

'Yeah, I can take holiday. Or unpaid leave. I can have the whole summer if needs be, everything pretty much shuts down.'

'I'll pay you,' Minel said immediately.

'You don't have to.'

'Yes I do, and that's the end of it.'

Faith thought for a moment. 'I'll stay with my parents I guess.' At least if she was busy here all day she'd be too tired to force herself to spend much time with them.

'You can stay here with Paul and I. There's plenty of space.'

'It's OK. I don't want to impose.'

'Won't Rob mind you spending the summer here?' Minel asked.

'Probably,' Faith admitted, 'but I'm fairly certain he minds the fact that he proposed to me and I said no, broke up with him and came here the next day a lot more.'

'What?!'

Faith sighed. 'You'd better make some more tea.'

'Sounds like you could do with some time away,' Minel said after Faith had poured out her tale of woe. 'Or rather, some time here. I know you're usually too busy to come and visit, but I do know how much you love it here.'

Faith looked out of the window. She could see the pool, glinting in the mid-morning sun. Paul was wandering around checking on a cement mixer.

'I did love it here,' she said slowly.

Her eyes drifted to the cork notice-board Helena and Ravi had covered with photographs; of themselves, of Minel and Paul, of Rik and Minel, most of them as children, a few as teenagers and a few more as adults. Rik was looking away from the camera in all but one of the photos. Typical Rik, she thought, refusing to co-operate just to irritate his parents. But in one of the photographs, which must have been taken a few years after she'd left, his eyes were fixed straight on the camera and he was smiling that radiant smile that lit up and transformed his face. Faith felt her heart contract and she forced her eyes away.

'What made your parents buy this place?' she asked Minel, not wanting to dwell on Rik any more. She'd never actually had that conversation with Helena and Ravi. It had been overgrown back then and probably in quite a lot of disrepair. There are project houses, she thought, and then there's this place.

'They must have thought it had a lot of potential,' Minel said. 'But you know my mum. She told me that they hadn't so much chosen this place, as it chose them. She said from the moment they set foot on the drive she could just *feel* it, like the place was telling them they had to come here.' She rolled her eyes. 'My dad and I used to laugh at her for it, but she was absolutely adamant. I think she had a lot more of an audience for all that rubbish in Rik.'

She would have done, Faith thought. Rik wasn't anywhere near as fanciful as her but he had spent enough time on this land, getting to know it and later shape it, to have cultivated a far stronger sense of place than his sister. Minel was never really one for immersing herself in the world around her the way she and Rik did. Her friend preferred to establish and abide by the rules than test and experiment with them. She's a born teacher, Faith thought, she found her vocation — and her husband — early on, and she's never had to question either of them.

'It surprises all of us that he hardly ever comes back here,' Minel added absently.

24

It surprised Faith too. She hadn't been able to bear coming back, not for many years, but Rik had no reason to stay away.

She supposed she would have to get used to Hollyhocks without him, even if she wasn't entirely sure how one could exist without the other. And she knew there would be memories waiting around every corner to assault her, emotions swirling just below the surface that she hadn't ever allowed to see the light of day. She still had no idea how she was meant to deal with them.

'Why doesn't he?'

'Too busy chasing adventures elsewhere, I suppose.' Minel shrugged. 'He travels a lot, and he's got himself some super-hot girlfriend up in London, although how she puts up with him constantly flitting about I don't know.'

Faith flinched again. 'What does he do?'

'He's a graphic artist,' Minel said. 'You can ask him yourself,' she carried on, still watching the puppy who was now gambolling at the end of the lawn, chasing an invisible quarry. 'He'll be here next Monday.'

Faith's stomach lurched, and she felt the hairs on her arms beginning to stand on end. 'Huh?'

'He's coming to help Paul,' Minel said. 'I wasn't sure I'd be able to talk him into it actually, but I didn't have to work too hard to persuade him in the end. He works freelance so he can stay here and help Paul with the labouring. We can't manage this alone and we couldn't afford to pay anybody other than a few local teenagers. At least I've saved him the trouble of having to think of a present for Mum and Dad himself.'

Faith gripped the table, watching her knuckles whiten.

'You don't mind, do you?' Minel asked. 'I just assumed — you guys were so close once, I thought it would be nice to have us all together again. I'm sure he's looking forward to catching up with you.'

I'm sure he isn't, Faith thought darkly. 'He knows I'm coming?'

'Of course,' Minel said. 'Why would that be an issue?'

Faith felt momentarily annoyed at her friend. How could she not know it would be an issue? Oh right, because she'd never told her, and from Minel's easy tone she assumed Rik hadn't either. Good as his word on that, at least, she thought wryly.

'It's not an issue,' she said firmly.

'So is next Monday OK?' Minel asked. 'You can sort out work and get ready to make a start?'

It wasn't OK in the slightest. But leaving Rob had left her with a definite sense of needing something — anything — to change. Maybe addressing the still unfinished business of Rik would help.

Chapter 3

When Faith arrived at Hollyhocks the following Monday morning she noted with alarm that her heart seemed to have upped sticks and moved into her mouth. It had been kicking around in that general vicinity all week, and as she'd stared blankly at her computer screen, listening to her boss grumble about the wildly late notice she was giving for her unpaid leave, she had put Rik's name into Facebook over and over again, but not once had she been able to hit 'enter'.

I can't even look at him on a computer, she realised. How on earth am I going to look at him in the flesh?

It had been bad enough going over the plans with Paul, because they had been annotated in Rik's unmistakeable spiky hand and Faith had felt like she'd taken a physical blow to the solar plexus. She had nodded gormlessly as Paul explained she would need to drain and fill in the pond and dig a new one, then move the rockery to the other end, and finally work through the borders and vegetable garden before finishing by re-turfing and removing the dandelions from the yellow speckled lawns.

She had nodded again when Paul had admitted sheepishly he and Minel hadn't maintained the garden since Ravi and Helena pushed off because they assumed it would all get trashed by the construction work anyway.

She only remembered later that dandelion roots were absolute monsters, invasive and dogged, insinuating themselves into the ground and taking hold so firmly that she'd broken many a fork and trowel trying to remove them. The lawn was a good day's work in itself, heaving all of those up and then removing every last tendril so they couldn't simply start the cycle all over again.

As she surveyed the mature borders and climbers, the Alpine plants spilling jubilantly out of the rockery, obscuring the stones almost completely, the suddenly enormous-looking, very deep pond, flecked with the diminutive green leaves of duckweed, and the relentless dandelions turning the lawns from acid-green to jaunty yellow, she half thought about getting back into the Land Rover and going home again.

There was so much to do — an overwhelming amount of work, most of it intensely physical, and she didn't have a clue where to begin.

I'm going to need an army, she thought frantically as her head reeled with the enormity of the task ahead of her. She bent down idly to stroke Minel's new puppy, which had rocked up and was sniffing eagerly at her ankle. She would go round to the site, she decided, and see if Paul was willing to discuss getting her some help, and if Rik was there she would just — well, she'd cross that bridge when she came to it.

She could hear a great deal of high-pitched giggling and lots of general rowdy hubbub. Turning the corner past the stone wall, she found a rabble of excited-looking teenage boys spilling all over the patch of already broken turf Paul had marked out with pegs and string, shifting and lurching all over the place in constant collective motion, occasionally cannoning off each other, dropping the butts of hand-rolled cigarettes and eating rather a lot of crisps.

Minel's puppy had followed her and he leaped yapping out onto the site, whirling around and around, his head going this way and that, his eyes popping out of his little head at all the excitement of so many new people. 'Come here,' Faith yelled at him, as he belted around snapping at ankles, hoovering up crisps and throwing himself bodily in the air to reach the packets. 'Come *here*!'

Paul, who was by the cement mixer, had noticed the commotion. 'Get him out of here,' he called to Faith. 'Take him back to the house.'

The little terrier, however, was so hopelessly worked up Faith couldn't get her hands around him. Every time she got close he would spy somebody new to harangue and whisk away, barking his tiny head off, then he vanished altogether.

'He went that way,' Paul said, gesturing towards the drive. Faith hurtled down it, desperate to stop the puppy before he reached the main road. She scanned the drive anxiously then spied the puppy sniffing about at the edge of the copse and shot forward, scooping him up into her arms and chiding him affectionately.

'You gave me a scare,' she murmured. The puppy, entirely unconcerned, squirmed happily in her arms and rolled over, proffering up his belly to be scratched.

Faith smiled. 'You are a charmer,' she sighed, rubbing the soft fur and watching the expression of unfiltered joy on the puppy's little face. From this angle his needle-like teeth were visible in his jaws and the resemblance to Tackle was so uncanny the hairs on the back of her arms began to prickle and a wave of something indefinable yet oddly familiar washed over her. It was almost déjà vu and she blinked and examined him a little closer, to reassure herself she hadn't accidentally scooped up an aged and shrunken Tackle instead.

But the terrier in her arms was still a puppy.

The person who had materialised by her side, however, was very much a grown adult. She hadn't seen or heard a thing but she would have known Rik was standing next to her if she'd been blindfolded and had her ears plugged.

Faith's heart, already roused by the sprint to the drive, cannoned back into her mouth and her stomach twisted and shot upwards too, and she wondered for a terrifying moment if she was going to be sick. She leaned forward automatically, clutching the puppy, and took a couple of deep breaths. The hairs on her arms were now standing fully on end like the spines on a cactus. The puppy, feeling her hands tighten too much on his furry body, yelped.

'Hi Faith,' Rik said, glancing at her and then dropping his eyes to the puppy before passing them straight over her to a point in the middle distance. 'Minel said you'd be here.' He didn't sound thrilled about it, but he didn't sound disappointed either. He just sounded matter-of-fact. 'Long time no see.'

'Yes,' she said breathlessly. No see indeed, but now she was seeing and it was an almost unbearable combination of feeling like she was seeing him for the first time but also, that she'd last been with him just yesterday. He had always been tall, but he had filled out since she'd last seen him and underneath his fairly close-fitting black t-shirt she could see his lean, streamlined muscles had become more defined. But not too much, she noted before she could help herself, he still looked like he would move gracefully and silently, which he clearly did given that she hadn't heard him approaching. Still a ninja, she thought with a bittersweet combination of relief and pain. His jaw was darkened by stubble but she could still see his almost haughty bone structure underneath, and his thick eyelashes still curled relentlessly upwards over his very dark brown eyes, eyes she'd once thought she could read like a book. But there was no trace of the restless energy he'd always carried around with him, the sense he was working very hard to stay still. That had been replaced by a more forceful presence altogether and she could practically feel the heat emanating from him.

'She said you'd be here too,' Faith said, her voice sounding distant and unfamiliar to her own ears.

He nodded. 'I do live here,' he said as if she didn't already know that. 'At least, I used to. Paul wanted some help. From somebody older than sixteen.'

His eyes finally met hers. Faith could almost hear her heart hammering away in her chest and her lungs were squashed and constricted, like she needed to yawn to draw in enough oxygen.

'OK then,' he said. She steeled herself and forced her face into an expressionless mask. 'I'd better get going. See you later.' And as quickly as he had appeared, he was gone.

Faith gaped at the empty space beside her.

That was all she was going to get, nine years of absence and heartbreak and it was just 'see you later'?

She stood motionless for a few moments, expecting Rik to come back so they could pick up their conversation, but then the puppy started squirming and wriggling in her arms and she supposed she'd better take him and herself back to the garden.

As she wandered past the site she could hear loud guffaws and was half tempted to stop and see what all the ruckus was about, but she suddenly didn't feel like putting herself at the mercy of Paul and a bunch of teenagers in front of Rik. She trailed on and set the puppy down on the grass, then looked into the murky depths of the pond.

He'll come over in a bit, she told herself reassuringly. *Or I'll go down to the site and grab him and we can take a few minutes. He's not just going to leave me hanging like that, not Rik, that's not how he is.*

How he *was*.

Chapter 4

This, Faith thought as she stared at the half-drained depths of the pond, the disturbed water swirling darker and murkier than ever, is a total nightmare.

She put her lips around the end of the hose pipe again and sucked as hard as she could, pulling and pulling until she was completely out of puff and then clamped her thumb over the end of the pipe, preventing any more air from leeching its way inside and undoing her good work. She took a few deep breaths and returned to the attack.

Her face was burning and her eyes were practically bugging out of her head with the effort as she sucked once again, drawing the painfully tenderised flesh on the inside of her cheeks against her teeth as she coaxed the reluctant water ever closer to her mouth. This was the third time she'd had to restart the siphon this morning and it was getting harder to create the necessary vacuum between the hose and the water. She gave it one last, almighty suck and felt filthy pond water flooding into her mouth, and she flung the hose down triumphantly and watched the dark greeny-brown liquid begin to pump out of the other end. She spat out the liquid, grimacing, and seized a bottle of water, rinsing out her mouth and spitting that out onto the lawn too. Then she ran the hose down to the nearest drain, listening to the contents of the pond gush into the depths below.

Thank Christ that was over. Now, back to the nightmare.

This wasn't panning out at all as she had expected. She was already way behind, completely thrown after seeing Rik again and her parents were acting weirder and more stilted than ever.

Faith could have cut the atmosphere at home with a knife, in fact she'd been half tempted to just to see if there was anything alive in there. Judith and Jeff made polite conversation over dinner, but it would all become strained and Faith felt sure it was loaded with double-meanings.

I know all about double meanings, she thought, I specialised in them once. Something's going on. But she couldn't put her finger on it and any time she asked her mother Judith insisted she was fine and returned to drinking her apparently bottomless cup of tea.

She had barely seen Minel, who was finishing up at school before the summer holidays and seemed tired and distracted. Preoccupied, no doubt, by her and Paul's struggle to conceive, and Faith wished more than anything she could say or do something to help, but she felt it would be tactless to inquire and Minel seemed reluctant to discuss it much.

At least she had Sara, or so she'd thought. But the one time she'd seen her usually wisecracking friend she was vacant and distant and even looked different, like she was fading round the edges. Sara had always been so earthy and vibrant, a glorious ruby-red rose, sexy and provocative but sweet to the very core. But her petals were curling and drying out at the edges. She had deeper lines over her forehead than Faith remembered, her usually shiny dark hair was distinctly less glossy and Faith had even spotted the odd tell-tale flash of grey at the roots.

Sara was the one person Faith had thought she could rely on to provide a positive, sassy spin on her current dismal situation, even if it would mean she had to avoid mentioning the suddenly extremely pressing situation with Rik.

What was she going to do about Rik?

She wasn't sure what she'd expected from him. Defensiveness, maybe. An awkward, strained atmosphere. That would have been fine, she could handle a strained atmosphere. She could have handled it — very nicely — if he'd just tried to turn it all into a big joke. In fact she could have handled anything, anything at all, except — nothing.

A big, fat, gaping great hole of nothing.

He'd looked disinterested and mildly affronted any time she'd crossed his path, dismissing her with a nod or shake of his head or making an entirely boring, closed statement and turning away. His eyes always seemed to be elsewhere and if he was forced to look in her direction, he looked straight through her as if she wasn't even there.

It's almost like he's annoyed with me, she thought in bewilderment, or he's blaming me for something. And if he is, if he's really trying to turn this all around onto me and make out it's somehow my fault we haven't spoken in nine years then he's prepared to stoop even lower than I thought he would.

The worst part was, it actually seemed to be working. Faith found she couldn't ignore him. She had fully intended to occupy the moral high ground and remain cool and distant and composed and watch him slowly become more agitated until eventually he would just spit it all out, like the cold, rancid pond water she had just spat onto the grass. And then she could have made an informed decision about whether or not she was prepared to allow him any wiggle-room into her life or finally tell him straight that he'd disappointed her beyond all repair. Either way, she would be able to feel the weight of whatever Rik-related trauma she'd been carrying around with her all these years lift away, leaving her free to carry on with her life as if he were nothing but a minor blot in the far distant horizon.

But as it was she found herself scanning his face desperately for a flicker of recognition, for a moment of warmth, for just the slightest inkling that she'd once meant something to him. The blanker and more inscrutable he became, the more anxious she was to prove to him and to herself that she had at one point mattered to him, and belonged here at Hollyhocks.

And then there was the small matter of her disloyal eyes.

Are you that shallow, she fumed at herself, that despite everything he put you through you're sidetracked by the fact that he's still hot? Hotter than ever, her eyes would insist, he's turned it up by several degrees, don't you think?

'It must be nice for you guys, catching up again,' Minel, who had popped home for lunch and unwittingly saved Faith from yet another predictable and borderline troubling argument with her own ocular nerves, remarked. They both watched Rik cycle off down the gravel drive, bouncing the bike slightly to test his suspension. 'Aren't you joining him for a lunchtime jaunt?'

He hasn't offered, Faith wanted to say. 'He seems quite busy,' she said by way of explanation. 'We haven't really talked much.'

'He's got loads of work on,' Minel said guiltily. 'He's straight back over to the cottage after dinner, burning the midnight oil. He never complains,' she said quickly, 'you know Rik.'

I don't, Faith wanted to scream, *I don't know this shell of a stranger at all. He looks like Rik and sounds like Rik and moves like Rik but I get the feeling if I put my hand on his shoulder it would just crumble and disintegrate beneath my fingers — he would turn to dust.*

Sara had turned up and as she walked over, cackling to herself about something, Faith's face lifted. Maybe Sara had just been tired the other day, she thought hopefully, and now she's back to normal she can inject some much-needed comic relief into this otherwise joyless situation.

But whatever it was that had amused Sara, it had faded by the time she joined them. 'Hey,' she said wearily. 'What's for lunch?'

'Sandwiches,' Minel said. 'Come up to the house. It looks like a bakery in there.'

Half-cut loaves of bread and various fillings were cluttering up the marbled countertops. Minel scraped together some offcuts and dumped a plate unceremoniously in the middle of the table. 'I made fifteen rounds of sandwiches for those teenagers this morning,' she said. 'You guys can just take what you're given.'

'So Faith,' Sara said, still in that same weary tone. 'You never did tell me what happened with Rob other than you saying "I don't" to his offer of "I do".'

'It just ran its course,' Faith said. 'With hindsight I should have ended it when we moved, but I thought I should work at it. It turns out,' she said glumly, 'that's not the kind of work a relationship needs. You shouldn't have to work at wanting to be with somebody.'

'Was it that bad?' Minel asked sympathetically.

Faith shrugged. 'It wasn't bad. It was just boring. So boring.' She chewed on a particularly thick crust reflectively. 'We were more like brother and sister, and not in a fun, having adventures together kind of way.'

'I never had adventures with Rik,' Minel said, wrinkling her nose a little at the thought. 'Other than winding up Mum and Dad of course.'

No, Faith thought. He had adventures with me, instead. If Rob had been anything like Rik, then maybe — then maybe he would have broken my heart too, she reminded herself irritably.

'How do you mean, brother and sister?' Sara was leaning forwards in her chair.

'Lots of low-level bickering, but again, not the fun kind,' Faith said. 'More the repetitive, tedious, why can't you be a different person kind. And we never had sex.' She flushed guiltily. 'Although that was really more my fault than his.'

'Why not?' Sara looked more interested than ever.

'I just didn't want to,' she confessed. 'It felt completely wrong. I had to steel myself any time we did go through with it and there was no real feeling in it on my part.'

'That's normal though,' Sara said. 'After a while. It's not like it was at the beginning.'

'I'm pretty sure it shouldn't be less appealing than doing the washing up.'

'Did you at least talk about it?'

Faith shook her head. 'I thought about it but I knew he'd be really hurt and upset and I'd feel too guilty.' She hung her head. 'I know it's cowardly of me but I couldn't face it and there was really nothing he could suggest that could solve the problem, because it wasn't that I didn't *want* sex, I just didn't want it with him.'

'So even if he'd dressed up or something, tried role play?' Sara was still going.

'Dress up as what?' Faith asked. 'A mountain biking ninja?' Don't go there, she warned herself. 'It wasn't a visual thing,' she said. 'He didn't put on weight or lose all his hair or dramatically change his appearance. It wasn't the way he looked, it was just him. He wasn't the right person for me.'

'So what attracted you to him in the first place?' Minel wanted to know.

'We got along well enough,' Faith said. 'He was funny, and sweet, and considerate, and he really seemed to like me. He did all the chasing, and he seemed so keen and so genuine and I had been single for ages and I just thought, why not at least give him a chance?' She sighed. 'I can't say Rob ever really set my world on fire, even right back at the beginning, but at least I knew he'd never…' she tailed off.

'Never hurt you,' Minel finished knowingly.

Faith nodded.

'Doesn't sound like the greatest reason to get together with somebody.' Minel sounded very gentle.

Sara sat back in her chair, looking defeated.

'Do you think,' Minel said, still in that gentle tone that made Faith want to lay her head on her shoulder and cry, 'that you were attracted to Rob because you felt safe with him and knew he'd never do what that awful guy at uni did?'

Faith felt a familiar stab of guilt. Minel and Sara still didn't know, to this day, that the tale of her great heartbreak over her university boyfriend wasn't true. Or rather that it was true, but it wasn't poor Joel, whose name she so easily took in vain, who had shattered her heart into a million tiny pieces and prompted her to vow never to allow anybody to hurt her again.

'Rob was your first boyfriend since Joel, wasn't he?' Sara mused. 'Your first serious boyfriend full stop.'

'He was,' Faith confirmed. 'There were a few other guys at uni — just flings really. Nothing serious. And then nobody for ages, and then I met Rob.'

That, at least, was true.

'It sounds like you never really gave Rob a chance,' Minel was saying. 'There has to be a spark somewhere, and that only really comes from being prepared to take a risk on somebody. After all,' she said wisely, 'if you truly feel they're not capable of hurting you then you obviously just don't care about it enough and that's never going to lead to fireworks.'

Fireworks are all very nice, Faith thought, until they blow up in your face.

Sara was picking at the corner of a sandwich, her face very downcast. 'So you don't think you can get that spark back? Once it's gone, it's gone?'

'I'm not saying that,' Minel said. 'But if it was never really there in the first place then it's hard to see how it can suddenly materialise at a later date. Mind you,' her tone turned gloomy, 'I'm not really a fountain of wisdom on that topic at the moment.'

Sara patted her on the shoulder. 'Still struggling with Paul?'

'I didn't know you and Paul were struggling,' Faith said. 'Other than the baby thing.' She couldn't really think of a better way of putting it. 'Infertility' sounded so final. So clinical. So *real.*

'The baby thing,' Minel apparently approved of the phrasing, 'is becoming a bit of an issue elsewhere. I want us to go and have tests. Find out why we don't seem to be able to get pregnant. Paul doesn't want to.' She put her head in her hands. 'He won't even consider it. He wants us to just keep trying, he says he's sure it'll work one of these days but I think he's just afraid that if there is a problem, that it might be him.'

Faith could see how for an undisputed alpha male like Paul, the prospect of fertility issues could be daunting. He would undoubtedly see it as a failure, a gigantic dent in his masculinity.

'I'm so sorry that you're going through this,' she said to Minel, wishing she could offer her friend more in the way of comfort.

'I am too,' Minel said bleakly.

'God, aren't we just a gigantic cloud of doom,' Minel said.

'Maybe we're having mid-twenties crises,' Faith said.

'Late twenties, in my case,' Sara corrected.

'Well, look on the bright side,' Minel said hopefully. 'We can't stay like this forever. Things have to get better soon.'

Just when things couldn't get any worse, it rained. Faith watched from the shelter of the greenhouse on Thursday as huge droplets hammered into the half-filled remains of the old pond, slowly but surely pushing the water levels back up. Thanks to the loose earth she had begun to shovel into it, it was now a cocktail of rainwater, sludge and grime. I'll have to drain it again, she thought, start all over from the very beginning. Oh, why didn't I cover it with a tarpaulin?

Because that would have involved going to the site to find one, and that would have involved seeing Rik. His blankness was sliding towards open hostility and Faith could no longer bring herself to face him.

You have to, she decided. Cover the pond up now and at least it can't get any fuller. You can leave it to settle and drain it again at the weekend. Without any more disturbance from the rain the earth will slowly sink back down and you won't have to siphon pure sludge.

She reached for the battered old Barbour of Helena's she'd pinched from the house that morning, and tugged it on. She put the hood up, and thought at least she would have no peripheral vision so if she stood directly in front of Paul her eyes wouldn't be able to hone in on Rik. Faith already knew his rain-soaked clothes would be clinging to his body and his hair would be wet and pushed back out of his face and that would make his high, haughty cheekbones and his eyes, which would no doubt be flashing with outrage at the horrendous conditions, more noticeable and dominant. And of all his many extremely redeeming features, she thought, his eyes are — were — the most irresistible of them all.

Just don't look at him, she ordered herself. Go and get it over with and don't let your own eyes wander.

She stomped off towards the site, shoving her hands in the pockets of the coat and shivering. She'd completely forgotten to check the weather forecast that morning, just assuming it would once again be hot and sunny, and she hadn't bothered bringing a jumper. Underneath the coat, which appeared to no longer be waterproof, she was wearing denim cut-offs and a loose-fitting white vest, which was probably the worst thing she could have chosen. If it weren't for Helena's trusty if inadequate Barbour she'd be doing a pretty convincing imitation of a contestant at a wet t-shirt competition.

She rounded the corner and scanned the site for Paul but he was nowhere to be seen. Rik had his back to her and was talking to one of the teenagers, and she completely forgot her resolve and allowed herself a moment to admire the way his soaked t-shirt clung to the outline of the muscles in his back.

'Looking for something?' one of the teenagers asked eagerly and Rik, alerted to her presence, turned and saw her shifting from one foot to the other at the edge of the site.

'What do you want?'

She pushed her shoulders back defiantly, feeling the hairs on the back of her neck beginning to stand on end. He had some nerve talking to her like that.

'I need a tarpaulin,' she said, hoping she sounded brisk and businesslike, not soggy and intimidated. 'To cover the pond. It's filling back up and I don't want to drain it again.'

'Get one from the hay barn,' Rik said. 'There's a few at the back.'

Oh, not the hay barn. Faith quailed a little as he shot her another ferocious glare. Grumbling, she stormed off in the direction of the barn. She glanced at the corrugated metal doors and felt a pang of something very bittersweet, and pushed it away. These doors, she remembered, were a nightmare to open at the best of times. She wasn't even sure she'd be able to manage it with the metal stiffened and soaked by the incessant rain and they looked like they hadn't been opened in the best part of ten years.

Well, she thought in a pathetic and misguided attempt to rally herself, you know they were opened at least once in that time.

She heaved at the rusting red metal and listened to several ominous creaks. The doors held firm. She tried again, but despite more creaking they still wouldn't budge. The Barbour was soaked now and the heavy material was clinging to her skin, overheating her as she exerted herself once more. 'Useless thing,' she muttered, taking it off and casting it dismissively onto the floor beside her where it lay crumpled and defeated in a soggy heap. 'Useless doors. Why does nothing around here actually work?' She gave them one more heave, and when they once again refused to move she lost her patience and delivered a hefty kick to the right-hand door.

There was a deafening, metallic grinding noise, then the door gave way completely and fell off its hinges, toppling with an almighty groan. She had just enough time to leap out of the way with a terrified yelp before it landed, on the exact spot she'd been standing just a fraction of a second ago, with a spectacular crash, sending muddly gravel-flecked water all over her.

'What's going on?' Rik, alerted by the din, had appeared next to her and Faith felt her temperature drop like sand through an egg timer as she realised just how close she'd been to being squashed flat by corrugated iron.

'Faith?' Rik looked at the stricken door, then at her pale face. 'Are you OK?'

She nodded dumbly.

'What happened?'

'The door fell off.' She took a couple of deep breaths and looked around for something to hold on to while she steadied herself. There was only the other door to hand, and something told her it would meet the same fate as its counterpart if it had to take any more strain.

She was suddenly aware she was freezing. Her knees sagged and she lurched a little, desperate to right herself, and looked frantically at Rik.

He shot forwards and put his arms around her and she clung onto him gratefully, feeling the warmth from his body seeping instantly into hers. He pulled her head against his chest and she put her hands up by her ears, burrowing her face into him.

She'd done exactly this the very first time she'd met him and all of a sudden she was seeing it all over again, like a montage in a movie. How she'd come skidding up the gravel drive on her bike to see Minel and almost been knocked flying by a furiously barking Tackle, who had proceeded to mount her leg the second she put her foot on the ground. How she'd been intercepted by a wiry, brown-skinned, black-haired boy who had dissolved into fits of high-pitched, strangely infectious giggles. He had eventually composed himself to apologise for Tackle's advances and explained the terrier just really liked pretty girls, then introduced himself as Minel's brother Tariq, or Rik for short. Then he'd admired her bike and somehow talked her into attempting to jump off a makeshift ramp over the largest of the potholes, which she had insisted was impossible until he'd seized her bike off her and proved her wrong, flying over the crater with inches to spare. She, however, hadn't made the jump and instead crashed heavily to the floor with her bike on top of her, and Rik had pulled her to her feet and put his arms around her while she shook from head to toe with shock and fear and relief. Then he'd taken her up to the house and made her a cup of tea, liberally sweetened with sugar, and watched her through doe-like, chocolate-brown eyes as she'd drunk it and told her he had never met anybody else with the guts to even try a jump like that. And that, she supposed, had been the start of all of it. It certainly had been for Rik, who had told her years afterwards he'd basically fallen in love with her the moment he met her.

And just as his presence had calmed and reassured her that and so many other times before, it was working its magic now and the churning in her stomach and the violent shivering was already lessening. His heart was beating against her right palm, steady and even. He bent his head and his breath was hot against her ear.

'You're OK,' he said.

She could feel the words as well as hear them, they were forming and resonating right beneath her forehead and reverberating through her skull. I know I'm OK, she thought through a swirling haze of overwhelming, poignant relief and recognition, because you're here.

You're here, and I'm here, and I'm home.

She tightened her right hand automatically.

His heart paused for a split-second, then it quickened noticeably.

She dropped her hands and stepped away from him, almost losing her balance again in her haste to put some space between them.

'Do you need to sit down?' Rik asked.

She shook her head. Her drenched vest was clinging to her front. Oh for god's sake, she thought, can this get any worse? She shivered.

'You're cold. Where's your coat?'

She gestured towards the fallen door. 'Under there.'

'Do you want my t-shirt? It's soaking too, but at least it's not...' His eyes ran down her and she thought, there goes any chance that he didn't notice my current completely exposed state. 'At least it's not see-through,' he finished.

'No,' she said again, steadily this time. 'I'll go back to the house, Minel can lend me something. And make me a cup of tea.'

'With sugar,' Rik said.

She smiled. 'Two spoons and a Kit Kat.' Sweet tea and chocolate had always been her and Rik's solution to the post-fall shock. Until they'd found a better one.

He looked at the door again. 'Looking at the size of that it's more of a three spoons situation. Did it just come off by itself?'

'I gave it a few heaves,' she said, 'and then a bit of a kick.' She winced. 'Sorry. I was just a bit wet and impatient. I'll pay for the damage.'

'Don't be silly.' He shook his head. 'I'd forgotten they were so hard to open. We should have replaced them ages ago. I'm just glad you weren't hurt.'

'I don't think that barn likes me very much. It obviously wants to punish me for something,' she said wryly.

Something flashed in Rik's eyes and she instantly realised she'd gone too far. She flinched internally as his face slid back into that impassive mask.

'Go back to the house,' he said. 'I'll sort out the pond for you.'

He turned away, and Faith felt any residual warmth draining away.

'Thanks,' she said hopelessly.

But he had already gone into the barn. Faith thought about calling after him, then decided that was quite enough for one day and, crossing her arms firmly over her chest in case she ran into any curious teenage boys, she slunk dejectedly up to the house.

Chapter 5

Thank goodness for manual labour, Faith thought on Friday as she heaved her shovel into the small but growing pit she had begun to dig. She had a huge plastic bucket next to her, slightly floppy with open handles, into which she was hefting wet mud and stones before dragging it across to the bright yellow skip and hauling it up and over, again and again until she felt like her arm muscles were on fire.

The repetitive motion and the almost constant pain were cathartic, and she found the more she dug and flung and shifted and hefted, the calmer and more orderly her mind became. With her whole body otherwise occupied she felt anchored, the aches and pains and sense of satisfaction she was gaining from the digging helping to ground her after the freefall that had been yesterday afternoon.

She had felt so tired by the time she got home she had eaten in stony silence, her mind as exhausted as her body. And then she had gone upstairs to her old bedroom and ransacked the drawers and units, scrabbling desperately through old pieces of paper, folders and ring-binders, looking for anything drawn and annotated in a spiky hand. But she'd thrown them all away, she remembered, she had systematically removed any trace of Rik from her life in the foolish hope she could also remove him from her heart.

She'd also thrown away her vast collection of notes about Hollyhocks, including detailed descriptions and classifications of the plant and animal life it hosted. Years of time and effort, a labour of true love, both entirely valueless and worth more than gold. Why hadn't she kept them? Quite apart from the fact they would have come in extremely useful now she was once again reshaping the landscape to which she had once so irrevocably belonged, surely even at that age she could have visualised a time when she might look back at them fondly?

Maybe I knew more than I thought at seventeen, she mused, because they would still rip my heart out right now.

It was ripping anyway, tears were once again pouring down her cheeks, and she had curled up in her creaky single bed and cried herself to sleep. When she woke she had known, without even looking at her phone, that it would be 3am and she had cursed the insomnia that had plagued her sporadically for near enough the last decade, as the tears began to flow again.

I miss Rik, she thought hopelessly now, as she dug. Having felt that strangely moving connection with him yesterday, that complete peace and rightness when he was holding her close while she was all adrift, knowing he was just round the corner but worlds away, hurt more than ever. *I don't want to think about him, but I can't stop myself either.*

'I need a distraction,' she said to Minel's puppy who seemed to have decided that she was his true mistress and was forever hanging around worrying at her ankles. 'You're good company,' she told him and the puppy sniffed at her ankle approvingly then spied a patch of particularly sloppy mud and pelted off to roll around in it.

'Thanks for looking after this little guy for me,' Minal said, walking over and going to pick up the puppy before noticing his mud-plastered coat and recoiling. The puppy sniffed her dismissively then wandered back to Faith. 'He likes you better than me,' Minel sighed, then she noticed the devastation around Faith. 'This is progress, yes?'

'It sort of has to get worse before it can get better,' Faith said, 'but have a little faith.'

'I'll have a little Faith with my tea,' Minel said. 'Come over to the house. Sara's coming over for a catch-up.'

'Have you noticed anything about Sara?' Faith asked as she and Minel headed up to the house after she'd given the puppy a brief but very splashy wash.

'How do you mean?'

'She seems a bit down,' Faith said.

'She's probably just tired,' Minel offered as she swept a fresh pile of clutter off the table and gestured to Faith to sit down.

'Maybe,' Faith agreed. 'I wondered if she was having problems with Tony. She reminded me of myself a bit —' she pulled a guilty face — 'when I was in the doldrums with Rob.'

'They've been together a long time,' Minel pointed out. 'One doesn't exactly sit and gush about one's lover's finer points when you've been together for nearly ten years and have to listen to them on the toilet every morning.' She giggled. 'I probably sound the same about Paul, but it doesn't mean I don't still love him.' She looked at Faith kindly. 'I know you must still be hurting about Rob, sweetheart, but please don't do that thing of assuming all men are the same.'

Faith flinched. 'I don't still do that.' She remembered only too well the long evenings she'd spent after too much wine discussing the failings of men with her long-suffering friends, so heartbroken after her Rik's betrayal that she'd tarred his entire gender with the same brush.

Minel put a cup of tea in front of Faith and sat down opposite her.

'I was actually going to ask you,' she said, 'if you'd noticed anything similar about Rik.'

So it's not just me, Faith thought with relief. He is acting weird, with all this blankness and irritability and general get-lost vibes. She'd only seen him once today, and her hope that yesterday might have mollified him a bit had been well and truly dashed when he'd been more abrasive than ever.

'It's hard to say.' She blew absently on her tea. 'I haven't seen Rik in years so I'm not the best person to judge but he definitely seems to have changed quite a bit.'

'It's not so much that he's changed,' Minel said. 'More that he's reverted. He reminds me of how he was after I left home.'

'How was he?' Faith asked, madly curious to find out how Rik had handled the entire situation after she'd left. She'd been completely incapable of asking Minel about him and on the odd occasion her friend had mentioned him it was to complain about him being in some horrendous teenage strop which she had deduced must be about a girl.

'Oh, he was a nightmare,' Minel sighed. 'So angry, and obviously really hurt about whatever it was that went down. He barely said a word to any of us, just spent all his time crashing around the place, slamming doors and chucking bikes around at that quarry and coming back all covered in cuts and bruises and going to parties and getting into fights. Tackle was the only one who would put up with him — no wonder he was so devoted to that bloody dog. And Jason,' she added. 'They were inseparable, even more so than before.'

That's odd, Faith thought, that Jason would forgive Rik so easily. But male friendships were a law unto themselves, perhaps to Rik's closest male friend it really was 'bros before hos', or whatever ghastly expression they would have used back then.

'Then he went to college,' Minel was saying, 'and he seemed to calm down a bit and he was much more bearable when he came home. But he doesn't come back much. I was hoping,' she said wistfully, 'that being back here for the summer might help us all get to know each other again.'

'Not working out quite how you expected?'

Minel shook her head. 'I actually think,' she pondered, 'that you not being around much after I went to college didn't help his mood. Not that I blame you,' she said hastily. 'You only really hung out with him because of me and after I left, you weren't exactly going to come back just to listen to him moaning about girls and watch him pulverise himself on some stupid bike.'

'No,' Faith said darkly. 'I was not.'

'Although for a while we did all think something might happen between you two.' Minel giggled and Faith tried to ignore the sudden heaviness in her gut. 'Everybody knew he had a huge crush on you. We were all placing bets on when you would finally get around to crossing that line, especially after that horrendous display at my birthday party…'

Faith had nurtured the vain hope they'd all have forgotten about Minel's 18th by now.

'I don't really remember much about that party,' she lied. 'It was so long ago.'

'It was,' Minel agreed, 'but are you sure you didn't end up getting bit too drunk and gropey with Rik?'

'No!' The word was out of Faith's mouth too quickly and far too emphatically.

Minel held up her hands. 'OK. Whatever. I mean, you did say you didn't remember much…'

'I would have remembered that,' Faith said grimly. Oh hurry up, Sara, she thought, come and save me from this excruciating conversation.

As if by magic, the kitchen door opened. Faith heaved a sigh of relief, then the breath caught in her throat as she saw the person who had come in was Rik.

He scowled in her general direction and nodded at Minel.

'We were talking about my 18th birthday party,' she announced gleefully.

'What about it?' He really did look completely blank. That's his default expression now, Faith thought.

'Don't you remember?' Minel teased.

Faith stared at the table and wondered if anybody would notice if she slipped silently under it. Where was that puppy when she needed him? She'd take a dog biting and/or humping her ankle over this torture any day.

'All I remember,' Rik said, 'is waking up with the worst hangover of my life, covered in sweat with Jason spooning me.' Faith's lips twitched involuntarily and she opened her mouth to say something then remembered the context of the conversation and slammed it shut again.

Sara came in. Oh thank god, Faith thought, but Minel was relentless.

'Do you remember my 18th birthday party, Sar?'

'Oh Christ.' Sara looked long-suffering. 'You're not going to start on at me about getting off with Paul again, are you? It was a joke,' she intoned wearily. 'And no, I didn't enjoy it and no, he didn't try anything on with me afterwards, and no, I don't consider him unfinished business.'

'I remember that,' Faith said, seizing on a possible diversion. She giggled. 'That really was disgusting. You looked like you were eating each other alive.'

It was Minel's turn to scowl.

'And you, Min,' Faith went on eagerly, 'and — what was his name again?'

'Gabe,' Sara chipped in and Faith dissolved into peals of giggles — 'weren't you so drunk you had to stop snogging him to be sick on his shoes?'

Minel groaned with mortification and Faith chortled merrily, accompanied by Sara who seemed to have perked up quite considerably. 'Poor guy,' she gasped.

'It was his tongue,' Minel wailed. 'It was like a washing machine. Round and round and round.' She grimaced and put her hands over her eyes.

'Not even you puking all over him put him off,' Rik said and Faith noticed that his face had also lightened considerably. 'Every time he stayed over with you I had to shove socks in my ears. To think I was pleased when Mum and Dad said we could move into that cottage,' he sighed. 'I didn't realise I would have to listen to a herd of elephants in the room next to me.'

'Wildebeest,' Faith corrected him, remembering the term he'd used at the time.

'Yes, wildebeest,' Rik agreed, and he banged the table emphatically, making Minel jump. 'Thundering away. Galloping.'

'Stampeding,' Faith offered.

Minel screeched in protest. Sara cackled.

'I don't know what you were doing in there,' Rik said, 'but with the benefit of hindsight and some actual experience to draw on, let me tell you, you were doing it all wrong.'

'We need to change the subject,' Minel protested. 'Before Paul comes in.'

'Rik,' Faith said, seizing the chance to get at least one of her questions answered while he seemed to have temporarily forgotten his animosity towards her. 'What happened to Tackle?'

'Didn't Minel tell you?'

'Tackle wasn't really that big a part of my life,' Minel said, also sounding relieved at the subject change.

'He died,' Rik said. 'A couple of years ago.'

'Oh.' Faith looked at him with genuine empathy. 'I'm so sorry.'

Rik shrugged. 'He didn't suffer.'

'But you must have been upset?'

He nodded. 'A bit. In a way it was a relief because I would have hated to have to watch him shuffle around into his dotage. His heart just gave up one day. It had taken all the excitement it could handle, I guess. But it did feel a bit like the end of an era and he was my last link with —' He stopped abruptly.

With me, she thought. That dog was his last link with me. Rik's eyes had gone very soulful and the blank expression had been replaced with something infinitely more poignant.

I hurt him, she realised. That's why he's angry.

He did miss me.

Her chest tightened. The silence hung in the room, Minel and Sara were both temporarily muted. Maybe they can feel it, Faith thought. Whatever is in this room with us, it's threatening to swallow all of us whole. We're all dumbstruck by our mutual sadness, even if none of us really know what the other is carrying around with them.

'Did you think about getting another dog?' she managed eventually.

Rik shook his head. 'I didn't actually take Tackle with me when I left home,' he said. 'I thought about it, but technically he wasn't mine and it didn't seem fair on him. Hollyhocks was the only home he had.'

I know how that feels, Faith thought. Tackle wasn't the only stray Hollyhocks took in.

He wasn't the only one who fell hopelessly in love with you.

The new puppy wandered into the kitchen, his tiny tail wagging frantically at the sight of his beloved. He shot over to

Faith and collapsed at her feet, sighing happily and closing his ferocious yellow eyes.

'This little guy,' she nodded at the puppy at her feet, 'reminds me of him.'

'Me too,' Rik said. 'It's almost spooky. He's got the same facial expressions and everything. When I saw you,' he went on slowly, 'holding him on the drive, for a moment I actually thought the corporeal ghost of Tackle had just materialised right in front of me.'

'He needs a name,' Faith said, looking down at the puppy again because the unexpected openness of Rik's face coupled with the news of Tackle's passing was drawing such a deep mourning from her she wasn't entirely sure she wasn't going to burst into tears there and then. 'I doubt Minel would go for Tackle 2.'

Minel snorted derisively. 'Absolutely not.'

'Grandson of Tackle,' Rik said dramatically.

'Bit of a mouthful,' Faith said dubiously. 'GT.'

Rik nodded. 'I like it.'

'Do I get any say in this?' Minel demanded. 'I can't have a dog called GT.'

At the sound of his new name, the puppy looked up.

'That's settled then,' Faith said. 'Plus you've had him for weeks and spectacularly failed to name him.'

'It's not even a name! It's just initials.'

'Initials are huge right now,' Rik said. 'We chuck them around all over the place up on silicone roundabout.'

Faith sniggered at his affected tones. 'You need glasses to pull off the hipster vibe, Rikki.'

The endearment was out of her mouth before she could stop herself. She waited for Rik to shut down instantly, to turn away, make his excuses and leave. For his eyes to drift away to that point in the middle-distance. And as she watched they did drift, but over her, not lingering or assessing but just noticing, as if he had only just realised for the first time that she was even there at all.

Silence had once again engulfed the room.

Say something, she commanded herself. Anything. And whatever you do, don't take the fact he finally seems to have at least noticed you without prejudice as an open invitation to just *gawp*.

But her eyes had done exactly that and they wandered over Rik's face, noting that he mustn't have shaved in a while and the darkness of his jaw made him look older and gave him more of a feral than a hipster edge. But there was no concealing the boldness and beauty of his features which in rare repose looked like they had been carved out of stone. That was why he looks so radiant when he smiles, she thought wistfully, not that I've actually seen him smile since I got here, but it was always that contrast, the way his smile floods his face with light and animation. He was wearing a faded grey t-shirt and his shorts were a little loose and had slipped down so she could see the waistband of his pants. Why, she pondered, was it currently the trend for men to flash their underwear and more pertinently, why did all those infernal teenagers look completely ridiculous wandering around with the waistband of their fake Calvin's on show but Rik somehow managed to make it look both like it had happened by accident, and the hottest thing on the planet?

Although actually, she conceded, even as a teenager Rik had pretty much constantly had the waist of his pants on show. Even back then she'd found her eyes, and then eventually her hands, irresistibly drawn to his hips and stomach, trailing her fingers over them and feeling him tremble, listening to those excited strangled noises he would be unable to stop himself from making, watching his eyes getting darker in his face as his pupils expanded.

'Do I have something on my shorts?' Rik asked pointedly.

Faith started and tore her eyes away. What was she playing at, mentally undressing him in front of Minel and Sara? Heat rose in her cheeks and she looked down at the puppy again, but she could feel Rik's eyes boring into the top of her head and she blushed harder than ever.

'No,' she squawked. 'I was just thinking about — um.'

'Yes?' Sara prompted, sensing mischief.

Faith gulped. 'What were we talking about earlier?' Something neutral and non-incriminating, she was sure of it, because there had been that momentary flash of a familiar rapport with Rik before she'd got all carried away and started staring at his crotch.

Minel chipped in eagerly. 'My 18th birthday party.'

'Yes,' Faith said, then she remembered and added quickly, 'I mean no, not that —' But Minel seemed to have been reminded of whatever point she'd been trying to make before she, too, had become side-tracked. 'I was talking,' Minel went on happily, 'about that disgraceful display you two put on.' She looked reprovingly at Rik. 'That you —' she pointed accusingly at Faith — 'claim you can't even remember.'

Sara cackled again. 'Oh I remember that. Disgraceful,' she agreed, 'much worse than me and Paul.'

'What display?' Rik was back to blank.

'Oh, don't tell me you don't remember either,' Minel sighed. 'You remembered me and Gabe, and so did you.' She looked at Faith again. 'And Sara and Paul so I don't see why you wouldn't also recall your part in that debauched little gathering.'

'I only remembered Sara and Paul because you went on about it for about six months afterwards,' Faith said. 'And you being sick on Gabe because who could forget that?'

'Gabe, hopefully,' Rik said drily and Faith smiled despite herself. Maybe I should admit that I do remember, she thought. Get rid of that gigantic elephant in the room, laugh about it like it's ancient history and meant nothing, and maybe once it's out in the open and we both admit to it we might be less stilted and tense around each other — and we might not have any more moments like that one just then, she added grimly — and then eventually we might actually get round to talking about the real issue at hand here.

'But I don't know what you two are talking about,' Rik carried on and Faith felt her bravado melt away at the conviction in his voice. 'I vaguely remember something about a hose pipe, but that's basically it.'

His memory, she thought, is very selective these days.

'Oh come on,' Minel exclaimed. 'You don't remember practically devouring each other in front of all of us?'

Faith forced herself to look surprised. 'What?'

'During the Spin the Bottle game,' Sara said patiently. 'You and Rik? Not ringing any bells?'

Faith shook her head. 'None at all. Are you sure that wasn't with somebody else?' Aha, she thought. Here's an opening I can take. She turned to Rik and steeled herself to say the dreaded name. 'Didn't you end up with Sophie Barnes that night?'

He shrugged. 'Can't say I remember that either.'

Sophie Barnes, Faith thought furiously, is anything but forgettable.

'Why do I know that name?' Minel mused. 'Who's Sophie Barnes?'

'She went out with Jason for a few months,' Rik said.

A few months? Faith frowned. So Jason must have carried on going out with Sophie even though — or *maybe*, she thought, maybe he didn't know. Maybe he never found out and that was the real reason he seemed so willing to forgive Rik. Because he didn't realise there was anything to forgive in the first place.

'Sophie Barnes!' Minel snapped her fingers. 'Of course. Huge boobs. But I thought,' she frowned. 'I thought she was going out with you?' She turned to Rik.

He shook his head. 'No.'

'She was,' Minel insisted. 'She stayed here a few times — I heard you, god, talk about a herd of wildebeest, you are in no position to judge me.' She folded her arms sternly.

All right, Faith thought. Now we're really getting somewhere. Let's see what he says to that. Her heartrate had picked up again and she was half worried everybody would hear it, thundering away like the proverbial herd in her chest. Her mouth was dry, and she swallowed hard.

Rik looked sheepish. 'She did stay here a few times, but not with me.' He winced, as if he knew he was saying something he shouldn't. 'When she and Jason started going out her parents wouldn't let them spend the night together, so she told them she was staying with you — sorry Min,' he added, 'took your name in vain a bit there. Anyway, they stayed at the cottage and I just banished myself to the hay barn.' He giggled. 'Good thing I did by the sounds of it.'

Faith's hand tightened involuntarily around her tea cup.

'So that wasn't you?' Minel asked, seemingly similarly confused. 'It was Jason?' A look of horror crept across her face. 'I was listening to *Jason*?'

Rik looked highly amused. 'Yep.'

Sara dissolved into giggles. 'Spotty totty,' she crowed. Faith felt a flash of deja vu through her shock and confusion, and the floor of the kitchen seemed to tilt underneath her feet.

'Jason,' she repeated robotically.

'Yes,' Rik said. 'You remember Jason? Had a massive crush on Sophie, they got together at a party while his folks were away. You were there,' he added harshly, then his eyes flickered again and he looked past her to a point on the wall behind her. 'I think.'

Oh, I was there, Faith thought. You know I was.

Her hand tightened again and the cup, unable to take the pressure, slipped out of her grasp and fell onto the floor, shattering with a loud clash and sending shards of enamel flying. Faith watched as if she were dreaming.

'Are you OK?' Minel was all concern. 'Did you cut yourself? Stay there,' she said. 'I'll get a dustpan and brush.'

Faith sat, frozen to the spot, as Minel swept up the pieces of the cup. Rik was also looking at her questioningly and she could feel the colour had drained from her face, leaving her pale and wan. Jason, she repeated to herself over and over again. I didn't see Rik. I saw Jason.

No. I saw Rik. I'm sure of it.

But I didn't actually *see* him.

It was early in the morning and the sun was coming in through the window and all I could see was outlines. The outlines of two people, and one of them was definitely a girl, and that told me all I needed to know.

All I thought I needed to know.

Oh my god, she thought. What have I done?

She got to her feet. 'I have to go.'

Sara frowned. 'I only just got here.'

'Stay for dinner,' Minel said immediately. 'We can all catch up — it's nice, isn't it?'

It's not, Faith thought. It's unbearable.

'Sorry,' she said, already edging towards the door. 'I just remembered — I promised my mum — I have to, um —' she put her hand on the door handle and gripped it firmly, half afraid it would melt away beneath her fingers and she would just crash straight to the floor and shatter like that cup. 'I'll see you on Monday,' she squeaked and she shot out of the kitchen and hurtled headlong across the garden, ignoring the whoops and yells coming from the site, flinging herself onto her bike, slamming her feet onto the pedals, forgetting her helmet entirely.

What, she thought again, have I done?

Chapter 6

The three years that passed after Faith moved to Westchester were the happiest of her life. From the moment she first came to Hollyhock House she was magnetically drawn to it and in return it opened its sleepy, sandy, sweeping self up to her as if it wanted to embrace her in the same way it had engulfed the entire Panesar family. Faith adored all of them, she could spend days on end enjoying girly fun with Minel and being welcomed by Helena and Ravi. They were an odd couple to Faith, the artistic, ethereal middle-class hippy and the brusque, severely handsome doctor, but despite their almost constant affectionate bickering they had a very warm, loving relationship that seemed to spill over into every part of Hollyhocks.

And then there was Rik, with whom Faith bonded almost immediately and to an even greater extent than she had with Minel. They rode bikes together constantly, argued and debated the finer points of life, read books and tinkered with computers, and all the while they roamed Hollyhocks and the surrounding areas like nomads. He took her to a small disused quarry in the middle of the woods where he practiced jumps on his bike, one of those curious secrets of the English countryside that history had long forgotten. Their desire to know the land soon turned into a desire to shape and change it, wanting to impose some of themselves so they, too, would become a part of its heritage. They dug the pond together, Faith worked on the garden while he read or drew, and they carved out steps into the quarry to bounce their bikes over.

Faith's own home life was a stark contrast to the euphoric freedom she enjoyed at Hollyhocks. Her parents seemed to be constantly arguing, never in front of her, but she heard muttering and strained voices behind closed doors. They had begun to discuss potentially moving away from Westchester or 'WC' as she and Rik had sniggeringly dubbed it, but Faith blocked her ears, refusing to even consider it. Here, at last, she felt she had found her home, even if it belonged to somebody else.

Judith and Jeff, but Judith in particular, disliked the Panesars intensely. Faith had wondered if her mother was racist but the only one of the lot she seemed to even remotely tolerate was Ravi. She scowled at Helena's floaty dresses, trailing hair and vague air, and she considered Minel basically a younger version of her mother.

But it was Rik for whom her mother's real venom was reserved. She didn't seem happy about Faith spending so much time with a boy, and such a boyish boy at that. She was constantly coming home late and muddy and usually scraped, grazed and bruised, and the contrast between the open, heady freedom of Hollyhocks and the tight confines of her home and Judith's obvious disapproval turned Faith into a caricature of a stroppy teenager. She huffed pointedly and grunted monosyllabically if her mother tried to find out what she'd been up to, before flying into a rage and peppering her outbursts liberally with choice words. Judith in turn blamed her attitude on Rik and decided he must be a bad influence.

In fact, the most recent source of Faith's angst had been that she and Rik had gone from being touchingly close to arguing wildly with an increasing loaded tension. Faith had found herself becoming hopelessly provoked and when he became particularly animated she would find herself completely fixated by his demeanour and gestures and to her alarm, it made her want to actually hit or shove him, release her aggravation in a physical form.

He in turn had found the ultimate weapon with which to torture her, which was to insist she secretly fancied him. Faith had hated it, it made her ears burn and her stomach churn uncomfortably with what she supposed must be revulsion, because it felt a lot like nausea but as unpleasant as it was there was something about it that was almost addictive.

And so they took this strangely horrible, strangely compelling atmosphere with them into Minel's 18th birthday party, held in the early summer.

It was one of those epic, heady evenings when everybody seemed full of adrenaline and Hollyhocks hummed with magic. Faith avoided Rik and his mob of spotty friends, who seemed to find their increasingly choice exchanges completely hilarious, and instead decided to find herself somebody to snog, preferably in front of him, so he could stop all this stupid nonsense about her fancying him once and for all.

At a certain point later on, everybody who hadn't coupled off or vomited gravitated towards the far end of the barn, where most of the bales of hay had been piled and covered with tarpaulin. Minel was lounging next to a group of girls Faith recognised from the year above. She smiled at her friend, who had obviously had a few too many Bacardi Breezers. Minel's dark hair was flopping into her eyes and she had a cigarette burning between her fingers, but from the length of the ash Faith guessed she'd forgotten all about it.

Rik appeared next to her and Faith sighed pointedly. He passed her a bottle of vodka and she took a tentative swig, wincing as the liquor burned down her throat.

He took it from her, deliberately taking a much bigger swig, and she giggled as he spluttered a little. 'Very cool, Rikki. Are you dressed as a ninja?'

He was all in black, and his eyes were very dark in the dull yet garish light of the barn. He did look a bit like a ninja, lean and wiry and graceful, like he would make no noise at all when he moved. She could see the waistband of his — also black — pants above his belt and she averted her eyes quickly.

'I like your, um…' he fixed his gaze on her camisole, which she'd had to sneak past her mother in a carrier bag and change into because it was rather lower cut than her usual vest and t-shirts and showed off her cleavage, or at least the closest she could manage to one thanks to an equally illicit push-up bra.

'I'm up here,' she said irritably, waving at her face, and Rik tried and failed to look guilty. 'Now, your pustular friend,' she began, thinking too late that all of Rik's friends were spotty.

He frowned. 'Which one? They're all a bit challenged in the complexion department, aren't they?' He gave her the smug smile of a person who didn't share that particular problem.

'I don't know. About this tall,' she gestured. 'He's been following me around all night.'

'He fancies you,' Rik confirmed.

'I thought you didn't know which one I was talking about?'

Rik shrugged. 'They all fancy you. They have that, and excess sebum, in common.' He pushed the bottle at her.

'Stop trying to get me drunk so you can loosen me up for your vile friends.'

Rik looked outraged. 'No way. Not those idiots.' He grinned. 'How drunk would you need to be?'

He took another swig and giggled so infectiously Faith suddenly wanted to hug him, which made a change from wanting to body-slam him. 'You're cute, Rikki,' she said. She must be drunk. 'For a kid.'

'Here, give me that!' Paul, his eyes glittering with mischief, took the bottle. Faith and Rik both stared, impressed, as he easily downed the lot without so much as a wince and twirled the bottle around his fingers. 'Let's play Spin the Bottle.'

'Yes!' Minel, who had a thumping great crush on Paul, shrieked in delight. She squinted at Rik. 'You can't play. You're too young.'

'No I'm not.'

'Yes he is,' Faith insisted. But she would play, she decided, and she would snog the face off whomever she happened to spin to infuriate Rik. As long as it wasn't one of his spotty mates.

'What if you and Rik spin each other?' Paul asked Minel, who looked revolted. He began to laugh. 'I think he should play just so we all see what you guys will do if that happens.' Vindicated, Rik smiled innocently at Faith and she ignored him and went and sat down next to Sara.

Somebody had switched the music to a Prodigy track and the thundering bass shook the barn.

'Birthday girl goes first,' Paul announced.

Minel spun Jason Denby, Rik's other best friend. Faith choked with glee at the expression on her face.

'Absolutely no way!' Minel stormed.

'You have to,' Faith crowed. 'Spotty totty,' she snorted and she and Sara laughed so hard tears ran down their cheeks.

Minel leaned in and pecked Jason briefly on the pock-marked cheek.

'Cheating!' roared Paul. 'It has to be on the lips!'

Jason winked at Minel encouragingly.

Grimacing, Minel pressed her lips to his, her eyes crossing a little. Jason looked thrilled with himself and spun Sara, who sighed and puckered up, then cackled wickedly. 'My turn!' She grabbed the bottle and spun Paul. Everybody made a big 'whooooh' noise. Sara and Paul were good friends and very similar, both alphas.

'Come on then,' Paul grinned.

Sara leaned in and he grabbed the back of her head and stuck his tongue down her throat, very obviously hamming it up for the whooping crowd. That's what I'll do, Faith thought, exactly that, all exaggerated and clearly not taking it seriously, but it will still drive Rik bananas.

'That's revolting,' Minel said irritably.

Paul spun and landed one of the younger girls, who in turn got one of the spotty teens and mystifyingly, looked extremely pleased about it. Everybody else groaned in disgust at the frenzied display.

Once they had finally finished the girl apologetically spun one of Paul's friends, who then spun Faith. As she stood up she realised he was at least two inches shorter than her and could barely focus. Bloody hell, she thought irritably, I can't snog him, I'd have to actually bend my knees. He looked equally disinterested and leaned up for a quick peck. Faith was hit by a waft of the distinctive, sweet smell of weed and grimaced.

'This is getting boring,' somebody complained.

'Spin me, Faith,' one of the spotty teens yelled, and Rik shoved him roughly.

Faith spun, hoping she didn't land one of the kids.

The bottle landed on Rik.

Faith's stomach gave an almighty lurch of protest. 'Oh come on,' she grumbled. 'What are the chances?'

Rik, who was still shoving back and forth with the kid who had wanted Faith to spin him, stood up and grinned at her, almost bouncing on his feet.

'I can't kiss *him*,' Faith said, breathless with outrage. 'It's practically incest. Is this bottle rigged towards the minor citizens? I'm not doing it!'

'You have to,' Minel was looking distinctly queasy. 'Sara and I had to kiss Jason.'

'Look mate, if you want to swap,' Jason said to Rik. 'I don't mind completing the hat-trick.'

'No way,' Rik said. Faith wanted to kick him, or preferably just shove him over. He'd be on at her all evening about this, the rest of her life, probably.

'All right, let's get it over with,' she sighed, stepping reluctantly towards him. It was only a kiss, what harm could come from one kiss?

She was going to have to stand on her tiptoes and she put her hands on his shoulders to steady herself and felt him shiver almost imperceptibly beneath her palms, the infinitesimal amount of friction generated warming her skin through the thin material of his t-shirt. He bent his head and she felt a cold rush of air in her nostrils as she drew her breath in sharply, with a very slight whooshing noise that caught in the back of her throat. From this very, very close range she could see his pupils had almost completely dilated and she felt something rising horribly, no, not horribly, *gloriously* from the ground below her, seeping in through the soles of her feet and taking all of her upwards with it.

His lips on hers were soft, but his intention was a forcefield all of its own.

Time slowed down. The music dulled and faded, the chatter and hubbub around them slipped and lurched down to a low, pulsing frequency. For a split-second even the air around them stopped moving and all the minute dust particles from the hay that had been drifting and floating and spiralling around hung suspended, frozen specks of stardust.

Of course, she thought. It's *you*.

Then she softened her ramrod-straight body and let herself just fuse into him, tilting her head back and parting her lips eagerly. She felt herself actually jolt physically with excitement, setting off a chain reaction of shockwaves from the top of her head to the tips of her toes. His face looked completely blissful, his eyes closed rapturously, almost as if he was dreaming. Her hands crept up into his hair, feeling it soft and springy under her fingers, and she closed her eyes to the increasingly staring crowd and let her other senses take over.

His tongue dancing over hers was unbelievably intoxicating, setting off previously unknown nerve endings and filling her with wild energy. She could feel blood roaring around her head and Rik's hands moving on her waist and the sound of his breathing in her ears, and her own heart racing and his hammering away underneath her chest which was straining right up against him. And most of all she could feel an overwhelming sense of rightness, as if something had just clicked into place. Oh, she had wanted to get her hands on him all right. She twisted her fingers into his hair, pulling at it to get him closer, and she heard him exhale sharply and more blood rushed to her head as he kissed her harder. Everything about him felt so amazingly alive, so perfectly in tune with her, like he had been made to do this with her. She curled her tongue round his to draw him into her, wanting to feel his breathing quicken and his body tremble in the places where it was pressed up against hers —

'Whoooh,' screeched Sara and a few of the other girls and all the spotty teens joined in. The noise was deafening.

Faith's eyes flew open and she squirmed out of Rik's grasp.

'That was disgusting,' Minel breathed in horrified fascination, and she giggled and toppled sideways on her hay bale.

Faith sat down abruptly next to Sara. Her hands were shaking.

'You've got to spin again, mate,' one of Rik's friends roared. 'Come on, wakey wakey!' She heard a fair bit of shoving and yelling and one of Sara's terrifying older friends got to her feet sighing and complaining. 'Don't even think about trying that with me, you little shit,' she screeched and Faith felt overwhelmed with relief when she sat back down.

The game went on with much hilarity and competition among willing couples to put on the best show. Faith sat reeling, staring at the floor and occasionally touching her lips as if to check they were still there.

Was this what all that arguing and goading had been about? Was this where they were meant to go? Surely not, not Rik, he was too young and silly and annoying and they were friends and he was Minel's brother and her mother hated him. So then why was she fighting so hard to stop her eyes drifting over to him, why did she desperately want to see the look on his face now and that other look, the way he'd looked so completely, so beautifully transported as he had kissed her? She'd kissed boys before, that wasn't the first time by any means, but that had been — that had felt — that had felt like — really? Rik?

She finally stopped forcing her eyes downwards and they shot to him as if they were magnetised. He was staring straight at her, oblivious to the noisy banter going on around him, and as soon as her eyes met his he smiled, a genuinely delighted smile that brought yet more colour to her already flushed cheeks. She looked down again hastily, but not before she had noted with extreme relief he didn't look in the least like he was gloating or crowing at her expense.

After a while everybody lost track of who had spun last and just started jumping in and grabbing the bottle.

One of Paul's friends, a handsome sixth-former Faith knew was called Gabe, spun Minel.

'At last, somebody decent,' Minel hiccupped and she kissed him extravagantly until everybody was bored senseless.

Paul turned to Ella, a girl he'd spun earlier, who was now sitting on his knee. 'This game is bust.'

The haybarn, released from Paul's chaperonage, erupted into a frenzy of shouting and laughing and snogging.

Rik, who had shot straight over to Faith's side, eyed the carnal carnage all around them. 'They need a cold shower.'

So do I, she thought, clenching her hands to keep them from just grabbing him. Shame there isn't one in here, I'll have to just use the — oh.

'Shall we get the hose pipe?' she asked Rik slowly.

He looked puzzled for a moment, then his face lit up. 'Yes. *Yes*. You are an absolute *genius*. Let's do it.'

'Do you really think we should?' She was always the one who got nervous about their more wayward ideas and his confidence and reassurance always gave her the final push.

'We're doing it.'

She nodded, her heart crashing against her ribs, and he took her hand, intertwining her fingers with his and locking them together. His palm fit straight into place, warm and dry against hers.

They slipped out of the side of the barn and he pulled her straight to him and kissed her, his enthusiasm almost knocking her off her feet. Faith felt the cold metal wall of the hay barn door behind her and leaned against it, putting her arms around his neck and kissing him like she was possessed. He moved against her restlessly and she arched her body up to him, squirming underneath his hands, which were creeping up her sides and rucking up the fabric of her vest. He had her pressed so hard up against the barn her head bashed into the metal, setting off a gong-like ringing noise.

'Sorry.' Rik paused and put his hand behind her head. 'Did that hurt?'

She had barely noticed. I have done some fun things with him, she thought, but this is far and away our best mutual effort yet. Why did I never think of this before?

Just next to her she could hear voices floating out from the door. Why were they out here again? Oh right.

'Hose pipe,' she reminded him.

It was pitch dark outside but they both had excellent night vision — honing it had been one of their projects over the winter — and made short work of connecting the hose then Rik turned on the tap.

'Come on.' He pulled at her hand again and, giggling wildly, they dragged the hose into the barn. Faith gulped, but it was too good an opportunity and she took a deep breath and put her thumb over the end, sending a spray of water all over Minel and Gabe.

Minel screamed. Faith shoved the hose at Rik and ducked behind him as he aimed it at Paul and Ella, then turned it on to the room at large. Couples were breaking apart, choking and spluttering, and the onlookers were hysterical at the scene.

'Come here,' Paul bellowed, advancing dripping towards Rik and Faith.

Rik dropped the hose, leaving it spewing wildly as it writhed frantically here and there, and grabbed Faith's hand again, pulling her out of the barn. Paul, Gabe and a few other boys came flying out, followed by a still-shrieking Minel and Ella. Faith ran as fast as she could, Rik lending her some speed, his hand still locked against hers. They both knew the land like the back of their hands and soon lost their pursuers, disappearing over the fence into the copse and leaping over the massive fallen log at the centre.

Rik slid down behind the log and pulled her down with him. She could still hear yelling and shouting and a great deal of laughing in the distance, but she knew she and Rik were out of the water — literally.

Under any other circumstances they would have crowed for at least an hour over their mutual brilliance but instead they just launched themselves at each other and she twined herself around him as joyously as an otter, letting him pin her to the ground with the weight of his body. She felt like she had crashed through a door to a new and wildly exciting side of him and she didn't care in the slightest that she was gasping frantically and her teeth clashed against his and a few stray sticks from the woodland floor were pressing uncomfortably into her back. Rik pulled her top all the way up and his hands were so light and they moved as gracefully as the rest of him and it was almost unbearably exciting, her nerve endings were jumping and firing and suffusing all of her with heady, raw energy.

'Oh Faith,' he said in wonder, tearing his mouth from hers momentarily, 'it *is* you.'

'Did you forget?' she asked, affronted.

'No!' He giggled. 'I've just wanted this forever and I'm a bit worried I'm dreaming it.'

If this is a dream, Faith thought, it's the best one I've ever had.

'You're not,' she said. 'I can pinch you, if you like.'

'You can do whatever you want to me,' Rik said fervently and she felt several jolts of something very primal and pulled his head back down to hers.

When a pair of headlights swung into the gravel drive at 10.58pm, Faith knew it would be Judith arriving to pick her up at eleven on the dot.

'I had better go,' she said reluctantly.

Rik pulled a regretful face. 'She can wait a couple of minutes, can't she?'

Faith shook her head. 'You know what she's like. Any excuse to ground me.' She adjusted her vest anxiously. 'Do I look like I've been up to no good?'

'God yes.' He sounded so blissfully happy about it she couldn't help giggling. Her skin was still warmed and sensitive from his hands, her lips were fuller and more swollen than usual, her cheeks were glowing and her own hands carried an energetic imprint of him, a whole new knowledge of somebody she'd thought she already knew inside out.

'Seriously Rikki. She's not going to know just from looking at me, is she?'

'Turn around,' he instructed, and she felt him picking some stray twigs out of her hair. 'You're good,' he said. He brushed his hand lightly down her back, removing the final detrius from her vest. 'And you're gorgeous,' he sighed, 'and sexy, and Faith — you're not going to regret this, are you?'

She turned back to face him. His eyes were very wide and black in the gloom.

'I really, really like you,' he said. 'Much more than I've ever liked anybody else. I've never really liked anybody else, to be honest. I really want to be with you.'

I really want to be with him too, she thought. I can't believe how much, but —

'I don't want to tell anybody about this,' she said firmly. 'Minel would die laughing and your spotty friends would be nudging each other grinning and yelling obscenities in the hallway at school and it would be a *nightmare*. I don't need all that, I've got exams this year and —' God, could she sound any more like her mother? 'So don't tell anybody. No talking about me with your mates, no bragging, no nothing.'

'OK,' he said, looking startled. 'I won't tell anybody. I won't do anything in front of anybody. But does this mean you want to?'

She could see hope rising in his eyes, then he smiled at her and she felt her heart leap and she nodded slowly, almost reluctantly.

'Yes,' she said. 'I want to.'

Chapter 7

On Saturday Faith decided she needed a break from Westchester, to get her thoughts in order, so she drove back to the flat to collect her things. It was torture. The Land Rover choked and spluttered, and Faith watched as her hands shook on the steering wheel until she practically had pins and needles.

She had hoped Rob would be out, but of course he was on the sofa watching TV, and his delight at seeing her quickly slipped into indignant self-pity as he plaintively asked her to explain, yet again, why she was leaving.

She found she didn't have the patience for it and snapped at him too harshly, then felt worse than ever at the hangdog expression on his face.

'You look different,' he said sorrowfully as he watched her throw her clothes into bags and boxes.

She wasn't sure how to respond to that, so she tipped her entire underwear drawer into a waiting cardboard box, watching the waterfall of plain, sporty knickers and bras, all blacks and whites and greys, form a pile in the bottom of the box. Rob had asked why she insisted on wearing such boring underwear. 'Why don't I buy you something pretty?' he'd suggested once, back in the days when he still noticed her underwear and what was inside it.

'You're not trussing me up like a Christmas turkey,' Faith had retorted.

What did he see in me? she wondered.

'I don't like it,' Rob said. 'Have you met somebody else?'

'When would I have time to meet somebody else?' she demanded. 'All I've done is work.'

He scowled. 'When I rang your office they said you'd taken leave.'

'You rang my office?'

'You won't answer your mobile.'

'That's because there's nothing left to say,' she said. 'We've been through it over and over. What new information can I give you?'

'I'm on leave doing a gardening project,' she said. 'All summer.'

'Where? Who with? Why?'

'With Minel, at Hollyhocks.'

'Who else?'

She shook her head. 'It's none of your business, Rob. No.' He had started to interrupt her and she held her hand up. 'What I did until last week was your business. I don't have to explain myself to you any more.'

She sent up a silent thanks to her previous self for never telling Rob about Rik.

Even so, he'd suspected there was something about her group of friends back home she wasn't telling him, and on the rare occasions they'd come to Westchester Rob had complained afterwards that Faith had been behaving like she'd had something to hide.

Once she'd packed everything into the straining Land Rover she gave Rob a quick, reluctant hug. 'Take care,' she said. 'I'll pay my share of the rent and bills until the lease is up.'

'Please don't go,' Rob said. 'We can try again — *I'll* try again, Faith. Anything you want.'

You can't give me what I want, she thought. You can't be somebody else.

She drove back listening to the radio and singing along to all the songs, which by some horrible twist of fate seemed to be reminiscent of times long gone, and lost loves.

A car in front of her braked and Faith stood on the middle pedal of the Land Rover, feeling the car almost sigh with relief as it slowed down. She was just outside London, she noted, she was making good time. What time was it? She looked at the clock on the dashboard.

Two thirty.

The girls she used to ride track bikes with would be gathering at the velodrome in an hour's time for their weekly skills session. Faith hadn't been in a while, Rob had complained about her taking off on Saturdays and leaving him at home by himself. But she'd liked the gang she'd met there and she could probably do with some repetitive motion to help her process her thoughts.

The contents of her mind were as circuitous as the track she was headed for, going round and round with no beginning and no end.

The fact that her feelings for Rik seemed to be bubbling back to the surface, no matter how hard she tried to push them down. The jolt of familiar pain and sadness when she reminded herself how it had all ended, then the fresh shock of having an entirely different perspective on the crucial event that had led her to terminate their relationship before it really got started. Then she would find herself wondering what might have been had she confronted Rik instead of shutting him out, allowed him the chance to explain himself, and what would have happened if she'd accepted that explanation as the truth, as she was becoming increasingly convinced that it must be. And then she'd be right back to reflecting on everything she'd felt for him, and everything they'd been through, both before and after

Minel's godforsaken birthday party, and then the betrayal again, and on and on it went, round and round until she could swear she was making herself physically dizzy.

The track girls were delighted to see her, flocking around her in their shiny Lycra, talking nineteen to the dozen. Where had she been? What had she been doing? Was she back for good now? 'We need more riders,' Shaun, the coach, said reprovingly as he wheeled out a track bike for her to borrow. 'You need to commit, Faith.'

'She doesn't have to,' Lucy, one of the younger and more adventurous riders, interjected. 'She's welcome here any time.'

'All right ladies,' Shaun roared. 'Let's mount up.'

'Wonder what torture he's got in store for us today?' Crystal, who had acted as something of a mentor to Faith when she'd first come to the track, mused as Shaun began barking out orders.

'I'm going to regret this tomorrow,' Faith agreed.

The session was intense and Faith had no time to worry about being out of shape and out of practice. She could barely catch her breath as Shaun drilled them around the track, separately and in pairs, then had them swapping lanes and diving up and down the banks of the velodrome.

'My legs are in bits,' Crystal gasped as they once again set off around the track.

Faith swerved to avoid the rider in front and crashed straight into the barriers. 'Ouch,' she howled, as she slammed down uncomfortably onto the crossbar. 'That's my childbearing years over before they even began.'

'Concentrate!' Shaun bawled at her. Faith flicked him a V-sign as soon as he'd turned away. Crystal giggled. 'If he sees you he'll have you doing laps no-handed,' she warned.

They had a short break then Shaun rolled out the gigantic speakers. Faith loved riding to music. They turned it up so loud it shook the ground and Shaun, who was old enough to have appreciated early 90s rave when it was actually contemporaneous, shared her taste in music. 'All right ladies,' he shouted again, sounding rather like Paul addressing his mob of recalcitrant teenagers. 'Let's get this party started.'

They flew round the velodrome, and Faith felt her thoughts spiralling up and around her head like mini tornadoes. The hypnotic motion and the responsive, twitchy bike beneath her took up all of her physical focus and as she rode round and round, she slowly began to hone in on the most crucial of all the issues, which was the new information Rik had given her yesterday.

There are two possibilities here, she mused. One is that this is all a gigantic elaborate lie. Which, she admitted, wasn't likely. Why go through all the effort to think of a plausible alibi? If he did cheat on me, he clearly never cared about me, and if he didn't care about me, why would he care what I think of him now?

Which can only mean that he is telling the truth. And that would explain why he seemed to have genuinely no idea why I finished with him, and why he seemed so angry and hurt afterwards.

And it would explain why he's blanking me now, she thought uncomfortably, and why he's acting like I'm the one who should be taking the initiative, because if he really didn't cheat on me then I just dumped him for no reason whatsoever, with no explanation, and never spoke to him again.

Because of course if he was telling the truth then maybe he really was in love with me, and maybe he really was that sweet, heartfelt boy I thought he was after all.

If that all is the case, she thought even more uncomfortably, then what I did must have absolutely ripped his heart out and I can't blame him in the slightest for never wanting to see or hear from me again, and I can understand why he never comes back. And I can also understand why he's come back now, because he must have thought if there was at least the slightest possibility he could get some answers from me, it was a risk worth taking.

So it looks like I do owe him an explanation after all. And that, she thought with resignation, is going to make rejecting Rob's proposal and leaving him the very same night look like a teddy bear's picnic in comparison.

'What shall we do now?' Lucy demanded as the final tune — or 'banger' as Shaun insisted upon referring to them — finished. 'I'm totally pumped. Let's go out.'

'I can't,' Faith sighed regretfully.

'Oh, don't tell us your boyfriend won't let you,' Lucy grumbled. 'Honestly Faith that guy sounds more like your dad.'

He did a bit, now she thought about it. 'We split up,' Faith said.

Lucy and Crystal exchanged a high five.

'We were hoping you'd kick him into touch,' Crystal said. 'We miss you on the track and the last few times we saw you you really didn't seem happy.'

'You're not going to get back together with him, are you?' Lucy demanded.

She shook her head. 'No chance of that.'

'Then we need to celebrate your freedom.'

'I really can't,' Faith said. 'I'm skint and I have a car full of stuff parked out front. I only dropped in on my way from packing up the flat. I have to go home and sort it all out. But as soon as I've got a bit of cash, we'll go out.'

'Not me,' Shaun said quickly. 'Can't think of anything worse than you lot out on the lash.'

'Do you promise?' Lucy demanded.

'I promise,' Faith said. 'I really have to get going, but I'll definitely be back.'

Why did I let Rob stop me from riding bikes, Faith wondered as she drove home. And talk me into saving for a house I didn't want, and encourage me in a job I didn't like. It wasn't his place to help her follow her dreams, she acknowledged, but it really hadn't occurred to her just how much he was firmly putting himself in the way of them.

His arguments had always seemed to hold more weight than hers. Money. Security. The sensible option.

But I have never thought money and security are more important than living life, she thought. When did I let his worldview become mine? And why?

She had intended to go straight home, but then she remembered the pond and forced herself to drive reluctantly past her parents' house and along the winding lane to Hollyhocks. At least once she'd drained that pond full of nightmares she could have a cup of tea with Minel, who would hopefully insist upon feeding her because she was starving.

But what if Rik was around? She might have concluded explaining herself was the only possible option, but that didn't mean she was ready to do it just yet and definitely not dressed in sweaty Lycra, doing a fairly passable impression of a human condom. Hopefully he'd forgotten the flicker of humanity he'd displayed in the kitchen on Friday and be so affronted by her mere presence he'd disappear straight back off to the cottage to stick pins in a voodoo doll of her, or whatever he did over there at night.

She set the siphon going, then began to scrape up all the mud and sludge and rocks scattered around and pack it all into bags to hulk across to the skip on Monday. Dank pond mud oozed out from invisible gaps, covering her with stains and streaks. She wrinkled her nose in disgust.

GT, sensing her presence, came yapping towards her delightedly and she crouched down to cuddle the puppy. He was so pleased he launched himself bodily at her and Faith, caught off guard, lurched backwards and collapsed into the almost-drained bottom of the pond. GT followed her, sending flecks of mud flying with his scrabbling paws. He lay down and rolled in the sticky substance and Faith watched the expression of transported ecstasy on his little face. 'I thought dogs had sensitive noses,' she said. 'How can you stand this stuff?'

'GT!'

Oh no, that was Rik.

She lay down on her back, ignoring the filth and hoping the puppy wouldn't betray her whereabouts. But GT was far too small to get out by himself and was leaping up and down, his head popping out of the top of the pond like a very muddy jack-in-the-box. She heard Rik laughing and another sound, the tinkling, almost bell-like tones of an unfamiliar woman.

That must be the super-hot girlfriend Minel had mentioned.

Hollyhocks hates me, Faith decided. It's the only possible explanation. Why else would it try to kill me with that godforsaken door and make my job so difficult and now somehow get me plastered in this rancid stuff before rudely and unexpectedly flinging me in front of Rik and the super-hot girlfriend? It hates me all right, she thought, and I have a feeling I know why. After all, Rik belonged to Hollyhocks before I did. It's well and truly on his side and it's not going to forgive me until I tell him the truth.

Either that or I'm a mud-coated idiot in skintight Lycra with a guilty conscience.

'I'll get him,' Rik said. She could hear footsteps approaching and she seized the puppy and threw him out of the pond. 'Oh, there you are,' Rik said to GT. 'How did you get up from there?'

Any second now, she thought, he's going to look down and find me lying here. I'm going to have to style it out.

'Oh, hi Rik,' Faith, standing up, said airily, as if she always grubbed around in the bottom of cesspits.

The super-hot girlfriend clapped her hand over her mouth in horror. Of course she was stunning, Faith thought with resignation, why wouldn't she be? She had a sheet of gleaming dark hair that fell to her slender shoulders and her long heavy eyelashes curled enticingly above china-blue eyes. She had porcelain skin, artfully flushed cheeks, seashell-pink lips and there was nothing modest about the mesmerising, flowing curves of her cleavage.

'Hi Faith,' Rik said blandly, as if he, too, saw nothing out of the ordinary about her rising from the pit of a pond liberally coated in its contents like a much, much less alluring version of Buffy the Vampire Slayer. 'This is Lucinda.'

'Hi,' Faith said, plastering a big smile on her face and automatically reaching out her hand. Lucinda stepped back, appalled. Faith looked down and saw that it was also plastered, but in filth.

'This is Faith,' Rik said to Lucinda. 'Our gardener.' As if that explained everything.

'Oh right,' Lucinda said, clearly befuddled. 'Do you roll around in it or something?'

'Not voluntarily. I went in after GT.'

There was a long, heavily pregnant pause. Faith waited for Rik to say something else, possibly elaborating that Lucinda was his girlfriend and the hands-down love of his life and responsible for the most mind-blowing sex he'd ever had, but he stayed resolutely silent. Which was really all she needed in the way of confirmation.

Lucinda herself meanwhile was still daintily gagging over the close encounter with Faith's mud-covered hand.

Awkward, Faith thought, doesn't even come close.

'I'll take him down to the hose and wash us both off.' Faith broke the silence eventually and clicked her fingers at GT, who obediently shot to her side.

'At least somebody can get that puppy in hand,' Lucinda said, and Faith saw telltale scratches on her delicate ankles. How do those things hold *those* things up, she wondered, looking once again at Lucinda's magnificent chest.

'We do have a shower, you know,' Rik said. 'You don't have to use the hose.'

'I'll drip mud all up the stairs,' Faith said awkwardly. 'I can't exactly strip naked in the kitchen.'

Lucinda blanched, as if the very prospect of whatever lurked beneath Faith's mud-plastered human condom was both unthinkable and unspeakable. Once again Rik looked disinclined to come to her rescue.

'I'll head back,' Faith mumbled. 'Tell Min I'll swing by tomorrow to check on the pond.' She turned to Lucinda. 'Nice to meet you, Louisa.'

'It's Lucinda.'

'I'm so sorry,' Faith said. 'I'm terrible with names.'

'She's weird,' Faith heard Lucinda say to Rik as she took off across the lawn. 'Where did you find her?'

'We were friends when we were kids,' he said.

'Were you close?'

There was a pause.

Whatever Rik says to that, Faith thought, I'm pretty sure I don't want to hear it. She dropped her head, and walked towards the waiting embrace of the Land Rover.

Chapter 8

The day after Minel's birthday party Faith did not regret crashing headlong through the boundaries of friendship with Rik. In fact she thought of virtually nothing else. She replayed the evening over and over in her head, from the second he first kissed her and brought the reality of her feelings for him into blazing, glorious technicolour to the euphoric expression on his face as she'd finally kissed him goodbye.

'I had no idea,' she'd gasped to him, forcing him to pause in his ongoing wrestling with the fastening of her bra. 'No idea you ever saw me as anything other than a friend.'

Rik had looked at her incredulously. 'Are you joking?'

'I mean you are a boy,' she'd conceded, thinking of Judith's endless lectures on the subject of boys all wanting only one thing. 'So I suppose you must think about this with every girl who comes within a hundred miles of you.'

'I don't,' he'd said. 'Just you. Just you and always you, from the moment I first met you.'

'Then why didn't you ever say anything?'

He sighed. 'I didn't think you thought about me like that, and I was worried if I tried anything on with you you wouldn't want to hang out with me any more. I'd rather stay friends with you and never take it any further than not see you at all.'

That was sweet, she thought, really sweet actually, but —

'What about all that rubbish about me fancying you? You've been on about it for months.'

Rik looked sheepish. 'I didn't mean it. I didn't really know what else to do so I just hoped some of it might magically go from my head to yours and become true.'

'But earlier,' she continued. 'If you were really worried about losing me as a friend — why did you kiss me like that?'

'I fancy you so much I had to take a shot,' he said. 'And you must like at least something about me to put up with me.' As if to prove the point he kissed her again and Faith supposed that would probably do for now, because more jolts of that primal something were ripping through her and she didn't really know what to do about it all.

But now Rik was on the hunt for some answers, and he pulled away again. 'I didn't think you saw me this way either.'

'I don't,' she said automatically, then realised her hands, which were pushed up underneath his t-shirt and creeping over his hot, smooth skin might beg to differ, and so might the rest of her. 'I mean, I didn't.'

But now she was thinking about it, she had always liked watching him ride his bike and been struck by aggressive and graceful he was, and she did love making him laugh because he had such a radiant smile. In fact, she had consciously admired just about every part of Rik, but never with the awareness that she could now feel flooding through every part of her.

'I don't really know why I never thought about you like that,' she said eventually. 'Bit slow on the uptake, maybe, when it counts. I think it's safe to say I will definitely be thinking about you like that now.'

'Good,' he said fervently.

After that the conversation had taken a very different turn, as Rik had confessed to her quite candidly exactly what had been on his mind every time they'd locked horns in the last few months. And she in turn had shyly admitted to the knot of tension and excitement and longing in her core.

'All right,' he'd said, sounding like he was congratulating her, or himself, or possibly both of them. 'So we should do something about this.'

'We can't have sex,' she'd squeaked, knowing she was in no way ready to cross that line just yet. 'I hope you don't think just because we're here that I'm going to —'

'I don't think anything,' he said hastily. 'I don't expect anything at all. It's completely your call. I'll do anything you want.'

'I don't really know,' she swallowed awkwardly. 'I don't know what I, um…' She didn't want to tell him she'd never let anybody past the final frontier of her waistband before.

'You don't know what you like?' Rik guessed.

She swallowed again and nodded.

'That's OK,' he said. 'It'll be fun to find out.'

He made it sound like an adventure and she thought yes, that's how it should be. An adventure. That's what he and I do.

'Yes,' she said. 'It will be fun.'

But the next day was Monday, which meant school, which meant facing up to all the chatter and gossip about Minel's birthday party.

'So,' Minel demanded immediately as soon as she'd cornered Faith in the corridor. Her eyes were glittering with mischief, rather like Rik's did, Faith noted, and she swallowed nervously. 'What was *that* all about then, at my party? You and my *brother.*'

'What, you mean with the hose pipe?' Faith hoped she could feign innocence.

'Not the hose pipe,' Minel said patiently. 'That *horror show* that was you two practically bonking in front of all of us.'

Gah, Faith thought, did she follow us to the copse? 'You were watching?' She should have denied it, she had to deny it.

'Nothing happened,' she rambled untruthfully. 'We were just talking…'

'We all saw you,' Minel interrupted, 'We thought you were going to rip each other's clothes off and start shagging there and then in the middle of the hay barn. Is that what you two have been getting up to, off on your bike rides?' She snorted with mirth.

'Oh that,' Faith said dismissively, as if she had forgotten all about it. 'Just thought we'd put it on for the crowd, like Sara and Paul did. And you and Gabe.'

As if on cue, a bunch of uniformed boys marched past, Rik among them. Faith flushed as his eyes caught hers, and he paused, a smile beginning to creep around the corners of his mouth. She felt suddenly hot and fidgety, and she hoped she wasn't shuffling or squirming in a compromising manner.

'Here he is,' Minel said jubilantly, 'your boyfriend.'

Rik had opened his mouth to say something and Faith cut him off quickly. 'I was just explaining that the Spin the Bottle stuff was a wind-up,' she said. She forced herself to look appalled at the memory. 'Bloody awful wind-up,' she said, hating herself when she saw a flash of hurt in Rik's eyes. 'I'm not going there again.'

Rik's eyes narrowed. 'Yeah, you're not exactly my type either,' he said disdainfully. His mates rumbled in protest and Rik shoved the closest one to him, sending them all cannoning into one another like a spotty pinball machine. 'At least Sophie Barnes didn't have to run home with Mummy at 11pm on the dot.'

Faith felt the blood draining from her face and she gaped a couple of times, but no sound came out.

Faith wanted Rik to ring her to say he'd only been joking about Sophie Barnes, but he was clearly annoyed, or it was true, because he didn't phone. They ignored each other pointedly at school and she decided that he wasn't interested in her any more, presumably because she couldn't hold a candle to the magnificent Sophie Barnes. And now he would have decided they weren't even friends any more. It had obviously all got too weird.

But on the first day of the holidays there he was, knocking at her front door, looking far too excited and already a bit sweaty and roughed up from the ride over which he must have completed in record time. Faith's mother's lips had tightened pointedly as she sat at the kitchen table drinking tea and eyeing this young man with windswept hair and sparkling eyes which were fixed almost hungrily on her flustered, uncharacteristically clumsy daughter.

Rik was wearing his usual summer attire of faded khaki shorts, and an old t-shirt, covered in oil, which seemed to repulse Judith even more. Faith, on the other hand, thought he looked almost indecent.

'Shall we go to the quarry?' he asked eagerly. She nodded.

Judith cleared her throat pointedly. 'Don't you have coursework?'

'It can wait,' Faith said vaguely.

'When will you be back?'

'I don't know.' Faith scowled. 'When do you want me back?'

This was embarrassing, being given a curfew in front of Rik, but her mother would never let her out otherwise. 'Six o'clock. And be careful,' Judith said meaningfully. 'You really should get a helmet.'

And mess up my hair and have Rik laugh at me, Faith thought. No way.

They rode off together and she felt horribly nervous. She didn't open her mouth once and he seemed content with silence, although he was very chipper and upbeat, zooming and zig-zagging ahead of her along the tree-lined roads, pulling wheelies and flicking V-signs at irate motorists.

He's going to act like it never happened, and that we're just mates going for a bike ride, she thought, feeling disappointment and humiliation coursing through her in waves. So much for him worrying that she might regret it. He had obviously changed his mind about her, and now she was going to have to pretend it had all meant nothing.

The idea of Rik realising just how much she'd opened herself up to him was beyond excruciating. She'd been so convinced he was genuine, she could have sworn she had even tasted his raw vulnerability on her tongue.

She should go, but she wanted to lose herself on her bike until the shame and mortification had passed, although she didn't want to talk to Rik so jumps were out of the question. Once they got to the quarry she turned her bike immediately and dropped in to the gravel pit.

'Faith, wait!' Rik sounded anxious and she ignored him, but she'd forgotten to check for the huge stones, which were constantly shifting and becoming dislodged, sometimes dangerously. One monster had fallen, and she only saw it when it was too late. She cannoned into it full pelt and flew in a graceless arc over her handlebars, slamming face-first into the ground.

Rik sprinted over and she felt him pull her bike off her. She could taste blood in her mouth as she sat up.

'That's pretty bad,' he said. 'Rinse it.' He handed her some water and she poured it over her face, wincing as it hit her raw, bloodied skin. He took her face in his hand. 'You've cut your lip. You might have some gravel in there. Let's get you back home.'

They rode back very slowly, and Rik stayed close to her. He took her bike from her and put it in the hay barn, then he put his arm around her and they walked up to the cottage. She felt weak and shaky, the adrenaline draining away as the shock set in. She had fallen off enough times by now to know it always took a while to kick in for her, much longer than it did for Rik.

'Sit down,' he instructed, and she curled her legs under her and waited while he got the first aid kit from the bathroom. 'Are you cold yet?'

'A bit.'

He located an old hoody from behind the sofa and gave it to her, and sat down next to her and put his arm around her shoulder. 'It's OK,' he said. 'I'm here. You just have to ride it out until it's done its thing.'

She gritted her teeth as nausea slammed in, beginning in the pit of her stomach and curling outwards, tendrils of chilling wrongness, disorientating and battering, leaving her feeling isolated and vulnerable and like nothing was as it should be. Her head began to spin and she leaned forwards slightly. Rik stroked her hair and murmured comforting nonsense in her ear. She closed her eyes and took his hand and breathed in his presence next to her.

After a few minutes she felt better, and sat back up. 'All done.' She squeezed his hand gratefully, her animosity forgotten. 'Thanks Rikki.'

'Let me sort this out for you. Hold still.' She tried not to wince as he put TCP on some cotton wool and dabbed at her lip. 'Oh your poor mouth,' he said, 'you're all messed up, but no gravel.'

'Do I look like a clown?' she asked, feeling that her already full lip was considerably swollen.

He smiled. 'No. You look as beautiful as ever.'

It was ridiculously nice to be told she was beautiful, especially by him. He was looking pretty beautiful himself, his dark eyes soulful and soft with concern, and her nostrils were full of his scent, which seemed to be making her a dizzy again in a far more pleasant and exciting way.

She ran her tongue over her lip tentatively, tasting the TCP and the metallic tang of blood. His eyes followed the movement and she saw that his pupils had dilated. Her heart began to pound insistently.

'It looks better already,' he said, moving towards her. 'Do you want me to make you some tea? Does it hurt too much for me to kiss you?'

What hurts, she thought, suddenly remembering what she had conveniently forgotten, is the idea you might go off and snog Sophie Barnes again. All her disappointment and rage and humiliation came surging back and she scowled at him furiously. 'We are not doing that.'

'Why not?'

'You know why not,' she snapped. 'I'm going now,' she said, getting to her feet, 'so you can ring Sophie right now as she's much more *your type.*'

'What?' He looked horrified. 'That was all rubbish, you know — I thought you knew. You were doing it too, weren't you?'

'Didn't sound like rubbish to me.'

'I thought you wanted to keep us quiet?' he said. 'I wasn't just going to stand there and take it from you, that would have made Minel more suspicious than ever.'

He was right, she thought. Minel would have smelled a rat a mile off if Rik's quick wit and killer put-downs had suddenly deserted him.

'You didn't have to go that far,' she said, weak with relief.

'Sorry,' he said instantly. 'Of course it wasn't true. I just thought you'd give it straight back, you said it was *awful*,' he reminded her, 'I was expecting you to say I'd drowned you in saliva or something.' He pushed at her shoulders gently to sit her back down, and crouched down in front of her. 'Have I still not convinced you that I'm crazy about you?' He leaned forwards and kissed her very gently, mindful of her sore lip, and Faith felt herself beginning to melt. 'I have been,' he said, 'since the second I met you and there is literally nothing I wouldn't do to be with you, so you can stop worrying about anything like that right now.'

She thought when he was this close to her and looking at her like this there was pretty much nothing she ever could worry about, except maybe —

'You haven't told anybody, have you?'

'Not even Jason. I did tell Tackle,' he admitted, 'but he can't talk, so that's OK. Oh and my mum knows,' he said absently.

'What?' Faith sat bolt upright and winced as her head swirled threateningly. 'You told her what we got up to? Jesus, Rik.'

'Not that,' he said, still sounding patient. 'I told her a while ago I had a thing for you. Or rather, that I'd always had a thing for you and I didn't really know what to do about it. And she was all, you know my mum,' he imitated a breathy sort of voice, 'but how do you *feel*, Rik? On the *inside*?' He looked a little distracted for a second, then seemed to pull himself together, 'So I said you make me laugh more than anybody I know, and no matter how much time we spend together we always have lots to say to each other, and I never get bored of being with you, and any time you fall off your bike I just want to look after you,' he smiled unselfconsciously, 'and you just seem to *get me* and you're the most beautiful girl I've ever seen and I fancy you rotten, or words to that effect.' He raised his eyebrows and Faith giggled, feeling unbelievably touched. 'I said we seemed to click and you just make me really happy.'

'What did she say?' Faith asked, fascinated at the idea of such an open and frank conversation with a parental figure. She had thought it was practically obligatory to hide absolutely everything remotely approaching genuine emotion from her parents, the way they did from her.

'She said it sounded like you might be the right girl for me,' he said, putting his hands on her knees, and she stroked his hair absently. 'And that she would be very happy if you were, although if you didn't feel the same way about me I should just accept it, but there must be a reason you wanted to spend so much time with me, so I should be patient.' Faith felt her heart swelling again. 'And then she lectured me for about half an hour about being careful and gave me the facts of life speech *again.*'

'My mother is not a fan of the facts of life,' Faith sighed, thinking how nice it would be if Judith ever seemed interested in her feelings or even recognised that she might have them. 'Her entire spiel is basically that if I ever let one of *those things* near me I will become pregnant and die of an STD instantaneously. I learned everything I know about sex,' which wasn't much, she acknowledged, 'from magazines and Sara and my mother's Mills and Boons.'

Rik leaned forwards and kissed her again and a surge of that primal energy rose up in her and she pulled him to her and urged him to kiss her much harder, feeling him trembling as he did so.

'Do you want to go upstairs?' he asked.

'Don't get your hopes up.'

'It's not my hopes that's up,' he grumbled and they both shook with laughter. 'Of course I won't. Whatever you want.'

'Yes.' She felt a thrill of anticipation as he took her hand and led her up to his room, which was covered with comics and magazines and piles of clothes and loose bits of paper with scribbles and drawings all over them. Tackle plodded in after them.

'He can't watch!' Faith squeaked.

'Look what I taught him. Only took a couple of weeks.' Rik looked ridiculously pleased with himself. 'Face the wall,' he instructed and Tackle obediently lay down with his head underneath the window.

'That's brilliant,' Faith said, delighted. Rik was never normally shy of discussing his own brilliance with her in exhaustive detail but he clearly had other things on his mind. He shoved another pile of assorted junk off his bed and pulled her down next to him. Faith thought again how unbelievably exciting this was with him, in a completely different league to any of the snogging sessions in which she had partaken before. Rik was so obviously and unashamedly enjoying himself that it was impossible for her to feel uncomfortable or embarrassed about anything, and the thorny little details like what to do about all the saliva and teeth-clashing and the weirdly exciting muffled noises they were making, or the occasional awkwardness of things getting tangled or snagged or pressed up against, just didn't seem to matter in the slightest.

'You are really turning me on,' he said after a while. 'You are just the best kisser and you look,' he had pulled her top off at lightning speed and fumbled his way around the fastening of her bra for considerably longer but finally managed to get that off too, and his eyes were like saucers as he stared at her. 'You look *so* gorgeous,' he said.

'You're really gorgeous too,' she said, looking at him so unselfconsciously dishevelled in just his shorts, his hair sticking up all over the place from where she'd been grabbing and tugging at it. 'But I meant it earlier. I'm not going to have sex with you. We can just do, um,' she didn't want to use any of the phrases the kids at school threw around, they were all so clinical or revoltingly euphemistic and made everything sound so soulless.

'Foreplay,' Rik said in a doctorly voice. 'Titillation.'

'I'll titillate you,' she said. 'With my not quite a handful.'

'Perfect, perfect handful,' he said. 'I think I like them more than I like you.'

'You're not really winning me over here, Rikki. That's technically an insult.'

'Come here,' he said, reaching out for her, 'and I'll make it up to you.'

Faith's mother, alerted by the dreamy state her daughter returned in, not to mention the cut lip and the inevitable lateness, went berserk. She wasn't even mollified by the fact Faith was so completely blissed out after an afternoon with Rik she couldn't even pepper her protests with choice words and snarky insults.

The following day she told her mother she was meeting Minel and shot off to Hollyhocks looking for Rik but he wasn't there or at the quarry.

Faith was busy with gardening jobs most days, but Minel invited her over for dinner on Wednesday night and Faith squirmed a little awkwardly at the table, staring at Rik for as long as she felt was reasonable without arousing any suspicion.

Afterwards they went back to the cottage and she sat and willed Minel to go to the toilet, even making her friend a cup of tea in the hope it would prompt her, but her bladder held firm. Then, just as she was about to give up hope completely, Minel finally excused herself and she threw herself at Rik.

'Can't we just tell Minel?' Rik asked. 'This is stupid, sneaking around.'

'No! We can't tell her yet,' she said.

He frowned. 'She won't mind. She'll probably find it funny.'

Faith still couldn't bear the idea of being a laughing stock among her friends. She shook her head. 'Just wait a bit,' she said.

'That's all I do, wait around for you,' Rik said indignantly and she was worried he really was annoyed and kissed him as hard as she could, and he seized the back of her head, pulling her to him. 'Luckily for you,' he said softly, 'I'd wait for ever.'

Minel returned and she and Rik leaped guiltily apart, and then she heard the unmistakable sound of her mother's car, revving on the drive.

Chapter 9

'Morning sunshine,' Paul bellowed as Faith scurried past the site on Monday, ducking her head and hoping this would magically conceal the rest of her.

'Morning big guy,' she said quickly. 'Morning, whatever your names are.' She waved in the general direction of the mob of teenagers.

'Morning sexy,' one of the teenagers yelled back.

'Knock it off,' Paul rumbled. 'Good weekend, Faith?'

'Not really.' She'd spent all of Sunday torturing herself alternately about the magnificent splendour of Lucinda, and the impending conversation she was going to have to somehow manage with Rik. At least he wasn't currently on site, and she could be on her merry way and bury herself — literally — in the pond until she'd finally come up with a plan of action.

'Get to work then,' Paul said. 'Good to catch up, pleasantries are now officially over. Back to it, you lot.' He turned to the teenagers and Faith sped off to the pond.

'One week down, six to go,' Paul roared after her.

It had only been one week. Or several lifetimes, depending on how you looked at it. Faith picked up her shovel and began to dig, ignoring the bags of slurry she'd set aside on Saturday. She could worry about them later. She could worry about all of it later, including how she was supposed to relandscape an entire garden in just six weeks when she'd done practically nothing other than create a gigantic mess in one-seventh of her allotted time.

When to talk to Rik, and where to talk to Rik, was the order of the morning. Actually when wasn't really an issue, it had to be today, because she'd barely slept a wink since Friday and she couldn't cope with yet another night of lucid, sweaty dreams in the brief intervals in between lying resolutely awake, staring at the ceiling and going through it all again and again, the confrontation ahead of her each time becoming greater and more terrible than ever before. And she didn't want to risk her theory about Hollyhocks hating her turning out to be true, and finding out what new and messy or life-threatening punishments it had in store for her.

So today it must be, which led to the rather more difficult question of where. It couldn't be on the site in front of Paul and the garden gang, but that was basically the only place she saw Rik.

She could go and bash the other door of the haybarn down, and hope he once again came to her aid and then hit him with it while he was temporarily jolted out of his usual blankness, but then he'd realise she'd done it on purpose and she doubted he'd be so forgiving of her a second time. And the kitchen was out of the question because the walls would loom in on her, and Minel might be there and Paul would probably come in and the last thing she needed was an audience while she stammered and gulped and cried and whatever the hell else she was going to do.

I need to get him away from Hollyhocks, she decided. She could try and run into him on his lunchtime bike ride, assuming he was going out today, but she didn't actually know where he went and she'd probably just end up roaming around fruitlessly.

So the only possible scenario was to go down to the site just before lunch and ask him to come out on the bike with her.

Which would involve some degree of persuasion, she was willing to bet, and that would have to happen in front of Paul and the boys.

However I look at this, she concluded, it's going to be a rocky road. As if on cue, she unearthed another massive boulder, and she dropped her spade and heaved at it with both hands, pitching her weight back and forcing it out of its earthy prison, then dropped it on the small but ever-growing pile at her side.

By half past twelve Faith could stand it no more and she dropped her shovel with a loud clang onto the now significant pile of rocks and dusted herself down.

She shot out of the garden towards the side of the barn, where her bike was leaning with her helmet dangling from the handlebars, and shoved it on her head firmly then grabbed the bike and wheeled it down to the site.

'Off for a ride?' one of the boys smirked. He made it sound moderately smutty. Those teenagers could make anything sound moderately smutty. Rik had his back to her over by the cement mixer and was laughing at something Paul must have said. Good, she thought, Paul's softened him up, time to go in for the kill.

'Rik.'

He mustn't have heard her, because he said something in response to Paul and they both laughed again. What's so funny, Faith thought irritably. Doesn't he realise he has better things to do than just stand around laughing like he hasn't a care in the world?

'Rik!' Faith practically screamed. Several of the boys closest to her winced and giggled. Rik, finally, turned and looked at her. His eyes, still softened and lit from the laughter, fixed on her for a moment and she felt her cheeks warming, then they slid seamlessly back into that distant expression. 'Oh, hi Faith,' he said, just a shade short of tonelessly. 'Didn't see you over there.'

'You had your back to me,' she said pointlessly.

Rik's eyes slipped to her bike. 'Going for a ride.' It wasn't a question, he wasn't inviting an answer, and he made to turn back to Paul.

'You're coming too.' Perhaps taking a very authoritative tone would work.

'I'm good, thanks,' he said, still in that disinterested tone. 'See you later.'

Evidently it would not work.

'I need to talk to you.'

'What about?'

She sighed heavily. 'Not here.'

'What's wrong?' one of the teenagers yelled. 'Did he not return your calls?'

More like I didn't return his, Faith thought.

'I don't think they need to hear this,' she said to Rik, nodding at the teenagers who all looked thoroughly interested.

'I'm sure it can wait then.' Rik had apparently decided the conversation, such as it was, was over and he turned back to Paul.

Faith dropped her bike and marched straight over to him. She put both hands on his shoulders and yanked him round to face her. Her palms tingled at the contact. A few of the teenagers whooped and cheered.

'Go and get your bike,' she said through gritted teeth, 'right now, or I swear, I will spill my guts here on the site after all.'

'You'd better go, mate,' Paul rumbled. 'She's got one hell of a bug up her arse about something.'

103

'Well?' Faith asked, her eyes fixed on Rik. Her fingers were digging into his shoulders and she could feel his muscles underneath. She dropped her hands quickly.

'All right, come on then,' Rik sighed. He scowled at her and stormed off across the site and she went back and picked up her bike and leaned against it for a moment, weak with relief. Thank god that was over.

Now she just had to somehow manage the rest of it. She got on her bike and freewheeled down to the drive, taking her hands off the handlebars to do up her helmet. Rik came out of the barn and her bike lurched threateningly to the right and she grabbed frantically for the handlebars.

'Well that was embarrassing,' Rik grumbled as he joined her and they rolled down the drive together. 'Where do you want to go?'

'I don't know,' she snapped back. Was she supposed to have thought of that too? 'Where did you go last week?'

'I did some hill reps.'

'Let's go up Fox Hill then,' she said. 'We can stop at the top. And don't even think about putting those in or I'll snap them in half.' He had reached into his pocket for his headphones.

She set off, spinning her legs determinedly but Rik overtook her instantly and soon they were climbing the winding hill. The sun shone brightly overhead, sending brilliant rays through gaps in the lush canopy. Workmen had cut back the sections nearest the road but above them the trees were free to spread and grow as they saw fit. Gnarled branches were reaching towards one other, drawn perhaps by a primal knowledge of a kindred, until at certain points they touched, creating a living roof over the dead grey tarmac.

Rik reached the top considerably ahead of her and he put his bike down. She stood up on her pedals to get herself up the final slope and rolled to a halt in front of him.

'What is it then?' His eyes were as flinty as the rocks she'd spent all morning digging up. He should never look at me like that, she thought and a surge of grief shot through her, hot and visceral.

She put her own bike down and sat on the grass verge. 'I wanted to talk to you.'

'Go ahead.'

Overhead she could hear the distinct yaffling call of a green woodpecker then, a couple of seconds later, the higher-pitched laughter of its mate. Bickering and laughing, like all the best couples.

If you can siphon out that pond — twice — she urged herself, then you can do this.

'Rik,' she said. 'I do remember Minel's party.'

He exhaled loudly.

'You remember too, don't you?'

'I do,' he confirmed, but he didn't sound particularly happy about it. 'I remember all of it, quite vividly as it happens, and the part I remember the most was you telling me you wished you'd never met me.'

Oh Christ, Faith thought. Now I wish his memory really was more selective.

'There was a reason for that,' she said in a small voice.

'I guessed there might be,' he said. 'I was actually hoping you might enlighten me at some point. But don't let me push you,' he added sarcastically, 'if you're not quite ready yet. It's only been nine years.'

This was new too, she thought, this acidity, the sarcasm. Did I do this to him, she wondered. Did I turn his sweetness knowing and sour?

'I had a bit of trouble at home,' she said, thinking she might as well begin there because she'd never actually told Rik what had happened with her parents and she could see with hindsight that had affected her judgement, that was one of the reasons she'd been so quick to assume the worst. 'Quite a bit, actually. I came home after that weekend — after I'd been with you,' she hoped he'd know to which weekend she was referring, because she couldn't really bear to spell it out, 'and my mum told me she and my dad were getting divorced.'

'OK.' He digested this for a moment. 'And this came as a shock?'

She nodded. 'I had no idea,' she said sadly. 'I knew they hadn't been getting along well but I didn't realise it was that serious. I felt really guilty,' she admitted, 'because I was so distracted by you I really hadn't seen it coming. It took all the wind out of my sails. I literally couldn't think about anything else, not even you. My mum was heartbroken, and I was too, and so hopelessly, powerlessly, vociferously angry at my dad.' She took a deep breath. 'They made me promise not to tell anybody,' she said, 'but my dad had — he had an affair, and my mum found out somehow and that was why.' She paused, feeling familiar waves of sadness wash over her, and guilt at betraying her parents' confidence. 'I felt like I owed it to my mum to be there for her.'

'I can see why you would feel like that.'

'She was devastated of course. But I really didn't want them to split up.' She hung her head. 'She wanted to move to London to live with my aunt, and take me with her while my dad organised selling the house. I couldn't stand the thought of leaving here so I pleaded with her to go for counselling and eventually she agreed.' She sighed. 'It must have worked, to some extent, because they did stay together. But it took a long time and that was pretty all-consuming for me.'

'It must have been,' Rik said gently and she felt a wave of gratitude towards him for being able to muster up some sympathy for her. But then his voice hardened again and he went on, 'But I still don't see what that has to do with me.'

'I came here,' Faith said, feeling that her heartrate had quickened and swallowing down the sudden rush of nausea it had brought along for the ride. 'To Hollyhocks,' she added. 'To see you. It had been a few weeks since Jason's party and I hadn't seen or spoken to you since.'

'I remember the party,' Rik said curtly. 'You don't have to give me any more context.'

'I kind of do,' Faith said desperately, 'so you understand — anyway, I hadn't spoken to you and I knew you'd been trying to ring me and must be wondering where I was, especially after...' she tailed off again. 'I hadn't been ready to see you, I knew I would just tell you everything and that would be going against what I'd promised my parents and it all felt very precarious and up in the air and such a mess.' She sighed. 'But I had really missed you and all I wanted was to be with you.' She bit her lip. 'I came over early one Sunday morning, very early actually, nobody had really got up yet except Minel who answered the door and she told me...' Faith took another deep breath and blundered on, 'She told me you were upstairs with some girl. With Sophie.'

'Sophie,' Rik repeated, as if he'd never heard the name before.

'I thought Minel was joking,' Faith said. 'She said you had a girlfriend, was talking about how you'd been acting totally loved-up and I just assumed you'd told her about you and me and she was trying wind me up but then I went upstairs into your room and I saw — I saw…'

Something approaching enlightenment was drifting across Rik's face. 'You saw Sophie?'

Faith nodded. 'I saw Sophie and you — at least I thought it was you. It was really sunny,' she said quickly, 'and I couldn't really make out faces or anything and to be honest I wasn't looking that closely but I saw two people and one of them was definitely Sophie because I saw her hair and the other one…' She could feel hot tears prickling behind her eyelids but pressed on regardless, 'I mean — who else could it have been but you?'

Rik shook his head. 'You didn't check?'

'Why would I check?' Faith asked. 'I didn't know you were conspiring with Jason. I had no idea about all that, I'd been in a totally different zone for weeks, I'd forgotten all about Jason and Sophie and pretty much everything other than my parents, and you. And then Minel was full of chat about you and her, and I saw what I thought I saw and what else was I supposed to think?'

There was a long, long, painful silence. Faith stared at the ground and twisted her hands together, wringing them absently, then she looked back up at Rik and saw that he looked equally shellshocked.

'So why didn't you say something?' he asked eventually. 'Why didn't you ask me what was going on? Why didn't tell me you'd seen her in my room?'

'I didn't think I had to,' Faith said quietly. 'I assumed you would figure it out.'

'A bit tricky,' Rik said, 'seeing as I didn't actually do anything in the first place.'

'Well, I know that now,' Faith said. 'But like I said, what else was I supposed to think?'

'I don't know,' Rik said. 'I don't get why you wouldn't be upfront with me then I could have told you what really happened and then...' His mind was wandering, she realised, he's coming to the same conclusions I've come to this last weekend, that if I'd just asked him straight up what was going on we wouldn't have had to go through any of this, back then or now, and instead we would be — we might be — we could still be —

'I didn't say anything to you,' she said, 'because I really didn't want you to know how much it had hurt me. I was devastated. The only possible thing I could salvage from the whole mess was not to lower myself to telling you or showing you just how much I cared about you.' She sighed. 'So rather than give you an earful I thought it would be better if I made it all out to be a bit of fun on both our sides, which is what I assumed it must have been to you.' He opened his mouth to contradict her but she cut him off. 'Rik, what other explanation could there be?'

'Loads of them.'

'Such as?'

'Such as it *didn't actually happen* in the first place?'

Faith could feel herself becoming annoyed. 'Minel told me she'd stayed over a few times. She called her your girlfriend. She said she'd *heard* you. And she was in your room and there were clothes all over the floor...' She could still remember her reaction to the scene, the sickening lurch in her stomach, the disbelief, the tugging in her chest as if her heart were physically sinking and pulling at all her arteries and veins on its relentless way down. And then that unbearable pressure behind her eyes that told her she was going to cry, much like she was feeling now actually.

Oh god, she really was going to cry. She was going to bawl her stupid tortured heartbroken little eyes out right here and now in front of him. It was going to be a fountain of misery, tears would spray almost vertically from her ducts straight onto him, soaking him and knocking him bodily to the ground with their velocity.

They were coming now, she could feel them beginning to gather and collect, spilling silently down her burning cheeks, and she put her head in her hands and stuffed her palms into her eyes, hoping to stem the flow but it was unstoppable, a tirade. She gave a horrible, snotty, choking sort of sob that turned into a groan and pressed into her eye sockets once more then gave up altogether and dropped her hands into her lap, watching droplets splash down upon them, huge and distorted like summer rain.

Rik was silent but she could feel his eyes on her. 'I'm so sorry,' she choked out, 'that I didn't give you a chance to explain. I did think about it, but all I really wanted was for it not to be true and I couldn't see any way it couldn't be true and I was so worried you would find a way to talk me round.' She gave another gasping, juddering sob. 'We never actually did have the conversation about whether or not we were boyfriend and girlfriend, and spell it out that we weren't going to see other people. And,' she wiped her face absently, 'as shallow and horrible of me as it was, I was a tiny bit embarrassed about the fact you were younger than me, you know how that stuff seemed to matter back then, and I was mortified that my "toyboy",' she mimed quotation marks, 'had cheated on me.'

'I did notice that my age bothered you,' Rik said.

She sighed. 'It did a bit. But I had decided it wasn't an issue any more because you and I were just obviously meant to be.'

110

She waited for him to counter her, to tell her she had indeed been naïve and romantic in thinking that anything could be 'meant to be' at such a young age but once again, he didn't say a word. Once upon a time Rik knew the exact right thing to say to me to make me feel better, she though hopelessly, now he knows exactly when not saying anything will hurt the most.

'You do believe me, don't you?'

'Yes,' he said reluctantly. 'I believe you.' He sighed heavily. 'Why didn't you at least say you just wanted to go back to being friends?'

'How could I?' Faith asked. 'How could I go back to being friends with you after that? Could *you*?'

There was another long, long silence.

'Well.' Rik sounded defeated. 'I guess we'll never know.'

But we could, she thought, a tiny flash of hope through her misery. We could now.

'Do you think it's too late,' she said in a very small voice, 'to say I want us to go back to being friends now?'

He made a dismissive sort of noise.

'You obviously came back here for a reason, Rik,' she said. 'And so did I,' she added hastily, wanting to be honest with him. 'One of the reasons I came back was in the hope I might get some answers out of you. Losing somebody who was such a big part of my life really affected me. I wondered what I did, or didn't do, to deserve that kind of treatment from my best friend and it still bothers me now. Or it did,' she admitted, 'until a few days ago.'

Rik laughed humourlessly. 'I hoped I'd get some answers out of you too. Instead I came back to you acting all weird and seeming like you were actually pissed off with me and wondering what that was all about. At least that makes a bit more sense now.'

'Likewise,' Faith said, glad he seemed to be willing to be open with her too. 'Much more sense. I can completely see why,' she said, reaching out to touch his arm tentatively. 'I do get it now, and I totally understand why you've been so distant.'

'Yeah,' he said, sounding resigned. 'I get it too. A bit. I think.'

'But look, Rik,' she tightened her grip on his arm and he looked down at her hand. She dropped it abruptly. 'Now we know — now we both know what the situation is, or was,' she was aware she was making a hash of this but carried on regardless, 'don't you think maybe we could try and put it behind us? At the end of the day neither of us really did anything wrong, it was just a horrible set of circumstances and if we take that part away, we're left with the fact that we used to really care about one another.' She hoped he wouldn't think she was suggesting anything untoward and added quickly, 'I mean we were such good friends. And I missed you,' she said candidly, thinking that she at least owed him that. 'I've often wondered what you're up to, what you're doing with your life. It would be nice if we could be,' she thought hard about how best to put it. 'If we could at least acknowledge each other's existence, without accompanying bitterness and resentment and accusing glares and blank stares.'

She studied his face for a moment. He was looking down at the ground and his brows were drawn together, his long eyelashes lowered. Without the stubble, she would be able to see spiky shadows of them on his high cheekbones. He's thinking right now, she thought. He's thinking about what to do and he's wondering if whatever we had is worth opening up a can stuffed to the brim with worms, if he can get over all the anger and sadness and betrayal that I once thought I could never see the end of. He's wondering if whatever is at the bottom, is worth the effort.

He's going to say no, she thought with anguish. He's going to say it's been too long, too much time has passed, he accepts my explanation but it's all ancient history and that's where it should stay and that will be it for this summer, that will be it for me and Rik forever...

'I mean,' she said, 'I'm here now.'

He looked back up at her and she could see resignation in his eyes, and irritation, and sadness, and something else too, something else very familiar that she hadn't seen in him so far, until now.

'Yeah,' he said. 'Looks like I'm here too.'

Chapter 10

After her conversation with Rik Faith knew she didn't have anything left in her. She felt as drained and depleted as the now-empty pond, and about as fragrant, thanks to all the digging and the mountains of bags stuffed full of rancid slurry she had to get to the skip.

She couldn't carry on without some form of help. Firstly to shift the bags, but mainly with Rik. The cocktail of memories and emotions and new and shocking revelations was simply too much for her to handle by herself. She could just about manage it, she decided, if she had at least one other person with whom to share it all. And that had to be Rik, as he was the only other person involved here and she didn't feel like going over the whole scenario with Minel, or Sara, or anybody else who would be coming in cold.

He was always in it with me, she thought, and like it or not he's in it with me again now. This has been as big a shock to him as it was to me. He's the only one who can move forwards with me now.

And if he chooses not to, if he decides to write it all off and pretend it never happens, if he continues to look right through me and act like the only purpose of my existence is to cause him irritation, then I just can't stay here.

If that cynical, dismissive person is who Rik really is now, then I'm out. I can't watch somebody who looks so much like somebody I used to love act like a callous, bitter stranger.

I'll have to tell Minel I can't handle it and she'll be disappointed and let down and have to find somebody else and I'll have to go back to work and put up with staying with my parents and commuting to London, spending hours on end on a train staring blankly out of a small window.

And even that stultifying little scenario was better than the thought of a summer here without anything other than ambivalence or moderate hostility from Rik.

I have to move on, she thought regretfully. At least we both know the truth now, and that's got to be better than not knowing, surely.

GT, as if reading her thoughts, snuffled approvingly and nudged her ankle hopefully. She nudged him right back, and he growled then adjusted himself so his other side was in the sun and went back to sleep.

Two days had crept past since their soul-sapping conversation on Monday, and in that time she'd chosen to leave him be, thinking that as she'd had a weekend to digest the new information before she acted on it, she'd extend him the same courtesy. But that had meant avoiding the site and not asking Paul or the teenagers for any help, which meant the bags of slime were rising to unmanageable levels, and so today she would have to go round to the site and get some of those teenagers to shift them for her.

Time to test the water. Again.

She pushed her shoulders back and marched across to the site. Paul was roaring at one of the boys, a chunky-looking youth who had paused with a handful of crisps halfway to his mouth. 'Put them away,' Paul was yelling. 'Doesn't your mother feed you? What do you want?' His gaze had fallen on Faith, hovering at the edge of the site.

'I need some help,' she said. 'Moving bags of stuff from the pond.'

'Why can't you move them?' Paul was clearly not in an obliging mood.

'There's too many of them and they're really heavy. I only need to borrow a couple of this lot for a few minutes.'

Paul grumbled something under his breath.

'Sorry,' Faith said. 'I didn't catch that.'

'It was pretty unrepeatable.' Rik had overheard and he was shaking his head. He was covered in cement dust and his hair was sticking upwards in a messy sort of quiff. She felt her insides squirming, then they turned weak with relief as he smiled at her and gestured to the two teenagers nearest to him. 'Come on, you can both help too.'

Oh thank you god, she thought, and thank you Rik. You're not going to spend all summer hating me after all.

He fell into step next to her and they wandered back to the pond. 'Here,' she announced, pointing towards the bags and buckets she had filled with the pond slop. 'I need that in the skip.'

The teenagers were shoving each other and giggling more than ever.

'Why are they doing that?' Faith asked Rik warily. 'Do I have a phallic-looking mudstain on my forehead?'

'They're trying to work up the courage to talk to you,' he said. 'But they're too afraid of me to try.'

'He doesn't like us talking about you,' muttered one of the shuffling teens.

'Go on then.' Rik gestured at the teenagers. 'Get on with it.'

'What have they been saying?' Faith didn't know if she really wanted to know but she was curious why Rik would care what they said. 'I guess it wasn't flattering?'

He smiled again, a genuine smile that reached the corners of his eyes. It was the first time he'd truly smiled at her since she'd got here, and she caught her breath and reached automatically for GT who was always close at hand. He nipped at her affectionately.

'I think they think it's flattering,' he said. 'But they're only young and they get most of their information from the internet so they have strange ideas about what constitutes a compliment. Luckily, they've got me and Paul to set them straight. Do you want to ride again at lunch?'

'Really?'

'Really,' he affirmed. 'It would be nice to actually catch up with you, Faith, find out what you've been up to all this time.' He frowned. 'I could do without the embarrassing shouty preamble, if that's OK with you?'

It had been embarrassing, she conceded, and quite shouty and when she'd yanked him round to face her she'd been so wound up she genuinely hadn't known if she wanted to kiss him or take a swing at him. Although she was pretty sure whichever avenue she'd chosen, it would have ended the same way.

'No more foreplay,' she agreed. There was an awkward — well, awkward for her, anyway — silence. Faith wanted the ground to open up and swallow her whole. 'God, sorry,' she gasped. 'Don't know where that came from. I was just thinking about —'

What had she been thinking about?

'Thinking about?' Rik prompted, clearly not willing to let her just leave the thought hanging.

'James Bond!' she said triumphantly. Her dad had been watching it last night. 'That's where it's from.'

'What?'

'That thing about foreplay.' I need to stop this, she thought. I'm just making it worse.

'Right,' Rik said, as if this were an entirely rational discussion.

117

'I need to get on,' she said quickly. 'I'll see you at lunch.'

By unspoken agreement they headed back up Fox Hill again. Faith felt her legs burning from yesterday's efforts, and as they reached the top she bashed Rik's rear wheel with hers and held up her hands for a time out.

Once they had sat down she had no idea what to say to him. It's an odd sort of limbo, this, she thought, because on the one hand we know — knew — each other so well small talk is really out of the question, but on the other hand I haven't seen him in nearly a decade and I have no idea how we're going to bridge that gap. She really wanted to ask him about the super-hot Lucinda but she supposed that might sound like she was fishing.

She took her helmet off and shook her hair out absently.

'So what do you do now?' he asked. 'For work?'

'I work for a local authority in London,' she said.

'Doing what? Land management?'

She shook her head. 'Communications. Writing up minutes of meetings, sending out press releases, that kind of thing.'

Rik looked surprised. 'Do you enjoy it?'

Faith sensed she'd disappointed him in some way. 'Not really,' she said, 'but it pays the bills and Rob — my boyfriend — wanted us to buy a house.'

'I always thought you'd go into garden design,' he said, sounding regretful. 'Or become a TV gardening expert. I kept expecting to see you pop up during the Chelsea Flower Show, gushing about daffodils.'

'They're not in flower that late. They're spring blooms,' she corrected. 'Brought into life by the first welcome rays of sunshine after the relentless grey and bitter frosts, but they can't handle the radiance of a real summer.'

'See?' he said. 'You'd be a natural. How come you didn't carry on with the gardening?'

She sighed. 'Too risky, I suppose,' she said eventually. 'Competitive, low pay, hard work, difficult to make a career out of it.' She didn't really feel like discussing why she'd abandoned her passions so comprehensively. 'What about you? What kind of graphic art do you do?'

'Very graphic, as it happens,' Rik said. 'Porn, mostly.'

'God, really?'

'No,' he said, laughing a little at the shocked expression on her face. 'Websites, logos, that kind of thing. The occasional graphic novel.'

'You mean comics.'

'Comic,' he agreed. 'I still love them. Not ashamed.'

'Minel says you travel a lot.'

He nodded. 'I can do most of my stuff remotely, and I pick up clients all over the place.'

'Whereabouts?' Faith felt a pang of envy. She would have loved to have travelled, she always thought she would, actually, with Rik. They'd agreed they would take off, doing all the usual student trails, which invariably involved Laos, Cambodia and Vietnam then Australia and New Zealand for all that outback biking.

And she'd always quite fancied South America, trailing down the Amazon and stopping off in La Paz, that mythical-looking city in the clouds. She and Rik would have sat somewhere on top of the mountains, gazing down at the metropolis below with swirling white masses floating above it and they would have wondered aloud what it would be like to just jump straight through them and feel that collected rainwater and mist soaking their skin.

'All over, really,' he said. 'I spend quite a bit of time in Germany. Hamburg, mainly.'

'Do you speak German?' Faith asked.

'Ja!' Rik boomed, and she started. He giggled. 'Apparently I sound quite dictatorial, and my grammar is awful.'

'It's quite a dictatorial sort of language,' she said, wishing she spoke more than just English. She'd always liked the idea of learning a language but she'd forgotten all her GCSE French within seconds of the exam and on the rare occasions she had been abroad she'd always relied on the good old 'speak English loudly and slowly' school of communication. 'Where else?'

'Slovakia, although that wasn't for work.' Faith presumed he must have had a central European girlfriend and felt another stab of envy. 'Sweden.' Had he notched up a blonde Viking conquest too? she wondered automatically. 'Singapore, Japan, the States…'

Jesus Rik, she thought, just how many women have you slept with?

'Sounds fun,' she said, noting that now her tone was a little acidic.

'I always thought you'd travel too,' he said. 'You seemed keen on the idea.'

'It seemed too risky.'

'What's risky about it?'

'I don't know,' she said. 'Didn't have anybody to go with, I suppose, and I don't speak any languages, and it's expensive.' She must sound like a total bore.

'So what have you been doing then?' He was looking a little confused. 'Other than writing press releases?'

'I got into track cycling for a while. I used to meet up with an awesome bunch of girls every Saturday for a skills session. But

I stopped.' God, she thought, I don't just sound like a bore, I sound like an old woman.

'Was that too risky too?' Rik asked. 'Worried you'd bore yourself to sleep with all that mindless round-and-round?'

'Actually it's very enlivening,' she said, affronted. 'And it definitely does good things for the mind, the centrifugal force just pulls all the stuff you don't want out and sends it on its merry way. Clouds dispersing to make way for the sun, seeds scattering to implant themselves into the waiting ground.'

'And you think you wouldn't be able to make it as a gardening pundit,' he said, sounding amused. 'You'd be like that woman we used to laugh at on my parents' dreadful food and drink show, sniffing wine and getting pissed live on air and talking about "wheelbarrows of watermelons". And we would all be very proud. We'd turn to each other and say "I knew her when she was a mere dandelion, now she's a blazing sunflower".'

Faith giggled. 'More of a dandelion still,' she said self-deprecatingly. 'Although at least dandelions have those *roots*.' Which she would have to break her tools and probably her arm heaving out.

'Sounds like you have too, if you're buying a house with your boyfriend.'

'Ex-boyfriend,' she corrected automatically.

Rik looked startled. 'You're moving in with your ex? Ron, was it?'

Ron! He made him sound like somebody's granddad, sitting on the sofa reading his newspaper and blowing his nose on ever-present tissues and droning on about cars. Actually that wasn't far off the mark, she conceded grudgingly.

'Not any more,' she said. 'We just split up.'

'Oh. Sorry.'

She shook her head. 'It's fine.'

'What happened?'

'He asked me to marry him,' Faith said regretfully.

'What a bastard.'

She smiled absently. 'He wasn't a bastard. He just wasn't very —' Very what? 'He was a bit too sensible,' she said eventually. 'He wanted security and stability and to settle down, and I didn't.'

'I would have thought you liked sensible,' Rik said. 'Well actually I wouldn't have, but I wouldn't have thought you thought gardening and travelling were risky either.'

She knew what he was saying and he was echoing the thoughts she'd begun to have herself recently. 'I did get very risk averse,' she conceded, 'after that shock with my parents and everything. I got a bit too focused on making sensible choices.' She frowned, because she hadn't actually consciously thought this at the time, but there had been that strange moment just before Ron — Rob! — had proposed when everything had gone a bit blurry and slow-mo. 'When Rob actually got down on one knee and popped the question — in front of all our friends, which was highly embarrassing — I just had this moment.' She could remember it a little more clearly now. 'I thought, is this what you want your life to be? Safe, sensible boyfriend, safe, sensible husband, safe job, safe life, *quiet* life…' She shook her head, it was like a pendulum at the moment. 'I thought, no. Enough is enough.'

Rik was watching her very intently and she thought she could see a flash of something in his eyes, something a little bit less disappointed. Or was he just confused? 'That probably made no sense,' she said. 'I'm a bit absentminded these days. Even more than I used to be. I follow trains of thought quite happily, just drift along taking whatever comes up.' She giggled. 'Like Tackle. I wish I'd seen him again before he died.'

'He adored you,' Rik said. 'We had that in common.'

She felt a wave of sadness, drifting over on an invisible breeze, and the hairs on the back of her neck stood on end. Rik was silent too, his eyes very soulful, and she swallowed awkwardly. You're going to have to get used to this, she told herself sternly, you'll be chatting away with him quite happily and then suddenly something will remind you of the way things used to be and you'll have to deal with it, you've got to learn to let it go. Think about something else.

An image flashed into her mind of a naked Rik, lying back underneath her, gasping at her to —

She felt a jolt in her groin. Stop that, she told herself firmly. *That* had never run its course, after all. They hadn't had a chance for the novelty to wear off, it was only natural, surely, that being around him might provoke some of those sorts of feelings. It didn't mean anything, he had the super-hot Lucinda after all.

And she was hardly a catch, she conceded, sweaty and dishevelled and downbeat and a little bit *curvier*, although that wasn't the right word because her lean frame didn't lend itself to curves and instead she had just picked up a bit of a belly and her thighs touched at the top and her breasts had grown a cup size. He might like that, actually.

'Rik?'

'Yes?' His eyes were still misty and faraway.

'We should get going.'

Hollyhocks must have joined Rik in forgiving Faith, because she made steady but noticeable progress with the pond that afternoon. Maybe it really was punishing me, she thought ruefully. It knew the truth and it wanted me to know too so it persisted in conspiring against me, forcing me into awkward and uncomfortable and downright exposing situations with Rik until all the pieces of the puzzle finally fell into place. The rain had made the ground softer and more malleable, and she dug easily, feeling a new strength in her body as she hauled stones aside and burrowed deeper into the no longer resistant earth.

'I've told Paul to get you some help,' Rik said, as she wandered past the site to say goodbye once her shift was finished. The sun was lower in the sky, and the halo-ish effect it created around his body made Faith's eyes hurt in more ways than one. 'He can't spare any of that lot so we need to get somebody else in.'

She glanced past him to the mob of teenagers, who were all rolling cigarettes and talking enthusiastically about their upcoming night at the pub.

'He did offer right at the beginning,' she said. 'I should have taken him up on it. I really had no idea how hard this would be.' She pulled a guilty face.

'You'll do a great job,' Rik said and she felt a surge of fresh hope at the conviction in his voice. It really is going to be OK after all, she thought hopefully. We'll have a lovely, fun summer and at the end of it I'll wish him well and we'll both move on knowing we can be a part of each other's lives.

She smiled happily at him, squinting a little against the sun.

'Help will be very welcome,' she said. 'That rockery is going to be a nightmare to shift.'

Help arrived the following morning in the form of an extremely tall, very blonde young man with bulging muscles who introduced himself as Henry but the teens immediately and inventively dubbed 'Lofty'. Faith guessed he couldn't have been more than twenty. 'There you go,' Minel said gleefully as Faith took in her new apprentice. 'You asked for help, we got you He-Man.' Lofty, she explained, was the son of one of her senior colleagues and doing manual work over the summer while on holiday from Cambridge. 'Clever and handsome,' Minel nudged Faith pointedly. 'You're welcome.'

'Bit young for me,' Faith protested. 'And a bit,' she eyed the strapping youth who was currently hefting two of her gigantic bags of slime effortlessly. 'Bit plastic-looking.'

Lofty, who seemed to find Faith mesmerising, couldn't have been happier about the arrangement. He relayed her endlessly with tales of his antics at Cambridge, in a deep but distinctly plummy voice that belied his privileged roots.

Rik came over to check out the newest addition. 'I'm pretty sure I drew him in at least three comics,' he hissed to Faith, who was thinking how much more attractive he was than the conventionally handsome young buck she was supposed to be supervising. Rik still hadn't shaved and his hair was now practically grey with dust, and he looked feral and a bit rough round the edges. He's still going to be gorgeous as an old man, Faith thought wistfully, the grey brought out his skin tone and made his eyes sparkle more enticingly than ever.

'I know what you mean,' she murmured back. 'He's like a caricature, isn't he?'

Rik looked vindicated. 'Ride again at lunch?'

She nodded.

He glanced at Lofty again. 'Let me know if he gives you any grief.'

Lofty, however, couldn't have been more charming. 'Can't have a lovely lady like you dragging all this around,' he said gallantly to Faith. She hated being called a lady, it sounded so old and pompous. He beamed at her winningly. 'I'm at Cambridge,' he said.

'I know,' she said. 'You told me several times.'

'I'm studying astrophysics,' he said.

'Stardust,' she said dreamily.

'Actually,' he said earnestly, 'you're not far off the mark. We study the physical and chemical nature of stars and other heavenly bodies.'

He has a heavenly body, Faith thought, if you like that kind of thing. Every muscle in his body seemed to bulge and strain as he easily hefted yet another bag over his shoulders. His vest rode up as he did so and she saw that he, of course, had the waist of his pants on show. White Calvins, and she bet his were the real deal. Lofty was good-looking, she conceded, but he was heavy and cumbersome, it looked like an effort for him just to shift his significant mass into the correct alignment.

I would hear Lofty coming a mile off, she thought, crashing and stamping around. She never heard Rik coming except of course when he actually *was* coming, because she had learned the warning signs pretty quickly, like the way he would shake and...

'You need to hang around this evening.' Rik had turned up again, either to supervise or to gape at Lofty. Faith leaped guiltily and shifted on her feet, looking around for GT to calm her, but for once the puppy had gone to pester some other ankles. Would you stop being so grotty for a moment, she told herself sternly, and concentrate on the fact you're supposed to be his friend?

They had gone up Fox Hill again at lunchtime and further out, not stopping this time but instead chatting as they rode. It had reminded Faith of all those times they had headed out together with no destination in mind, no real idea of how much time was passing, and no particular topic of conversation on the agenda. It was those times that had seen their burgeoning friendship turn into a deeper bond, through incidents and hitches like getting completely lost and having to find a way home, falls and cuts and grazes, and punctures and various other mechanical failures. Those were the times, she thought, when we realised how well our minds worked seamlessly together to solve problems, we never blamed or got annoyed with each other, we just got on with it and got each other through it. And that is why, with the benefit of hindsight, I fell in love with him, slowly and over time, so subtly and seamlessly I never even realised. It was only when we kissed at that stupid party that it all caught up with me.

'We're having a few drinks,' Rik said, mercifully oblivious to her train of thought. 'You're not busy, are you?'

'Can't think of anything I'd rather do.'

'Faith is a *heavenly* name,' Lofty said, returning for another load. 'You do look rather saintly, I have to say.'

She rolled her eyes. Lofty might be able to read stars and other heavenly bodies but he couldn't read women at all.

Lofty toiled off and Rik mimed sticking his fingers down his throat. '*Saintly*,' he said, aghast.

I'm still a sinner, she thought, when it comes to you.

'See you later,' he said and he slid off, giggling.

Faith turned back to her charge. 'When you're done, we need to start the rockery.'

'Just point me in the right direction,' he said raffishly.

'Thanks Lofty.'

'Henry,' he corrected. 'Or you can call me Harry if you prefer. For short.'

'It's not really shorter,' Faith said. 'It's got the same amount of letters. Lofty suits you just fine.'

Chapter 11

It was quite a crowd that assembled at Hollyhocks that evening. Sara and Tony had arrived and taken up position at the head of the swimming pool. Lofty was lounging next to them wearing a white ribbed vest that emphasised his bulging muscles, and the teenagers were all floating about chortling and drinking lurid-looking alcopops and looking at their cracked mobile phones.

Faith had gone home to shower and change and put on a very bright yellow vest and dark khaki shorts, which clashed becomingly with her sunkissed skin. She left her hair down and didn't bother with makeup, because her newly-acquired tan made her green eyes glow in her face. I look quite pretty, she decided, if you ignore all the scratches on my arms and legs.

Or so she thought, until Lucinda walked in looking sleekly elegant in white jeans, a black silk camisole and sky-high, diamante-studded heels and Faith instantly felt childish and silly. Sara had also pulled out all the stops and was wearing a pretty tea dress with cherries printed on it, which emphasised her gloriously feminine figure, and a pair of matching cherry-print sandals. Only Paul and Rik were letting the side down, still in their labouring clothes, cracking open bottles of beer in two deck chairs, side by side.

'Oh hello Faith,' Lucinda said, with a smile that didn't quite reach her eyes. 'Didn't recognise you without the mud coat.' Her eye fell on Lofty. 'Who's that?'

'My temporary assistant. I think Minel considers him a late birthday present.'

'I can see why,' Lucinda swooned. Rik had noticed she had arrived and came over to greet her. Lucinda looked marginally annoyed at his appearance.

'Hey Lu.' Rik kissed her briefly and turned to Faith. 'We won't lose you in the dark,' he said, looking at her vest.

'Wouldn't get lost anyway,' Faith said. 'I've got excellent night vision.'

Rik's eyes met hers and Faith knew exactly what he was thinking. I can see us, she thought, and so can he. He can see us right now, giggling madly while we navigated our way around that copse in the pitch black, telling each other what obstacles we could see, or sense. Occasionally reaching out to grab hands when one of us stumbled. Feeling that sense of adventure, of taking a risk, safe in the knowledge we were both there for each other.

He can see it and he feel it too. What we were, what we stopped being, what we lost.

Faith was about to reach out and touch his face, then she remembered that she was right next to Lucinda, who was eyeing Lofty up again.

GT, wildly overexcited by the amount of people present, was dashing back and forth beside the pool, occasionally throwing himself into the water before clambering out and shaking himself off, sending droplets cascading all over the floor. Minel nagged Paul to get up and turn the sausages. Hearing the magic word, GT launched himself at the barbecue, slamming his nose against the metal legs.

'Not the brightest, is he?' Lucinda said to Rik.

Rik laughed. 'But very cute.'

'Maybe he's an acquired taste,' Lucinda said. 'I'm more of a cat person.'

Of course you are, Faith thought, because cats are sensuous and captivating and discerning, and dogs follow you around with their tongues hanging out and roll in their own shit.

'Ah, my lady boss.' Lofty had stopped gazing into the middle-distance affectedly and smiled at Faith.

Faith rolled her eyes. 'Sara, have you met Lofty?' she asked her friend, who was also staring at Lofty in detached fascination.

'Harry,' Lofty corrected, sounding plummier than ever. He gave Sara the benefit of his piercing blue eyes and flexed involuntarily. 'I'm at Cambridge.'

Sara bubbled over with giggles. 'Who brought the doll?' she murmured to Faith.

Thank goodness, Faith thought. I was starting to think there was something wrong with me, but Sara gets it. 'Lofty's been helping me out with the pond. He's studying —' she had forgotten again and looked at Lofty for guidance.

'Astrophysics,' he said patiently.

'Astro what now?' Sara said.

'Planets and stuff,' Faith translated. 'Heavenly bodies. I think he thinks his falls into that category,' she hissed to Sara.

'Does he?' Sara hissed back.

'How would I know?'

'You're not tempted to find out?'

'As if. I'm literally the most chaste and lonely person around this swimming pool. I think even the teenagers have had more action than me.' Faith stopped abruptly. To her astonishment Sara's eyes had filled with tears.

'Oh Sar.' Faith stood up quickly and whisked her off to the greenhouse. 'Come on in,' she told Sara, ushering her towards the quiet cosiness of the back of the structure. 'What's the matter?'

'It's Tony,' Sara sobbed. 'We haven't had sex in nearly a year.'

'What?' Faith knocked over her bottle of Smirnoff Ice — talk about reliving my teenage years, she thought ruefully — and watched it fizz all over the greenhouse floor.

Sara sat down and put her head in her hands.

'I knew something was up with you,' Faith said. 'You've lost your spark.'

'I haven't had my spark in a long time.'

'A year,' Faith said in horror. 'Why?'

'I don't know,' Sara wailed. 'He won't talk about it. At first it was just "I'm tired", or "maybe tomorrow", and then tomorrow never came, and neither did I,' she laughed humourlessly, 'I started trying to push him on it a bit, find out what was bothering him, but he just clammed straight up. He won't discuss it at all. Flatly refuses.'

'Have you tried subtly seducing him?' Faith asked.

'How would I do that?'

'God, I don't know.' She thought for a moment. 'Go to bed naked? Jump him first thing in the morning? Give him a bit of dirty talk?'

'I have tried in the morning,' Sara said, 'but he just gets up and goes off for a shower. And probably a wank,' she said, suddenly furious, 'he stays in there for long enough.'

'Go and get in with him,' Faith suggested.

'He locks the door,' Sara groaned, and she put her hand over her eyes again. 'I'm starting to feel like a sex pest. What's wrong with me? Why doesn't he want me?'

'I can't begin to think why,' Faith said. 'Is he stressed about something? Like money or work?'

'Not that I know of,' Sara said. 'Work's OK. We're not flat broke. We get by.'

'Did anything happen?' Faith asked. 'Maybe he drank too much one night and couldn't perform, something like that?'

Sara frowned. 'I don't think so. I can't really remember the specifics of the last time we had sex. At the time I didn't know it was going to be the last time. He just doesn't want it at all, which makes me wonder — was he forcing himself before? Just to keep me happy?'

'Oh sweetheart,' Faith said. 'You poor thing.'

'I feel so unattractive,' Sara said, and Faith was horrified to see fresh tears rolling down her cheeks. 'I know sex doesn't equal love but it's important to me. I'm not a knockout, but I always feel like a queen in bed. Plus there are many benefits to a good seeing-to. Improved concentration, better circulation, glowing skin and hair...'

'You sound like an advert for shagging,' Faith giggled. 'Fresh breath and a healthy glossy coat.'

Sara laughed too. 'It's true though,' she said.

'I wouldn't know,' Faith sighed. 'I haven't had sex with anybody since Rob and I can't say I was bouncing with *joi de vivre* or glossy hair afterwards. Not lately, anyway. Ugh. I miss it.'

They sat together glumly, sharing Sara's drink. 'We need more booze,' Sara said, getting to her feet. 'Come on. Let's go out there like the pair of chaste losers we are and hold our heads up high.'

Faith watched Sara and Tony and now she knew, the tension between them was obvious. Every time Sara turned towards him or laid a hand on his arm, he visibly tensed and moved away. What was his problem, Faith wondered? Why would a man just go off sex like that — and not even talk to his girlfriend about it? She shook her head. Thank goodness for

Minel and Paul, the shining beacon, the talisman of what a couple could be if they were lucky enough to meet at the right time and continue to grow together.

Like she and Rik might have done.

Speak of the devil. He had wandered up, brandishing a bottle of vodka.

'Having fun?' Faith asked breathlessly.

'Not really. Minel and Paul are talking to Lucinda about interior design,' he pulled a disgusted face, 'and I had to sit and listen to Tony and tall, blonde and steroids talk about weightlifting. I've been looking for you all over the place.'

'Why?'

'To talk to, of course,' he said. 'Where did you get to?'

'Just cackling in the greenhouse with Sara,' she said airily.

'Something tells me that conversation would have been far more interesting than what I just had to endure.'

One of the teenagers slipped on a puddle of stray water left by GT from one of his many missions into the pool. He yelped as he attempted to right himself, windmilling his arms before landing in the pool, sending a fountain of water up the sides and all over Rik.

Rik pulled his soaked t-shirt off. Faith tried and failed not to stare at the way the light from the candles Minel had set out flickered on his skin, casting shadows across the muscles in his chest and stomach. How can Lucinda be ogling Lofty when she has *that* at home? she wondered.

Sara wolf-whistled. Rik flung his t-shirt in her direction and she caught it and wrung it out before clutching it to her chest exaggeratedly.

'Oh, grow up,' Faith heard Tony say.

Paul had escaped the interior décor chat and wandered over to help the spluttering teen out of the pool. The teen skulked back to his sniggering mates, most of whom had pulled out their mobile phones to film his undignified swim.

Paul patted Rik's shoulder. 'Been working out, mate?' He puffed his own considerable chest out pointedly. 'You don't look as scrawny as you used to.'

Rik rolled his eyes. 'You mean since I last worked on site with you, when I was eighteen?'

'Has it been that long?' Paul looked nostalgic. 'That was a fun couple of years, having to put up with your attitude over the school holidays.'

'I was never as bad as that lot.' Rik gestured at the huddled youths.

'You were much worse. Until I whipped you into shape.'

'You look in pretty good shape now,' Sara said. 'I barely recognise the skinny kid who was always first in line when Min and I did the sandwich run.' She ruffled his hair affectionately.

Faith stayed silent, unable to join in with the references to a time that had not involved her. They must have had fun, she thought wistfully, and stayed a tight group while I was noticeably absent.

Watching her friends enjoy a shared history that didn't involve her was almost as painful as watching Rik and Lucinda enjoy a shared present, and possibly future, that was equally exclusive.

Lofty wandered over. 'Talking about working out?' He eyed Rik dismissively. 'You could use a bit of bulking up,' he said. 'If you want me to run you through some of my drills, just let me know.'

Minel and Lucinda had also drifted over to join them.

'Why are you half-naked?' Lucinda demanded.

'So everybody can tell me I need to work out, apparently,' Rik grumbled.

Lofty had pulled off his own t-shirt and was flexing away merrily, talking completely to himself about his rigorous daily workout routine. Lucinda nodded approvingly, then turned to Rik. 'Maybe you should,' she said playfully.

'Don't be ridiculous,' Faith, finally jolted out of her reprieve, snapped before she could help herself. 'You're fine the way you are,' she said hotly to Rik. 'More than fine.' *Shut up*, her brain sirened.

Lucinda's face darkened. 'You should go and get dressed.' She turned back to Minel before Rik could respond.

What does he see in her? Faith wondered. Lucinda was utterly gorgeous, there was no disputing that, but she seemed to have a complete sense of humour failure.

She wondered how Lucinda felt about Rik when he came home sweating and covered in mud after an afternoon mountain-biking, then hastily distracted herself when her thoughts automatically turned to how she would feel about Rik were he to come home to her sweaty and excitable and covered in mud.

Minel was laughing at something Lucinda had said. Traitor, Faith thought, and she knew she was being unfair. Minel was so warm and friendly towards everybody and she had no idea how Faith felt about Rik, not that it would have made any difference because Rik was here with Lucinda, not her. She really needed to stop thinking about him as anything other than a friend. Even though he wasn't helping matters, standing there with his top still off — which she was willing to bet was entirely down to him refusing to acquiesce to Lucinda talking to him like a naughty child.

He looked up and caught her watching him and smiled completely unselfconsciously, a secret sort of smile that felt like it was meant only for her, and her heart started soaring and floating inexorably upwards and expanding like it were her own personal sun, sending rays of warmth and light all around her body.

Then she realised Minel and Lucinda were standing next to her.

Rik must have been smiling at Lucinda, not her. She felt a wave of disappointment crash over her, and felt suddenly tired and defeated.

'I'd better head off,' she said to Minel.

'You can't drive,' Minel said immediately. 'Stay at the house.'

Faith didn't fancy waking up to the Rik and Lucinda show. 'I brought my bike,' she said. 'It'll only take me ten minutes.'

'Rik and I should turn in too,' Lucinda said, unnecessarily smugly, Faith thought. 'We've got a christening up in London tomorrow and we need to go to IKEA.'

'Sounds fun,' Faith said automatically, thinking the only thing that could glorify IKEA for her would be giggling away with Rik over those implausible names.

Lucinda marched over to Rik and put a perfectly manicured hand on his bare shoulder, tightening her fingers possessively. 'Shall we go?'

'I'm not going to bed,' Rik said indignantly.

'You're being very childish,' Lucinda hissed. 'We have to go to IKEA and —'

'IKEA?' Rik looked disgusted. 'I'd rather nick myself shaving.'

'You'd have to start shaving first,' Lucinda snapped.

'Why are you going home so early?' Rik asked Faith, who shrugged and averted her eyes, sticking her hands in her pockets.

Aware his mistress might be deserting him, GT appeared at Faith's feet, shoving himself determinedly between them and rubbed his little furry body approvingly against his beloved ankle.

'Sorry, baby,' Faith sighed to the puppy. 'I'd love to take you home and curl up in bed with you, but I think there's at least one woman here who might have something to say about that.' He was Minel's dog, after all, she reminded herself. 'But don't worry, I'll be back on Monday and you can wrap yourself around me again as soon as she turns her back.' She smiled at the puppy affectionately.

There was a long, heavily strained silence.

'Um, who are you talking to?' Lucinda shrilled. Minel looked utterly scandalised and even Rik was temporarily lost for words and just staring at her and she didn't even want to begin to read the expression on his face.

'Him, of course,' Faith said, gesturing towards her feet. 'GT,' she prompted. Lucinda still looked completely lost. 'The dog?' Faith said, wondering if Lucinda was a bit tapped.

'Oh god.' Rik shook his head a little and went off into fits of giggles. 'Didn't see him down there,' he said, doubling over with mirth. Lucinda looked more po-faced than ever.

'Who did you think I was talking to?' Faith said, confused, then she remembered the last person she'd addressed before GT distracted her was Rik and felt a crash of mortification wash over her. Even Minel was sniggering, but Lucinda most definitely didn't seem to think it was funny and neither did she.

Crimson with embarrassment, Faith shoved GT away and stormed off, hearing Rik and Minel still laughing helplessly behind her.

Chapter 12

By Monday Faith had begun to see the funny side of the excruciating incident by the swimming pool with Rik and Lucinda. She would have to apologise to her, she supposed, but maybe Lucinda would also see it for what it was, a genuine mistake, and it might even break some of the seemingly endless ice between them.

She arrived early enough to catch Lucinda before she drove off but to her surprise Lucinda, resplendent in denim hotpants and an immaculate white cami, clearly wasn't going anywhere. 'I thought I'd hang around for a few days,' she said to Faith, looking far from thrilled to see her. 'Watch my man in action.'

Get some action, more like, Faith thought as she eyed Lucinda's radiant face. *I'm not apologising to you now.* She stomped off to the garden.

She couldn't even be bothered to joke with Lofty, who greeted her eagerly and with several unintentionally comic asides. She sent him off to move the rockery, and picked up her shovel. After a couple of intense hours she decided to wander up to the house and make some tea. GT had shot out delightedly when she showed up and was now dozing in the still early morning sun, one eye on her in case she dared run out on him again.

Minel wasn't in the kitchen but there was bloody Lucinda, wafting around looking far too happy and most definitely at home.

'Hi Faith,' she said, sounding much more chipper. 'Come for a tea break?'

'Hi,' Faith mumbled, avoiding eye contact. Stop being so childish, she ordered herself. 'I won't be a minute.' She flicked on the kettle and reached for a cup, deliberately ignoring the new-looking bone china Lucinda had chosen in favour of the cracked stripy mugs she was willing to bet were older than she was.

'Good weekend?' Lucinda asked conversationally.

'Yeah,' Faith said. 'Went to a track meet. I ride bikes,' she said by way of explanation. 'What about you? How was your christening?'

'Lovely,' Lucinda said, 'although we were a bit late.' She giggled. Ugh, Faith thought, no prizes for guessing why. Does she have to be so obvious?

'Get up to much else?'

Lucinda giggled again. 'Just spent some time catching up with Rik,' she said, and sighed dreamily. Faith sloshed water into her cup and half thought about flinging the kettle at Lucinda's despicably smug face. I hate her, she thought helplessly, and it's not her fault in the slightest.

It wasn't just that Lucinda got to sleep with Rik, she thought longingly, it was all of it. She got to *be* with him, to do all those normal everyday things that suddenly seemed so much better when he was around. She got to spill the contents of her mind at him without censoring herself and she could just reach out and kiss him whenever she wanted and she got to wake up in the morning with his arms around her and — no, she wasn't going there.

'Sounds nice,' she said to Lucinda noncommittally, stirring the tea and squeezing out the bag, before tossing it towards the bin. It missed.

'It was,' Lucinda said, still in that dreamy tone of voice. 'Gosh, he must have missed me after all. Oh, I'm sorry,' she said, sounding very genuine. 'How thoughtless of me. Rik says you've just broken up with your boyfriend. Awful having other people shoving their happiness in your face. I know when I split up with my last boyfriend I couldn't bear to be around a happy couple for months. I hope I don't sound too smug.'

You do, Faith thought, but that's only because you are. She poured milk into her tea. 'It's fine,' she said. 'Don't worry about it.'

'How's it going in the garden?'

'Slow progress,' Faith said. 'Glad I've got Lofty doing all the heavy lifting for me.'

'I don't blame you,' Lucinda said. 'Bit of a dreamboat, isn't he?'

'Not my thing,' Faith said. 'But he's good value, I suppose.'

'I'd be half-tempted myself if I wasn't with Rik,' Lucinda said conspiratorially, and she winked. Faith wanted to be sick into her tea. 'I'd best go and find him,' Lucinda said. 'Missing him already. Hope he's still got a bit of energy left.' She floated out of the kitchen, giggling.

Faith stormed furiously back down to the garden, kicking several stray plant pots outside the greenhouse on her way. They made a satisfying clattering noise and she picked up a metal watering can and hurled it across the lawn, watching it catch the sunlight as it bounced upon landing.

Rik didn't show up to ride with her at lunchtime and Faith hung around with Minel instead, giggling at GTs antics and eating the raspberries that were starting to ripen on the tangle of canes next to the greenhouse. Then, as she returned to the rockery, she was greeted by a beaming Lucinda who was wearing the same denim shorts but had changed into one of Rik's t-shirts. Faith didn't want to think about what circumstances had led him to take it off in the first place.

'I thought I'd give you a hand,' Lucinda said.

'Not much happening here really,' Faith said dubiously. 'Digging, shunting, that kind of thing. Not really much fun for you.'

'I don't mind.' Lucinda smiled persuasively. 'It's better than loafing around by the pool while you all toil away. Also, it would be nice to spend a bit of time with you, Faith. I have the feeling we didn't really get off to a great start.'

That's your fault, Faith thought irrationally, with your acquisition of *my* man. Even though he absolutely isn't.

Lucinda was still smiling, her china blue eyes lit prettily and her dainty lips stretched over her perfect teeth. 'What can I do?'

Faith plastered a smile on her own face. 'Why don't you start going through these?' she suggested, gesturing at the reams of potted plants that she had ordered in. 'I've got a list somewhere of what's going where.' She dug around in her pocket and pulled it out, brushing some stray compost off it. 'There. If you can sort them and then water them, and let me know if any look like they're struggling, that would be great. Thank you.'

'No problem.' Lucinda took the scrumpled piece of paper and smoothed it out. Faith sent Lofty over to help Paul for the afternoon then picked up her fork and began to attack one of her infernal piles of earth, which was rock-hard and tightly packed. I can just pretend it's Lucinda's face, she decided, and the afternoon will fly by.

'This looks like hard work,' Lucinda, who was watching her, said sympathetically. 'Look, Faith, I hope it's not too weird, having me around.'

'Of course not,' Faith said.

'I mean, I know you and Rik have a bit of history,' Lucinda said idly.

Faith flinched. Did she really? He must have told her everything after all — oh, why had he told her? Talk about making things awkward.

'Yeah, we were all good friends when we were kids,' she said.

'Faith, it's OK,' Lucinda cut her off and flashed her a kindly sort of smile. 'I know about you and Rik. He told me.'

That still wasn't conclusive. 'Seriously, don't worry about it at all,' she said firmly. 'It's not weird in the slightest.'

'I think it's quite sweet, that you two are still friends,' Lucinda, undeterred, carried on. 'I certainly wouldn't want to be within a million miles of any of my exes, let alone working with them.'

Faith had a vision of spending all summer stuck with Rob and shuddered exaggeratedly.

'Suppose it's ancient history now,' Lucinda remarked.

Faith shoved her fork viciously into the mound of earth, feeling the iron prongs protesting as she rammed it forcefully down with both her feet, then heaved it back and forth. One of the prongs gave way and she tossed the fork aside irritably and reached for another one. She was going to get through all of Helena and Ravi's tools at this rate and the bill to replace them would be astronomical.

Lucinda fingered a rose thoughtfully. 'You obviously meant a lot to each other.'

Faith shrugged. 'Pretty formative time, one's teenage years. We all helped to build one another. Minel, Sara and I were like sisters under the skin. Sisters from another mister,' she said idly.

'Doesn't sound like Rik was very brotherly,' Lucinda observed, still petting the unfortunate rose, which Faith could

142

swear was already beginning to wilt. 'I never did *that* with my brother.' She shot Faith a cheeky, conspiratorial look.

'He wasn't into cycling then?' Faith said evasively. 'That's what Rik and I were into.'

'I wasn't talking about the cycling.'

Why is she still pushing this? Faith wondered. What does she want from me? She raised the new fork threateningly and, presumably cowed by the fate its predecessor had met, it slid into the ground without protest.

'How old is your brother?' she asked Lucinda, hoping to change the subject.

'He's older than me,' Lucinda said. 'Thirty.'

'Lucky you,' Faith said. 'I'd have loved a sibling. Bet he had loads of hot mates.'

Lucinda laughed. 'One or two,' she confided. 'Although obviously I wouldn't have dreamed of acting on it. You're an only child?'

Faith nodded and Lucinda looked at her sympathetically. 'You must have been lonely, growing up. I can see why you spent so much time here.'

'Who wouldn't?' Faith asked, sweeping her arm around the land. 'It's like something from a dream.'

'It's just stunning. A little bit magical.'

Faith nodded eagerly. 'I couldn't believe this place, the first time I came here. I had never seen anything like it. The space, the setting, the peace and quiet, the wildness spilling out just beyond the drive. Heady clouds of cow parsley lining the road, the way the trees almost touch together to form a roof over it, so close that squirrels can jump from one to another. The freedom,' she said yearningly. 'Minel and Rik moved into the cottage not long after I moved here,' she said, 'and we had so much fun, all of us. Helena and Ravi were so trusting. They gave us free run and I knew every inch of this place like the back of my hand, from the stream that cuts off this land from next doors to the secrets hidden down in that copse. The more I knew it, the more I felt it knew me too. Do you know, from time to time I was sure this place was enchanted. Some days I could actually feel the magic, just beneath the surface, vibrating on a frequency just beyond our reach, drifting in from the copse along with the scent of the wild garlic...' She supposed she must be sounding like a mad hippy and stopped abruptly.

But Lucinda looked transfixed. 'I always wanted to find fairies living at the bottom of my garden,' she said, 'I doubt they come in as far as north London.'

'There are some lovely parts of London,' Faith said. 'North in particular. Hampstead Heath and Primrose Hill. You'd definitely meet some fairies up there.'

'Picnicking on toadstools,' Lucinda agreed. 'The red and white ones. I don't know what they're called.'

'Fly agaric.' Faith thought maybe she could warm to Lucinda after all. 'Very poisonous, and hallucinogenic in small quantities. Not that I'd know, and I couldn't imagine hallucinating anything more magical than Hollyhocks.'

'Magic,' Lucinda repeated. 'Obviously worked on you and Rik.'

'Only for a bit,' Faith said, thinking she'd often suspected the same herself. 'Not long at all,' she added wistfully.

'Of course.' Lucinda nodded. 'Silly of me really, thinking it would still be weird.' She pulled her phone out of her pocket and sighed. 'Even while I'm on leave, they still bother me. So sorry Faith. I have to go and reply to these emails.'

'What do you do?' Faith asked. She didn't actually know, shame on her for not even finding out something so basic about Lucinda. She was almost starting to think perhaps she wasn't such a horrendous bitch after all.

'I'm a journalist,' Lucinda said absently. 'Always on, even when I'm off. I was glued to this ghastly thing all weekend.' She frowned at her phone.

All weekend? Faith thought as Lucinda marched off. But surely she'd spent all weekend 'catching up with Rik?' Something felt distinctly off, she was prickling a bit. She surveyed the ground meditatively. What was it? Her hackles were undoubtedly up, she almost felt like she'd been had in some way. But how? She hadn't told Lucinda anything she didn't already know — she'd barely done any of the talking until she started waxing lyrical about Hollyhocks.

She poked tentatively at the ground again. She was a press officer, she was always having to fend off nosy journalists. Something about Lucinda must have reminded her of work, she concluded. That was all it was. She raised the fork, and watched the ground shift around to make way for the inexorably descending iron prongs.

The romantic diatribe to Lucinda about magic had awakened something within Faith — reawakened, anyway — because she was treated to a night of steamy and astoundingly graphic dreams about Rik. She lurched awake at 3am, her heart pounding, drenched in sweat, after another toe-curling but frustratingly inconclusive encounter with him.

I need to get a grip, she thought. Lucinda was still floating around, although her appetite for girly chit-chat with Faith had thankfully dissipated just as quickly as it had arrived, and she rode alone on Tuesday, hoping the relentless churning of her legs as they powered her up hill after hill would somehow ease her equally relentless internal torment. GT, instinctively attuned to any bitch on heat, had leaped on her ankle so many times she'd had to banish him to the greenhouse so she could get on with some work. He howled plaintively if she tried to put him in the house, out of sight, and the noise drove Paul crackers.

'Sorry if you're the wrong person to put this on, but I need to get laid,' she sighed to Sara that evening over a bottle of Prosecco at the Blacksmith's. They had appropriated the table at the end of the garden and were sharing a plate of mezze, Faith eating most of it because she seemed to be constantly starving and Minel's sandwiches barely scratched the surface at lunchtime. 'All my appetites have increased exponentially,' she confessed.

'At least if you do I can live vicariously through you.' Sara popped the last olive into her mouth. She had touched up her roots and was wearing a bright red sundress. 'How bad is it?'

'Bad,' Faith said.

'Anything prompted this?' Sara inquired.

Faith thought how perceptive Sara was and how honest she'd been with her about her situation with Tony and how desperately she wanted somebody with whom to talk to about it all.

'Oh Sar. I'm in a muddle.'

'About?'

'About Rik.'

'What about Rik?' Sara frowned. 'What — you had him in mind as a potential outlet for your current rush of blood to the…' she tailed off.

'Something like that,' Faith admitted. 'Seeing him again threw me a bit.'

'He's grown up, that's for sure,' Sara mused. 'Very easy on the eye, especially after the tops-off zone on Friday. It was practically raining abs over there in amongst all that swimming-pool water. Is that what's got you thinking about him?'

'Not really,' Faith said. 'That's actually not the first time I've seen Rik with his top off. Although it is the first time in a very long time.'

Sara sat up very straight. 'Don't tell me you did more than just eat his face off at Minel's birthday party? You said you didn't even remember.'

Faith sighed. 'I do remember. And I didn't tell you what happened after that,' she said, still feeling residual pangs of guilt for keeping something like that from her friend. 'We didn't tell anybody but yes, there was some tops-off action and that wasn't the only time.'

'Ohhh.' Sara's eyes were sparkling again. 'Oh. You and him, eh? What happened? Why didn't we know?'

'You would have done, I expect, if it had gone on for much longer,' Faith said. 'I was a bit embarrassed about it at first, him being younger and Min's brother, I thought you'd all laugh at me.'

'Oh, we would have,' Sara said, 'but we'd have been pleased for you, god knows you needed some fun, and Rik was a good kid, bit annoying and lippy but obviously that didn't bother you.' She looked delighted to have a new piece of gossip to mull over. 'I can't believe you didn't tell me.'

'Didn't go on for very long,' Faith said again. 'Not that much to tell.' Not much and so much.

'Come on then,' Sara said. 'Dish.'

'We were friends for ages,' Faith said, 'and then there was Minel's 18th. And after that,' she could still remember the impact of that kiss, that feeling of discovering a new side to her friend. 'We hung out a bit. Messed around.'

'How messy did it get?'

'About as messy as it can get,' Faith admitted. 'It got quite messy in your house once actually. But then I ended it and I basically never spoke to him again.'

'Why?'

The million-dollar question. 'I thought he cheated on me,' she said. 'I was absolutely sure he did, actually, but it turns out,' she sighed again. 'It turns out he didn't after all.'

Sara frowned. 'So why did you think he did — what happened?'

Faith explained briefly. 'I didn't think to check,' she said. 'I just assumed it must have been him and if it wasn't for that conversation we had in the kitchen last week, I would never have realised.'

'Oh,' Sara said.

'Oh indeed,' Faith said. 'Which means that what actually happened was, I dumped Rik for no reason whatsoever with no explanation and I haven't spoken to him, until this summer, in nine years.'

'Oh.' Sara's eyes grew very wide.

'I've told him now,' Faith said hastily.

Sara ate a few olives and Faith waited patiently for her to hone in on the most pertinent of the facts she'd just given her.

'Did you shag him?'

Always focused on the important details, Faith thought with amusement, and she nodded.

Sara gasped. 'Really? You went *all* the way?'

'All the way,' Faith confirmed. 'Just one night — well, most of the night actually. And the next morning.'

Sara looked taken aback. 'Christ. You two didn't do things by halves.'

'We were teenagers.'

'Agonisingly horny teenagers.' Sara chortled merrily. 'But hang on — I thought you lost your virginity at university? To that guy who cheated on you. Joel.'

Faith shook her head. 'No. It was with Rik. Joel was just a fling. I made up all that stuff about him cheating on me — well I didn't make it up, I just swapped his name for Rik's. The rest of it is all true. At least I thought it was true.'

'All right.' Sara held her hands up. 'Let's get this straight. You were with Rik, and then you dumped him for cheating on you, and now it turns out he never actually cheated on you at all and this is the first time you've seen him in nine years and you're getting on — how are you getting on?'

'Pretty well,' Faith said. 'Not at first, but all things considered, we're OK. Which is kind of the problem,' she admitted. 'Because it's reminding me of all the things I liked about him in the first place, and now I no longer think him a heartless faithless bastard, it's quite hard not to —'

'Not to think about what might have been?'

Faith nodded.

'Do you still have feelings for him?'

'It's hard to say,' Faith said. 'It's all been very emotional and confusing but there does seem to still be a bit of a spark. On my part, anyway.'

'The spark that wasn't there with Rob?'

'The very same.'

'And now you want to re-enact your sweaty night of teenage passion?'

Faith snorted. 'There are definitely some sweaty teenage feelings going on here, yes. But it's not just that. It's more that he was such a big part of my life, way before anything happened. And then the spark happened and he was already pretty much my favourite person in the whole world. It was all so perfect — I thought afterwards, it was just too good to be true. And now it turns out he didn't cheat on me,' she sighed. 'I have a horrible feeling that I basically threw away the best thing that ever happened to me for no reason whatsoever.'

'That,' Sara said philosophically, 'is a gigantic kick in the balls.'

'If I had balls,' Faith agreed and they giggled. 'It certainly puts a different perspective on things and now I keep getting all these reminders of Rik and me, all the fun we used to have, how close we were,' she sighed. 'I missed him, and I missed it around here, and I missed me, the way I used to be, before my parents nearly got divorced and Rik broke my heart. I was so happy. I knew myself, I knew what I wanted to do with my life, I thought I would probably do most of it with Rik because we were so —' she tailed off again, too sad to continue.

'What are you going to do about it then? Have you told him any of this?'

Faith shook her head emphatically. 'No, and don't you go blabbing either. He's with Lucinda, as we both know only too well. Bitch,' she said enviously.

'Bitch,' Sara agreed happily. 'Don't worry, I'll keep it to myself.'

'I have a horrible feeling the more time I spend with Rik this summer, the harder it's going to get.'

'Don't hang around with him then.'

'Not sure I can do that,' Faith admitted. 'I just need to let the spark bit go and concentrate on being friends.'

'It'll fade,' Sara said. 'Just think about it as a silly crush. Focus on the things you don't like about Rik and avert your eyes during any future tops-off zones.'

'There aren't many things I don't like about Rik,' Faith protested. 'Top on or off.'

Sara smiled. 'You'll find some, I'm sure. Nobody's perfect. Focus on the flaws and find yourself somebody else to re-enact your crazy teenage memories with. An actual teenager, if needs be. There's enough of them floating around.'

'Not sure I'm prepared to stoop that low,' Faith said.

'It'd be like being in a timewarp,' Sara said.

'It already is,' Faith said grimly.

Chapter 13

Lucinda was conspicuously absent on Wednesday morning and as soon as Faith took up her position in the garden Rik appeared, bouncing on his feet and clearly very excited about something.

I hope he's glad because she's pushed off, Faith thought cattily. I know I am.

'What are you all hyped up about?' she asked.

'Paul has given us all tomorrow off,' Rik announced. 'Something about an order of slabs not arriving in time.' He giggled. 'I think one of the teenagers put in a prank call to the supplier to get a break from him.'

Faith sniggered. 'Are you sure it wasn't you?'

'I wouldn't dare,' he said. 'He's got a traffic cone in the back of one of his trucks and I wouldn't put it past him to make me wear it as a dunce's hat if I did mess with his schedule. He is not amused. Anyway, we can't do much until they arrive on Friday and he doesn't want to pay them all to stand around smoking fags so that means I get the day off too and although I really should catch up on work, instead I'm going to check out a mountain biking place not far from here. A friend of mine — of Jason's, actually — has just taken it over.'

'Oh that sounds fun,' Faith sighed enviously. 'I haven't ridden any trails in years.'

'Come with me,' Rik said. 'Let's go and get lost and muddy and pretend we're teenagers again.'

'I'm not sure Paul would like that.'

'He won't mind,' Rik said. 'You're making great progress.' He cast his eye over the ruins of the garden and paused. 'Or something. Plus technically he's working for me and Minel, not that he'd see it that way, but I don't mind pulling rank on him just this once.'

'Are you sure?' she asked, thinking there was probably nothing in this world she'd rather do than spend the day getting lost and muddy with Rik. Other than actually relive their teenage years, of course. Even so, it was a close second. 'I'm pretty out of practice.'

'You'll be fine,' Rik said. 'It's like riding a bike.'

They left early the next morning, loading both bikes into the back of the reluctant Land Rover. Rik had to shout over the roar of the engine as Faith pushed the protesting car down the motorway. 'How long have you had this car?'

'Since just before I left home,' she yelled back.

'You're not tempted to swap it for something a bit more —' Rik lurched and grabbed the door handle as the car bounced merrily over a crack in the road. 'A bit more roadworthy?'

'It's perfectly roadworthy,' Faith insisted. The Land Rover let out a dissenting whine and she gunned the engine irritably. 'Drives just fine.'

He looked around at the battered interior. 'I suppose it has a rustic sort of charm.'

'The guy I bought it off,' Faith said airily, or as airily as she could manage given that she was shouting at the top of her lungs, 'said it was practically a magnet for girls. That was actually his nickname for it,' she giggled, 'the magnet.'

'Does it have the same effect on men?' Rik asked.

She shook her head. 'It didn't on Rob. He hated it. He was a bit of a car nut,' she elaborated. 'Used to read dreadful magazines full of borderline pornographic images of girls draped over gas-guzzling supercars. He flatly refused to get into this. We used to have to take his car everywhere.' Every weekend, when they used to spend endless hours on motorways, driving to visit his equally car-obsessed friends. She felt a wave of relief that at least that wasn't her life any more.

Rik reached up to hold the handle above the window and Faith found her eyes riveted to the outline of the muscles in his arm. She forced her gaze back to the road. It's going to be a long summer, she chided herself, if you carry on swooning over him every time he so much as moves. And you might as well get into practice getting a grip right now before you have to watch him getting all hot and sweaty and excited on his bike.

'Does Lucinda ride bikes too?' she asked, hoping she didn't sound like she was fishing.

'No,' he said. 'Not her thing. She thinks it's dangerous.'

'Rob did too,' Faith said. 'Every time there was a news story about a cyclist getting hit by a car he'd send it to me. He used to nag me worse than my mother. I got so fed up it was actually easier just to stop,' she said ruefully. 'Hence me being out of practice.'

'Didn't you miss it?' Rik asked.

She nodded. 'So much.'

'If I have to go a week or two without getting out I swear it affects my mood,' Rik said. 'I get much more irritated about little things that wouldn't normally bother me.'

Like the fact that Lucinda is a gigantic bitch, Faith thought hopefully. 'I do too,' she said. 'Rob was starting to regret his insistence that I stop, because he certainly found me harder to live with.' She sighed. 'I felt like I spent all my time looking out of windows. On the train on the way to work, sitting in my office, on the train home then in our flat, which didn't have a garden, or in the car, driving somewhere,' she scowled irritably.

'It reminded me of when I was at school, and I just used to stare out of the classroom window wishing I was on the other side of it.'

'You aren't the indoor type,' Rik agreed. 'Do you really think you'll go back to all that?'

'Well, I won't go back to Rob, obviously,' Faith said. 'But I have to pay the bills somehow. And right now, when I have no relationship and no home to speak of and absolutely nothing to my name other than this car,' she patted the steering wheel affectionately, 'my bike and a couple of boxes of clothes — doesn't feel like the right time to quit my job and go back to college and start all over again.'

'What better time?' Rik countered. 'What do you have to lose?'

She couldn't really think of an answer, and fortunately the car provided a distraction in the form of a sudden lunge to the left. Faith grabbed the steering wheel with both hands and wrestled the vehicle back under control, feeling a great deal of resistance. 'I think I've blown a tire,' she said apologetically.

'Roadworthy indeed,' Rik sighed. 'You'd better pull over.'

She pulled on to the hard shoulder and Rik leaped out of the car next to her. 'I can do it,' she insisted but the mechanic must have tightened the wheel nuts with hydraulics last time she'd had the car serviced, because no matter how much she heaved against the wrench, she couldn't budge them an inch.

'Give it to me,' Rik said exasperatedly. She handed him the wrench and tried not to stare as he made short work of taking the wheel off, then passed him the spare wheel, which she'd removed from the underside of the Land Rover.

'Thanks,' she said as he put it on and handed the wrench back to her.

'Nine years later,' Rik said wryly, 'and I'm still fixing your punctures for you.'

'I could have done it myself,' she protested.

'Yeah, yeah.' He smiled at her and she felt a pang of something very bittersweet. There are few things in this world, she thought, as romantic as somebody fixing your punctures for you. 'Come on, get back in. It should get us the rest of the way in one piece.'

Once they had turned off the motorway and hit the smaller country lanes, the Land Rover, content to be back in its rightful domain, settled right down and Faith admired the rolling hills beyond the gardens and houses they were passing. 'Nice part of the world,' she said wistfully.

'Very,' Rik said. 'Simon — Jason's mate — grew up round here. He used to ride this place as a kid and basically became an accountant with the sole ambition of making enough money to buy it.'

'Good for him,' Faith said. 'Following through on his dreams like that.'

Simon, who was blonde and well-built and distinctly attractive — if you liked that sort of thing, Faith thought absently — greeted Rik warmly and his blue eyes lit up when he saw Faith. 'Don't tell me you've traded Lucinda in for a more outdoorsy model?' he asked, eyeing her khaki shorts and faded black vest.

Rik laughed. 'This is Faith,' he said. 'She's an old friend.'

'Not that old.'

'Older than me,' Rik pointed out.

She shrugged her shoulders. 'Negligibly.'

'How come it's negligibly now, but when we were teenagers it was "significantly"?'

156

'It reduces with time,' she said. 'By the time I hit thirty we'll actually be the same age.'

'So have you guys come to ride, or just flirt?' Simon cut in. He grinned knowingly and looked at her with more interest. 'Sure Rik hasn't traded Lucinda for you?'

'We're women, not cars,' Faith said loftily. 'Also you must have met Lucinda — therefore you can't possibly think I could hold a candle to her.' You can thank me later, Rik, she thought. I took one for the team there, pointing out how much more attractive than me Lucinda is.

Simon ran his eyes over her very brazenly and she shuffled uncomfortably, not enjoying the scrutiny. 'I don't know,' he mused. 'I wouldn't be so hard on yourself if I were you.'

'Rik,' Faith said, 'shall we go?'

He started and looked guilty. Oh god, she thought, was he actually *comparing* me to Lucinda?

Simon pulled out a map and began explaining the layout. Faith tried and failed to pay attention, and as she snuck a glance at Rik she noticed he looked equally distracted.

'So,' he said as they left the tiny ramshackle hut that served as an office building and surveyed the landscape liberally peppered with woodland. 'Where first?'

'Let's just have a look around, shall we?' she suggested, and put on her helmet. She followed him down a long, wide gravel track, avoiding potholes and pulling her bike up underneath her over the occasional ledge. Oh this is fun, she thought, feeling the wind in her face and bending her knees automatically as she landed the final jump.

Rik pulled out the map Simon had given him and studied it for a moment. 'Looks like there's some good stuff in there,' he said, gesturing to a copse to their right.

Simon had worked hard, Faith realised as they entered the copse via a steep descent, made bumpy and challenging by gnarled tree-roots. They crossed a narrow wooden bridge, which rattled and shook beneath their wheels, then plunged into the cool dimness of the copse. The track twisted and turned, through steep curved ascents and sweeping downhill sections more twisted tree-roots, the odd jump and more of those wooden bridges.

At the centre was a wonderfully bumpy, arched bridge that sloped off to one side, and she hurtled down it and yanked her bike around to the right, following a section marked out with the slender trunks of fallen silver birch, and back up to the top of the copse to begin the circuit again.

Rik was right, she thought. She hadn't forgotten a thing, her balance was as honed as ever and she felt as attuned to her bike as if it were a living being, shifting her weight with the trails, using her knees as suspension and automatically pitching herself to the back of her saddle down the bumpy descents.

And there was something else she hadn't forgotten either. She felt as attuned to Rik as if they had last ridden together just yesterday. They took it in turns to lead the way and set the pace and they rode for hours, occasionally pausing to discuss the next section or obstacle, but mainly there was no need for any verbal communication. He's got a lot better, she thought. He's not as silly and reckless as he used to be, he doesn't get so bent out of shape and he makes it all look effortless.

'I think there's a trail here,' he called to her after a while, as they climbed up a steep grassy bank that ran next to what she had assumed was a stream. He paused, and looked at the map. 'It's marked out.'

Faith squinted through the trees. It was a stream, a very narrow rocky one and it looked all but impassable. The entrance was practically a sheer drop. She eyed it dubiously. 'I can't ride that.'

'Yes you can.' Rik went ahead of her and she watched as he went down the bank sideways, then dropped his bike straight into the stream. It was all rock, and from here she could see it got even narrower towards the centre and had several terrifying-looking ledges to negotiate.

'Come on,' Rik yelled.

Cursing, Faith slammed her heels down, pitched her weight as far back as she could and gritted her teeth.

She dropped into the stream with an emphatic splash and muddy water immediately soaked her to the top of her calves. The first part of the stream was bumpy but wide, but it soon became so narrow she couldn't really see how she could get her bike through it. If I'm going to die, she thought, I might as well enjoy it. She released her vice-like grip on her brakes and let the bike do the hard work for her, feeling the suspension and the grippy tyres absorbing some, but not nearly enough, of the bone-crunching impact of the many drops. The trail widened fractionally, then there was another series of almighty drops, each one shaking her to the core as she landed and soaking her with fresh backspray. Her bike lurched and juddered and she gripped the handlebars so hard her knuckles had turned white, but by the time she cannoned down to the bottom and out into an unexpectedly deep pool of muddy water, she could feel the blood roaring around her head and she was grinning from ear to ear.

'Jesus,' she gasped as she rolled to a halt next to Rik. 'I need to ride that with stabilisers.'

'That was harder than I thought it would be,' he conceded, looking a little taken aback. 'Good fun though.'

'The best,' she agreed enthusiastically. 'Shall we do it again?'

'Oh god yes. I had forgotten,' Rik said suddenly, 'how well you ride.'

Faith blushed beneath the mud splattered across her cheeks. 'Thanks.'

'I always thought so,' he said. 'You're seriously fast, and your handling is still better than mine. And you're fearless.' He was looking at her with something approaching awe.

'Not so fearless today,' she said ruefully.

'Even more so,' he countered. 'If you haven't ridden much in a while.'

Simon looked surprised when they finally rolled back to the office hut, giggling and sweating and plastered with mud. 'I thought you guys must have left hours ago,' he said. 'I was just about to lock up.'

'I'm glad you didn't,' Faith said. 'We'd have been stuck out there all night.'

'Wouldn't that be a shame,' Simon said archly.

Faith was grateful she was already beet-red from all the exertion. I might not look sexy, she thought wryly, but at least nobody can see me blushing yet again.

She took off her helmet and shook out her black curls, which were soaked with sweat.

'You look like you had a good time,' Simon said approvingly.

She nodded. 'This place is awesome.'

'Come back whenever you like. You don't need to bring him,' he said conspiratorially, nodding in Rik's direction. 'I can show you around instead.'

Rik snorted dismissively. Faith's lips twitched. 'Thanks,' she said to Simon, then she gave him her most radiant smile. He reeled visibly.

'Time we were off,' Rik said pointedly.

'What's your rush?' Simon asked easily. 'You're both welcome to stick around.'

'I need to eat,' Rik said and Faith suddenly realised she hadn't eaten since this morning and was absolutely starving.

They stopped at a pub on the way home and Faith, who had started to become chilly in the draughty old Land Rover, felt the warmth seeping back into her body, leaving her glowing with contentment.

'Whereabouts in London do you live?' she asked Rik.

'Nowhere, any more,' he said. 'I'm here for the summer then I'm going to Cornwall for a bit. I have a client up there who wants me to come in-house for a few months.'

'That sounds nice,' she said, thinking how lovely it would be to be by the sea. All that gorgeous chalky soil, bursting with cornflowers and poppies and other, far rarer wild blooms. 'What will you do, just rent somewhere for a bit?'

He nodded. 'Shouldn't be too hard, especially outside of holiday season.'

'Is Lucinda going to come with you?'

Rik was silent and she had the distinct impression she'd touched a nerve.

'I don't know,' he said finally. 'I'm only down there for a few months and she works in London.'

'Long distance can work,' Faith said. 'Rob and I did it for a few years before we moved in together. It was fine.' Actually, it was probably the reason their relationship had lasted as long as it did. Only seeing Rob at weekends had prevented her from getting to know him as well as she could have, and she'd overlooked all the little warning signs of the bigger issues to come. 'Lucinda seems nice,' she said. She seems anything of the sort, she thought, then reminded herself that if she wanted

161

to be friends with Rik she would need to muster up some positivity about and interest in his significant other. And it was hardly Lucinda's fault. It was the fact he had a significant other in the first place that was the real kicker here. 'She said she's a journalist?'

Rik nodded. 'She works for a newspaper, that's how I met her actually. I went in to do some design work for them.'

Faith wasn't sure she could stomach some nauseating story about their eyes meeting over a malfunctioning laptop or something equally clichéd.

'She's been with the same company for a while and they've got quite a few titles. She's very ambitious,' he said. 'She's aiming to be an editor by the time she's thirty.'

'She seems like the sort of person who focuses on what she wants,' she said, remembering how skilfully Lucinda had questioned her in the garden. She still felt like she'd been duped in some way there, but she pushed the thought away.

'She's really focused, and she works very hard,' he agreed. 'She's always staying late and taking on extra shifts and she's the first to volunteer for any weekend work or to cover stories that are breaking out of hours.'

'That's the way to get ahead,' Faith said. 'Not sneaking days off to go mountain biking. Although I could see it might be tricky if she was living in Cornwall,' she mused. Perhaps that was the issue.

'We haven't been together long,' he said. 'It feels like a big step.'

'It's very different from just dating,' Faith agreed. 'It's nice at first, but once the novelty of having each other around all the time wears off you get a much better idea of who they actually are and that can be tricky. Well, it can be if you're me and

Rob,' she conceded. 'I'm sure you and Lucinda will be fine.' She hoped she sounded encouraging, not accusing.

'So when you moved in with Rob,' Rik said, 'you must have been pretty serious about him?'

'Yes and no,' Faith said. 'It was more circumstances. Rob was living and working in the Midlands, and I was sharing a flat in London with a friend from uni. He came up to see mutual friends most weekends and that's how we met. It evolved quite slowly but we got to the point where we realised we weren't going to go any further only seeing each other once a week, so we talked about it and he was really keen for us to move in together somewhere halfway in between.'

'And you were too?'

She tipped her head from side to side thoughtfully. 'We'd been together for about two years by then. I had a couple of flings at uni but nothing I wanted to take any further, because,' she had hoped to escape today without bringing this up again, but Rik looked so open and receptive she thought she could chance it, 'I was pretty wary of getting involved with anybody, after what I thought had happened with you. And then all of a sudden I was in my mid-twenties and in a two-year relationship and all around me my friends were moving in with their boyfriends and talking about getting engaged and it seemed like the obvious next step. But then he wanted to take the *next* step and I didn't, and now I'm pretty much right back at the start again, only on the wrong side of my mid twenties,' she added ruefully.

'Don't tell me you actually do think you're getting old,' Rik said.

She watched as a waitress cleared their plates away. 'I'm not old,' she conceded. 'But there's nothing like a relationship ending to make you re-evaluate your life and I have come to the rather depressing conclusion that I've been just drifting along. It's not even like I'm advancing my career, like Lucinda,' she said fretfully. 'I hate my job. I was trying to get promoted but only because Rob was keen for me to push for a payrise so we could save for a house.'

'When you were at school and thinking about the future, what did you think you'd be doing at this age?'

I thought I'd be with you, Faith wanted to say.

'I thought I'd be a garden designer. I had actually started thinking about it before Rob and I split up. We did have some savings and I thought I could use them to retrain.'

'So why not?'

'Well, I'm having to use the savings to pay the rent on the flat,' she said gloomily. 'I couldn't leave Rob with all the bills for the rest of our tenancy. And I'm not exactly flush so if I want to study I'll have to go back to work and start saving again and that'll take ages —'

'Get a loan,' Rik said. 'Or do an apprenticeship, or work part-time while you're studying. There's always a way.'

'Plus,' she said awkwardly. 'I'm making a bit of a hash of Hollyhocks.' There were moments when she could feel things were coming together, flashes of inspiration and glimpses of how it might all look once she'd finished, but in the main, it was still an almighty mess.

'You did a pretty good job of it first time around,' Rik said. 'You transformed the place, and I remember you did a pretty good job of the other places you worked on too. You might be out of practice but you thought you were out of practice on the bike and you didn't seem to have any problems today.'

That was true, Faith thought hopefully.

'I'm sure,' Rik said softly, 'you still have that magic touch.'

Her stomach fluttered.

Rik picked up his phone and he frowned. 'I'm running late.' He typed out a message quickly.

'Do you need to head off?' she asked, hoping she didn't sound too flustered.

'I'm supposed to be on a call with somebody from the States this evening,' he said. 'Got confused with the time difference. Do you mind if we go?'

'Of course not,' she said. 'Let's get the bill.'

Faith rang Sara when she got home. 'I just had a cycle down memory lane with Rik.'

'Not a ride?' Sara asked hopefully.

Faith giggled. 'Not that kind of ride. Strictly friend zone. We even discussed the fragrant Lucinda. But I can't say focusing on his flaws is really working for me.' She sighed. 'Apparently he doesn't have any, other than the aforementioned bitch.'

'Of course he does,' Sara said. 'Just give it time. And in the mean time, get laid.'

'About that,' Faith said. 'What are you doing on Saturday night?'

'I'm not shagging you.'

'No,' Faith giggled. 'I'm going out in London with some friends from the track after our training sessions. Why don't you come? Might cheer you up, take your mind off Tony for a while.'

Sara's voice sounded eager. 'Sounds just the ticket. Shall we take Minel too?'

'Why not?' Faith said. 'More the merrier.'

165

Chapter 14

When Faith had said 'more the merrier' she hadn't reckoned on quite how many more. Minel instantly said she wanted Paul to come too. 'We haven't been out together in ages,' she said persuasively as Paul took a break from bollocking the recalcitrant teenagers and gratefully downed a pint of water she had brought him. 'And all you've done is work. It'd be nice to spend some time with you.'

'All right,' Paul said. 'I suppose there is still life in the old dog yet.'

'I'll come,' Rik said and Faith's heart leaped. Then she realised that meant she would have to put up with bloody Lucinda too.

'What about us?' one of the teenagers demanded.

'Absolutely no way,' Paul said. 'You're all wildly underage and a total liability.'

'I'm not,' Lofty pointed out.

Faith thought about Lucy.

'You can come,' she said to Lofty. 'But you lot,' she glared at the excitable rabble, 'can save your fake IDs for another time.'

'You look hot to trot,' Lucy said as Faith came out of the track changing rooms, running her fingers through her newly-washed hair which was clinging to her scalp but already beginning to separate into spirals. They were all buzzing after the skills session. At the end Shaun had divided them into categories so they could race, and Faith had actually won her round before being thoroughly pulverized by Lucy.

Faith had been going to wear her usual faded denim shorts and a vest, then she'd thought if Lucinda did join them she would instantly feel shabby and scruffy. In the depths of her still-unpacked boxes she'd unearthed a long white peasant top which she'd put on over skinny jeans and the one pair of heels she owned, which were made from glittery black leather. She'd roped in her trusty push-up bra to make her breasts work a bit harder and put on a black choker necklace.

'You look like a very sexy fairy,' Lucy said delightedly.

'I've brought you a present for this evening,' Faith said. 'Let's go and meet everybody.'

They met at one of those identikit pizza restaurants that had long, marbled tables and an endless menu and everything was noisy and rowdy and a little bit messy.

'This is Lucy and Crystal,' Faith gestured at her friends, 'and this is Sara, that's Minel and her husband Paul and this is — oh you look nice,' she blurted out before she could help herself.

Rik was wearing dark blue jeans and an orange t-shirt with a picture of a small cardboard robot on the front. She'd barely seen him in anything other than dusty and tattered labouring clothes so far this summer. The lurid orange was practically glowing against his dark skin and eyes. He looks vaguely ridiculous and ridiculously gorgeous, she thought. Even up here in town where everybody was far more glamorous and polished and put-together than in Westchester he stood out through the force of his presence alone. Although his height and beauty weren't exactly helping him slip under the radar either.

Certainly not with Lucy.

'I'm not sure nice really covers it.' Faith recognised the predatory expression on her friend's face. Do I look at him like that, she wondered? Like I want to eat him? 'What's under that?' Lucy asked, flicking the robot idly.

Rik smiled easily, as if he were entirely used to this kind of attention. Which he probably was, Faith thought irritably. 'Lucy,' she said quickly, turning her friend in the direction of Lofty. 'This is —' *Shit, what was his actual name?*

'Harry,' Lofty said, flashing his most charming smile.

Lucy looked him up and down, then her gaze drifted to Rik again. 'You didn't tell me you were bringing me two presents tonight,' she chided Faith. 'Where do you hide them all?'

'He's not for you,' Faith said, hoping she didn't sound shrewish. 'He has a girlfriend.'

Lucy shrugged and turned to Lofty. 'Well, you can start by buying me a drink.'

Lofty took her arm and steered her off in the direction of the bar.

'Your friend seems nice,' Rik said.

'She's a force of nature,' Faith agreed reluctantly. 'When I grow up, I want to be just like her.'

'Looks like Lofty's in for a good night,' Sara observed. 'At least someone is.'

Faith touched her shoulder reassuringly to remind Sara that she wasn't in for that kind of good night either. Rik's presence was the ultimate chaperonage. She wouldn't be able to look at anybody else with him around even though Lucinda was mercifully absent.

Crystal, who had been exchanging pleasantries with Paul and Minel, drifted over. Faith introduced her to Rik. 'Crystal is my track mentor,' she said. 'She initiated me into the art of mindless round-and-round.' Crystal looked blank. 'That's his interpretation of track cycling,' Faith elaborated.

Crystal looked affronted. 'Have you ever even been on a track?'

Rik shook his head.

'It's pretty hardcore,' Faith said. 'You probably couldn't handle it, Rikki.'

'Track cycling,' Crystal said firmly, 'is the ultimate test of skill, speed and control. No brakes, no gears, no fancy stuff or interruptions to hide all your bad habits and there's nothing tame about those banks.'

'There isn't,' Faith chipped in. 'First time I rode track I honestly thought I was going to die and Crystal had to hold my hand all the way round.' She smiled affectionately at her friend.

'Also,' Crystal announced grandly, 'we all ride commando.'

Faith giggled, remembering the first time she'd worn padded cycling shorts, known as a chamois, and complained about her pants getting tangled up in all the fabric. Lucy, Crystal and the other girls had howled with laughter. 'Nothing comes between a girl and her chamois,' Lucy had said, still chortling merrily.

Rik turned to Faith. 'I'm absolutely not allowed to say anything to that, am I?'

'Nothing at all,' she confirmed. 'Anything you said would just sound incredibly creepy.'

'But it's OK for you to talk about riding dressed as a — what did you call it?'

'A human condom,' Faith said. 'Yes, that's totally acceptable.'

Crystal giggled. 'Lycra isn't the best look. But it helps with speed, and you're super-fast.'

'I am without the wind resistance,' Faith said. 'Which is finally going.'

'What are you on about?' Rik asked. 'Wind resistance?'

'I put on a bit of weight,' Faith said. 'But thankfully all the hill reps and that leaden ground is seeing it off.'

'Can't say I noticed,' Rik said.

'You wouldn't have noticed,' Faith said patiently. 'You hadn't seen me in nine years and I was hardly going to look like a seventeen year old.'

'Actually,' Rik said. 'I thought you looked just the same, only maybe a bit more —' He looked a little troubled. 'You just look like you.'

The hairs on Faith's arms had begun to prickle, and she swallowed hard, because his words had provoked a powerfully bittersweet sensation within her. She felt like she knew exactly what he meant. He had changed, and despite his protestations she knew she had too, but she'd felt from the second she'd laid eyes on him again that he was still so very *him*, only more so, somehow.

Faith sat between Crystal and Rik at dinner, enjoying watching them finding each other pleasantly interesting and she thought they could both see what she saw in each of them, and they in turn both seemed to see exactly what each other saw in her. And as always, she and Rik just seemed to unconsciously gravitate towards one another, picking up each other's thought trains and running with them, occasionally leaving Crystal looking a bit perplexed. It reminded Faith of the way Minel, Paul and Sara used to look when she and Rik would take group conversations off onto tangents of their own, and Minel would complain that they talked in riddles and were in their own little world and huff that Faith was *her* friend first.

'What now?' Lucy asked once their table had finally been cleared away. 'Shall we go dancing?'

'Yes,' Faith said instantly. 'Not to one of those poncy, up-their-own backsides places,' she said. 'Let's go somewhere good and cheesy with a fair to middling chance of 90's rave.'

'I know just the place,' Lucy's eyes lit up. 'You'll love it.'

'Where is it?' Rik asked, looking at his phone. Not Lucinda, Faith thought sadly, I like it far too much sitting next to you chatting and giggling and making Crystal laugh with our silliness, as if you and I were a couple. That's a bit unhealthy, she chided herself, but without Lucinda prowling around that was exactly how it felt.

'Jason's up in town,' he said. 'He wants to join us. Where?' he asked Lucy and she gave him the address.

'What's he up to nowadays?' Faith demanded.

'He's an accountant.' Rik was still typing. 'He's getting married in a couple of weeks.'

'Oh wow.' Rik's long-time sidekick had been so sweet, he deserved it. 'Who to?' Not Sophie, surely. If everybody else had made it other than her and Rik it would finish her off.

'Lily,' Rik said. 'Awesome girl. He met her at uni.'

They piled into taxis, which dispensed them outside an ecclesiastical-looking building not far from Tottenham Court Road. 'This used to be a church,' Lucy said, as they queued outside the building. 'Now it's the church of rave.'

Inside, the building had a huge central dance floor with a DJ booth at the top, and grand-looking staircases on either side. The bar was located at the back of the room and was heaving, so to save time they all bought two drinks and Rik disappeared off to find Jason. Faith drank quickly, desperate to start moving. The music was absolutely as Lucy had promised, right up her street, and she was still full of a charged energy from the track session and the general mood of the evening, which was merry and raucous and a little bit silly.

'Come on,' she yelled at Lucy, Crystal, Minel and Sara. 'Let's dance.'

'Why are girls always first to the dancefloor?' Sara asked as they wound their way through the heaving crowd. 'Girls on the dancefloor, boys at the bar.'

Faith had only meant to dance a bit, wanting to see Jason and not needing any excuse to be near Rik, especially in Lucinda's absence. But as song after song blared noisily out of the speakers, the bass shaking the floor and her insides, she couldn't tear herself away and they danced on and on, giggling and shouting to one another and occasionally being chatted up.

Minel got tired quickly and went back to Paul. After a while the music changed to the sort of poppy RnB that came with beats that seemed designed for one purpose alone. The entire crowd as one began bumping and grinding and Faith felt quite shocked.

Lucy, next to her, had no hesitation whatsoever in grinding herself vigorously against Lofty. Faith felt a pang of envy as she watched her supremely confident friend work her magic. I would feel ridiculous doing that, she thought, and I'd look it too.

Sara had been appropriated by an enthusiastic-looking youth and was being bounced across the dancefloor by his relentlessly thrusting pelvis. Her eyes were practically popping out of her head. Faith dissolved into hopeless giggles.

'This is quite fun,' she told Faith as she jerked past. 'I'm rather enjoying this.'

Giggling, Faith made her way over to the bar, liberally cannoned around by gyrating couples. She was flushed and sweaty, and her hair was falling all over the place. She pushed it out of her eyes irritably, bouncing on her feet to try and see over the crowds of people flocking around the bar.

'Faith!' Rik had appropriated a stool from somewhere and shot his hand out and grabbed hers, dragging her over to him.

'Jason,' he said to the man next to him, 'you remember Faith, don't you?'

Jason's skin had cleared up and he, too, had filled out but his face was as open and friendly as ever. 'Of course I do,' he said. 'Hey Faith. Good to see you again.'

'Good to see you!' She hugged him delightedly. 'I hear you're getting married. Congratulations. She's a lucky woman.'

He smiled. 'Thanks. Looking forward to it. Looking forward to all the table planning and flower chat being over with,' he said conspiratorially.

Seeing Faith was still being battered and buffeted by the constantly moving crowd, Rik steered her in between him and Jason, perching her on the end of his seat.

'What are you up to now?' Jason asked, and Faith gave him the brief version. Rik was watching the cavorting on the dancefloor. Sara was being humped into view again, eyes bugging more than ever but still giggling happily as her consort continued his apparently never-ending thrusting. 'He's got stamina,' Rik noted, 'the lucky bastard.'

Faith felt giddier than ever and couldn't stop laughing.

'Even Paul and Minel are at it.' She watched her friends indulgently as they moved together, perfectly in tune, oblivious to the heaving and shunting that was going on all around them. 'They're so sweet,' she sighed.

'Are they having any luck getting pregnant?' Jason asked.

Rik shook his head.

Faith squeezed his arm. 'You'll be an uncle one day.' He would be a great uncle, he'd be a great dad, actually…

'Lily wants to crack on after the wedding,' Jason said. 'I'm up for it. I love kids.'

'Me too,' Faith said. 'I want loads. A whole bunch, following me around like a gaggle of puppies, arguing and answering back and generally driving me to distraction. Not stuck up in their bedrooms for hours on end,' she added disgustedly, 'watching TV and playing nicely and never making a mess.'

'My mum used to just kick me and my brother out in the garden and lock the door,' Jason said nostalgically. 'We tore the shit out of each other. Good times.' He smiled brightly.

'Kids need to be mucky, and noisy, and silly, and outside as much as possible,' Faith said firmly. 'That's what childhood is for.'

'Riding bikes,' Rik agreed and she saw that he was looking at her affectionately. 'Getting into scrapes, and making a hash of clearing them up.' She smiled and he held her gaze, his eyes soft on hers, bringing a warmth to her stomach and her already flushed cheeks.

He pushed her off the seat. 'Let's go and dance like all the cool kids.'

Faith wasn't going to say no, although — 'I'm not doing that,' she said, watching Sara giggling with fascination as her young suitor performed a freakish-looking figure-of-eight with his pelvis.

'I don't think it's supposed to do that,' Rik said. 'He must be double-jointed.'

He steered her by her shoulders through the crowd, bouncing a little on his toes behind her. The music was deafening and she had to shout over the racket.

'I'm not twerking,' she yelled. 'My legs are far too stiff for that, or slut-dropping, or,' what other crazy names were there for overtly sexual dance moves? 'Daggering,' she shouted.

He laughed. 'Do you even know what that is?'

'I can guess,' she said, eyeing the bumping and grinding all around her. 'Does all this this make you feel old and prudish or is it just me?'

'I can't hear you,' Rik yelled.

Faith stepped a little closer to him and stood on tiptoes, raising her head to his ear and putting her hand on his shoulder. He slid his arm around her waist and she felt his presence flooding into her in the places her body was pressed against his and forgot completely what she had been going to say.

'Rikki?'

'Yes?' He had bent his head down to her ear and she leaned her head against his. She drew her breath in sharply and Rik moved his head against hers, very affectionately, like a cat rubbing against a beloved owner.

You're still mine, she thought possessively. Somewhere, underneath, you know you're still mine just like I'm still — I'm always — yours.

The music changed, thankfully, to a more dancy if slower-tempoed number. But again it was the kind of song made for two, dreamy and mournful with occasional slow, beat-heavy breaks. Rik put his other arm around her, seemingly entirely content to dance with her despite the intimacy of the song, and Faith felt her entire being fill once again with bittersweet sadness. But because Rik didn't seem to be going anywhere she let herself flow against him, putting her arms around his neck and wishing she could just kiss him right here and now and never let him go. He was watching her, his dark eyes very soulful, and she closed her eyes, not wanting to read the expression in his, just wanting to let go for a moment and pretend that this was actually real. Without her eyes to guide her she had to rely entirely on her other senses, which had of their own accord just tuned effortlessly into him.

The song ended too soon, replaced by a rowdy and upbeat number, the DJ clearly fearful of actual full-frontal shagging erupting on the dance floor. Faith opened her eyes reluctantly and saw that Rik's were heavy and far-away. Misty, almost, he was looking at her without really focusing and his pupils were very wide and her heart rate instantly quickened madly.

She stepped away pointedly and pushed her hair back. 'Need a drink,' she said to him, and he nodded dreamily and followed her back to the bar. She didn't dare look at him again, unable to take the acute mixture of emotions swirling through her. They rejoined Jason, who was chatting to Paul, Minel and Crystal, and Faith shifted herself so she was further away from Rik and leaned on the bar.

Rik pushed his way in next to Jason, who must have assumed Faith was out of earshot. 'You two look pretty tight,' he said pointedly.

Rik laughed. 'I haven't seen her in nine years, mate, I'm allowed to catch up with her.'

'Lucinda doesn't mind?'

She didn't catch what either of them said, the crowd beside her had erupted into noisy laughter, but when Rik said, 'No, I haven't,' she was both glad she hadn't overheard and wished more than anything that she had.

'Might make things awkward,' Jason was saying. 'Never a good idea to talk about the ex with the current missus.'

'Yep,' Rik agreed. 'No point telling her when I'm working with Faith all summer.'

No point telling her? But hadn't Lucinda said — she'd definitely said Rik had told her everything and she'd seemed to know quite a bit about it. Or had she? What had she actually said? Referred to him as an ex and accused him of being less than brotherly. And then they'd giggled about fairies and magic, and Lucinda had joked that it must have affected her and Rik, then she'd said…

Oh no.

What had her exact words been? Not for long, something like that? Something she had still thought was fairly noncommittal but if Lucinda didn't know, if she'd just been guessing, and fishing, that would have been the confirmation that she needed.

Faith felt all the energy drain out of her body. It was like somebody had chucked a bucket of ice all over her. She'd dropped herself right in it, and Rik too. Bloody Lucinda, she fumed, I knew she was a bitch.

She had to tell Rik. Lucinda was clearly suspicious and she had to warn him, let him know he was in for an uncomfortable confrontation and a nasty shock. She felt a flash of shame. What had she been thinking, dancing with him like that? Sloping off to ride bikes with him, entertaining her wistful little fantasies, searching his face and analysing his words for any possible inclination that he might still have feelings for her? He's not an object, she lectured herself furiously, he's a person, with a heart and a life and a girlfriend and he's moved on, and you should too.

She felt completely sober and extremely tired, and to her relief Paul and Minel appeared, both yawning and saying they were going home. 'I'll come,' Faith said instantly and Sara said she would and then of course Rik said he would and Jason too, and it took ages, and all Faith wanted was to go home and sleep and wake up in approximately three hours time plagued with insomnia and self-doubt and probably horniness from yet another erotic dream about Rik, especially after that dance.

He caught up with her on the way to the train, and began chatting easily with her again, but she had completely closed up and cut off all his attempts, collapsing gratefully into the nearest seat. Rik and Jason sat down opposite and Faith cursed. She'd have to listen to them bantering away all the way home.

'Where's Sara?' Faith got up and stalked off down the carriage, finding her sharing a table seat with Paul and Minel.

'Hold me,' she wailed and Sara put her arm around her and squeezed her shoulders sympathetically. She didn't ask Faith what was wrong and she felt a surge of gratitude to her friend. If she hadn't told her about Rik she'd be firing all sorts of difficult questions at her right now.

Paul and Minel were murmuring to one another, Minel nestled easily in his strong arms. They seemed oblivious to the rest of the carriage. She leaned against Sara, and closed her eyes again. 'Wake me up when we get there.'

She didn't sleep, but the rocking of the train was soothing and Paul and Minel's chatter and Sara's closeness seemed to calm her. Sara was happy enough occasionally interjecting into their conversation, squeezing Faith reassuringly every now and again.

There are advantages to being twenty-six after all, she thought. You can take comfort in the little things, like the company of good friends, the sound of light rain on a train window, and the certainty that no matter what happens, even if your world feels like it's falling apart all over again, there's always somebody out there like Sara who will be there for you.

Chapter 15

As the long, hot summer of her seventeenth year dragged on Faith was increasingly frustrated by how hard it was to get any time with Rik. Thanks to part-time jobs, her parents rigid curfews and fondness for grounding her, and Minel wanting to dissect both her relationship with Gabe and Paul's every word with Faith, they seemed to have gone from spending all their time together to finding it virtually impossible to be alone. Matters weren't helped when he and Minel went on holiday with their parents for two weeks. Faith thought she might go through the roof with all the waiting around.

Sara was also struggling, burdened as she was with a short-tempered Faith who had taken to coming to her house just for something to do, only to loaf around in her friend's back garden grumbling about being bored and trying and failing not to think about Rik being surrounded by suntanned, bikini-clad girls.

'You need a boyfriend,' Sara tried one day when Faith was being particularly insufferable.

Faith scowled. 'Hardly.'

'Charlie thinks you're fit,' Sara went on. Charlie was a friend of Sara's latest boyfriend, Flynn, who was a few years older and fully ingratiated into the polo set. Charlie, who Faith had met once or twice, was so posh he could barely speak, his words slurring plummily into each other as if he were constantly drunk. Which he may well have been, as all he and Flynn seemed to do was hang around in pubs.

Pubs were no fun, Faith thought darkly, unless Rik was there with her so they could pretend to argue while groping each other's legs under the table. And when that was no longer enough they would sneak off around the corner past the cool stone wall, once night had fallen and everybody was too drunk and rowdy to notice their long absences. Not that anybody would question it if they did notice, everybody would have assumed they were just entertaining themselves in any of their usual ways.

Faith felt increasingly guilty for not enlightening Sara as to what 'usual ways' her and Rik's entertainment involved these days.

Would it be so bad if her friends knew?

She could finally join in her and Minel's worldy conversations about their sex lives, although something told her Minel in particular would not be enthralled to hear some of the more pertinent details. She was almost certain she was ready to say goodbye to her virginity, but she could have still done with some moral support and somebody with whom to discuss things like, what to wear? What if it hurts? How could she make sure it lived up to expectations? How, exactly, does one become 'good in bed'?

'Faith?' Sara's voice interrupted her brooding.

'Huh?'

'I was saying Charlie thinks you're fit. Shall I tell him you'll be out on Friday with me and Flynn?' Sara was holding her mobile phone, frowning at the screen.

'Isn't, um, Min back on Friday?' Like she didn't have it emblazoned on her brain.

'Good point. I'll text her and see if she wants to come too.'

'And Rik,' Faith said before she could stop herself. Heat rushed up into her cheeks just at the mention of his name and the ever-present pulse in her lower belly thumped once or twice. She glared accusingly at Sara's back garden, which was completely paved over. 'It's too hot. You need more plants in here. And you should pull up some slabs and put in a pond.'

'Go ahead,' Sara invited.

And then I can get Rik over to help me and we can spend the entire day rolling around Sara's house and nobody will suspect a thing, Faith thought gleefully.

'What did you get up to while I was away?' Rik asked as she led him into Sara's airy living room.

'Nothing,' she grumbled. 'I don't know what's up with my mother but she's over my shoulder constantly, and it's driving me bananas. She even asked me the other day if I had a boyfriend. Only she couldn't use that exact word, she was so obviously disgusted, so instead she asked me if I had a "b-friend".'

'What did you tell her?' Rik asked.

'I said no, of course. What about you? How was your holiday?' How were the suntanned girls in bikinis, she wanted to ask.

'Awful,' he said. 'It went on forever and I had to put up with my parents and Minel asking me what was wrong a thousand times a day and lots of muttering about raging hormones.'

'They were probably right,' she said irritably. 'Unless you met some pretty girl to help you out with them, obviously.' The resplendent figure of Sophie Barnes loomed into her mind.

'Of course I didn't. Is that what you're worried about?'

'It's just that —' She gulped. 'I missed you.'

Oh please, she thought, don't let him trivialise this. Not everything is a silly joke. She'd never admitted to any actual feelings for him before.

'That's good, isn't it?'

'Not if you didn't miss me.'

'I already told you I did. Didn't you get my texts?'

'Yeah but —'

'But?'

'That's just a couple of texts.' She scowled.

'I couldn't exactly fly home to tell you to your face.'

'No but —'

'Yeah but no but,' he said softly. 'I think I should just show you.' Thanks to the considerable amount of practice they'd both put in Rik had discovered just the right way to kiss her to make her practically dissolve with hollow, weak-kneed longing. Faith felt her whole body, along with her residual irritation, melting.

'Has that convinced you?'

'No.'

'Oh OK.' He edged her vest up and Faith obediently held her arms up over her head so he could take it off. Thanks also to the considerable practice he could now unhook her bra at the first attempt. 'Let's see what will.'

The stones on Sara's patio were a pale creamy-white and the sunlight bounced straight off them and back upwards, illuminating the garden with an almost blinding light. Faith wished Sara had a lawn that she and Rik could go and lie on, as it seemed a shame to be indoors on such a perfect summer's day, but neither of them wanted to get dressed and so they stayed on the living room floor, their clothes scattered far and wide from Rik's enthusiastic brand of undressing.

If my mother could see this, she thought, she'd go absolutely ballistic. She'd tell me you can't trust boys, that if you let a boy take your clothes off you're giving him the green light to do whatever he wants, it's like she doesn't realise there's so many possibilities, so much you can do together without having sex.

'What are you going to do next year?' Rik asked. 'About university?'

Faith still didn't know. 'I want to go to horticultural college,' she said, 'and my mother wants me to go to a *real* university and get a *proper* degree, and every time we talk about it we end up arguing so I'm kind of avoiding the issue.'

'You should just go to college,' he said instantly. 'Who cares what your mum wants you to do? It's not her life.'

'I know,' she said, 'but as she keeps pointing out, she and my dad will be funding me, or helping fund me, at least.' She grimaced. 'And she might have a point that mowing lawns and weeding isn't exactly well-paid.'

'There's loads of ways to make money gardening,' Rik countered. 'And even if you don't, you can always do something else on the side, or go back to university later on.'

Those were the exact points Faith had made continually and repeatedly to her mother, but for some reason now she was playing devil's advocate herself. 'Or I could study English and find a decent job and do the gardening on the side,' she said, echoing her mother's arguments. 'I don't know. What are you going to do?'

'I'm going to study graphic design and then go travelling and then get a job where I can do both at the same time.'

'I want to go travelling,' she said. 'But I can't see how I could ever afford it, especially as I'm going to have to get myself into a lifetime's worth of debt just to get a degree in order to allow me to get a job that pays me enough to pay it all off by the time I'm seventy.'

'You can work at uni, and during the holidays,' he said. 'We both can, we can save up and go together. For a year at least.'

Her heart soared. A year. A whole year of dossing around with Rik, riding bikes and having adventures and swimming in the sea and discovering new places together. Meeting new people and speaking haltingly in foreign languages, giggling at each other's awful pronunciation, and getting into scrapes and bailing each other out and looking after each other when they got food poisoning from dodgy street vendors. Camping under the stars and staying in grotty hostels and overnight train journeys across continents sharing a tiny cabin and listening to the miles roar past under the all-encompassing cover of speed and darkness, knowing they would be somewhere completely different when the sun finally rose again.

And all without anybody hanging over her shoulder nagging her about — well, everything under the sun. She couldn't think of anything she wanted to do more.

'It's a pain that you're a year below me,' she said. 'I'll have to wait around for you, I suppose.'

'That'll make a change,' Rik said. 'I've done all the waiting so far. I had to wait for years just to get to first base with you.'

Faith kissed him. 'But now you get to do that all the time. And you get to go to second base with me too, and,' she dropped her voice dramatically, 'third.'

'It was worth waiting for,' Rik said.

She put her head on his chest. The bright, golden light streaming in through the patio doors was bouncing off his skin and the air around them was very still, entirely content to just be.

'I should probably tell you,' she said slowly, 'my parents are going away this weekend. All weekend.'

Rik sat up. 'And leaving you home alone?'

She nodded. 'All by myself.'

'That won't do,' Rik said. 'All kinds of undesirable types might come knocking. I'm surprised your parents are actually leaving you alone.'

'So am I,' she said. 'But I've persuaded them not to pack me off to my aunt's house in London for the weekend by promising religiously — literally, actually, my mother made me swear on the Bible — to keep myself out of trouble and to ask Minel if she can come and keep me company.'

'Oh, she'll be busy,' Rik said, 'trying to pull Paul, now she's dumped Gabe at last.'

'Has she?'

Rik nodded. 'Over the phone. Lame or what? But let's not talk about her.' He stroked her hair reflectively. 'So what do you want to do this weekend then? Can I come and keep you company instead? I would love to stay the night with you,' he said dreamily. 'And see how beautiful you look in the morning.'

All right, she thought determinedly. Time for that conversation.

'Have you ever, um,' she felt suddenly awkward, because part of her didn't want to know the answer in case it was the wrong one. 'Have you ever done that before?'

'Done what?'

'The sex.' She giggled slightly.

Rik shifted a little and Faith held her breath, hoping desperately he would say — 'No.'

'Oh good,' she said delightedly. 'I haven't either.'

Rik looked highly relieved.

'I probably could have,' he said, 'if I had wanted to.'

Faith held up her hand. 'I don't need to hear it.' She scowled at the thought of Rik with anybody else. 'I'm just glad you didn't.'

'I am too,' he said quickly, sensing he was walking a fine line. 'I always wanted it to be with you.'

Faith nodded. 'That's right,' she said vehemently. 'That's how it should be.'

Chapter 16

After their night out in London Faith had fully intended to keep away from Rik to work herself up for the inevitable uncomfortable conversation, but Monday was so sunny and the air was so full of enchantment, and Rik so obviously happy to see her, that she couldn't face it. One more day, she promised herself. *One more day in this weird limbo we seem to have arrived at, in which we are behaving like long-lost friends who are gravitating towards one another and becoming closer and more attuned, just as we did for years before we crossed the line.*

'Paul will be down on you like his tonnes of bricks if you keep sneaking over here,' she said when Rik turned up to visit her yet again.

'Tonnes and tonnes and tonnes,' he agreed. 'We're up to our eyes in them over there. Come on. Lunch time.'

They rode out onto 'the big road' and Faith wondered if the time was right to suggest the quarry, but no, she still wasn't ready for that. Rik took her further out than before, up and around and down and up again, but when they got back she was amazed to notice they had still only been an hour.

'I must be getting stronger,' she said delightedly.

'You are,' Rik said. 'Compared to how slowly you crawled along when you got here.' He smiled cheekily. Faith's heart failed. *I just adore him,* she thought. *It's going to kill me to let him go again, when all this is over.*

After they had finished up Rik fell into step next to her as she headed up to the house to say goodbye to Minel and GT. 'Stay for dinner,' Minel offered. 'Sara will be round in a bit.'

Faith helped her knock up a lasagne and salad and giggled as GT kept trying, and failing, to leap up onto the side to steal food from her hand. 'I need to train him,' she sighed.

GT brought over a length of rope and begged Rik into playing tug-of-war. Faith watched him with the puppy. He'd be amazing with kids, she thought. We'd have great kids, me and him.

'You are going to neuter GT?' Faith said to Minel.

'Of course.' Minel looked affronted. 'Completely irresponsible, having a dog like him carousing around. He'll be worse than that infernal Tackle.'

'The neighbours did try to restrain him once,' Rik said. 'They bought an electric fence that you bury around the parameters of your land and fitted him with this awful collar, that gave him an electric shock every time he crossed it.' He giggled infectiously. 'Tackle did not care. He would jump over the fence, lie down twitching for a while until the shock had passed, and then just get up and go.'

'I felt a bit like Tackle as a kid,' Faith said. She caught Rik's eye and flushed. 'A weird combination of left to run wild, and pegged in by an invisible fence.' To be fair she and Tackle had also shared a mutual desire to be as close to Rik as possible and a fondness for humping his leg, but she wasn't saying that one out loud.

'When we have kids,' Paul said, 'they won't be allowed to run wild and get up to all sorts of mischief.' He tapped the table emphatically. 'They'll do as they're bloody well told.'

'Slave driver,' Faith said, but she felt pleased Paul was discussing children so openly, without any of the usual loaded tension. 'You were the worst of all of us,' she said, 'you great hypocrite. You led all of us astray, especially Minel.'

Paul laughed. 'Fair point,' he said.

'When we have kids they'll run wild around this place just like we did,' Minel said to Paul firmly. 'We all turned out OK. Just think,' she said, her face radiant, 'one day there'll be a whole bunch of them running around here, exhausting us poor parents, probably trashing that lovely summerhouse we're building for them like we trashed the hay barn. A new generation.' She looked wistful and hopeful, and Faith reached out and squeezed her shoulder, too moved to speak. That is what we're building here, she thought. A legacy, a gift for a new generation, and I'm a part of it.

Sara wandered in full of smiles and hellos. Faith was about to pull her aside and ask for the latest news on Tony, because Sara had seemed far more upbeat lately, but then she clocked Minel and Paul exchanging a glance and her heart skipped several beats.

'Now we're all here, we've got something to tell you,' Minel said, taking Paul's hand.

Faith caught her breath. Could it be?

'I'm pregnant,' Minel said, and she burst into tears.

Faith flung her arms around her and felt Sara wrap her arms around the pair of them. A few tears escaped from her own eyes. 'Oh Min,' she said. 'You wonderful woman. You miracle worker.'

Rik and Paul exchanged a high five. 'I did a bit too,' Paul pointed out, and Faith giggled and turned to him. 'Congratulations,' she said, and he held out his arms and she squeezed him and blinked back more tears.

'How far gone are you?' Sara looked misty-eyed too.

'Not very,' Minel said. 'Just a few weeks. I only took a test this morning. I felt a bit off and thought it must be my period but then I realised I'd thought that when I felt rough last week too. And sure enough. I'm pregnant. I'm actually pregnant,' she said again, 'I can't believe it.'

'How are you feeling?' Rik asked. 'Sick as a dog yet?'

'Fine, so far,' Minel said. 'A bit tired and bloated, but other than that, I feel great. I almost wish I did feel sick,' she said a little anxiously, 'because that might make it more real.'

They sat down to eat, talking nineteen to the dozen about the baby and Faith felt a lifting in her chest as she realised here, again, was a part of the legacy of Hollyhocks to which she belonged. The day the new generation began, she was here, sitting around this very table, having dinner with her best friends and the man she wished she was creating her own new generation with.

Everything was so lovely and happy it was even more of a wrench for Faith the next day when she knew she had to talk to Rik. Lucinda mustn't have said anything yet, because he was upbeat as ever, but she knew it wouldn't be long and she couldn't have him hearing it from her first. When he showed up with his bike at lunchtime she shook her head. 'Let's just stay here and eat the vegetable garden instead.'

Rik wavered, then nodded. 'OK. What have you got in there?'

'Let's see. Oh look,' Faith noted delightedly. 'The raspberries are going bananas.' She examined the canes which were top-heavy and laden with fruits that had turned from a pale green to deep red practically overnight. She rummaged around underneath and unearthed a few stray strawberry plants that were similarly heavy with fruit. 'It's like a fruit salad down here,' she said, picking one of the strawberries and examining it closely. She bounced it in her hand gleefully, then ate it. 'Not for you,' she said to GT.

He sniffed at the canes and lifted his leg disdainfully.

'For Christ's sake, you horror.' Faith shoved him away gently.

She ripped a few fruits off the canes and handed them to Rik, then picked a few more for herself and sat down with him. GT lay down too and stretched his body out, his little hind legs splayed inelegantly like a spatchcocked chicken.

Rik threw a raspberry in the air and caught it in his mouth. 'Anything else in there?' he nodded at the canes.

'There's tomatoes, and baby cucumbers, if you fancy a salad?'

She picked a few of each and they ate them contentedly. 'Don't you think it's amazing,' she said wonderingly, 'that all of this came from practically nothing? A few seeds, soil, a bit of water and air and you can grow enough to sustain you. It's like this place wants to nurture us,' she said, sweeping her hand around. 'To fuel us, give us some of itself because it knows we want to nurture it in return...' Rik smiled indulgently and she thought she'd better stop waxing lyrical with her flights of fancy because last time she'd done that it had landed her in a bit of trouble, which she was now going to have to address.

In the distance somebody fired up a lawn mower. The smell of freshly-cut grass drifted over. Rik's face looked very open, his eyes gentle and content, and she felt her breath catch in her throat.

Tell him now, she urged herself. You can't just work it into a conversation about vegetables. Just tell him straight.

'Rik, look,' she said. 'I have to talk to you.'

'We're talking right now, aren't we?' He smiled easily.

She took a deep breath. 'I overheard you telling Jason that you hadn't told Lucinda about you and me. Other than that we were friends.'

'Yeah,' Rik said thoughtfully. 'Might make it a bit awkward for her, and for you. I mean, it was ages ago, but still.' He smiled again, apparently unconcerned.

'About that,' she said. 'I think — I mean, I may have, dropped you in it a bit.'

'What do you mean?'

'She came over to chat last Monday,' Faith said miserably, 'and asked if it was weird for me having her around, and I said of course not, and then she said,' she gulped.

Rik's eyes had darkened. 'What did she say?'

'She said she knew about you and I — said you'd told her, she knew we had been, that we were,' she still didn't really know how to describe it. She'd never called him her boyfriend, they hadn't used those words with one another, but to all intents and purposes. 'She referred to you as my ex, said it sounded like our relationship hadn't been sibling-like, she seemed to know,' she bit her lip, 'and I did try to fend her off, I didn't say anything, just said we were friends and cycled a lot but then she sort of — got me.'

'Got you how?'

'Oh, got me rambling on about this place,' Faith sighed, 'my usual stuff, flower analogies all over the place. I told her I always thought this place was a bit magical, and she seemed to know what I meant, we had quite a nice chat actually and then she brought it back to you and me and all I said was that it hadn't lasted long, but I suppose for her that must have been confirmation.'

Rik looked furious, and Faith quailed.

'I'm so sorry,' she wailed. 'I feel awful. I've landed you right in it, she's going to be annoyed that you weren't straight with her, it's all my fault, I should have just kept my trap shut. Too easily distracted,' she said vehemently, 'with my vague hippy theories, idiot that I am. I'm so sorry. I hate to think that I've got you into trouble. I knew straight away,' she acknowledged, 'that I'd said something I shouldn't. I could just feel it, you know, all prickly and like my hackles were up. If you want, I can talk to her.'

'Don't be ridiculous,' he said indignantly. 'What was she doing, pumping you like that? If she wanted to know if anything had ever gone on with us, why didn't she just ask me?'

'I assumed she did ask,' Faith said slowly.

'She asked if we were close and I said yes, we were very close once but I hadn't seen you in years. She didn't ask any more. If she'd asked me directly, of course I would have told her.' He looked more incensed than ever. 'God, I feel like — I feel like I've got something to hide, and I haven't. We were young, we didn't do anything wrong, neither of us should feel bad about that.'

'Well, I do a bit,' Faith said, and he looked at her irritably and she added quickly, 'but only because it turns out I treated you really awfully.'

There was a long, loaded silence. Faith wanted to ask him what he was thinking, but Rik in turn seemed to expect something more from her and he waited, letting the air hang between them, punctuated only by the faint hum of a bee, until she couldn't stand it any more.

'I'm so sorry,' she said, 'that I didn't give you a chance to tell me the truth.'

He sighed. 'I am too. I still don't know why you didn't.'

'I was in a pretty bad place, after my dad had the affair. My mum was so vicious,' she winced. 'So adamant that men weren't to be trusted, that they would let you down, they were all the same. I'd had two weeks of that pretty much nonstop and then I saw you and it was just,' she closed her eyes tightly. 'It was just the final nail in the "all men are bastards" coffin.'

His eyes were a little less gentle. 'If we'd only just met each other, I could understand it but we were friends, best friends,' he sighed heavily. 'And I really was *so* in love with you. I couldn't even remember a time when I *wasn't* in love with you.'

Faith wondered if she was going to cry. 'I really was in love with you too,' she said softly.

She stared out over the greenhouse, softening her gaze and letting the greens and reds inside and the riot of colour around it blend into a kaleidoscopic blur. Rik was silent too and she found she didn't feel the sadness so much knowing that he was right there with her. This wasn't the conversation she'd expected to be having with him, but she was glad all the same.

Rik flicked a stray stalk back into the veg patch. He was wearing a black t-shirt that had seen better days and a great deal of cement and dust, not to mention the wrong end of several of Paul's tools. His hair, including the mess of ever-increasing stubble, was wilder than ever and the sun had turned his skin another shade darker.

'Call me naïve, but I actually thought, after we got together, I thought that was it. I thought we would travel together and have adventures and scratch our itchy feet and get married and knock out a bunch of kids,' he said all in a rush. 'I was a bit of a romantic as a kid and I was totally sold on the idea of you and me.' He glared at her hotly as if already regretting his outburst.

Faith blinked rapidly. 'That's exactly what I thought too,' she said softly. She couldn't bring herself to say any more.

'It's messing with my head,' he said, still sounding annoyed. 'You being here. Especially with GT knocking around too looking like the image of Tackle. I feel like — like I'm in a...'

'A timewarp,' Faith said.

'Yes! A timewarp.' He frowned again. 'When I saw you on the drive it was like I was looking at the same girl who rolled up one day with her bike. But also it was like I was seeing you now, but more — I don't know. Something.' He was clearly frustrated at his uncharacteristic inability to find the words. 'And I'm still half convinced you're just not going to show up one day. I'll come down onto the site and there'll be this big space where you used to be, and I'll start to wonder if you were ever really here at all. Then off we go on the bikes again and it's just like it always was, before...' he tailed off.

Faith once again felt such a strong surge of affinity with him it was almost physical. That was exactly how she felt too — it was like she was having three relationships with Rik, the friends they had been, flashes of the heady intensity of their brief time as more than friends, and one with him now, which was reminiscent of both at times and at the same time, still completely new and loaded with the fear that it might all suddenly end again, like it had never really begun. This is crazy, she thought. But at least it's not just me.

'I'm sorry,' she said, not really knowing what she was apologising for but knowing he still sounded almightily annoyed and that somehow that had to be her fault. 'We don't have to hang out. We don't have to go out, ride the bikes — we don't have to do any of it. I can just keep out of your way.'

Rik looked exasperated. 'If I wanted you out of the way, I'd just stay out of the way,' he said. 'I'm not telling you this like it's some massive problem for you to solve for the both of us by shutting yourself away again, removing yourself like you were never part of the equation. We're friends, you're a part of this,' he swept his hand over the garden, 'after this summer it's not like we'll never see each other, unless you take off again.'

'I won't,' Faith said quickly. 'I'm a bit past that now.' In more ways than one, she acknowledged. She might have wanted to run away and hide at the very beginning but now the idea of just closing the door on Rik and on Hollyhocks was unthinkable.

They sat in silence again, much more companionably this time, and Faith let her thoughts swirl up and amass, waiting to see what appeared. It didn't change anything, she acknowledged, there was no hope that he might still feel the same way about her. That much was obvious. But he also had made it pretty clear that nobody would be closing any doors at the end of this summer, they would still see each other, they could be friends, or at least have a knowledge of each other's lives.

It was validating, in a way. They'd never discussed their actual feelings for one another then or now, other than that first awful conversation, when he'd said very little about it. Sometimes she wondered if she'd dreamed the whole thing herself, or just lost it all, scattered like wildflower seeds, but seeds could eventually have roots, and so could she.

She didn't have to lose him altogether, all over again.

'I'd better get back to it,' she said eventually. Rik nodded and they both stood up. Faith forced herself to meet his gaze, which was level and steady.

'I really did love you,' she said, a little sadly. 'I hope you know.'

'I don't really think you did,' he countered, 'because if you had, I don't think you would have been so quick to think the worst of me.'

'Believe me,' she said. 'I did. I suppose I was scared, maybe, or just young and confused, but mainly I was just so very much in love with you and I think,' she felt a tugging at her heart

195

even as she said the words, 'I think a part of me will always love you.'

It was about as close as she could get to expressing how she truly felt, but Rik was still looking at her as if he was waiting for something, anything else that she could offer him, and without any words left in her she didn't really know what she could do next, other than to try and show him just what he meant to her.

She stepped forwards and he didn't move away, or towards her, he didn't move at all, frozen to the spot, frozen in time, maybe, and she stood up on tiptoes and kissed him, her lips soft as butterfly wings, just once. Just for a second.

Just long enough for the memory of how his mouth had once felt against hers, the taste of him, the heat of his raw energy, to rush back up into her consciousness.

She stumbled away and turned to GT, snapping her fingers and pointing at her heels and as if by Hollyhocks magic he for once got the message and fell in behind her, and she and the dog walked back to the rockery together. The second she knew, just by feeling it, not needing to look, that Rik had gone, she grabbed the terrier and buried her face in his wiry coat, and cried.

Chapter 17

The weekend Faith's parents headed out of town was to prove momentous not just for her and Rik. When she showed up at Hollyhocks he told her, with an expression of faint disgust, that Minel and Paul had finally got together.

'Oh,' she said delightedly. 'About time.'

Rik grimaced. 'I wish they'd keep the noise down.' He shuddered, then shot her a sly look. 'At least I won't have to listen to it tonight.'

'Oh are you staying at Jason's?' Rik's best friend had invited them to a house party, as his parents were also out of town.

'Only if you're there.'

They spent the party entertaining themselves ingratiating a lovestruck Jason with the ever-admired Sophie Barnes.

'Reckon we've done enough?' Rik asked as he and Faith watched Jason and Sophie, who were now in full flow, finishing each other's sentences and exchanging admiring looks.

'I think so,' she agreed.

'So we can go?'

So this is it, she thought.

A full moon was blazing up in the sky, giving off a silvery glow. Faith nudged Rik. 'Don't sprout fangs and claws.'

'It's not me you need to worry about,' he said, following her gaze. 'Tackle always goes mental on full moon nights. We'd better not let him follow us back to yours.'

But she didn't want to go back to her house. We don't belong there, she thought, looking at Rik. If we're going to do this, it can't be in my poky little bedroom with the walls and ceiling looming in on us.

'I don't think we should go to mine.'

'Oh.'

'Let's go to Hollyhocks,' she said decisively. It has to be there, she thought, that's where he and I met, that's where we became ourselves and that's where we first came together, that's where we need to be.

'If you like,' Rik said, 'but Minel and Paul...'

She smiled at him ecstatically. 'Not the cottage. I don't want to hear that awful din either or have to explain myself to your nosy sister. Let's go to the hay barn,' she said excitedly, 'nobody's going to come in there and bother us, we can get some blankets from the cottage, and there's those cracks in the ceiling so we can watch the moon, and Tackle can come and find us once he's finished his marauding and pillaging.' It was perfect, she thought, it was exactly what she wanted to do.

Tackle was mercifully absent when they got back and rounded up some blankets and cushions from the cottage, and they climbed up to the top of the stack of bales. The moon glowed encouragingly overhead through the cracks in the ceiling. In the silvery glow Rik's eyes looked black and the light on his skin made him look so beautiful she found she had a lump in her throat.

'So,' he said, finally a little lost for words.

'So,' she echoed.

He kissed her and she lost herself in him, letting him pull their clothes off and scatter them far and wide, lying back naked and completely exposed beneath him as his eyes drank her in. She could tell how excited he was, too excited even for foreplay, she suddenly wondered if it really was going to hurt.

'So,' he said again. 'Do you want to?'

'Do you have condoms?'

He nodded.

She could smell the slightly musty sweetness of the hay piled around them and something a little acrid, petrol he must have spilled when filling up the lawn mower. The moonlight splintered around a narrow crack in the roof and in the distance she heard a fox shrieking.

'Yes,' she said matter-of-factly. 'I want to.'

It took a while to work out how it would all come together. Faith was surprised how exposed she felt and how logistically awkward it all was. Rik was as gentle and careful as he could be, but it was still uncomfortable.

'Sorry,' he said sheepishly. 'I got way too carried away.'

'It's OK.'

'I'm so glad that was with you.'

She stroked his hair, which was damp with sweat. 'I'm glad it was you too, Rik. It was always going to be you.'

They lay in silence, staring up at the moon through the cracks in the ceiling, watching as time held still.

The balmy air brushed calm across her heated skin, soothing her tension until all of her felt fluid and resonant with life.

She could feel Rik next to her, his energy rolling off him in waves, drawing an answering pulse from within her.

Inside the stillness, everything was in motion.

She reached out for him at the exact same time as he turned to her.

When Faith woke soft light was streaming into the haybarn. She guessed it was early, around six, because it was still chilly and the air smelled fresh and inviting. The dawn chorus was in full swing, birds shrilling and cheeping and singing melodically, repeating their refrains over and over again, occasionally changing in pitch and tone. She could hear the trilling of a blackbird and the low cooing of woodpigeons, and the distinctive 'teacher, teacher' notes of a great tit.

I wonder what they're saying to each other, she thought.

Rik was still asleep, his eyelashes casting spiky shadows over his cheekbones. Not even sleep could soften those, but he looked peaceful and much younger and almost angelic. She could feel the air humming with a kind of earthy magic, but it wasn't tranquil and dreamy and softly cherishing, like it had been last night. It was vibrant, awake. More forceful. Did we do that, she wondered? Did we change the frequency? It still felt evocative, but she shivered, realising that without the blanket she must have kicked aside at some point during their brief doze, she was cold. She must have moved away from Rik.

Well, that was a mistake.

She shifted back over to him, huddling into him for warmth, and he stirred and blinked. 'You look beautiful in the morning,' he said dreamily.

'You look sexy in the morning,' she countered. 'And the afternoon, and the evening, and at night, and at 3am, especially at 3am…'

'Last night,' he said, suddenly intent. 'All of yesterday. It was all.' He paused. 'It was so much more than I thought it would be,' he said softly.

In the end all they had really had to do was tune into that pulse of energy and it had guided them all the way.

Even through the awkward bits, even though it still took a couple more attempts until Rik managed to hold on long enough for her, grasping her hand and tightening his fingers around hers until his knuckles were white.

Once she had truly surrendered and let it all take over her the intensity had been shocking, the connection far more profound.

'You know I love you, don't you?' he said. 'I've always loved you.'

Of all the things he'd said to her, this was the nicest, but she felt that magic tighten and tremor again. It must just be going through its evolutions to prepare for change, just like she and Rik had changed until they had arrived at the point they were at now, the point at which she supposed they must always have been meant to be.

'I love you too,' she said softly.

He kissed her and pulled her on top of him. 'It's been hours.'

Tackle, alerted by the disturbance, shuffled over to see what was going on. But as his ferocious yellow eyes took in the scene his intuition told him there was no place for him in the ensuing mayhem and, without any prompting at all, he sloped off and faced the wall.

'So can we tell everybody now?' Rik asked as they finally left the haybarn. Faith was looking at Hollyhocks, which was just beginning to stir in the still-early morning light. The birds had died down now, finished their showboating and gone about the serious business of the day, whatever that was. Eating and flying and resting and twitching — they did twitch a bit, the way they hopped across the ground on both legs, tiny powerful movements that propelled their entire feather-light bodies inches into the air. And they would be watching for predators, Faith thought as Tackle shot out behind them and ran yapping into a small gathering of thrushes, which all took flight and dispersed across the cloudless sky.

'Yes,' she said, squeezing his hand. 'Although you know Minel will make our lives unbearable, she and Paul will be wisecracking all over the place and in front of your parents, and Sara too.'

He shrugged. 'I don't care. It doesn't really bother you, does it?'

It did, but she didn't want to tell him, because she knew it would make him think less of her. 'Of course not,' she said, kissing him quickly.

Her mother was sitting at the kitchen table when Faith got home. Does she ever move? Faith thought agitatedly.

'Where have you been?' Judith asked.

'Just out,' Faith said. 'Sorry I didn't answer the phone earlier.' She assumed they must have phoned. 'I was in the shower and it had stopped ringing by the time I got to it.'

'Who were you out with?'

'Some friends.'

'Sit down,' Judith instructed.

Faith slid into a chair. 'Don't worry,' she babbled a little frantically. 'I didn't do anything.'

'It's not about that.' Judith said. Faith gripped the table, realising her mother's cheeks were red and her eyes very puffy. Judith began to talk, and Faith watched her knuckles turn white as her world imploded.

It took Faith two weeks to recover from the bombshell Judith and Jeff had dropped on her. In that time she didn't ring Rik, even though she knew he'd rung several times while she was out riding her bike, spinning mile after mile as she contemplated the future she was so powerless to influence.

But slowly her thoughts crept back to the parts of the future she could control. On Saturday morning she woke just before sunrise with an unmistakeable feeling of excitement in her stomach. Judith and Jeff had shocked all her joy away with their sudden announcement, but she could feel a new resolve within her, and along with it, at the top of her mind, was Rik.

Today, she thought. I'll go and see him today. We'll tell Minel and we'll go public and I'll be able to see him whenever I want, kiss him in front of everybody, stay with him at the cottage, hold his hand at school. I'll tell my parents I'm going to study garden design and that's the end of it and there's absolutely nothing they can do about it — now they'll know how powerless I feel, because it's my life. And I'll go travelling with Rik and have that life I want so much.

She might not be able to persuade her parents not to self-destruct, although there was always a chance her pleas might help, but she could at least make sure they didn't take her down with them.

She fidgeted around the house, avoiding eye contact or conversation with her parents, until 8.30am when she could wait no longer. Everybody would probably be asleep at Hollyhocks but she'd go anyway, she could hang around in the hay barn until they woke up or see if the cottage was unlocked — Rik and Minel often forgot to lock it at night — and even sneak up to Rik's room to surprise him. That would be fun, she thought eagerly, she could creep straight into bed with him and wake him up in just about the best way possible.

'See you later,' she called as she let herself out the back door.

Judith, gazing into the murky depths of her tea cup, didn't even bother asking where she was going. Faith felt a flash of guilt. Maybe she should stay with her mother today. Keep her company. It was just one more day.

But her heart was already racing, and she knew she couldn't hold out any more.

Hollyhocks looked dormant in the early morning sunshine. Faith avoided skidding up the gravel drive, anxious not to create a racket and wake anybody up, and instead dismounted silently from her bike and leaned it against the side of the hay barn. She ran up to the cottage on light feet, keeping an eye out for Tackle on his way home from goodness knows where.

But Hollyhocks was as still and as golden as if it had been put under an enchantment.

Faith tried the cottage door, praying it would be open. It was locked. She sighed and looked up at Rik's window. For once, he had drawn the curtains.

She knocked softly at the door.

It opened almost immediately. Minel was wearing a fluffy cream coloured dressing gown and a cup of tea. She blinked several times at Faith.

'Were we meeting up today?' she asked blearily. 'Did I forget again?'

Faith shook her head.

'Oh right.' Minel looked a little confused. 'Is something wrong? Only Paul's here and I was just going to go back upstairs.' She gestured at another cup of tea on the side.

'Actually,' Faith said, 'I came to see Rik.'

Minel frowned. 'At six am?'

'It's nearly nine o'clock.'

'Whatever.' Minel pulled a face. 'I'd just assume any bike riding plans you've made are cancelled now he's got a girlfriend.' She grimaced.

Rik must have told her already. 'Very funny,' Faith said. 'I'm sure you have lots more to come but let's save it for another time, shall we? I'll go kick him out of bed.' That's the last thing I'm going to do, she thought, and almost giggled.

'I wouldn't go up there if I were you,' Minel warned.

'It's nothing I haven't seen before,' Faith said teasingly.

Minel looked more confused than ever. 'Seriously, Faith. He's got some girl up there — and from the racket that was coming out of that room last night,' she paled, 'I would not expect him to take kindly to being kicked out of bed by you.'

Faith stared at her blankly. 'What girl?'

'That Sophie girl,' Minel said. 'The one with the massive,' she gestured at her chest.

'Sophie?' Faith repeated, parrot-like.

'*Huge* boobs.' Minel sounded awestruck.

'No,' Faith said.

'They are,' Minel insisted. 'She must be a D-cup at least.'

'Min!' Paul's voice came booming down the stairs. 'Where's that tea?'

Minel looked down at the tea again. 'I need to take this upstairs.'

'What do you mean, Sophie?' Faith said. Her voice had begun to waver. 'You're not joking?'

'Of course I'm not joking,' Minel snapped. 'Paul and I are exhausted, having to listen to that all night. Must be his twisted idea of revenge.' She mimed retching. 'She's been over here a couple of times this last week. I suppose somebody was always going to take pity on him in the end.'

'A couple of times,' Faith was back to her parrot impression.

Minel nodded. 'I've never seen Rik like this before. He's properly loved-up. Such a relief to have a break from his usual attitude.'

Faith felt a sharp pain in both palms, and realised she had involuntarily clenched her fists so hard her nails were digging in to her own skin.

'Anyway.' Minel yawned. 'I'm going back to bed. You can go up there if you want, but if I were you, I'd steer well clear.' She disappeared up the stairs, the ancient wood creaking softly beneath her bare feet.

Faith stared after her. Minel must have been joking — she had to be joking. Of course she was joking.

It wasn't her usual style, admittedly, but there was absolutely no way she couldn't be joking.

Minel had one lame sense of humour.

Faith nodded decisively and kicked off her trainers to follow her friend up the stairs.

The timber felt hard and smooth beneath her feet, but not cold. The latch of Rik's door clicked softly as she pushed it open.

The heel of a shoe brushed against her bare foot as she stepped into the room. A high-heeled shoe.

Right next to a red dress, tossed casually across the floor.

Faith's eyes followed the trail of clothes across the room, to Rik's bed where two figures were silhouetted by the morning sun blazing determinedly through the thin curtains.

The figure closest to her had long hair, spilling out over the pillow.

Faith clapped her hand over her mouth.

Nobody stirred.

She turned, and ran straight down the stairs and out of the door, not even realising as she did so that her exit from the house was as silent as the entry she had planned.

The loss of Rik as a friend was almost harder to bear than the loss of Rik as a boyfriend, but she told herself they couldn't have been that good friends in the first place if he was prepared to use her like that, and that she must have imagined them to be closer and more attuned than they actually had been.

With no resistance left in her, she allowed herself to be talked into studying English at university instead of garden design. She'd planned to use the garden at Hollyhocks as part of her portfolio of evidence, showing how she'd transformed it over the last few years, but she could no longer bear to carry around such a strong visual reminder of what she had once had, and so suddenly lost.

If I don't have to look at anything that even remotely reminds me of Rik, she thought hopefully, maybe I can just forget him.

She purged her room, flinging away anything that might possibly remind her of a ninja boy with soulful brown eyes who had told her he loved her as the sun streamed in through the cracks in the roof of a haybarn.

But she couldn't forget completely, and she found herself thinking of him at the most inopportune times, reminded by anything and everything, and most poignantly any time she detected just a hint of that earthy magic that occasionally seemed to linger on a particular kind of summer's day, vibrating on a slightly higher frequency, just out of reach.

Chapter 18

The next day Faith headed straight for Rik, stepping carefully over the paving slabs which were still settling, and greeting him with a warm smile. 'Morning Rikki,' she said brightly. 'Morning big guy,' she nodded to Paul, then turned back to Rik. 'Shall we ride at the quarry at lunch?'

He was looking a bit tired, still unshaven, hair still sticking up all over the place, still a bit feral, still unspeakably gorgeous, she thought longingly. GT must have sensed her from the road, because he was already frolicking delightedly at her feet, nosing her ankles and climbing up frantically, desperate for a cuddle. She picked him up and he shoved his little face against hers, resting it on her shoulder. It was cloudier today, the odd cartoonish cumulus drifting across the sky. They would get darker and greyer as the day wore on, she knew. Tomorrow, this place would be drenched. Got to let it clear, Faith thought, ready for the sun again.

'Yes,' Rik said eagerly, sounding distinctly teenager-ish despite his rugged appearance.

'I'll come back at lunch,' she said.

'Four weeks down, three to go,' Paul shouted after her.

Nobody seemed to have told the garden that. It looked worse than ever, the half-dug new pond still needed hours of labour and the ground was now so dry the impending rain would just roll around on the surface, barely penetrating and softening the earth below, and she'd once again be faced with endless hours of lugging slurry. At least the rockery was all but finished, and she'd planted up some borders and ordered in turf to replace the dismal remains of what had once been a grandly sweeping lawn. She would get there. She would. She pushed aside the very real fear that she might not, and picked up her spade.

The path to the quarry was very overgrown. Nobody must have come here in years. Once so easy to navigate that Rik and Faith could ride down it side by side, it was littered with fallen branches, shifted stones and briars that were creeping inexorably closer together. One day they would just close it off altogether, barring any entry, a tangle of thorns and whiplike branches with serrated leaves and heavy, slowly ripening fruit. Faith felt thorns tearing her bare legs, adding to the carnage from GT. 'We need to cut this back,' she shouted up to Rik, who nodded and shoved a gigantic snakelike briar away.

The quarry itself lay sleeping like a craggy, gravelly giant. The day had warmed up beautifully and the sun, currently in between the gathering clouds, was streaming through the thick, forest-green canopy, bouncing off the flinty stones and illuminating tiny insects dancing overhead, turning them into little spiralling specks of stardust. It also was very overgrown, ivy was creeping determinedly up the barks of the trees surrounding it, and the splintered trunk of an ancient sycamore, against which she and Rik had often rested, had rotted away almost completely.

New beech saplings, in their infancy when she and Rik had ridden here last, had sprung up and were sporting lighter green, almost transparent leaves. The ground was thick with years of beechnuts, their discarded shells crunching beneath the tyres that passed effortlessly over them.

Faith had only come back to the quarry once since she had ridden here with Rik last, and the lack of his presence had hit her like a physical blow, slamming into her gut, drawing great racking sobs from the very core of her. The silence had been deafening, the loneliness overwhelming, the emptiness engulfing. She had turned her bike immediately and fled, not looking back, half afraid she would see the ghosts of a ninja boy and a fairy girl and a yapping terrier still whirling round and around the pit, their spectral laughter bouncing off the catastrophically silent walls.

Something told her Rik hadn't been back here either. 'It looks OK,' he said. 'Still rideable. Just.'

'We'll have to come and tidy it up,' Faith said fretfully. 'Your new niece or nephew won't be able to hurtle around here on their balance bike if we don't keep it under control. We need to get rid of some of these saplings, or they'll obscure too much of the floor and the violets and primroses will have no chance.'

'The steps are still there,' he noted. It had taken them all of one of their Easter holidays to carve those out. They, too, were overgrown, the ivy creeping its way relentlessly down to the centre of the pit.

'Won't take long to rip that up,' Faith said. 'Once you start it comes up easily enough.'

'I'll leave you to it.' Rik swung his bike round and flung it down the steps.

Faith winced. 'Stones,' she yelled, 'remember the stones.'

Rik clearly hadn't and he hit one dead on, stalling his front wheel instantly and the back rose up, flinging him over his handlebars and sending him crashing down a couple of the steps. Faith yelped and dropped her bike, leaping down the stairs after him. 'Rik!'

'It's OK,' he said, getting to his feet. He knocked on his helmet. 'Maybe these things aren't so pointless after all.' He picked up his bike again and Faith heaved the offending stone away.

'You idiot,' she grumbled. 'Why didn't you check it first? Are you sure you're OK?' She could see he had cut his knee and crouched down. 'You're bleeding.'

'Just a scratch,' Rik insisted.

'There might be gravel in it. I can't really see.' She put her hand on his knee and peered a little closer. 'There's a fair bit of blood,' she said. 'Have you got any tissues?'

'Do I look like somebody's grandma?'

She sighed. 'You pick the weirdest things to get offended about. We need to clear this up, get the stones out.' She pulled her water bottle from the cage on her bike and poured some over his knee, watching it mingle with the blood and turn it from a dark to a lighter red. He inhaled sharply.

'That must sting,' she said sympathetically. 'Sit down.' She sat down next to him and took off her trainer. 'I'll have to use my sock,' she said. 'Don't worry, they were clean on this morning.'

Rik took off his helmet and put his head in his hands as she pressed lightly on the cut. 'Yeah, there's some in it,' he said, and she stroked his calf soothingly as she pressed harder. 'This won't take a moment.' She twisted the sock and he put his hand over hers, tightening it involuntarily. She worked her fingers over the cut gently, not wanting to hurt him any more, but she could feel one stone was lodged and she would have to pinch it out. 'Ready?' she asked.

'Yep.'

She yanked the stone out in one swift movement and Rik gasped. 'All gone,' she said, shaking out the sock and taking off her other trainer. 'You can use this one until we get back to the house. I'll patch you up there.'

Rik, who had paled a little, nodded obediently.

Faith folded her sock over and pressed it against his knee again. She remembered the post-fall shock well, the physical impact of all the adrenaline just rushing away and the fear of what might have been and the relief that it hadn't been so much worse creeping in. It was a horribly vulnerable, isolated feeling — unless you happened to have Rik and a free afternoon to hand, of course. 'You shouldn't be such a show-off,' she said. 'Are you cold?'

'Not yet.'

'Want to wait it out here?'

He nodded and she took his hand and put it over the sock, and put her arm around his shoulders. He breathed a couple of times then put his head between his knees and she stroked his hair, feeling him shivering slightly. 'It'll pass,' she said softly, 'just keep breathing.'

Rik said nothing and she continued to run her hands over his hair, twining her fingers in the ends, pulling gently, working out some of the cement dust. He shivered again, and she put her arm around him again, pressing her body into him for warmth, then she rubbed her hands up and down his arms, generating friction to help his circulation return to normal. After a couple of minutes his skin became clammy and she reckoned he was probably feeling sick as a dog right about now, so she ran her hand up and down his back, very slowly so as not to distress him, all the way down to the waistband of his shorts and then back up again to the nape of his neck.

Funny, she ruminated, she'd been dying to get her hands on him all summer and now she was actually doing it, all she could think about was calming him down, not working him up. She put her hand on his forehead, feeling it burning and soaked in sweat, and damped her hand with some water and put it back to cool him down. 'It'll pass,' she said again, 'it's nearly over.' He nodded almost imperceptibly and she put her arm around him again. 'You're OK, Rikki,' she said gently. 'I'm here.'

He took another deep breath and raised his head slowly, and she smiled affectionately. 'Better?'

'Much,' he said, and she saw with relief the colour had returned to his face. 'Thanks.'

'No worries.'

'I haven't done that in ages,' he said. 'I forget every time how horrible it is. I swear it gets worse as I get older.'

'At least it's over quickly. You need something to eat,' she said. 'Let's get you up to the house and Minel can make us some lunch.'

'I need a stiff drink,' he said, grinning slightly.

'No you don't,' she said. 'Paul will ban you from riding for the rest of the summer if you come back limping and half-cut. I'll make you some tea instead. Three sugars.'

Paul was merrily yelling away at Rik when Faith nipped over mid-afternoon to see how he was. 'You are not going out rampaging with her again,' he roared, pointing accusingly at Faith, 'until we're done here. If you mess yourself up smashing bikes around we won't finish in time.'

'Who wants tea?'

'Ten minutes,' Paul said, 'that's all.'

'How are you doing?' Faith asked Rik as he fell into step beside her up to the house.

'Fine,' he said. 'You patched me up a treat.' GT trotted along next to them, wagging his tail importantly. 'Shall we go back on Saturday and do something about those stones? Seeing it again has made me itchy for a bit of gravel, preferably not in my knee.'

'More manual labour? Count me in. Oh, hang on, I can't,' Faith sighed regretfully. 'Sara and I are taking Minel out for afternoon tea to celebrate.'

'What about Sunday?'

What about Lucinda, Faith wanted to ask. 'Sunday works,' she said. 'Can't imagine we'll be getting plastered and staying up late, what with Minel's condition and all.' She felt another surge of joy for her friend. 'I still can't believe it. Paul seems made up too, I'm so happy for them both.'

Rik touched her hand gently. 'You and Sara will be fairy godmothers.'

'I am going to lead that child so far astray,' she said happily. 'Even though I'll be over forty by the time he or she is a teenager.'

'So will I.'

What would she be like at forty? And him? It felt like ages away, a different era altogether, but time seemed to pass quicker with every coming year and she knew from listening to friends with children that it picked up even more once you had children, they went from tiny babies to tearaway toddlers to schoolchildren in the blink of an eye.

I can't picture it, she thought, because I have no idea what I'll be doing then, if I'll have met anybody I want to marry and start a family with.

Anybody else, that is.

Rik would probably take it in his stride, still confident in his path, whatever that might turn out to be. He'd be married by then, maybe to Lucinda, she hoped not but if that was what he wanted, then that was probably what he would get. Lucinda wasn't the only one who was focused and ambitious.

Minel was upstairs. 'She must be having a pregnancy nap,' Rik said. 'Best keep the noise down.'

Growing a baby must be hard work, Faith thought. All those tiny miracles happening inside, cells coming together and bonding, fusing and multiplying, slowly but surely building something out of nothing, flesh and blood and bone. Now that was magic. And people thought she was fanciful. You couldn't make that stuff up, the ability of the female body to create another entirely separate being inside its own self, with no intervention whatsoever other than the initial meeting of egg and sperm. No wonder men used to think women were witches.

I want to do that, she thought. I want to create life. I want to go on that crazy adventure with Rik.

'Do you ever think about kids?' she asked as she prepared a tray for the tea.

'Yeah,' he said. 'Of course. Especially when Minel and Paul started talking about it. Only natural, isn't it, to think about it?'

'It is for us,' Faith said. 'Women, I mean. First it's all about not getting pregnant, then apparently once you turn thirty it's like you have a gigantic clock sellotaped to your uterus, ticking noisily away and prompting even passers-by in the street to stop you and ask if you're getting broody. Not sure it's the same for men.'

'I don't think so,' Rik agreed.

'Do you want to have children?'

'Yes. And I don't want to be an old dad either.' He frowned. 'I know lots of men wait and wait, it's quite normal for them to be in their late thirties or even forties before they even consider it, but I want to have the energy for kids. I don't want to be sitting in an armchair reading my newspaper or wheezing around after them while they leave me for dust. But that does also depend upon meeting somebody you want to have children with.'

Or, Faith thought, it depends upon you meeting somebody you want to have children with, getting over them, and then meeting somebody else. He'd said yesterday he'd once wanted children with her. She could picture them, a rowdy, noisy, cheeky little rabble with dark hair and olive skin and maybe with his brown eyes, or her green ones, or light hazel, a combination of both. I want to meet those children, she thought longingly, those children I will never have.

'Do you want me to change your dressing?' she asked, wanting to put her hands on him again by any means necessary.

'I'll do it,' he said, getting up. 'It feels like it's stopped bleeding now. It's getting tight.'

'Must be healing already,' she said, feeling a little bit disappointed he didn't seem to want her to continue looking after him. 'I'd better get this tea out to Paul.'

Chapter 19

Faith drove to afternoon tea, and Minel and Sara complained nonstop as the Land Rover chugged noisily along. 'I didn't realise we were taking the scenic route,' Sara moaned.

It was very scenic though, Faith noted with pleasure. The cow parsley had long gone but the verges were still lushly overgrown and bursting with crimson poppies, their fragile petals translucent and tissue-like, interspersed with clumps of cheery oxeye daisies. Their little yellow hearts seemed to bob and wink cheekily as they chugged past. There were cornflowers too, deep blue pom-poms bursting from the top of their dark green stalks, and thistles topped with softly spiked explosions of shocking violet.

The hotel was lavishly opulent, the carpets soft and thick, silencing all footsteps, and the walls were painted a glowing peach with stencils of violets, daffodils and tulips at the corners. 'This place is famous for its assignations among married older gentlemen and their distinctly unmarried consorts,' Sara confided.

Faith was squinting behind her, wondering if she was actually hallucinating the familiar figure at the check-in desk.

'What the hell?' she hissed.

'Faith?' Minel's voice sounded far away. 'You look like you've seen a ghost.'

'Not a ghost.' Her voice wavered.

Minel followed her gaze, and Sara craned her neck.

'Oh my god,' she said. 'Faith, is that…'

'My dad.'

Faith watched as her father signed the check-in form, turning to the woman next to him. She looked a bit younger than him, probably in her mid-fifties, with poker-straight, ash blonde hair. Cliché straight out of cliché central.

'No!' Minel said but Faith ignored her and marched across the room. Anger was coursing through her and she felt so entirely filled with it, so suffused she half wondered if she was going to hit her father across the room.

'Hi Daddy,' she said loudly. 'And I don't mean sugar, in case you were wondering if this is a party for three.' She glared at the woman next to him.

All the colour drained from Jeff's face. 'Faith.'

'We haven't met,' Faith said to his companion acidly. 'I'm Faith. Jeff's daughter.'

'Faith,' her father said pleadingly. 'Don't….'

'It's weird,' she continued, talking to the woman, 'because you don't *look* like my mum and somehow here you are, checking into a hotel room with my dad.'

'Stop it.' Her father took her arm and she shook it off, livid.

'Get off me. What do you think you're doing?'

'I should go,' the unfortunate blonde said. She backed out of the hotel, turning on her heels and scuttling across to the carpark.

'Nice lady,' Faith said. 'Shame she didn't stick around.'

'Come on,' her dad said. 'Let's go and have a drink.'

She wanted to run screaming, then she thought no, not this time. He can explain himself to me then I'm marching him straight home to my mother and he can explain himself to her too, and I want to hear every single word. She followed him through the lounge and into the bar, a long, narrow, oak-panelled room with Oriental-print wallpaper and tastefully low lighting.

218

For want of anything better to do, she sat down and stared at her hands. Her head was running on a furious loop, in a mini timewarp all of its own only very much present-day, from outrage to confusion to hurt to disappointment to anguish for her poor mother.

'Drink this.' Her dad put a shot of something brown and sweet-smelling in front of her.

'I'm driving.'

'One of your friends can take you home.'

'I'm going to have to tell Mum. You know that, don't you?'

Her father took a deep breath. 'Faith,' he said, quite gently. 'Your mother already knows.'

She stared at him, some of her righteous indignation knocked out of her and replaced with yet more shock. 'You mean she knows about her? About tonight, and whatever you were planning on doing?' She shuddered. 'Ugh. I don't want to think about it.'

'About all of it.' Jeff took a sip of his own drink and fixed his eyes on her. 'She knows I'm here, she knows who I'm with, she doesn't know her personally, of course, but she knows I have a, um —'

'A mistress,' Faith spat. 'I think that's the word you're looking for.'

'Not exactly,' he said carefully. 'More of a friend with benefits?'

Faith wanted to gag.

'Your mother and I,' he began. 'We love each other dearly.'

'You've got a funny way of showing it.'

'Faith, please. Let me finish. We love each other dearly but your mother hasn't, how can I put this?' He thought for a moment. 'She hasn't loved me in that way for a very long time.'

219

'Oh, so this is all her fault now? She doesn't understand you?' Faith took a gulp of her drink, wincing as it burned its way down her throat. 'Change the record. Mum adores you. She worships the ground you walk on and I can't for a moment think why when this is how you repay her, for all of her loyalty, standing by you after everything you've done to her…'

'She has stood by me,' Jim agreed. 'She's not just stood by me, she's given me her consent.'

'No she hasn't.'

'Yes, she has. Your mother and I haven't been intimate in a very long time and she made it very clear to me that she had no intention of ever rekindling that side of our relationship. We had this conversation years ago.' He paused. 'The year before you left home. I was indiscreet and your mother and I were on the verge of divorce.' He sighed heavily. 'We discussed it, and she was very hurt, but she was also absolutely resolute that she had no interest in having any kind of physical relationship with me any more.'

Faith opened her mouth to leap to her mother's defence, but her father held up his hand to stop her.

'I don't suppose you're going to believe me if I say people can sometimes be compatible in many ways, but incompatible in one very fundamental way, and if that happens, then you have a choice. You can either choose to allow one of you to be persuaded into something that they don't want, or you can compromise.'

Faith took another sip of her drink and she studied her father's lined, familiar face. Part of her still refused to believe him. Her mother would never condone something like this, he was trying to put her off the scent, soon he'd be saying her mother was a very *private* person and asking her not to mention this.

It was just another line, another ruse, a way to cover his tracks. Her mother would never agree to this in a million years.

Then she thought about Judith sitting at the table staring at her tea leaves. The awkward way she continually asked her father about his golf weekends as if she was looking for information about something else. The way her mother was so strained when her father returned home, but at the same time so determined to carry on as normal.

Jeff was looking at her with sympathy, but also conviction. She put down her glass.

'So what you're saying is, you love Mum and she loves you but you aren't in a physical relationship any more?'

He nodded. 'I don't expect you to understand, sweetheart,' he said sadly. 'I don't want to sit and tell you how it feels to know that a door to something you once valued — once cherished — has been closed without you getting any say in it. I would never want to make your mother feel guilty, or ask her to do something she didn't want to do just to please me.' He shook his head. 'If she ever wanted to I would stop all this, in a heartbeat. But like I said, she's been very clear that she can't ever see a time when she may want to, and I know I must seem ancient to you but I still don't feel old enough for a life without physical intimacy.'

'Actually,' she said, surprising herself. 'I do understand that sentiment.'

He looked astonished. 'You do?'

She shrugged. 'It's one of the reasons I left Rob. We were pretty incompatible in that area.'

Jeff looked taken aback. Well, she thought, if he's going to gross me out whining about his sex life, or lack of it, he can stomach hearing about mine.

'I thought, I'm only twenty-six. I'm too young to be in a relationship that feels more like one between a brother and sister.'

She didn't add that Sara was also contemplating the same dilemma.

'It's not just about sex, is it?' she said. 'It's about feeling wanted, valued, *known*.'

'It is,' he said slowly.

'Mum's really OK with it? You know I'm going to have to talk to her about this?'

'You can try. I'm not sure I'd say she's OK with it,' he said, sighing heavily. 'It's complicated. If I were to ever find I had any real feelings for anybody else it would have to stop. But she understands that she can't ask me to just give up on a physical relationship altogether, and so, like I said, we compromise.'

Faith was astonished to find herself feeling suddenly compassionate towards her father. 'It sounds lonely.'

'It is lonely,' he agreed. 'But it's not as lonely as the alternative.'

She nodded, thinking that she could understand that too. 'It must be,' she said, 'because surely the best kind of connection is with somebody who knows you inside out, all your foibles and your flaws, and still wants to be with you.' She frowned. 'It's like the ultimate acceptance, really.'

'I think so, yes.'

'OK,' she said finally. She wrinkled her nose. 'I think it's going to take me a while to get my head around it.'

Her father nodded. 'Take all the time you need.' He gestured at their empty glasses. 'Do you want another drink?'

'I'm going to go back to my friends,' Faith said. 'You should probably go and sort out your affairs.' She paused. 'If you'll pardon the pun.'

Her father laughed sadly. 'I'm sure you're going to want to discuss this with your friends, but remember your mother is a very private person. I don't mind what you tell people about me, and I know you will want to discuss it with Judith. But I would hate to think of your mother feeling like people were talking about her.'

'Well,' she said. 'I'll think about that too.' She stood up. 'See you soon.'

'I hope so.'

Faith shook her head slightly and wandered back through into the lounge. All the anger had drained out of her body and she felt numb and extremely tired. Part of her still hated her father, but what he had said had resonated with her and she knew she needed to let it rest for a while, before she could really make up her mind what she thought about it all.

'Are you OK?' Minel asked. 'What happened?'

Faith sat down. 'I need to think about it,' she said. 'He explained some things. I feel like I need to sleep on it before I tell you, because it's not really my stuff to tell, if you know what I mean.'

'You don't have to tell us anything,' Sara said gently. 'We're here for you.'

Faith yawned, suddenly exhausted. 'I need to get some sleep. I'm done in after last week and I need — I need.' She didn't know what she needed other than not to be here.

'Come back to the house,' Minel urged.

'I have to go home later,' Faith said. 'My mum.' She couldn't leave her mother alone again, not knowing the true meaning of her dad's 'golf weekends'. 'You're going to have to drive,' Faith said to Minel. 'Sorry.'

Minel shrugged. 'No problem. Although how that heap of yours even moves is beyond me.'

They dropped Sara off and then Minel took Faith up to the house, sitting her down at the table and insisting she drink a cup of hot, sweet tea. GT leaped up onto her lap and curled up happily. 'You're always there when I need you,' she told the little puppy lovingly.

'Do you want to talk?' Minel's eyes were huge with concern. She wants to fix it all for me, Faith thought, and she shook her head. 'Not yet,' she said. 'I need to just let it sit. Please, Min.'

Minel nodded reluctantly. 'Take all the time you need,' she said. 'We're all here for you.'

Paul strode in. 'How was the cackling?' he asked. 'Did all the other customers run away screaming?'

Minel took him aside. 'She's had a bit of a shock,' she told him quietly, as Faith stared blankly at the wall. 'Just let her be.'

'How are you feeling?' he asked Minel. 'Still tired?'

Minel nodded. 'Really tired,' she said. 'Feel like I could sleep for a hundred years.'

'Early night tonight,' Paul said gently.

'Again.' Minel giggled. 'Not much fun, am I?'

'Nothing I'd rather do than lie up there with you and watch reruns of *Friends*,' he murmured, and Faith felt cocooned by the warmth of their love for one another. This was what a marriage should be. This was what she wanted and she wanted it with —

Rik came in and Faith was about to ask him if he wanted to marry her, or, more realistically, walk GT with her. They could go to the quarry and scope out what needed doing tomorrow and she might cry and she might not but even if she did, he wouldn't press her if she asked him not to. But then Lucinda came trotting in, looking weekend casual in navy chinos and a becoming pink blouse, the peachy colour illuminating her perfect skin, flushed like the petals of a peony, and Faith scowled.

'Hey,' Rik said. 'How was afternoon tea?'

Faith grunted noncommittally.

'That good?'

'Hi Lucinda,' Faith said reluctantly.

'Oh, hi Faith.' Lucinda smiled as delightedly as if she'd been reunited with her long-lost BFF. 'Nice to see you. You look pretty.' Faith glanced down at her white sundress and saw GT had left paw-marks and wiry, sandy coloured hairs all over it and it was already crumpled.

'Hmph,' Faith said ungraciously.

Lucinda looked happier than ever.

'How's your knee?' Faith asked Rik.

'Fine,' he said. 'Just a scratch,' he added and caught her eye, grinning.

'What happened to your knee?' Lucinda asked sharply.

'Fell off the bike yesterday,' he said. 'I got a bit silly.'

'Let me see!'

'It's fine,' Rik insisted. 'Faith patched me up a treat.'

Lucinda was starting to look distinctly less friendly. She turned her china blue gaze onto Faith, who looked back at her blankly. What's your problem, she thought. I wasn't exactly going to leave him there bleeding and shaking until you turned up ready to sink your pearly pink claws into him.

She had had pearly pink nails. The woman. That woman. That bitch – but no. She wasn't culpable for whatever sordid arrangement she had made with Faith's father.

Or rather she was culpable, but that didn't make her a bitch, it just made her a woman who, for whatever reason, thought it was perfectly acceptable to hook up with married men.

Did she know he was married? Did she care? What kind of woman would do that?

Maybe she, too, was married to somebody who only wanted to offer her half a relationship, a Sara twenty years down the line. Maybe she was a widow. Maybe she was going through a divorce. Maybe she'd never managed to find anybody in the first place. Maybe her father had lied to her.

Or maybe she actually is just a bitch, Faith thought bitterly, watching Lucinda sidle closer to Rik and raise her face to his. He kissed her lightly on the cheek and turned to look out of the window.

Undeterred, Lucinda snaked herself still closer to him, coiling her body possessively around his. Get off him! Faith wanted to shriek, but instead she could only watch with revolted fascination as Lucinda ran her hand meaningfully down Rik's back and put her face right up next to his. She kissed his cheek again and Rik turned to her, and Lucinda launched herself at him, kissing his lips demandingly, winding her arm up around his neck to hold his head down to hers. Look away, Faith screamed internally, but her eyes were riveted to the horrific scene, much like a rubbernecker at a car crash, and she could only watch, bile rising in her throat, as Rik finally got the message and kissed Lucinda properly, her pleasure and satisfaction so blatantly visible she looked like she might erupt in his arms.

Rik pulled away awkwardly. Lucinda didn't release her hold on his neck. 'Let's go back over,' she breathed, writhing catlike against him.

Faith could feel her stomach pulsating, forcing acid threateningly up into her mouth. Jesus, she thought. I actually might be sick. She gripped the table and GT whined softly.

Lucinda was still waiting. Don't do it, Rik, Faith willed him, not when I need you more than I've ever needed you, and he certainly seemed to look puzzled, but he nodded and followed Lucinda as she practically danced out of the room.

Paul glanced over at Faith. 'God, love, are you OK?' Her lip was curled up at one side, baring her teeth like an Elvis impersonator, her nose was wrinkled and her brow was tightly knitted together. She must have physically recoiled, because her head was pressing back against her neck, no doubt giving her a fetching double chin. Paul looked momentarily amused at her expression. 'Don't know why she doesn't just mark out her territory by pissing all over him,' he rumbled disapprovingly.

Even Minel looked thoroughly sickened. 'Nobody wants to watch that. Especially a blood relative.'

More bile flooded into Faith's her mouth, and her stomach heaved. She got up and lurched.

Paul stood up too. 'Not on me,' he roared. 'Get to the toilet, love, quick!'

Faith pelted through the kitchen and into the downstairs bathroom and collapsed in front of the toilet, grabbing it with both hands. She retched noisily a couple of times, but all that came up was brown liquid, the cup of tea and that drink her dad had bought her, she supposed. Good thing she hadn't got round to actually eating anything or she'd probably have painted the walls.

GT, beside himself at his mistress's plight, nosed his way into the door, which she hadn't managed to shut properly in time. He sniffed at her and licked her face a couple of times. Only a dog, Faith thought, would want to lick me all over after I've just thrown up. If I had been sick all up the walls he would have probably cleaned it up for me. The thought made her heave again, but there was nothing for her to throw up and she sat back, weak and clammy, still clutching GT to her like a furry lifeline.

She stayed in there with him for a few moments, waiting for the heaving and retching to pass, then she got to her feet and stumbled out of the toilet. She hated being sick. She felt lonely and vulnerable and empty, isolated and adrift, the unsettling sense of something being wrong inside the very centre of her. Why the hell wasn't Rik here stroking her hair and cooling her forehead and telling her she'd be OK?

Minel was looking worried when she came out. 'What was that all about?'

'Delayed shock, I guess,' Faith said. 'On the plus side, I'm probably fine to drive. Time I was heading off.'

'Paul will take you,' Minel said. 'You are not driving in this condition.'

Paul, his face still concerned, nodded. 'Come on, let's get you home.'

'If you want to stay here,' Minel said, 'tonight, tomorrow night, all week, all summer. Whenever. We're here. I'll make up a room for you, so you know it's always there.'

'Thanks.' Faith's voice was weak and wavery after the vomiting.

Paul put his arm around her shoulders, warming her reassuringly. 'Where are your keys?' he asked, and Faith looked around for her bag, only to find its contents strewn across the floor and the bag itself half chewed up by an ecstatic GT.

'You naughty boy,' Minel chided.

Paul complained good-humouredly about the Land Rover as they wheezed home. Faith, not used to being a passenger in her own car, was thrown all over the place as it bounced merrily over potholes and humps in the road. 'It's not the smoothest ride,' she admitted, as her head banged against the roof for what felt like the hundredth time.

'Sure you're OK?' he asked as they pulled up outside her house. 'You do look like you had a nasty shock.'

'My parents,' she said.

'Not Rik and whatserface, then?' His eyes were very kindly.

'Of course not,' she said. 'What makes you think that?'

'Somehow,' Paul said, 'I was the only one who made the connection between Rik's Damien from *The Omen* impersonation and your sudden absence from our lives all those years ago.'

Faith stared at the gearstick.

'It was pretty hard to miss the atmosphere between you two when you first got back,' he pressed. 'And now you're suddenly joined at the hip again and you're looking at him like he's the best thing since sliced bread…'

Paul might be the strong, silent-ish type — when he's not yelling at teenagers — Faith thought, but he doesn't miss a thing. He's going to be such a great dad.

'I can't believe you picked up on it and Minel didn't,' she said eventually. 'Back then, I mean.'

He rumbled with satisfaction. 'She was probably a bit too close to the both of you,' he said. 'But to me it was as plain as the nose on your currently tearstained face that you and Rik were at it like rabbits.'

'Not really,' she said. 'Not for long, anyway. We had a — misunderstanding, and that was the end of it. It was years ago.'

'Hmm.' Paul didn't sound convinced.

'And that really was about more than just an *abominable* PDA,' she protested. 'My parents seem to have hit on some difficulties. Again.' She sighed. 'Looks like I really am reliving my teenage years. The worst parts of them, anyway.'

'I don't think you're the only one,' Paul said meaningfully.

'How do you mean?'

'I've known Rik a long time,' he said. 'Whatever went on with you two, it was obviously rough on him. He was a very angry young man for a while. He seemed to become a lot more negative and cynical.'

A broken heart will do that to you, she thought. I should know.

'But he seems much more like that idiot kid we all knew and loved, coinciding nicely with your reappearance.' Paul went on. 'Lucinda's certainly got her charms,' he said diplomatically. 'But I'm not sure she's quite his cup of tea.'

Neither, Faith thought, am I. She felt a leap of hope, then the reality of the afternoon came crashing in again.

'Now isn't the time,' she said to Paul firmly. She kissed him quickly on the cheek. 'Thanks Paul. I really appreciate it.'

'See you Monday,' he said. 'Don't be late.' She wouldn't dare. Paul might be kind and supportive and thoughtful outside of work, but on site he was still a monster and she wouldn't have him any other way. Yelling with, and at, him had helped bring her back to life as much as anybody and anything else, except maybe Rik, and she got out of the car and trudged reluctantly towards the house.

Chapter 20

Faith hadn't agreed a time to meet Rik on Sunday. She was looking forward to slogging around the quarry all day, thinking the manual labour would help keep her grounded while her thoughts about her parents formed and grew and took flight, hot air balloons floating around her head, knocking into each another, moving and dislodging one another until she was left with something remotely approaching a coherent dialogue.

But she didn't want to turn up too early and risk disturbing him and Lucinda doing god knows what, probably on the kitchen table. Instead she kicked around the house annoying her mother with her monosyllabic responses to any attempts to engage her in conversation, and drinking tea until she was sure her tongue was starting to change colour. This is awful, she thought, I literally have nothing to say her because there's only one thing I can think about, only one thing I want to ask her, and I'm not ready to do that yet.

She would have to stay at Hollyhocks. She only came home to sleep anyway, or rather, jerk awake at 3am, and it might be nicer if she knew Minel and Paul were down the hall if she needed them. And GT. He could come and sleep on her bed and protect her from her demons.

She packed a rucksack, folding and tucking pants, socks, bras, shorts and t-shirts one on top of the other, and putting a thin hoody on top for the evenings, which were beginning to develop just the faintest nip, a tiny hint of autumn thinking about creeping its sleepy golden tendrils around Hollyhocks and turning it from a rainbow of colour and green and sand to a narrower spectrum of blazing orange, pale yellow, deep red and burnished bronze.

She looked at the clock. It was only ten o'clock, she should give it a bit longer. Wait until half past, she ordered herself, and then you can go. Take the dog for a walk once you get there if it looks like Rik and Lucinda are set in for the morning. She made yet another cup of tea, and took it out onto the patio.

Of all the déjà vu she'd had this summer, this was definitely the worst. She was reminded horribly of the freefalling aftermath of the first time her parents had stunned her into passive, reeling shock. Her dad mustn't have told her mother about their conversation yet because she was going about her business quite oblivious to her daughter's turmoil. Faith thought grimly that Judith must be completely blind to her if she didn't realise something was wrong.

Why wouldn't she tell me, Faith ruminated, staring at her mother's pottering outline through the kitchen window. Why did she let me think she was the innocent victim, that my father's failing was the fundamental failing of all men, an inability to keep their base urges in check even when they had a happy home life to which they could anchor themselves?

She heard tyres skidding behind the back gate, and then it opened and Rik walked in. Faith gaped at him, the contrast between his still-unkempt appearance and her mother's immaculate back patio too much for her poor muddled brain to handle. She could count on the fingers of one hand the number of times Rik had come to her house. He had even asked her once if she had something she was hiding from him, the skeleton of a long-lost sibling in her cupboard perhaps, but Faith always used to feel so strongly he didn't belong in this tight, sterile little world and she hadn't needed yet more grief from her mother.

'What are you doing here?' she snapped.

'Come to get you. You're late.'

'We didn't set a time.' You were too busy sloping off with that randy cow, she thought jealously. She examined him for traces of a certain glow, remembering how blissful he always looked after she had finished with him and they had lain back together, staring up at the ceiling, or the sky, watching and listening to the world carrying on idly like it hadn't just all but shaken along with them. But her radar must have been all off, because she couldn't read his expression at all.

'I didn't realise you were struggling or I'd have hung around,' he said apologetically. 'Paul told me you'd had an upset with your parents and you could have done with a bit of company and hadn't needed to bear witness to any stomach-churning PDAs.' Faith smiled despite herself. 'We don't have to go to the quarry if you're not feeling up to it,' he said kindly. 'We can just head back and hang by the pool all day.'

'No.' She needed to do something more than just lie around and those heavy stones would be the perfect outlet for her fluctuating but increasingly restless energy. She could chuck them around to her heart's content. She was quite looking forward to the burning in her arms and the ache in her legs. At least she would know she was alive.

'You are coming, aren't you?'

'Of course I'm coming,' she said. 'I've packed a bag.' She waved it at him. 'Minel said I could stay a while, and I thought it might be a bit nicer than coming back here. I could use some company, even if it's only GT. I want to go to the quarry,' she said, getting to her feet, 'and kick the living daylights out of any unfortunate stone that happens to be in my path.'

'Not too hard,' Rik said. 'You'll break a toe and I don't think even whatever's going on for you now would save you from

233

Paul's wrath if his gardener was nobbled three weeks before we finish up.'

Was it only three weeks? Where was the time going? Three weeks, and Rik would be off to Cornwall and there would be no more lunchtime bike rides or yelling at Paul or oddly tricky, but nonetheless incredibly enlivening, conversations about the past and the future and everything in between.

Her mother stuck her head out of the door. 'I thought I heard voices. Oh hello, Rik.' Her tone cooled and her lips tightened.

You couldn't even call it stubble now, Faith thought, eyeing Rik's jaw, it's a full-on beard and he looks utterly ridiculous and mildly threatening and faint-makingly gorgeous and like my wildest fantasy and her worst nightmare, all rolled up into one.

'Hi Judith,' he said pleasantly.

'I'm off,' Faith said to Judith. 'Staying at Hollyhocks for a while.'

Judith eyed Rik suspiciously.

'With Minel,' Faith said.

'When will you be back?'

'Don't know.' Faith hadn't even thought about it. 'At some point, to get some clothes, probably. Where's Dad?' She had asked automatically, then remembered too late.

'Golf,' Judith said tonelessly and Faith saw her lips purse together once more. For a moment she felt a flash of pity for her mother. It couldn't be much fun, rattling around the house plumping cushions and settling, sighing, into them to read yet another bodice-ripper while her husband was off re-enacting the steamy contents with some other woman.

Feeling alive, if only for a moment, while her mother pushed it all down and swallowed it along with whatever else she was lugging about inside of her that prevented her from wanting intimacy with her husband in the first place. Maybe if I ask her, Faith thought, try and get her to talk about it, help her shake it up, bring it out of her, maybe that would help get the ball rolling and then she and dad might —

Then her eyes moved of their own accord to Rik, who was watching her very intently, as if he knew she was contemplating telling him to go without her. She studied his beautiful, wild face, the traces of crow's feet just beginning around those endlessly expressive dark eyes, his thick lashes curling upwards, his mouth which seemed made for smiling — or for other, more exciting things — almost obscured by that infernal facial hair.

She got to her feet. Rik automatically fell into place next to her. She reached out and took his hand, gripping it, needing to draw on his strength and use it to fuel her own. 'See you soon,' she said to her mother. 'You know where I am if you need me.'

Judith, her eyes on Faith and Rik's intertwined hands, closed the door.

'I don't want to talk about it,' Faith told Rik firmly as they rode back to Hollyhocks.

'Whatever you want,' he said, and they turned off down the track to the quarry. It was a bit more accommodating this time, the briars had already remembered their previous passage and parted company where they had begun to overlap.

Faith flung her bike down and pelted down the stairs, desperate to begin tearing up the ivy.

The first few tendrils clung stubbornly to the earth, as if pleading with her to leave them be, but she hauled determinedly and as she had predicted, once the first few acquiesced the whole lot seemed to give up as one, and she heaved and pulled and yanked, enjoying the faint crackling noise as the plant reluctantly released its hold on the steps. These steps belong to me, not you, she thought irrationally as she systematically uprooted the climber. Get off my land.

Rik had started moving stones and seemed content to work in silence. The ivy didn't take long to clear and she was soon binding the tendrils together and tying them into a tight knot and wishing it hadn't uprooted so quickly.

She leaped back down the stairs and began to heave at stones, ignoring Rik's protestations that he could do it. She wanted something solid and heavy in her hands, and she lifted even the largest boulders easily, tossing them disdainfully aside as if they were made of hollow plastic. She hurled one against the side of the pit, listening to the crash as it landed a little way up the side and rolled down, taking smaller stones and rain-like gravel with it in a glittering shower that flashed under the rays of the ever-present sun. She threw another, higher this time, generating a second tiny avalanche and watching the second stone thud mercilessly into the first, shifting it a little further with the impact.

She picked up another, and another, flinging them mindlessly against the wall, listening to the thuds and clashes and sprinkling and watching as the pit shifted and moved, changed its form and structure with each adjustment she made. It will recover, she thought, it'll bounce back, I could hurl every stone in here against that gravel slope and it would still regroup, begin to heal, nurture life once more in the form of the tiny green strands that poked out from the rubble here and there.

It can take it, she thought, and she threw rock after rock until they had gathered in a pile at the side of the pit. It wasn't enough and she began to pelt pieces of gravel at the miniature mound, watching them bounce here and there, pinging off the wall and settling back down into the pit.

I need a stick, she decided and shot up the steps, scouring the woodland floor for a suitable implement and picking up a twisted bough with moss on one side.

She ran back down the steps with the stick over her shoulder and began raining blows down on the pile of rocks, again and again, watching with a kind of detached fascination as the moss flew into the ether. The rocks resisted, then shuddered, then finally capitulated and rolled away until she had beaten her heap down to a scattering of rocks that littered the quarry floor, quailing beneath her as if wondering what kind of punishment she was going to inflict upon them next.

She dropped the stick, her breath coming in ragged gasps, her appetite for destruction temporarily satiated. She felt hot and flushed and she could feel the blood rushing around her body, roaring faintly in her ears, and her skin was tingling on the surface, the hairs on her arms standing up despite the heat. Now what, she wondered. Now what can I do?

Rik, who had been watching her wordlessly, touched her shoulder and she swung around and buried her face in his chest. He put his arms around her and she clung to him, and she could feel her heart pounding against her ribs and the heat of his body and she pushed her head even more insistently into his chest, opening her mouth so she could make a muffled sort of roaring noise right into his heart.

It's all lies, she thought. I threw you away for something that never actually happened, and all this time my parents have been living a lie too. Everything I thought I knew is wrong, and the only thing that makes sense in all of this is you.

It's always you.

Rik tightened his arms around her and she could feel that his heartbeat had quickened too. He felt very alive and full of a primal, dominant energy and Faith felt her body begin to change and adjust in response, softening and readying itself to just draw him into her. Her hands grasped his back, and she thought, he's what I need. I want that gravelly floor digging into my back and his body on mine and his voice in my ears. I want him over and over again until we're both spent and sore and bordering on numb, then I want to just lie back and watch the sky and let it all float away. That's how I need to let it all go, with him, always with him, because he's the one I do all this crazy messy uncomfortable soul-sapping life-affirming stuff with, because I love him. I've always loved him. It's always been him.

'Rikki,' she said into his chest.

Don't say it, some forgotten prudent part of herself warned instantly. He wants to, I can feel that he wants to because his heart is going like an express train and he's breathing a bit too fast, but he's with Lucinda and you're a mess and he's *with Lucinda*.

'What is it?' he asked, his heart still hammering away against her face.

Oh, he wants to, she thought again, I can read him like a book when we're this close. I still know every single way his body changes when he wants to give himself to me, subtle changes that might be imperceptible to anybody else but I know. If I just said it he would throw me down right here and neither of us would be able to take it back.

It can't be like this, she acknowledged. It just can't. I hate Lucinda but I won't become that woman in the hotel, I won't take another woman's man even if he should be mine, even if right now he's telling me with every part of him that he's always been mine.

Rik and I make each other stronger, not weaker. I won't let him do to Lucinda what I thought he did to me. That's one little twist I absolutely could not stand. She growled into his chest again, pouring out some of her frustration, then she shifted her head and pulled back. 'I need to breathe.'

He released her reluctantly.

Does he even know, she wondered? Am I here with actual Rik or sixteen-year-old Rik or even fourteen-year-old Rik or some weird combination of all of them? Does his head know what his body just told me?

'I can clear this,' he said, gesturing at the remains of her carnage, 'if you want to do some laps. Bit of mindless round-and-round.'

It's not mindless *round-and-round* I need, she thought, and almost giggled. Between me and Lucinda practically throwing ourselves at him he's going to start feeling like some kind of stud for hire. He's basically turning into Tackle.

She shook her head. 'No. Not today. I think I'm done here. I need to go back to the house, see GT. He'll be worried about me.' The dog could probably sense her distress even from this distance.

Back at the house Faith was knocked flying by a demented GT, who worried around her all afternoon, growling warningly at everybody to stay away from his mistress. She took him for a quick walk and almost immediately felt unbearably lonely, so she went back to the house and then just as quickly felt desperate for space.

She wandered back and forth, from the house to the pool to the greenhouse to the copse and back to the house again, but no matter where she went, she wanted to be somewhere else. Minel and Paul tried to carry on as normal, and Rik kept checking in but otherwise left her to it, but she could tell that she was affecting all of them and began to think maybe she shouldn't have come here after all. It'll pass, she soothed herself, once or twice reaching up to absently tug one of her own curls the way she'd soothed Rik after his fall. It will pass.

If she could just cry, she might feel better. Clouds were gathering overhead and the air felt impossibly close and stuffy, even the sky needs to let it all out, Faith thought, but right now it's as stifled as I am. She couldn't even get close, she just felt numb and dazed in between flashes of anger and confusion and wild irritation. She snapped at GT too sharply when he brought her a length of old rope, wagging his tail in the hope of a game of tug of war, and he cowed and she felt dreadful and wondered if his literal hangdog expression might spark something, but then he mounted her leg enthusiastically and she got annoyed with him all over again.

'What do you think, Faith?' Paul asked as she drifted vaguely back into the kitchen, the ever-present GT at her heels, to make her hundredth cup of tea.

'About what?'

'Breast or bottle?' Minel said. Faith stared at her blankly. 'The baby,' Minel prompted. 'We're just thinking about how we might feed him or her.'

'I don't know,' Faith said, turning to the kettle. 'Does it matter?'

'Breast is best,' Rik, who was sitting at the table doing something on his laptop, said in his doctorly tone.

'But if we bottle-feed,' Paul said, 'then I can be involved too.'

'But what about bonding?' Minel fretted. 'I could express, I suppose, but I don't know if I want to sit around milking myself like a dairy cow.'

'You'll probably appreciate it if I can get up and help out at four in the morning,' Paul pointed out.

'What are you doing?' Faith asked Rik.

'Just catching up on some work. I seem to have fallen behind a bit. A lot.' He frowned.

Too much sexy time with Lucinda, Faith thought.

She didn't feel like being inside, not that she was really doing too well outside, either. The closeness in the air was practically squeezing her from all directions, but hopefully the storm would break soon and she could stand out in it, letting the huge droplets of rain soak her skin, watching lightning illuminate the enormous sky and screaming wildly at the thunder like some godawful crone. She could shake her fist and pledge vengeance on anybody who had wronged her. Could she send a bolt of lightning Lucinda's way?

'Are you hungry?' Minel asked. 'I can make you something.'

Faith shook her head. She wasn't hungry, or thirsty, she didn't even want the tea but it had given her something to do. She stalked back out of the kitchen and then paused, and stuck her head back in. 'Sorry I'm being a basket case,' she said, addressing Minel but then looking at Paul and Rik so they knew she was talking to them too. 'Just got to put up with me for a bit, I'm afraid.'

'As long as you need,' Minel said immediately.

The afternoon dragged on interminably and Faith waited and waited and wondered what she was waiting for. Bed time, she supposed, but she knew all that would happen was that she would lie awake staring up at the ceiling and her thoughts would continue to plague her.

Why didn't her mother want her father? Why did they continue with their charade of a marriage and not just part ways? What kept them together? What had driven them apart? How did she fit into all this? She wasn't naïve enough to still think it must be her fault, but nonetheless she was, to quote Rik, a part of the equation and what was her role in it all?

What was her destiny, would she too find herself one day either in a soulless marriage or forced to look elsewhere for something or somebody to make her feel alive?

And then there were the other questions. What was she going to do about work? About finding somewhere to live? About Rik?

Help me, she pleaded silently, looking up at the still-darkening sky. Tell me, show me, something, anything. What is it I need to do?

The sky, entirely unmoved, carried on with its business.

'You're no help at all,' she said out loud, and then thought she actually probably was going mad.

The storm wasn't going to break, she finally realised, and neither was whatever was inside of her.

Chapter 21

For the next week Faith didn't know if she was in an actual timewarp or just suspended animation. With Minel so tired from the pregnancy hormones that she and Paul retired to bed not long after dinner every night, Faith was virtually alone with Rik and they were practically inseparable.

Paul seemed happy for him to come and help her whenever she needed it, turfing and digging and planting. She told Rik something had happened with her parents but she wasn't ready to talk about it, and he didn't press her. Nor did they, by entirely unspoken mutual agreement, mention Lucinda. Instead they talked in more depth about the passage of the last nine years, which Faith found uncomfortable as he seemed to have made a great deal more of them than she had.

'I know you don't want to tell me what's going on,' he said to her one afternoon. 'But if this is anything like what happened with your parents last time I really wish I'd been able to be there for you.'

'It was pretty awful,' she said. 'Very lonely, with Minel gone and Sara busy and you and I not talking any more. Although in a way that made it easier,' she said, 'because my mum was so humiliated and she was adamant she didn't want anybody to know. At least with nobody to talk to there was no chance I would let her down too.'

'You must have been really worried about her,' Rik said.

Faith nodded. 'I felt I had to make it up to her, give her the companionship and support my dad should have offered. She didn't really have friends, just people she badgered into doing charity work for the church. She's very proud,' she said reflectively. 'She wouldn't even talk to my aunt about it, she didn't want anybody to know how cut up she was. All she really had was me.' Faith sighed heavily. 'When I thought you had cheated on me, I could at least identify in a very tiny way with what she was going through. It was the first real connection I'd ever felt with her. We were in it together, two wronged women — or so I thought. And seeing how insistent she was about holding her head up high in public, not letting anybody know how she was really feeling, I guess I admired that, in a weird kind of way.'

She looked at him, shamefaced. 'I wanted to be like that. I didn't want you — didn't want anybody — to know how much what I thought you'd done to me had hurt me. I didn't want to talk about it because that would make it more real.'

She shifted absently, feeling the newly-laid acid-green turf giving beneath her feet.

'And I didn't want to get back in touch with you, or come back here,' she said. 'I guess I was still trying to block it all out, pretend none of it ever happened.'

He touched her shoulder gently. 'I know how that feels,' he said. 'I don't come back much either. Everything just reminded me of you. But I think,' Rik said slowly, 'it might not be like that now.'

She nodded. 'Yes, it's better now we're friends again. And I do want to be friends,' she went on, only half lying, because any Rik was better than no Rik.

'So do I,' he said.

At least we're moving forwards, she thought hopefully, even if it's not in the way I want. I suppose I'll really know we're friends when he finally starts discussing Lucinda with me, not that I'll want to hear it, but I can't just keep pretending she doesn't exist forever. And as their conversations moved from the past to the future, talking about what they might do after the summer was over and real life began again, it was getting harder to ignore the new elephant in the room.

We've replaced not mentioning our relationship, Faith thought, with not mentioning his.

In the evenings he stayed in the house with her instead of disappearing over to the cottage. Under the quiet cloak of the setting sun outside, and with Paul and Minel upstairs, all she wanted was to pull him down onto the sofa and wrap herself around him. She tried to read or watch TV, but she found she couldn't concentrate and she fidgeted and shuffled next to Rik on the sofa, GT strategically positioned between them by her in case her hands went wandering without her noticing.

'Do you know what I wish I hadn't done?' she said as she put down *The Country Diary of an Edwardian Lady*, because not even its sublime watercolours and verse could draw her in. 'I threw out all those drawings you did of Hollyhocks, and all the notes I made. Every single one. They reminded me of you too much too, but I wish I'd kept them. It was like my own country diary or nature journal.'

'Start them again,' Rik said instantly. 'Take pictures of whatever you want on your phone and I'll draw them for you.'

'They won't be the same,' she said.

'They'll be much better,' Rik said. 'Without all those warped perspectives and errors.'

'I liked all the errors,' she protested. 'And those plants and flowers have matured, or died, or variegated.' What she had wanted was the historical record, so she could pore through them and note how everything had changed. 'We'd have to start all over again from scratch and I've forgotten how it all looked before. I don't have anything to remind me.'

'But in however many years time,' Rik countered, 'you'll have the new set to remind you, won't you? It's all still going to change. You can't stop it.'

'Aren't you too busy with work?'

He shook his head. 'Never too busy for you, and you seem like you need something to occupy yourself.'

They worked all week, with GT snoozing contentedly between them among her piles of reference books, until she reluctantly took herself off to bed where she had lucid, troubling dreams until she woke at 3am, staring at the ceiling, waiting for the sun to rise so she could go out and start working again.

But as the week went on and she slept worse than ever, she became more tired and emotional and increasingly close to the edge. On Thursday night she thought about turning in early, but reasoned she would only wake up earlier still, and those lonely hours in the morning while everybody else was asleep were the darkest for her. She didn't have the energy to carry on with the notes and had to force herself to keep her eyes open through some superhero movie only to find herself bawling her eyes out for no reason whatsoever.

Rik turned the TV off and put his arm around her. 'What's Captain America done to warrant this?'

Faith didn't know herself and she shook her head weakly, pulling a blissfully unaware GT onto her lap. She watched her tears fall into the puppy's sandy coat, but he slept on and it made her cry harder than ever.

Rik stroked her hair but didn't say any more, and she cried hopelessly until she felt she had no more tears left. Then, feeling herself calming down a bit, she waited until her shoulders had stopped shaking with silent sobs and gave him a watery smile. 'Sorry.'

He carried on stroking her hair and she closed her eyes. GT shifted in her lap, but didn't wake.

'What was that all about?' Rik asked eventually.

'I don't know,' she said honestly.

'Fair enough.' He took his hand off her hair and she missed it immediately. 'Think it helped?'

'I don't know,' she said again. 'Hope so. I guess I'll know at 3am.'

'What happens at 3am?'

'I wake up,' she sighed. 'Every night, without fail. 3am on the dot. I've been doing it on and off for years.'

'You need some fun,' he said. 'Why don't you come out tomorrow night? Jason and a few of us are going for some drinks, his last days of freedom and all that.'

'Won't it be appallingly blokey?'

Rik laughed. 'I'm pretty sure girls are allowed too.'

'Isn't —' Time for the elephant to make an appearance at last. 'Isn't Lucinda coming?'

'What difference does that make?'

Shit, Faith thought. I sound like I'm treating it as a date.

'No difference,' she said quickly. 'Just thought you might like some time to catch up.'

'Hmm,' Rik said. 'Anyway, no. She's not coming. Doesn't want to drag herself all the way down here just to watch me get hammered and complain viciously about my hangover the next day.'

More fool her, Faith thought. 'OK,' she said. 'I'll come.'

The Blacksmiths was heaving. Rowdy mobs spilled out into the garden and lounged over the benches, which were crammed to bursting with empty and half-empty pint and shot glasses, cracked mobile phones and overflowing ashtrays.

Jason and his friends were at a far table, and as they approached Faith recognised Simon from the day she'd gone mountain biking with Rik. He got to his feet as soon as he saw her. 'I was hoping to run into you again.' He leaned in and Faith proffered her cheek, but instead he went straight for her lips and she stumbled against him awkwardly, caught off guard.

'Have I made you weak at the knees already?' he asked slyly as Faith righted herself.

'Don't flatter yourself,' she chided.

Rik muttered something about drinks and slid off, scowling.

Her tears the previous night must have released something, because Faith couldn't remember having so much fun. As Rik had promised, she wasn't the only girl, a charming redhead and her blonde-haired friend joined them. They were both younger than her and full of life, talking enthusiastically about their burgeoning careers and plans for the rest of the summer, and Faith felt imbibed with the joy and promise of being young and carefree and having her whole life in front of her. Which I do, she reminded herself. I'm twenty-six, not seventy-six.

Simon kept bringing her drinks and trying to barge his way into the conversation. 'He likes you,' the redhead noted, nudging Faith.

'He liked me a few months back,' the blonde said knowingly. They all giggled.

Rik had noticed Simon's advances too and was glowering at Faith from across the table. What's his problem? she wondered. I thought he was over all that scowling and hostility. He couldn't possibly be annoyed at her for talking to Simon. Not after that appalling clinch with Lucinda in the kitchen. If anybody was entitled to feel annoyed around here it was her, given that she was still hopelessly in love with him and had

248

spent all week practically immersed in him and he wasn't really showing any signs of being affected in the same way.

'So how come I haven't seen you around here before?' Simon had returned to the attack.

She twirled a lock of hair around her finger. 'I moved away a while ago,' she said, 'and I don't come back that often, but I'm here for the whole summer this time.'

'Are you now?' Simon dropped his voice meaningfully. 'That's a stroke of luck.'

'Is it?'

'Looks that way to me,' Simon said, still in a low tone. 'Why don't you tell me a bit about yourself?'

Faith answered his questions obediently, which included scoping out whether or not she had a boyfriend. 'I split up with somebody quite recently,' she said, 'and I'm not really looking for anything right now.'

Unless Rik was offering, of course.

Which wasn't likely given that he was currently looking at her as if she were a wasp in his drink.

'How long were you together?' Simon pressed on.

'Three years or so.'

'Sounds like you could use a bit of fun, after a slog like that.'

It had been a slog, Faith thought, an energy-sapping slog all round. Not just Rob, the commute, work, herself — she remembered how weak and jaded she'd felt at the beginning of the summer, before Hollyhocks had begun to work its restorative magic on her.

She felt like a different person. Stronger, but also a lot more able to be vulnerable, and more able to deal with things. Open. That's how I feel, she thought. More open, thanks to the way Hollyhocks and GT and Minel and Sara and Paul — and Rik, most of all Rik — had grounded and supported her. Maybe I should tell him, she thought, and say thank you and that might cheer him up a bit, and she turned to him only to find him talking distractedly to Jason and looking moodier than ever.

'So what do you think?' Simon asked pointedly.

She turned back to him. 'About what?'

'Do you think you could use a bit of,' he dropped his voice again, 'fun?'

His blue eyes were very clear despite the amount he had drunk, and he had a dusting of freckles over his snub nose and cheeks. Maybe I could, Faith thought, surprised to find herself even contemplating it, but she found his cheekiness and self-assurance quite charming.

Maybe a bit of fun is just what I need, God knows I'm practically climbing the walls after the turgidness of Rob and having to watch Rik chucking tools and bikes around and getting all hot and bothered with me at the quarry and hanging around with me in the evenings wearing far too many clothes and — and being with somebody else, she reminded herself very firmly.

'I don't know,' she said to Simon, the corners of her mouth turning up slightly in a secret sort of smile. 'Maybe.'

He took this as encouragement and redoubled his efforts, making her laugh with his anecdotes and increasingly outrageous asides. He's funny, she thought. But not as funny as Rik, when he's not impersonating a moody teenager. Where was he, anyway? He and Jason must have gone inside. 'I should probably spend some time with my friend,' she told Simon. 'I'll see you later. Maybe.'

'Definitely,' he said hopefully, and she laughed again and went off in search of Rik. She found him propping up the bar with Jason.

Rik still looked troubled, and Jason was nodding understandingly, always his sounding board, Faith thought. I should have taken that role off him, although Rik would have still needed somebody to complain about me to when I drove him crackers, which I appear to be doing right now with my general presence. Rik had noticed her and his expression hadn't changed, he looked more disapproving than ever. Faith shoved a drink towards him. 'What's rattled your cage?'

'Nothing.' Rik frowned at the drinks. 'On a mission, are you?' He sounded very acidic.

Faith gulped down her shot defiantly. 'As you said,' she sniped, 'I could use some fun.'

Jason disappeared tactfully off in the direction of the toilets.

Rik drained his own glass disdainfully. 'What have you done with Simon? Your admirer?' he prompted, and Faith flushed. Why should I feel guilty? she wondered indignantly. He's the one sticking his tongue down Lucinda's throat in the kitchen and making me heave my guts out in the process. How many double standards is he going to hit me with?

'Not that it's any of my business,' Rik said, 'but you might like to know that Simon gets through them.'

'You're right,' she said, thinking she didn't care in the slightest how many Simon got through. 'It is none of your business.'

'I just don't want to see anybody kick you when you're down.'

So that's why he's annoyed, Faith thought. He's just looking out for me. Being a good friend.

What a complete bastard. He should be raging with jealousy.

'Once again, as you yourself pointed out,' she said, 'I could do with some fun.'

'I don't think his brand of fun is really what you need, unless you want to end up crying on the sofa again.'

She flinched. 'What makes you think I'll be the one crying?'

'Call it intuition.'

That knowing tone — he must have replaced the patient, talking-to-a-small-child tone he'd used when they were teenagers with this condescending one. She wasn't sure which rankled more, the tone of voice or the fact that nine years later he still knew exactly how to push all of her buttons.

'I wouldn't worry about that, Rik.' She forced out a laugh that she hoped was more patronising and worldly than shrill witch. 'As my ex boyfriend will testify I'm hardly sitting pining my heart out and just waiting for that special somebody to notice me.'

What a barefaced, breathtaking lie, she chided herself. But he doesn't know that.

'You're right,' he said. 'You seem in just the right place for a one-night stand.'

'Who cares what place I'm in? I'm a free agent.'

'Oh, go and get off with Simon,' Rik snarled. 'You're probably exactly what each other needs.'

You're what I need, she thought desperately. 'Rikki, look —'

'And stop calling me that,' he howled. 'My girlfriend is still steaming mad at me thanks to you.'

'What?' Faith gasped.

'Why do you think she's not here?' he snapped. 'She's had enough of you ramming the fact you and I were together for about five seconds a hundred years ago down her throat.'

Faith shook her head. 'I don't know what you're talking about.' *Those aren't his words*, she thought, *I know they aren't. They've come out of his mouth but they're Lucinda's words.*

Was that what she'd been doing?

It absolutely wasn't. Rik had wanted to know why she'd left, and she'd told him. She'd given him the truth, not to win him back, but to help him make sense of it, give him the answers he needed so he could let it go. So they could both let it go.

'If the point to all of this,' she said when no new information was forthcoming, 'is that you would like to see less of me, then why didn't you just say so?' She glowered at him. 'Nobody's held a gun to your head. I've offered to stay out of the way.'

'You don't have to stay out of the way,' he said. 'Just maybe be a bit less, um,' he waved his hand irritably.

'A bit less *what?*'

'Your boyfriend is back.'

Simon had returned and was hovering nearby, looking madly interested.

'Don't let me interrupt you two *old friends*,' Simon said slyly.

Faith flushed again. 'I think I should go,' she said.

Rik rolled his eyes. 'What a surprise. See you in nine years.'

Faith shot him a filthy look and stormed off, muttering goodbye to a returning Jason as she went.

'Where are you going?' he asked.

'Home,' she said. 'Have a good wedding.' She paused, thinking she didn't need to take her mood out on him. 'I really am pleased for you, Jason. You're definitely one of the good guys.' She leaned in and kissed him on the cheek. 'Lily is a lucky woman.'

She set off along the winding road, feeling the fresh air hit her. God, she was quite drunk. And annoyed. And embarrassed. That had been mortifying.

Had she really been flaunting her former relationship with Rik in front of him and Lucinda, acting like she was entitled to a place in his life, a seat at the table, devoid as it was of any offers of close encounters of the 3am kind?

I'll definitely be awake at 3am now, she thought wildly, tonight and probably for the rest of my life, because one thing's for sure, I've well and truly blown everything with Rik now.

Chapter 22

Faith had half hoped Rik would come after her, but she was most definitely alone. Hollyhocks was dark when she got back and she used the light of her phone to navigate her way up the stairs to her room.

No more going out boozing and carousing and arguing, she told herself sternly. Just get yourself into bed and worry about it all night and every night for the rest of your life. She sighed heavily and changed into a very old vest and pair of checked flannel shorts and brushed her teeth, trying not to make too much noise so she wouldn't disturb the sleeping parents-to-be. Then she heard creaking coming from their room and winced. She must have woken them.

But the noise that came from Paul and Minel's room wasn't irritated muttering. It was weeping. She paused, tuning her ears in. Minel was crying, great racking sobs, and she could hear Paul murmuring something that she assumed was meant to be comforting, and then GT, who was all tucked up on the end of Faith's bed, woke up and started yapping.

'That bloody dog,' she heard Paul groan, and he came out of the bedroom, illuminated in the soft light of the bedside lamp. 'Oh, Faith,' he said, seeing her frozen with her toothbrush still in her mouth. 'We thought you were still out.'

She shook her head. 'I'm just going to bed. Is everything OK?'

'You'd better come in.' He opened the door fully and Faith saw Minel curled up on the bed, her face in her hands.

'What's going on?' she asked warily.

'I'm bleeding,' Minel's voice broke. 'I think I'm miscarrying.'

'Oh no.' Faith was beside her in a shot, her hand at her mouth. 'Since when?'

'I had some spotting yesterday,' Minel said. 'I rang the midwives and they said not to worry, but to come in if it got worse, and I just went to the toilet and,' she sobbed again, her shoulders heaving. 'It's pouring out. Masses of it.'

'You need to get her to hospital,' Faith said to Paul. 'Can you drive, or have you been drinking? Shall I call an ambulance?'

'I'll take her,' Paul said. 'I'm fine to drive. We'll go now,' he told Minel, rummaging in the drawers for some clothes. 'It might not be a miscarriage. We won't know until they check you out.'

'I don't want to go,' Minel said, and the pitiful defiance in her voice chilled the blood in Faith's veins. 'I don't want to.'

She doesn't want to have it confirmed, Faith thought, wishing she could say or do something to help but she could see that a dark stain was beginning to gather on the bedclothes where Minel was sitting and she had to admit, it didn't look good.

'You have to,' she said softly. 'They might be able to do something to stop it. They can do all sorts of things these days.' Could they? She didn't know, but it sounded like the sort of reassuring thing a person should say at a time like this.

She helped Paul get some clothes on Minel and ran to the bathroom. 'Do you have any sanitary towels?'

Minel gestured at the cupboard and Faith grabbed a few, shoving them at Paul. 'Ring me as soon as you know anything.'

He nodded. 'Where's Rik? Over at the cottage?'

'Still out,' Faith said, wincing as she remembered their argument. 'Don't worry about him. I'll let him know.'

'Thanks.' Paul took Minel's arm and led her gently out of the room. 'We'll be in touch.'

After they had left Faith stripped the bed and put the duvet cover in a bucket of cold water. She had a feeling Minel wouldn't want to be greeted by that stain no matter what her condition when she returned. She remade the bed with fresh linen, and looked over at the cottage, hoping Rik was home, but it was still in darkness.

GT was whining and pacing the corridor and she took him downstairs to let him out in the garden, bringing her phone in case there was any word from Paul. The puppy did his business then caught sight of something in the distance — a fox, Faith guessed — and launched himself after it.

She ran after him, cursing. 'Come back,' she yelled ineffectually, as GT disappeared into the hay barn, with its right door still prostrate in front of it.

Really? Faith thought. Do I need to face all my demons tonight? She had no idea if the lights still worked and she switched them on, crossing her fingers. For a second the barn remained in darkness, then slowly the lights began to flicker, illuminating the inside with an eerie, blue-ish glow.

It looked exactly as she remembered. The pile of bales at the corner, half-covered with tarpaulin. The stalls, empty bar a few old pieces of rusting metal, presumably Rik's work. The ancient lawn mower, which she and Rik had painted a fetching shade of orange, now warped beyond all repair. And there, on the jumbled pile of bales, she caught her breath, because in the faded light with the cavorting puppy at his feet, dressed all in black and with his head bowed so the now-voracious facial hair was completely indistinguishable from the shadows, Rik looked the image of his teenage self.

For a second she wondered she had actually gone back in time. When he looked up, would he be sixteen again? She clapped her hand protectively over her chest, conscious her vest was very thin and sagged a little at the neck. Rik finally looked up, and she was almost disappointed to see that he was still very much an adult and still looked very pissed-off.

'Minel's had to go to hospital,' she said. 'She's losing blood. They're worried it's a miscarriage.'

All the anger drained out of his face and he stood up. 'Is she OK? Do you think we should go?'

She shook her head. 'Paul took her. I think whatever the outcome, they're going to need some space.'

He swayed and reached out to the hay bales to steady himself. 'I think I drank too much.'

'Come up to the house and I'll make you some tea.' She scooped up GT and flicked the lights off.

He followed her unsteadily into the house and she put on a sweater and made him a cup of tea, putting a pint of water next to it. 'Drink that,' she said. 'And get some sleep. They don't need you crashing around, clutching your head and moaning tomorrow.'

Rik drank the water in one go and paled visibly. 'I definitely drank too much. I feel shocking.'

'I'm really sorry,' she said, meaning it. 'For being a bitch, and I'm also sorry if I have caused any upset between you and Lucinda. I didn't mean to, I promise.'

He sighed. 'I know. I came on a bit strong. Drunk, residual irritation,' he waved his hand. 'Still a bit confused by it all. We should probably tone it down a bit though, when Lucinda's around.'

So it was both of them now? 'Tone what down?'

'Oh, I don't know,' he said irritably.

'It's fine,' she said quickly. 'I can back off.'

Rik stood up, looming over her and she backed into the marble side, feeling it cold and hard against her back. She watched his eyes slide reluctantly into focus, fixing directly on hers.

'Can you back off?,' he said.

'Yes, of course, I just said —'

'No,' he said, 'that wasn't a statement, it was a question. *Can* you?'

'You're drunk, Rik,' she said.

He opened his mouth as if to contradict her, then lurched. 'Yes. I am.'

He sat back down and made an indecipherable noise that was neither question nor statement but seemed to amuse him no end.

Faith sighed pointedly.

'Oh, by the way,' he was still sniggering, 'Jason wanted me to ask you if you could come next Saturday. To the wedding. Lily's going ballistic over the table plan because somebody's other half can't make it. You'll have to sit next to Simon.' Now he was back to glaring at her accusingly. He lurched again and got up. 'I feel horrendous. Text me when you hear from Paul.'

He shot out in the direction of the cottage and Faith watched him go.

At least they'd cleared the air. A bit. Had they? She looked at her phone once more. Nothing. She was in for a long night, lucky there was no way she'd be able to sleep anyway. She picked up GT and went upstairs, turning out the lights behind her.

Paul texted her during the night to confirm Minel was miscarrying and they would be home the following morning. Faith texted him back, saying she'd let Rik know and make herself scarce. 'Be there when we get back,' Paul responded. 'She wants to see you.'

She sent Rik a quick message to let him know, and thought she might as well try and get some sleep. But every time she managed to nod off, she would wake what felt like seconds later, haunted by dreams about Rik disappearing around corners and down endless corridors, just out of her reach.

I'd better sleep with Simon on Saturday if only to stop all this, she found herself thinking after one particularly harrowing dream in which she'd pursued a teenage Rik halfway down a corridor she was sure she remembered from school, only for him to turn around and have become an old man, greying and exhausted. 'Just leave me alone,' he snapped and she woke sweating and clutching GT to her for all she was worth.

Minel looked pale and impossibly fragile when she returned. Faith hugged her, feeling her friend leaning weakly against her. 'At least we know I can get pregnant,' Minel said tonelessly, and repetitively, for the next hour, until Paul took her off to get some rest.

Rik looked pale and ragged the next morning. Faith supposed she must do too, she had barely slept, and Minel and Paul were also listless, almost catatonic. They all lounged wordlessly around the pool, occasionally drifting in to cool off.

Sometimes these sun-soaked late summer days would stretch out endlessly, oppressively, with not even a cloud to break the rays that were blistering mercilessly down on them. 'This is why we need a summerhouse,' Minel said, fanning herself furiously, and the effort seemed to completely exhaust her. Tears welled up in her eyes once again.

She got up, and Paul rose to his feet and put his arm around her. They went slowly into the house, which would be blissfully cool and shady, Faith thought wistfully, but they needed some privacy and she really should go home. Then she remembered her parents, and she could almost picture Judith waiting patiently at the kitchen table for her daughter to reappear, and she couldn't face that either. Sara was away with her sister for the weekend so she couldn't even go and grumble in her friend's back garden like the good old days.

She sneaked a glance at Rik, who was wearing sunglasses. She wasn't sure if he was still awake.

It was so hot she was starting to sweat, she could see beads of it forming on her chest, and feel it on her stomach too. She wanted to take her vest off and if Minel and Paul had still been hanging around she probably would have done, but she didn't really feel like sitting next to Rik wearing only a faded grey marl bra and her denim shorts.

'I'm going for a ride,' she told him. He didn't look like he felt like joining her. She sloped off, and because she had nothing better to do she stayed out all day. She rode out as far as she could, turning down every bridlepath or farm track she came across, hoping to put some distance between herself and Hollyhocks but finding herself always, frustratingly, looping back to within just a few miles of it.

She stopped for a rest and pulled out her phone. She had a message from Sara saying Minel had phoned her that morning to tell her about the miscarriage. 'I should be there with all of you,' she wrote fretfully.

'I think she and Paul need some space,' Faith responded. 'She knows we're all here if she needs us. How's it going with your sister?'

'Perfectly dreadful,' Sara wrote back.

Faith grinned to herself. 'That sums it up round here too.'

'What else have I missed?' Sara demanded.

'Nothing,' Faith wrote back. 'That's why it's perfectly dreadful.'

She rode to the quarry and sat on the top step and stared down into the pit, until the silence chased her back out onto the road again. The shadows were lengthening by the time she wheeled home, exhausted and starving.

There was nobody at the pool when she got back, and the kitchen and living room were empty. She had a flash of fear that they had all run out on her. Minel and Paul would be upstairs, she reminded herself. Rik was probably at the cottage, working or sleeping. He's still there, she told herself. Everybody's still here.

GT yapped from the sofa and she shuffled in and lay down, pulling the puppy into her arms. She would just rest her eyes for a bit, and then think about getting something to eat.

When she woke it was pitch dark. She checked her phone. 10pm. She could hear creaking from upstairs.

Somebody's home, she thought. Somebody's here.

You're not alone.

She glanced out of the window and across the garden, she could see a light on in the cottage.

I feel lonely, she thought, lonely for Rik but something tells me if I go over there right now with an olive branch I'm only going to end up feeling lonelier.

Just give it some time. It'll be OK, but you have to give it some time.

He's still here. We're all still here. Battered and bruised and broken, shattered into our factions, Paul and Minel in it together, Rik and I very much apart, but we're all still here.

Chapter 23

Paul returned to the site later on in the week and the work carried on as normal, if a little less carefree. Faith had hoped the new tension with Rik might have dissolved, but while they were still riding together every lunchtime and staying up at night working on the drawings of Hollyhocks, all their previously easy conversation had dried up.

He was clearly still troubled by something he couldn't or didn't want to express. She wondered why he still persisted in spending time with her at all. But in spite of the tension the silence with which their evenings now passed wasn't uncomfortable, nor was it particularly unwelcome.

After five weeks in which everything seemed in constant motion, they had both finally stopped spinning.

By Friday lunchtime Rik seemed to have mellowed and they rode to the quarry where she watched him gracefully sweeping round the gravel pit, swooping up and down through the corners, before skidding to a halt in front of her.

'Do you want to hang around here tonight, or go out?' he asked.

'Go out,' she said instantly. She had had just about enough of their mutual silent retreat. She wondered if it was odd, that they both just assumed they'd be spending the evening together.

He nodded. 'I'm up for that.'

'We can't stay out too late,' she warned. 'Big day tomorrow.'

'Tomorrow. Saturday.' From his expression she guessed he'd forgotten what day of the week it was. 'I can't this evening,' he said reluctantly. 'Lucinda's coming later.'

And there goes my Friday night, she thought sadly, and there goes the strange world Rik and I have been living in, just the two of us, right with it.

In fact there goes whatever weird little bubble we've both been encased in all summer. It's like something hit the earth the moment I cried in front of him on Fox Hill and all this time it's just been rolling downwards, taking me and Rik and all the conversations we've had and the thoughts and the memories and the noise and the silence, bundling us all up with it.

Now it's reached the bottom. Now it's burst.

So there goes my last weekend with him, because I'll have to respect his request and steer clear while Lucinda's around. And this time next week we'll be finishing up. The garden will be done, the summerhouse will be built, and it'll all be over.

Of all the ways she had thought this summer with Rik would end, of all the final conclusions, she would never have guessed the very last one, would have been silence.

But for once, there was truly nothing more to say.

Chapter 24

The Land Rover bounced over potholes as Faith gripped the steering wheel tightly, narrowly missing banging her head on the roof. Jason was getting married at one of those irritatingly discreetly concealed, showy country house places but the driveway was very much out of the Hollyhock House mould, and she cursed as she failed to notice yet another gigantic pothole. A crunch came from somewhere in the region of where her suspension had once been. Maybe she should think about getting a new car, after all.

At least she looked OK today. Her early night had mitigated the usual effects of the inevitable 3am wakeup call and she'd enlisted Sara to make her face up, hiding the shadows beneath her green eyes, which were flashing brilliantly thanks to her friend's artful hand. She had also let Sara put her hair up for once, twining it into an elegant knot from which curly tendrils were already beginning to escape, framing her face fetchingly.

Sara had been on good form this morning, Faith mused, full of resolve to once again try and persuade Tony to open up. 'I have a plan,' she'd said to Faith, her eyes sparkling. 'I'll give you a full debrief tomorrow.'

'So will I,' Faith had said.

Sara had raised her eyebrows. 'That sounds promising. Don't tell me you've finally stopped pining over Rik?'

'Still pining,' Faith had confessed, 'but now thinking maybe I do need a bit of a push to just let it go.' She thought of Simon. 'You never know,' she'd said to Sara. 'Maybe this summer will end with a bang after all.'

She parked up and got out of the car, tottering on the spiky heels Sara had lent her, which matched her dress. I look like a lady, she giggled to herself. Maybe I should have brought Lofty as a date.

Lucinda's silver gas-guzzler purred disdainfully past and Faith watched as she got out of the car, smoothing down her aquamarine dress. She looked stunning, her glossy hair sweeping in a shiny curtain down to her fragile shoulders which somehow still managed to hold up her magnificent, voluptuously soaring breasts. The shiny fabric of her dress clung to her slim waist before flaring out over her curvy hips. I can wear all the fancy dresses I like, Faith thought bleakly, but I'll never be able to hold a candle to her.

And there was Rik next to her, wearing dark blue trousers and a pale blue shirt. He hadn't bothered with a jacket, it was boiling hot and she pitied the groomsmen, who were milling around in morning suits laughing heartily and sporting delicate corsages of cornflowers and oxeye daisies in their buttonholes. Oh, wildflowers, Faith thought delightedly. They were beautiful, nestling prettily against the steel-grey lapels of the suits, a little flash of summer on a grey winter's day. I like Lily already, she decided. Then Rik turned to say something to Lucinda and she caught her breath, because he looked different — totally different.

He'd shaved, she realised. That stupid beard. Lucinda must have finally persuaded him to ditch it.

She hadn't actually seen his jaw or his impossibly high, haughty cheekbones all summer. Somewhere along the line she'd stopped noticing the beard, it had just become another part of him. Without it he looked much more like the teenager she remembered, his body still lean and graceful under his shirt. But he also looked a more accurate version of who he was now, without the chaos of hair his wilder edges seemed sharper and more defined.

She could just as easily be seeing him for the first time all over again, witnessing like a time lapse the passage of the last nine years, all the ways he had changed, and all the ways he had stayed the same.

Sensing her gaze, Rik caught her eye and nodded. He said something to Lucinda who turned and gave Faith an overly friendly wave, then steered him off firmly in the opposite direction.

The ceremony was short but moving, and Lily looked absolutely radiant in a simple cream dress. She had a crown of wildflowers in her dark brown hair, and she and Jason both gazed at one another adoringly and giggled touchingly as they stumbled over their vows.

Faith, still hopelessly adrift, stood next to Simon and tried not to watch as Lucinda slipped her hand into Rik's and smiled at him winningly. They looked good together, she thought in anguish, very classy and well-matched. They all filed out of the airy, hexagonal room into the corridor and reception area for drinks. Rik put his arm around Lucinda's satin-smooth shoulders and she leaned into him as if it was a given that he would always be standing next to her, as if she just knew where he was, without even looking. Does she feel him like I do, Faith wondered? Do the hairs on her arms prickle when he moves silently into range?

Does her infinitely feminine, luscious-looking body just melt into his like mine did? Does he find every inch of her as mesmerising as he once found every part of me?

How could she be threatened by our past? I only know what it's like to be loved by Rik as a boy. She's the one who knows what it's like to be loved by him as a man.

She felt a knot of pure misery swirl together in the pit of her stomach and rise up to the back of her throat. Was she going to be sick? No, she wasn't, she was going to cry. Again. She was going to bawl her eyes out and ruin Sara's lovely makeup.

Was the mascara waterproof? She choked back the first of the sobs and ran out of the hall, her stupid spiky shoes clattering and skidding on the marbled floor of the corridor that led to the blissful reprieve of the Ladies.

'You need these!' An attendant shot forward, holding a pair of plastic heel-shields.

'Not now,' Faith said, and flew past him into the toilet, shutting herself into the farthest cubicle and sitting down on the chilly seat, putting her head in her hands and wailing like GT after she'd booted him off her leg. She cried and cried and cried, sobbing and choking and heaving, her tears pouring like a waterfall down her face, soaking her stupid showy lovely dress and splashing onto the floor.

I'm crying an actual river, she thought, and she cried until she thought her heart had torn itself into separate pieces and she had no more tears left, her eyes stinging as they dried.

She heard the door go and stood up, flushing the toilet automatically so she could blow her nose and choke out the last of her strangled sobs with some modicum of privacy. She opened the door and went out to wash her hands and splash some cool water on her face, and who should be there but — of course, of *course*, because she was always there to kick her when she was down — bloody, bloody, bloody Lucinda.

'Hello Faith,' Lucinda said suspiciously. 'Are you OK?'

Faith nodded and turned to look at her reflection in the mirror, then winced and thought better of it. 'Such a lovely wedding,' she said, her voice wavering and watery. 'But you were right, you know, other people's happiness does set me off and I really miss Rob. My ex,' she said, as Lucinda looked blank.

'Oh.' Lucinda nodded. She looked marginally more sympathetic. 'You poor thing. I know just how you feel. It's awful, isn't it? Missing somebody so much you feel like your heart might just break altogether.' She examined her own, apparently highly pleasing, reflection.

'Enjoying the wedding?' Faith asked.

'Not really,' Lucinda confided. 'I'm desperate to get back to London. I've got a shift tomorrow and I could do without being tired and hungover. But Rik doesn't want to head back yet and so I suppose I should stick around.'

How can she consider it a hardship? Faith thought. How could she prefer sitting in an office talking on the phone to being here with Rik?

'He said he's got something to talk about with me later,' Lucinda said. 'He's left it a bit late but I expect he's going to ask me to come to Cornwall with him. Can't live without me after all.' She winked cheekily. *Hope she gets an eyelash in her eye*, Faith thought bitterly.

'Good for you,' she said tonelessly. 'Are you going to go? Will you be able to sort it with work?'

Lucinda shrugged. 'Well, I haven't said yes yet. But it'll be OK as long as I'm plugged in, which I always am.' She waved her phone. 'I miss the old days, when this job involved actually going out and meeting real live people, not just monitoring Twitter and rewriting *ghastly* press releases from incompetent press officers who wouldn't know good writing if it hit them in the face.'

'I'm a press officer,' Faith said pointlessly.

'Oh, sorry. I'm sure your releases are just fine.' Lucinda smiled guilelessly.

'They're not,' Faith said. 'They're full of drivel.' She couldn't go back to that, she just couldn't. That life wasn't her, it had never been her. She was from a different world and she was going to start living in it, even if she couldn't live in it with Rik.

And she was going to start right now.

'I'm going to leave,' she announced, 'and study garden design then set up full-time.'

'Very hard physical work,' Lucinda said. 'I had no idea how much. You must be stronger than you look. Although your arms are bulking up, aren't they?'

Faith was quite proud of her newly-defined arms. 'Strong is the new sexy,' Faith said, and slid off towards the door. 'See you later.'

'I'm done here too.' Lucinda followed her out of the toilet. Rik was waiting for her. He caught sight of Faith's blubbered, wrecked face and his eyes darkened.

'Let's go and talk to Jason,' Lucinda said briskly, 'and then we really need to head off.'

Rik's eyes were still on Faith. 'What's wrong with you?' he demanded. 'You look like you've been crying.'

Faith shuffled in her hideous heels. 'Shoes are killing me.' She kicked them off, stretching out her toes and noticing she had livid weals where the horrid things had been pressing into her skin, pale from spending all summer shod in trainers or workboots. She had a tan-line, like the ones she used to get from the ankle socks she wore at school in the summer.

'Oh, hi gorgeous.' Simon had turned up.

'Rik,' Lucinda said pointedly. 'We really need to wrap this up.'

Faith reached up to rip her hair out of its infernal knot. It was giving her a headache, having it pegged back and constrained like that.

The music slowed and dulled, the babble of the guests and the odd tinkling laugh, appreciative roar and popping cork, all warped and muted. Faith's eyes darted from Simon, to Lucinda, to Rik, and her ears were filled with a low, resonant hum.

She could hear the air shifting around her hair as it burst free of the pins with a very audible puff, and floated and spiralled down to her shoulders, strand by strand.

It seemed to take forever.

Lucinda and Simon were both talking. Their voices slipped and slid around one another, indecipherable, syllables spilling together.

Faith's eyes stopped flicking and fixed on Rik.

And then just as suddenly as whatever had happened arrived, it left.

'I need a drink,' Faith said. She turned to Simon.

'Let's find Jason,' Lucinda prompted Rik.

Simon ushered Faith over to the bar and gestured for a couple of shots. Faith fired hers down instantly. She knew exactly what she was going to do now. She was going to get absolutely plastered and dance wildly and have lots of fun and she was bloody well going to shag Simon whether she liked it or not.

Then tomorrow she was going to kick him out and get up with a crashing hangover and start working on her portfolio for garden design courses.

It was about time she had a plan.

'I'd better have a Pimm's too,' she told Simon, who beckoned the barman again. 'Lots of cucumber and strawberries, please.'

A few more, she thought, and I'll be about drunk enough to just snog Simon right here on the dancefloor, in front of Rik and Lucinda, and that will show her once and for all that I'm completely over him and they can push off to Cornwall and live glamorously ever after.

She edged closer to Simon.

'Are you enjoying yourself?' he asked.

Not in the slightest, Faith thought, but that's going to change.

She smiled flirtatiously. 'I am now,' she said.

'Me too,' he said, 'now your so-called mate is over there arguing with his girlfriend and has temporarily stopped looking at me like he wants to punch my lights out.'

'Rik's just being a good friend,' Faith said, meaning it. 'He knows I've been through a bit of a rough time lately and he's just looking out for me. And I hear you,' she smiled teasingly again, 'have a bad reputation.'

'Oh, do you now?' He moved still closer.

'I do.' This is just complete nonsense, she thought, the sort of nonsense you talk when you're both gearing yourselves up to just throw yourselves at each other and it should be exciting and fun and loaded and my heart should be racing and my breathing should be coming quicker and my skin should be tingling with anticipation and instead I feel —

Nothing, she thought despairingly. There's no way I'm going to be able to bring myself to sleep with Simon.

This is pointless.

'I need the toilet,' she told Simon.

'Again?' He looked perplexed. 'You just went.'

'I've got my period.'

'Don't let me stop you.' Simon moved away from her pointedly. He's just figured out he's not getting any tonight, Faith thought. Well now he knows how I feel, only magnified by about one hundred.

Faith went and found Jason, who was sitting with Lily watching some of the more enthusiastic action on the dancefloor.

'Hey Faith,' Jason pulled out a chair. 'Come and sit down. This is Lily,' he gestured at his new wife, whose sweet face was alight with happiness. 'Mrs Denby.'

'Congratulations.' Faith kissed Lily warmly on the cheek. 'You look absolutely radiant and that was a beautiful ceremony. You did well,' she said to Jason. 'Remembered all your lines.'

'Jason says you're an old friend?' Lily said. She squeezed her husband's hand affectionately. 'You must have some tales about his antics back in the good old days.'

'Don't tell her, Faith,' Jason hissed comically.

'You'd want to ask Rik that,' Faith said. 'The only incriminating evidence I have involves their adorable habit of spooning each other after nights out.'

Lily giggled. 'Where is Rik? He and Lucinda were having a row last time I saw him.'

Jason rolled his eyes. 'He picks his moments.'

'Well, at least they're getting into practice for when they move in together and start arguing about him leaving the toilet seat up and her squeezing from the middle of the tube of toothpaste,' Faith said despondently.

'Hardly.' Jason snorted. 'He's not moving in with her.'

The ground tilted fractionally underneath Faith's bare feet.

'How do you know?' Lily chided.

'He told me,' Jason said. He looked awkward, aware he shouldn't be betraying confidences.

'Why not?' Faith demanded, knowing she was sounding far too interested and not caring in the slightest.

'It's none of our business,' Jason said firmly. 'Ask him yourself, if you're that bothered.'

'I am bothered.'

Lily was looking at Faith curiously. It's her wedding day, Faith reminded herself firmly. Don't try and hijack it.

But you might not get another chance to ask Jason anything, she countered, it's just a few moments, just ask him.

'Look, Jason, do you think Rik might —'

'You need to be talking to him, not me,' Jason interrupted.

'But is there any point?' She fixed her gaze on him. 'Or am I about nine years too late?'

The hairs on her arms began to prickle. Too late now, she thought. A Lucinda-free Rik had materialised next to them.

'It's never too late,' Jason said.

'For what?' Rik asked.

'We were just talking about whether we're too late to show off our dance moves,' Lily said quickly. 'Now everybody's plastered.'

She's perceptive, Faith thought, and bright, and something tells me I'm going to like her.

Lily smiled at Jason. 'You're right. All those dance classes we took don't have to go to waste. Let's hit the floor anyway.'

Faith watched them go. Rik was still standing next to her.

'Hey,' he said.

'Hey,' she responded. 'Where's Lucinda?'

'She left,' he said, not sounding particularly interested in discussing her.

'Sorry,' she said, not meaning it.

'I don't think she was enjoying herself much anyway.'

'Pity,' Faith sighed, watching the merriment on the dancefloor. 'It's nice here.'

He was looking at her crumpled, tearstained dress. 'What happened to your dress?'

'I just got it all mashed up crying in the toilets.'

'Why were you crying?'

'I must be getting my period, it always turns me into a hormonal mess.' That's the second time tonight, she thought, I've blamed my monthly cycle for something it hasn't done.

His hair was falling forwards, tangling with his long eyelashes, and his eyes had lost that flinty edge and were doe-like and dreamy. 'What would help?' he asked. 'Some painkillers? A drink?'

'A drink would be just the thing,' she said. She gestured to him to sit down with her and liberated a bottle of wine and a couple of glasses from the detritus on the table. 'Shall we get hammered?'

'*Hammered.*' he agreed fervently. 'Absolutely cross-eyed. Poleaxed. Plastered. Then we can carry each other home and pass out watching a movie.'

Faith nodded. 'Perfect. But what about Lucinda?'

Rik shook his head. 'She's gone back to London.'

'Aren't you going to go after her?'

'No.' He picked up his drink. 'I'm staying here.'

Chapter 25

Faith woke up, feeling something pressing against her face. She blinked a couple of times. Why could she see stripes?

She blinked again. Still stripes.

Something was pressing into her back too and she twisted her head round and saw it was Rik.

Where were they and why was everything stripey?

She realised she was staring at the back cushions of the sofa in the cottage.

She and Rik must have fallen asleep — or passed out, she conceded — after they got back from the wedding. She vaguely remembered them both falling through the front door, and him saying she couldn't go back to the house as she'd probably fall up the stairs, and them both agreeing they would fall up whatever stairs happened to be in their path, and finding it wildly funny, and then arguing about which movie they were going to watch.

That was all she remembered, so they must have just flopped out on the sofa.

Last night had turned out to be magical. There had been no more flipping back to the past, and for once she had given up projecting into the future and questioning and analysing and agonising over it all.

They had just danced and giggled and eaten and drunk and been merry all night and she'd fended Simon off, because why would she want him when she could be with Rik, why would she want to be anywhere else, with anybody else?

Rik stirred and she felt him moving against her. She still felt slightly drunk, the pounding head and churning stomach she knew were headed her way hadn't set in yet. God, they must have been plastered. She giggled to herself and the noise woke Rik.

'Oh thank god,' he said. 'It's you.'

He shifted awkwardly. She could feel the heat from his body where he was squashed up against her and the alcohol had the effect of making her feel like a layer of skin had been removed, leaving her hopelessly sensitive.

'I don't feel that bad yet,' he said, 'which means it's going to be awful later.'

'Awful,' she agreed, thinking he didn't feel anything approaching bad to her.

'Think if we went upstairs we'd be able to get back to sleep?' he asked.

They might, she thought, but more than likely she'd just lie there burning up all over for him and that could get awkward very quickly. On the other hand, the sofa was horribly uncomfortable. 'We could try,' she said dubiously.

Rik got up and clutched his head. 'Maybe I spoke too soon before.'

She got up slowly, feeling her own head swimming. 'This dress is done for,' she said. 'Can I borrow some clothes?'

They went upstairs and she took one of his t-shirts and a pair of shorts and got changed in the bathroom and brushed her teeth. Rik went in after her and came out with two glasses of water. 'I can still taste booze,' he said.

Soft light was pouring into the room from the open window. Rik hadn't bothered to draw the curtains and the room was lit with a golden glow. He had changed into a t-shirt and shorts too and looked sleepy and dishevelled, his hair rumpled and falling forwards into his eyes.

That'll help, she thought, him standing there looking like he just walked straight out of one of my wildest fantasies.

There was a telltale scratching at the door and then it caved in reluctantly, the latch so old and worn out by Rik slamming it around in teenage strops it barely caught any more. GT came bounding in, and he yapped joyfully when he saw his mistress and took a running jump towards the bed.

Faith giggled as he missed and made contact instead with the side of the mattress. She leaned over and picked him up and he cavorted happily all over her, covering her in kisses and gifting her with the odd sharp nip.

He sniffed at Rik and allowed him to rub his belly, then spied Faith's bare leg and flung himself down on it.

'That dog and your ankle need to get a room,' Rik grumbled.

If you think this is bad, Faith thought, you want to try watching you and Lucinda. Her stomach tightened at the very thought.

She shook GT off her ankle and he curled himself up in her arms. She hugged him happily. 'I love him,' she sighed to Rik.

'The feeling is mutual,' he said, watching GT snake his head over the crook of Faith's arm and close his eyes contentedly.

'I always wanted a dog,' Faith said. 'I know it sounds silly, but when I take him out for a walk, just him and me, I feel like we're in on a big exciting journey together. One girl and her dog.' She smiled affectionately, both at the dog and her own little flights of whimsy.

'That's how I felt about Tackle,' Rik said. 'He was up for anything. Literally anything,' he added, 'I caught him mounting a fox once.'

Faith sighed. 'I'm going to go into a decline when I have to leave GT here at the end of the summer.'

'You can't leave him,' Rik said. 'Minel might have bought him but we all know the dog chooses the owner and he's chosen you. You'll have to take him with you.'

She scratched behind GTs ears absently. He was right, she thought, she couldn't leave him.

'All right baby,' she said to GT. 'It's settled, then. You're coming with me and you and my ankle can live happily ever after.'

Rik pulled a bag out of his wardrobe. 'What are you doing?' she asked as he began to fling clothes in its general direction. 'You're not leaving, are you?'

'I've got to go to Hamburg tomorrow,' he said, still flinging. 'I missed so much work last week they want me out there where they can keep an eye on me.'

'What am I — what are we all going to do without you? What about Paul?'

'It's only a few days,' he said. 'He can get Lofty back in. He hasn't really got much choice and I haven't either. I've got to keep them sweet or I'm out of a gig.'

'How come you've got so behind?' she asked.

'Too many distractions, I guess.'

Like me, she thought, thinking how he'd stayed up with her in the house every night instead of going back to the cottage to work.

'And between you and me,' he said, 'I could do with a bit of time away from Paul's increasingly heavy and unwieldy tools.'

GT, always aware, whined softly. Faith hugged him again, horrified at how unpleasant the prospect of a week without Rik was. She watched him pack and began to feel drowsy again, and put GT at the foot of the bed and closed her eyes. She was already half in a dreamworld by the time Rik got into bed next to her.

He rolled towards her and put his arm around her and she was too tired and too glad of his closeness to even think about mustering up any Lucinda-based moral objection. He buried his face in her hair in an oddly touching, almost childlike gesture, and breathed in deeply, tightening his arm around her. She put her hand over his and squeezed it, then shifted back and settled herself against him just where she was meant to be.

When they woke again sunlight was blazing insistently through the window. Rik still had his arm around her and Faith felt strangely at peace even though her hangover had kicked in and she was horribly dehydrated.

'Let's go to the pool,' Rik said. 'I'd say we should go for a ride but I don't think I could even balance in this condition.'

They shuffled out, clutching their heads and griping companionably. Minel and Paul were already by the pool and Minel looked taken aback when she saw Faith. She eyed her clothes and her pale face. 'Lucinda,' she said. 'You've changed.'

'You look rough as hell,' Paul said. 'Good wedding, was it?'

'Very boozy,' Rik said.

GT had run on ahead of them and was scampering around chasing a pigeon feather, which kept being lifted by a very welcome breeze and deposited again just inches from his nose.

'So where's Lucinda?' Minel was asking Rik.

'She left.'

'Oh.' Minel didn't ask any more.

Faith dived into the pool, feeling the blissful relief of the cool water caressing her hot, aching body. She swam a couple of lengths and dived around underwater for a while, hoping her skin would absorb some of the liquid and start to feel better, then she swam to the side and drank another glass of water. 'What are you doing today?' she asked Minel, who was looking a bit more like her old self.

'Not much,' Minel said. 'Still need to rest up. And you need to rest too,' she said to Paul, 'as he's not around for most of next week.' She nodded at Rik, who had also got into the pool and was treading water and watching GT.

'Are Sara and Tony coming over?' Faith asked.

Minel shook her head. 'Just Sara, today. Tony's busy, apparently, doing what I don't know. Who wants to do anything other than laze around on a day like this?'

'I should go home at some point,' Faith said anxiously. 'I haven't been home since last Sunday morning. My parents will have forgotten what I look like.'

'Have you thought about that, much?' Minel asked gently.

Faith shook her head. Other things on my mind now, she thought ruefully. When did it all get so complicated?

It got a lot more complicated when Sara rolled up, her eyes red and puffy.

'We need to talk,' she said grimly, looking firstly at Minel and then at Faith. 'Not you two,' she gestured at Rik and Paul, who both looked unconcerned at their exclusion.

'I'll make some tea.' Minel, ever the hostess, bustled them into the kitchen and pulled out the chairs. 'What is it?'

'I tried again,' she said. 'With Tony. We were watching a movie and I just cuddled up to him, he said his shoulders were sore and I gave him a massage and he seemed to relax a bit, so then I thought, maybe if we just try.' She took in a shuddering breath. 'I said we didn't have to do anything, no pressure at all, but wouldn't it be nice to just be together, I could give him a proper massage. He clammed straight up,' Sara wailed. 'He said would I just let him have some space and watch the movie without climbing all over him like a bitch on heat.' She put her head in her hands. 'He made me feel like I was pestering him relentlessly when all he wants is some peace and quiet. I felt disgusted with myself, completely disgusted — and disgusting.'

Sara began to cry and Minel put her arm around her, murmuring soothing words as her shoulders jerked and shook.

'After helping you get ready yesterday,' Sara was saying, 'seeing you all dressed up and talking about pulling somebody, I just thought, I want that. Why don't I have that any more?' She looked at Faith again. 'Don't tell me you got laid last night or that will finish me off altogether.'

Faith shook her head. 'Definitely not.'

'Thank god. At least I'm not the only one who can't get any.'

'Glad to be of help,' Faith said acidly.

Sara gave a watery giggle. 'Did anything interesting happen at the wedding at all?'

'Nothing of note.'

'Why did Lucinda leave?' Minel demanded. 'How come you stayed over at the cottage with Rik?'

'You spent the night with Rik?' Sara was all ears.

'We just passed out drunk on the sofa.' No need to mention this morning's chaste love-in.

'So how come Lucinda pushed off?' Minel wasn't going to let it drop.

Faith shrugged. 'Ask Rik.'

'Why can't you tell us? Didn't he mention it?'

'He didn't,' Faith insisted. 'They looked like they were having a row about something, but that's all I know.'

Sara joined in the inquisition. 'You spent the whole night with him after his girlfriend stormed off and you didn't even ask why?'

'I don't know what you want me to say,' Faith protested. 'All I know is that she doesn't seem to like him spending time with me.'

Minel was frowning. 'Is she jealous?'

'Oh, I don't know,' Faith sighed, too hungover to think of a decent excuse. 'She knows we have a history, she's worried we're going to re-enact it I suppose.'

Minel sat down with a bump. 'What history would you re-enact?'

Faith gripped her teacup in her hand and stared down at it, watching the leaves swirl around before descending to settle at the bottom. If only she could read them.

Her mother could teach her how.

'OK, Min. No more keeping things from you. There's something I never told you. Rik and I did used to be closer than just friends.'

'What, when we were kids?'

Faith nodded.

'But I asked you just a few weeks ago and you said nothing ever went on. You didn't even remember snogging him my party.'

'I lied,' Faith said.

'And he said he didn't remember either,' Minel went on. 'I thought it was weird that both of you were so blank when you seemed to remember everything else about that evening.'

'I remember, and he remembers,' Faith confirmed. 'To quote Facebook circa 2008, "it's complicated".'

Minel pressed on. 'Were you having some kind of secret fling that none of us knew about?'

'Yes.'

'You were? For how long?'

'Long enough for them to deflower each other,' Sara chipped in. 'Several times, from what she told me.'

'Oh my god.' Minel looked lost for words and Faith could see that the cogs in her brain were working furiously. 'Tell me

283

everything. Well, maybe not everything,' she winced. 'You don't need to go into graphic detail about any deflowering, thanks. But I want to know. What — when — why didn't you say anything?'

Faith sighed. Here we go again. She was starting to get bored of it herself. 'So, your 18th birthday party…'

'Oh Faith,' Minel said when she had finished. 'Oh, that's a bit of a tale of woe, isn't it?' She frowned, clearly trying to make sense of it all. 'Poor Rik. No wonder he was so heartbroken.'

'Yeah,' Faith said sadly. 'Not just him, but yeah, pretty harsh for him.'

'I had no idea,' Minel breathed. 'I was so wrapped up in Paul, I suppose, and us finally getting together. And I was really very intolerant of Rik.' She looked guilty. 'I wish I'd known, I might have been a bit more sympathetic.'

'I'm sure he's over it,' Faith said. 'He's over all of it.'

'But Lucinda thinks he isn't?'

She shrugged. 'More that she thinks I'm not over it.'

'And are you?'

Faith could feel Sara's eyes on her.

'Do you still have feelings for him?' Minel was like a dog with a bone sometimes, Faith thought reluctantly, just like her infernal brother.

'That's not really relevant,' she tried.

Sara snorted.

'It sounds extremely relevant,' Minel said. 'How did you feel about him back then? If you hadn't jumped to conclusions about Sophie what do you think would have happened with you and Rik?'

284

'It's impossible to say, of course,' Faith said but she knew what Minel was asking. 'I was in love with him,' she conceded. 'He was with me too. He knew it before I did.'

'And what about now?' Minel asked again. 'Do you still?'

'Love him,' Faith finished for her. 'Yes. I do.'

The table fell silent. Even Sara had nothing to offer.

Faith watched the grandfather clock in the corner. Seconds ticked by.

'So what are you going to do, then?' Minel asked.

'What do you mean, what am I going to do? I'm not going to do anything. He's with Lucinda. He doesn't love me.'

'How do you know?' Sara asked. 'Have you asked him?'

'Of course not,' Faith exploded. 'What kind of question is that?'

'Have you even told him you're still in love with him?' Minel asked.

Faith shook her head. 'No, of course not. Again. He's with Lucinda,' she said patiently. 'She does exist, doesn't she? I didn't make her up?'

'Of course she exists. She's notable by her absence. She's not been around here that much recently at all.'

'She was there last night,' Faith said.

'But she's not here now,' Sara said, as if that weren't obvious.

'And he's been spending all his time with you,' Minel said. 'I can definitely see why she's suspicious.'

'There's nothing to be suspicious of,' Faith protested.

'Are you sure? What have you been doing?'

'Just riding bikes and talking and occasionally crying and giggling and bickering and drawing and writing and hanging out.'

'Hanging out,' Minel repeated, as if it were a euphemism.

'Ohhh,' Sara said. 'Oh. Yes!'

'Yes what?'

'He must still have feelings for you,' Minel said patiently, 'if he's sacked Lucinda off just to "hang out" with you.'

'Of course he doesn't. He hasn't sacked her off, she's been busy with work. In fact, she told me he was going to ask her to go to Cornwall with him.' Faith was thinking about Jason's cryptic comments. 'Although Jason did say he wasn't going to move in with her.'

'There you go then.' Sara looked delighted. 'He obviously told her he didn't want to shack up with her and she got the hump and stormed off. Case closed.' She dusted her hands with satisfaction.

'So now you can tell Rik how you feel,' Minel prompted.

'I can't,' Faith insisted again. 'Even if he and Lucinda did argue last night they're still together. What good will me telling him do? At best it'll confuse him, at worst he'll just tell me thanks but no thanks because, as I keep reminding everybody, *he's with Lucinda.*'

'So you're just going to let him go?' Sara challenged. 'You're going to let him push off to Cornwall, with or without Lucinda, without even telling him that you still love him? You're really prepared to be that self-sacrificing and noble?'

'I just want him to be happy,' Faith said. 'And if Lucinda makes him happy then fair enough.'

'I'm going to suggest that Lucinda probably doesn't make him happy,' Minel said, 'hence them barely spending any time together any more. That doesn't mean being with you necessarily would,' she went on. 'He might well be over it all and genuinely just see you as a friend. Or, he might still be just as in love with you as you are with him.'

'If he was,' Faith said, 'he'd tell me.'

'And he's probably thinking the exact same thing,' Minel said gently. 'Only Rik's already put it out there for you once, and he got his heart well and truly stamped on as a result.'

'You need stop wafting around playing the guessing game and hoping he will do all the hard work for you,' Sara announced. 'You need to tell him how you feel and then let him make up his own mind. Right now,' she went on. 'Instead of mooning around and whinging to us, why don't you take him on some bike ride and just put it out there?'

'He's going to Hamburg tomorrow,' Faith said, but her stomach was hollow with nerves all of a sudden. Should she? Could she?

'Even better,' Minel said. 'Gives him a bit of time to mull it over, and if he doesn't go for it you've got time to take it on the chin.'

She had to, she acknowledged, she needed a resolution one way or the other and Rik couldn't help her if he didn't have all the information he needed.

'Just one more thing,' Faith said to Minel. 'Can I buy GT off you?'

Minel looked relieved. 'You're welcome to him,' she said. 'I should have just got a Springer spaniel in the first place. These yappy little monsters you and Rik are so keen on drive me crazy. Run off with him and live happily ever after, take my brother with you, help yourself, take it all.' She waved her hand around the kitchen and smiled, and Faith thought how all Minel had ever wanted to do was make her feel like she belonged here, like she fitted in too, and she hugged her friend tightly, then Sara. 'Whatever happens,' she said, 'with Rik, with Tony, with the babies — we'll always have each other, won't we?'

Sara rolled her eyes. 'You're going to make me cry again with your soppiness.'

'Of course we will,' Minel insisted. 'Ignore her.' She nudged Sara.

Faith wandered out to the pool and appropriated Rik. 'Go and get your bike,' she said. 'Let's go out.'

'Where?'

She shrugged. 'Dunno. Let's see where the mood takes us. I'll just go and change.'

Chapter 26

Faith and Rik rode out to a pub and she bought them lunch and a jug of Pimm's. Rik still didn't mention Lucinda. Faith thought about asking what they'd fallen out about but then she decided that was just a roundabout way of trying to ascertain if he had any feelings for her and the only way she was going to find that out was if she just told it all to him straight.

Just like she should have done nine years ago.

'You're probably going to be sick of hearing this by now,' she said. 'But I wanted to talk to you about something.'

Rik nodded. 'Your parents, right?'

Her parents. It was still at the back of her mind, but the issue with Rik had become more pressing since then. But actually she did want to tell him about it, she realised, she'd value his perspective and she might as well get that out of the way first.

'The other weekend,' she said, 'when Sara, Min and I were having afternoon tea, I saw my dad. He was checking in to the hotel, which is apparently a hotspot for extramarital sex. With a woman,' she said. 'A woman who wasn't my mum.'

'He's at it again?'

'He is and he isn't,' she said. 'I confronted him, and he explained a few things to me. Finally.'

Once she'd finished Rik drained his glass, chewing thoughtfully on some ice. It crunched between his teeth, a vague reminder of the satisfying crunching noises she'd generated throwing stones around the quarry like a woman possessed. 'How long have they been doing this?' he asked. 'And whose idea was it, do you know?'

'I don't know,' she said. 'But I did wonder if maybe it was something that came up during counselling. Which makes me feel even worse,' she said, suddenly realising something, 'because if the counsellor did suggest it and I was the one who persuaded them to go to counselling in the first place, doesn't that make the entire miserable situation kind of my fault?'

'No!' Rik said, very loudly, and she jumped. 'It's not your fault. None of it is your fault. Whoever suggested that particular solution, the counsellor or one of them, they must have both agreed to it just like they had to agree to counselling in the first place.'

He was right, she thought, and she felt something lift, a lightening, a burden of guilt she no longer needed to carry around. Off it floated, up into the sky, and she nodded gratefully and drank some Pimm's, watching a young couple snogging ferociously at the table at the far end of the garden.

'I just keep thinking about my mum,' she said. 'And it's made me realise that's what I could turn into. If I'd stayed with Rob, or if I find myself another sensible safe bet of a man who I don't love enough to risk getting hurt by. If I live half a life, settle for half a relationship.'

The sun had moved overhead, carrying on its inexorable passage across the sky, which was once again beginning to darken and pull together, grey clouds expanding and attaching themselves to one another in preparation for release. A dog barked in the distance, trapped in one of the gardens of the few houses scattered around, maybe restrained by an invisible electric fence. A pair of birds flew overhead, huge and pure white. Swans.

Swans, she thought, mate for life.

'I want the whole deal,' she said. 'I want real love even if it is terrifying. Even if there's no guarantee it'll work out. Even if it means risking getting my heart shattered again.'

Rik's leg was very close to hers. If she just moved hers a tiny bit, just an inch or two, they would be touching. His eyes were still sleepy and narrowed against the sun, his eyelashes were curling determinedly upwards, and he had something caught in one of them. A wildflower seed, maybe, or a speck of stardust, frozen in time.

'I want all that with you,' she said.

Rik blinked and the seed or dust dislodged and floated off, spiralling upwards, lifted by an invisible wind.

'I've never wanted that with anybody but you,' she went on. 'You're the most compelling person I have ever met in my life. You make everything an adventure, the big things and the little things. You have such strength and integrity, you have the most amazing heart and beautiful soul, you make me feel like home is a person not a place.' She blinked hard. You can't cry now, she thought irritably, you have to be stronger than that, you have to tell him how you feel without making it sound like he owes you anything. 'It's still you, Rik,' she said, 'It's always been you.'

He didn't say anything but she could see she had moved him. The clouds were gathering at speed now, drifting into one another and merging seamlessly into one lowering ceiling of dark grey.

'Am I being out of line?' she asked him, suddenly feeling foolish.

Rik, for once, seemed completely lost for words. She had thought he'd always have a comeback, an answer for everything, but this time she truly had floored him, the final verbal KO, and so she studied the young couple intently for a while, letting him digest it all. The young man, becoming aware of her scrutiny, gave her a challenging look and she turned away, blushing a little.

Rik finally pulled himself together. 'When did you realise — how long have you felt like this?'

'Pretty much since the start,' she said. 'I came here wanting some answers but from the second I saw you,' she bit her lip. 'There was still so much there. I thought it might be emotional memory, unfinished business, that once I had the explanations I so desperately needed I could put it behind me and finally get over you.' She winced, digging deep into herself for the courage to carry on. 'That day at the quarry, it just all came crashing down, rather like that pile of stones I so comprehensively beat up. I knew I was in love with you. I don't think I ever stopped loving you. It's up to you what you do about it,' she said. 'But that's how I feel, and now you know.'

'Do you know, though?' he asked. 'If you really did love me — back then — you wouldn't have been so quick to think the worst.'

He's still stuck on that, she thought. Maybe I really am too late.

'I can't go back,' she said. 'But I can do now, what I should have done then. I can tell you exactly how I feel, even though it might be fruitless, and hurtful, and embarrassing, and you might end up telling me something I really don't want to hear. I still want you to know, because I'd rather feel embarrassed and hurt and rejected than spend the rest of my life wondering what might have been.'

'And what do you think might have been?' he asked. 'Back then, if you had just asked me what was going on, or seen that it was Jason with Sophie and not me. What do you think would have happened?'

'I don't know.'

'Neither do I.'

And we never will, she thought. So what is the point in keeping on going back there?

'I'm done,' she said. 'Thinking about it, wishing, wondering. I'm tired of living my life half in love with a person still stuck in time, of asking what if?' She looked at him levelly. 'I don't want to go back in time, Rik. I want who you are now. I want to know what we could be, now. But if you don't,' she pulled a rueful face, tipping her head on one side, 'if you really are in love with Lucinda, or if your path involves somebody else entirely, if it's just *not me* any more, then I need to move on and find out who I am when I'm not carrying around all these traces of you.'

Because it wasn't just Rik she had come back to find after all.

'Are you coming back to Hollyhocks?' he asked eventually.

She started. After that? After all that? She was just going to pour her heart out and he was going to give her — nothing?

But she'd put a great deal on him, a huge big deal, and he obviously needed to think, he wasn't saying anything but he wasn't saying no, either.

All I do is wait around for you, he'd told her once. It was her turn to do some of the waiting.

She shook her head. 'I need to pick up my clothes and reassure my parents that I'm still alive and I think we both need to let it sit, for a bit.'

Rik nodded reluctantly. 'Yeah. I suppose you're right. I just can't shift the feeling I'm going to go away and never see you again.'

'Whatever happens,' she said, 'I'll be around. I'll take you to the airport tomorrow — I absolutely insist, OK?'

He nodded obediently.

'And I'll come and pick you up,' she said boldly, 'if you want me to, and I'll never leave your side again. But if you don't want to,' she smiled wistfully. 'We can be friends. And if that's too much we can watch each other's lives even if we're not a part of them. I'm always going to want to know what you're up to. I'm always going to care.'

'I am too,' he said. 'Always.'

'Then that's something.'

'Yes,' he agreed. 'That's something.'

He was wearing another pale blue shirt when Faith picked him up, and she thought he had never looked more beautiful to her. She smiled brightly as he got into the Land Rover.

'Good night?' he asked.

'As ever,' she said, thinking how she'd stared mindlessly at the ceiling until she'd wondered if it actually might begin to cave in. He looked much livelier and Faith felt her heart twisting painfully. 'It's still a shock seeing you clean-shaven,' she said.

'Yeah.' He stroked his chin thoughtfully. 'Didn't go down well all round, that.'

'I quite liked it,' she said absently. 'Got used to it. It grew on me, much like it grew on you.' Also she'd definitely started to wonder what it might feel like against her skin — oh not now, she told herself irritably.

They didn't talk a great deal on the way to the airport and Faith gripped the steering wheel, watching her knuckles turn white, as the Land Rover juddered any time she tried to push it over 40mph. 'I hope I'm not going to make you late,' she said, gunning the accelerator furiously, but the Land Rover squealed in protest she thought if she gave it much more grief it might not get them there at all.

She pulled into drop-off and turned off the engine, which let out an audible sigh of relief.

'Will this thing even get you home?' Rik asked.

She smiled. 'I'll take my chances. Are you OK from here?'

He nodded. 'Thanks for the lift.'

'Just text me,' she said, 'if you want me to come and pick you up. If you think — if we might — just at least think about it, Rik.'

She yearned to lean over and kiss him, thinking she might never get another chance.

'Safe trip,' she said.

'Faith,' he said softly and he reached out and took hold of the back of her head. She drew in her breath and wondered if he actually was going to kiss her but instead he just leaned his forehead against hers, and she blinked once or twice, wondering if she was going to cry.

The second hand on the dashboard clicked noisily forwards.

A horn blared behind them, making them both jump, then an angry-looking driver from the car behind, who was waiting for the drop-off bay, rapped sharply on the window. 'Get on with it,' he roared through the window. 'Go and snog somewhere else. That's what long stay is for.'

'I should go,' Rik said.

She nodded, not trusting herself to speak, and he got out and opened the boot. 'See you soon,' he said, banging on the top of the Land Rover a few times, and the angry driver, who had got back into his car, revved his engine and hooted again. Faith shook her head, trying to clear it, then gunned the Land Rover and pulled away, forcing herself not to watch Rik through the rear-view mirror.

She looked at the speedometer, then the clock on the dashboard. Time ticked by.

Second, after second, after second.

Chapter 27

If this is Hollyhocks without Rik, Faith thought as she shivered beneath another of Helena's old Barbours, watching GT lounging contentedly from the shelter of the greenhouse, then I don't think I like it very much.

It had poured without a break since he left, the sky itself mourning his absence as much as Faith was. All the sunshine and the fun seemed to have melted away, and everything felt heavy and oppressive and impossibly dismal. Paul and the teenagers were in vile moods, soaked and miserable. She was turning into a teenager herself, checking her phone constantly in case Rik had rung or texted her, but she heard nothing.

There were traces of him everywhere, only this time they weren't distant nostalgic memories, they were very much in the here and now. There was constant empty space, the site without him, the cottage devoid of his presence, the house somehow less full and noisy.

She stayed in the cottage, in Minel's old room because she couldn't stand to be in his room by herself. GT moved in with her and kept her company at night, waking her constantly with his demands to be let out to go to the toilet and entertaining her from 3am onwards.

On Wednesday she, Sara and Minel went out for dinner.

'What's going on with Rik?' Sara demanded immediately. 'Did you tell him?'

'I told him everything,' Faith confirmed. 'Including that I still loved him, and said I'd pick him up from the airport if he wanted and never leave his side again.' She took a sip of wine. 'I guess now I just have to see what he makes of it all.'

'Did he say anything when you told him?' Minel asked.

Faith shook her head, feeling deeply despairing, 'I haven't heard anything from him at all.' She looked down sadly.

Sara patted her shoulder comfortingly.

'Anyway, enough about that. What's the latest on you and the T-bone?' Faith asked.

'T-no-bone,' Sara said and they all giggled again. Then her face fell. 'I'm going to have to leave him.'

'Do you think so?' Minel looked more anxious than ever. She doesn't like it, all this uncertainty, Faith thought. She wants to make it better for us all. Mother us out of it. This is practice for her too. She can't fix everything for us, she won't be able to fix everything for the baby she wants so much. She needs to learn to let us make our own mistakes and live our own lives.

'I don't really see what options I have left,' Sara said. 'He won't talk, I've tried every which way I can think of, we just plod along.' She blinked a couple of times. 'I love him,' she said, 'but I can't live like this. I love myself more.'

'It's a bit of a long-shot, but if he realises he's actually going to lose you he might finally address it, whatever it is,' Faith said.

Sara nodded. 'I feel a bit like I'm giving him an ultimatum but I don't see what other choice I have. If he does agree we have to end it,' she said vehemently, 'I am going out and getting laid immediately even if I have to do it with one of those awful teenagers.'

'I am too,' Faith said. 'If Rik doesn't want to. Got to get over him. Get under somebody else.' She giggled sadly.

So we'll all have a resolution one way or another. Sara will either get Tony to talk or she'll go and get some elsewhere; I will either have a chance of a future with Rik or not. Not all of us, she corrected herself, Minel still doesn't have her baby but she's got Paul and they'll keep trying and isn't that proof that life doesn't fit itself into tiny boxes, but that sometimes, you have to get through the hard, complicated, messy, painful stuff and if you have somebody who loves you like Paul loves Minel, or somebody who will cuddle you like Sara and GT cuddle me, you'll get through it.

Faith didn't hear anything from Rik on Thursday either and she supposed she had her answer. At least the sun had made a welcome return, drying the sodden ground and warming her skin and everybody's moods as they toiled away. She'd better pack her things and head home before he got back, just in case he still had Lucinda in tow. Besides, she still needed to talk to her mother.

It feels like the end of the summer holidays, she thought wearily. Back to school. Back to life, back to reality.

Faith texted Judith she'd be home for dinner, before packing up her things from the cottage. If Lucinda was still on the scene she wouldn't like it if she knew Faith had been staying there so she took care to remove all evidence of her presence, throwing out the spare toothbrush she'd used and replacing it with an identical one.

GT watched her mournfully as she locked the door behind her. 'You'll have to go back to the house,' she said.

He whined plaintively, too miserable to even sniff her leg. She looked at the puppy and thought, sod my mother. I need somebody to hold at night.

'Come on then,' she said, scooping him up. He rolled over happily in her arms, exposing his belly in anticipation of a scratch. 'You can come home with me.'

Her mother looked boot-faced as the yapping puppy bounded eagerly into the house, sniffing madly around the kitchen and lifting his leg against the table. 'Stop that!' Faith yelped, grabbing him up and rushing him out to the garden. 'You know perfectly well you go outside.'

'Is that a permanent fixture?' Judith asked, watching GT merrily launch himself at the anemones.

'Yes,' Faith said firmly. 'I'll have to find somewhere to live where they don't mind dogs.'

They made stilted conversation over dinner, then Jeff excused himself to go and watch University Challenge. Judith made a pot of tea and sat down at the table, looking at Faith expectantly.

'What is it?' Faith said suspiciously.

Judith examined the fading floral pattern on her china teacup. 'Your father said he saw you when he was in something of a compromising situation. I assume that, and your absence since then, are related?'

'They are,' Faith confirmed. 'But not exclusively. I've had other things on my mind too.'

'Such as?' her mother asked.

'Such as the realisation that I've been in love with Rik Panesar basically my entire adult life,' Faith said, suddenly feeling despairing and almost unbearably flat. She checked her phone automatically, but there was still nothing. 'Not that it matters,' she sniffed, 'because although he was once most definitely very much in love with me, he doesn't seem to be any more.'

Judith stared down at her teacup. 'I never thought much of him.'

'I noticed.'

'I saw the way he looked at you.'

And mustn't that have frightened you, Faith thought. 'I noticed that too,' she said. 'I'm sure the idea of your daughter discovering boys, and sex,' she ignored her mother's flinch, 'was truly terrifying for you but if not Rik, then just who would you have preferred me to have chosen? Somebody like Dad?'

Judith sighed.

'Somebody I wasn't attracted to?' Faith suggested pleasantly.

'Attraction isn't everything.'

'It's not,' Faith agreed. 'But it helps. I would have thought you of all people would realise that.' She picked up the teapot and poured herself a cup. 'Dad told me your arrangement.'

'Yes.'

'So why didn't you tell me? Last time, when you were thinking of getting divorced. Why didn't you say there was more to it than just Dad being unfaithful for no reason?'

'It's not an easy conversation to have,' Judith said.

'No truly useful conversation is. And it would have been a useful conversation,' she went on, 'because it turns out I have been carrying around some pretty misguided opinions about men, and relationships, and life in general thanks not entirely, but definitely in part, to you.'

'I take medication,' Judith said, 'and it has side effects.'

Faith frowned. She'd never noticed her mother popping pills. 'What kind of medication?' And then suddenly she knew. 'Anti-depressants.'

Her mother nodded and took a sip of tea.

'You had postnatal depression,' Faith said. 'After me.'

So it is my fault, she thought. It was my fault all along and I never even knew.

'I did,' Judith said. 'But also my own upbringing wasn't what you'd call nurturing and I'd certainly had episodes before. And I tried,' she looked at Faith almost imploringly, 'to keep it from affecting you, because I wouldn't change having you for the world, Faith. But I can't deny I found it hard, and your father found it hard, and I tried coming off the medication because I knew it was affecting our marriage, but the thought of being so out of control of my own emotions when I was trying to raise you.' She stopped talking and looked back down at the tea cup.

Faith felt a wave of sympathy for her mother and she touched her hand gently.

'I'm sorry,' Judith said, 'if it did affect you. It can be genetic,' she winced, 'and you're very sensitive and you could be so very emotional at times and I worried that meant you would end up like me.'

'You wanted to protect me,' Faith said.

Judith smiled weakly. 'Instead it looks like I drove you away.' She took another deep breath. 'I was so grateful to you for your company and your support after your father and I nearly split up.'

'I didn't do much,' Faith said automatically, because she hadn't, really. But then also she had. She'd thought all the time and concern she'd devoted to her mother was wasted but if it had helped, even in some small way, then that was something.

'You did more than you know,' Judith said. 'You persuaded me to go to counselling with your father, you encouraged me to try and find a way forwards. You stopped me from running away,' she went on, 'and although I can see the solution we came to is distasteful to you, it's also a compromise and that's what marriage is all about. Compromise.'

Faith wrinkled her nose automatically, but her mother's expression was similar to the one of resigned conviction she'd seen on her father's face after she'd confronted him. She eyed Judith for a moment, wondering if she should say any more, but already she could feel her anger at her mother drifting away.

She probably did think she was doing what was best for me, she admitted, trying to protect me from everything. Wrap me up in cotton wool and hope no harm ever came to me.

Just like I've been doing to myself all these years instead of living life the way I want to.

'I'm not going back to work,' Faith said. 'I'm going back to college to train in horticulture and then I'm going to set up as a garden designer and if it means I have to live in a caravan, or a shed in a garden, then that's what I'll do.'

Judith looked relieved at the change of subject. 'You can stay here as long as you want,' she said.

Faith nodded. 'Thanks,' she said. 'I'll think about it. And I appreciate it,' she added. 'It means a lot. This really is what I've always wanted to do.'

Judith sighed. 'You're old enough to make your own choices, Faith. And if that and Rik really are your choices, then your father and I will support you.'

'That all depends,' Faith said sadly, 'on whether I'm still Rik's choice or not, and right now it's looking depressingly like I'm not.' She stood up. 'I'm off to bed. Busy day tomorrow.'

'Sleep well,' Judith said automatically.

I will, Faith thought, until 3am.

She woke at three on the dot. GT stirred instantly and she reluctantly put on a jumper, knowing he would have to go out to the garden and she had no hope of getting back to sleep after that. She made herself a cup of tea as the puppy busied himself in the garden, then she scooped him up and carried him back to her bedroom.

Should she stay here? She would have to pay rent, but it wouldn't be anything like what it would cost her to rent on the open market and she was pretty sure she could persuade her mother to put up with GT. She noticed a freshly-chewed patch of skirting board and winced.

If she stayed around, she could be there for Sara like her friend had been there for her this summer. They could nurse each other through their heartbreak together.

But if she stayed around here she'd have to get used to Westchester without Rik. She remembered having the same thought at the start of the summer, when Minel had first asked her to come and work at Hollyhocks. Maybe this would be the first step to finally putting him behind him. Maybe now she could look what she'd lost in the eye, she could start to let it all go. And what better place to do it than here, who better to do it with than her best friends?

She picked up her phone, checking it automatically, her eyes sliding away with disappointment, then she stopped and stared. She blinked, and stared again. She had a message.

She opened it, her hands trembling. GT curled himself into her lap supportively.

He had texted her a flight number, the terminal and the time of arrival which was, she squinted, only four hours from now. Early flight. He must be up already. She looked at the time of the message. 3.05am.

And then her heart just exploded in her chest and she thought, he knows. He knows if I really meant it, that I'll be awake now tearing my heart out over him.

Oh Rik, she thought. This time I won't let you down.

'Guess what?' she said to GT, ecstatic. 'I think, I just think, he just might love me after all.'

GT sighed and closed his eyes.

Thank god for my predictable insomnia and GT's diminutive bladder, she thought, and then she texted Rik back quickly

saying she'd see him there. She set an alarm for 5am and shut
her eyes, knowing she would be back asleep almost instantly.

Chapter 28

Faith woke to the shrilling of her alarm, the excited pounding of her heart, and more snuffling from GT. She would drop him off at Hollyhocks before she left, she decided. She couldn't handle a car journey with him leaping about all over the back of the Land Rover yapping and chewing her admittedly already battered upholstery.

She showered and put on the nicest vest and shorts combination she owned, because she still had a bit of gardening to do and she and Rik were going to be late by the time they got back to Hollyhocks.

Oh god, what was she going to say to him? What if she was wrong? What if he was going to tell her he'd thought about it and thanks, but no thanks? They would have to drive home in awkward silence. You and him have got through worse than a car journey in awkward silence, she rallied herself.

She booted GT out and shoved him into the haybarn, knowing he would be whining and scrabbling at the front door within minutes and feeling mildly guilty about waking Minel, but not guilty enough to stay a second longer. The Land Rover was obviously in an obliging mood as she managed to scale the dizzy heights of 60mph on the M25, which she thought must be a personal best.

Despite the early hour, Arrivals was packed with yawning, blinking people milling around and watching for flight numbers. Faith saw that Rik's flight had arrived right on time but there was no sign of him, and she paced around, back and forth until she started to worry she was going to dig a trough with her restless feet.

Travellers were pouring through and Faith heard German accents and assumed they must be from the Hamburg flight, but there was still no sign of Rik and she recommenced her pacing, bobbing her head frantically over the embracing couples and families at the rails in front of her. Oh, where was he?

She checked her messages again. Nothing. She checked the flight number and the terminal for the hundredth time, and still no Rik. It had been forty minutes now. How long should she leave it? What if he hadn't got her reply and assumed she hadn't got his message and thought she was still at home and he'd gone and found a taxi and was on his way to Hollyhocks right now?

Then suddenly she saw him coming towards her. He hadn't shaved since he left and was dressed all in black, and as soon as he noticed her shuffling at the front of the rail his face lit up with that radiant, heart-stopping smile.

'Rikki,' she gasped. 'You're here.'

'I'm here,' he said softly.

She bit her lip and fidgeted, her stomach full to bursting with a tornado of butterflies, her palms clammy, her heart thundering.

'Sorry that took so long,' he said. 'I got stopped at immigration, who seem to have no idea what "racial profiling" means.'

He moved fractionally closer to her and she could feel the heat coming from him, rolling off him in waves, surrounding him like an invisible forcefield.

She should say something. In fact she should have a pithy speech all ready about how she was — about how he was — about how they should — but apparently her brain had disconnected from all rational thought whatsoever and all she could do was gawp at him.

'Oh god,' she gulped. 'You're so hot.'

For christ's sake, she thought. Is that the best you can do?

But it was enough for Rik, who moved forwards again and took hold of her head with both hands, and then finally, *finally*, he kissed her. Faith's eyelashes fluttered closed and her lips trembled under his as recognition rose joyfully within her, flooding her from the tips of her toes to the top of her head.

She seized him right back, kissing him furiously, desperate to get him as close to her as she possibly could. He felt full of that raw, primal energy, his mouth hot and insistent, his tongue dancing over hers in a way that felt vaguely familiar and shockingly new and it was making her head spin, sending blood coursing around her body and roaring in her ears. Her heart had taken off like an express train, hammering against her ribs and his was crashing just as fast in his chest. She could hear his shallow breathing in her ears, and her nostrils were full of the scent of him and her hands were full of him too, curling into his hair, wanting to draw him even closer still. I'm never letting you go, she thought. Not now, not ever.

Rik seemed to want to take in as much of her as he could too, his hands moved from her hair to her shoulders and then down the soft, bare skin of her arms, leaving a trail of goosebumps in their wake. He bit her lip, drawing a sharp gasp from her and a loud retching noise from just behind them.

Faith pulled away and buried her face in Rik's chest, her shoulders shaking helplessly.

'For the love of god,' somebody from the throng behind them said, 'get a room.'

'Yeah we need to go,' Rik said, and Faith, her head still firmly pressed against him, could hear he was giggling madly too. He put his arm around her hustled her swiftly through the airport. 'Where did you park?'

'Short stay.'

They had reached the lift, and he jabbed at the call button repeatedly while Faith put her head against his chest again, too impatient and overwhelmed and bursting at the seams with longing to do anything other than breathe him in. As soon the doors creaked open he pushed her in and kissed her again and she wound her arms around his neck and kissed him back until she could barely breathe. The lift stopped halfway down to the basement and an elderly couple who had been about to get in blanched and stepped back pointedly, and as the doors clanged shut again Faith thought it was just as well because it was all getting very X-rated. He had her pressed right up against the metal wall and she was arching her body up to him in a brazen invitation and there was a great deal of urgent grabbing and muffled gasping going on from both of them.

The lift doors opened into the basement car park.

'Where's the car?' he mumbled against her lips.

She gestured towards the darkened corner where the Land Rover was glowering, looking very much like it would rather not be interrupted.

Rik picked her up and she hitched her legs around his waist, hanging onto him like a monkey so she could kiss him as he carried her across the car park. He put her down on the bonnet of the car and pulled her right up against him and Faith felt a jolt of pure, electric longing shoot all the way through her and she made a strangled sort of groan deep in her throat. Rik put his hand in the pocket of her shorts, running his fingers over the soft skin of her upper thigh before fishing out her keys.

'We need to get in the car,' he said, burying his head in her neck and so he could kiss the delicate skin just above her collarbone, grazing his teeth over it, sending more sparks shooting through her. He edged his hand along as ineptly as a teenager, fumbling the key around the lock while his other hand had slipped underneath her top and was moving far more assuredly over her burning skin, sending all her nerve endings leaping and firing into life. Oh come on, she thought frantically, and finally he managed to get the door open and pulled her into the car and onto his lap.

His eyes were almost completely black as he stared at her.

'Do you think we'll get arrested?' Not that it mattered if they did, because there was no way either of them were stopping now.

'I won't last long enough for us to get arrested,' Rik said. 'Just to manage your expectations.'

She dissolved giggling, clinging on to his shoulders, giddy with euphoria.

'You really haven't changed,' she said. 'Not where it counts.'

They were both silent for a long time afterwards, and Faith curled herself up on Rik's lap and listened to the sound of their breathing and pressed her head into his chest so she could hear his heart beating, and then she closed her eyes and felt him underneath her and his arms around her. He stroked her hair and she wished she could freeze time and stay in this moment with him indefinitely.

'Oh, I missed you,' she sighed eventually. 'I missed everything about you.'

'I missed you too.' He kissed her forehead, which was drenched with sweat.

'That was worth waiting nine years for.'

Rik looked extremely pleased with himself. 'Yeah,' he said. 'That was quite something.' He leaned his head back against the headrest and she knew she hadn't seen anything even remotely approaching the blissful expression on his face all summer.

'I really do love you,' she said.

'I love you too,' he said. 'I don't think I know how not to be in love with you.'

Faith felt her heart pulsing and lifting and soaring, sending an entire fleet of hot air balloons floating all around her body.

'Oh, thank god,' she said fervently. 'I would have understood if you didn't but I am so, so, so glad you do. Did you talk to Lucinda?'

He nodded. 'I actually split up with her at Jason's wedding. Could have picked a better time I suppose, but I needed to be straight with her.'

She was astonished to feel a pang of sympathy for Lucinda. 'I do feel a bit bad for her. She's only human, it's not her fault she fell for you.'

'It wasn't that serious,' Rik said, stroking her hair again. 'She wasn't you. I should have ended it with her the second I saw you on the driveway again.'

'So why didn't you?'

Rik smiled ruefully. 'I was pretty angry with you, and at that time I had no idea you thought I'd cheated on you. I thought the only reason I suddenly couldn't stop thinking about you must be because I hadn't seen you for so long. Emotional memory, timewarp, whatever you want to call it. I didn't want to chuck away another relationship because of you.'

'So you really didn't know?' she asked. 'That I was still in love with you?'

'I knew you wanted to make things right, and that you did seem to have cared about me, back then and now,' he said.

'But let's just say I've been burned before.' He squeezed her absently. 'You really did break my heart.'

'You broke mine too,' she said. 'Unintentionally. God, what a waste, all those years we spent —' the thought made her sad all of a sudden and she tailed off.

Rik was silent too. There's still sadness here, she thought, and loss. But it looks like we're finally on the same page, finally in it together.

'It is a shame,' he said slowly. 'But although at first I was convinced that was completely your fault, I did realise that wasn't true. It was odd the way you literally disappeared straight after that weekend. I should have known there was something else going on.'

'You weren't to know,' she said. 'It was a complete shock to me that my dad was having an affair so there's no way you would have guessed.'

'No,' he agreed, 'but I knew you and I should have realised there was a reason you had just gone to ground. You weren't the only one who was a bit too proud.'

She ran her hands up and down his arms, which fit so perfectly around her. 'I'm so glad, Rik, I was so worried you were going to say it had been too long, or that you really had no interest in me any more.'

He kissed her forehead, then her cheek. 'It's always been you, Faith.'

'You could have told me,' she grumbled. 'At any point over the last week.'

'What, in a text?' He kissed her cheek again, then her lips. 'Not like this?' His lips were warm and soft and utterly irresistible. 'Or this?' Faith sighed as he kissed her again, slowly and deeply, turning the blood in her veins molten hot and all her joints heavy and fluid. His eyes were closed as if he'd surrendered completely to a daydream, either a long-forgotten one or one he'd had just seconds ago.

'OK,' she said shakily when they finally broke apart. 'That is a better way to tell me than by text.'

'We had better stop,' Rik said reluctantly. 'I think we'd be pushing our luck trying to get away with another round.'

She put her head on his chest again and they stayed there a little longer in contented silence until she felt her eyelids becoming heavy. 'We had better head off. This is way beyond the remit of "short stay" and Paul will be foaming at the mouth if we're any later.'

'Can I drive?'

'You want to drive my car?'

He grinned wolfishly. 'I quite like it.'

'I knew you would.'

Paul appeared the second Rik cut the engine, brandishing a trowel in a manner Faith could only describe as threatening. It had rained that morning, a passing shower in preparation for more later on, and the sun was blinking through clusters of greying clouds. The scent of flowers and damp foliage was rising in the air, sweet and fresh and heady.

'What took you so long?' he demanded as they got out of the Land Rover. 'You were supposed to be back ages ago.'

Rik grinned wickedly. 'Just catching up.'

Paul looked at Faith suspiciously and she treated him to a radiant, face-splitting smile. 'Well at least you've cheered her up,' he rumbled. 'She might actually do something about that mud-pit she calls a garden now.'

'I need Rik to come and help me this morning,' Faith announced, 'because it's going to rain later,' she sent up a silent thanks to the ever-unpredictable British summer, 'and I really need to finish up before it does.'

Paul harrumphed. 'All right then. Push off and finish the garden, and whatever else you need to finish.' He looked momentarily amused. 'About time you two got your act together.'

Faith thought she had never had such a perfect day. They hauled up the last of the dandelions and put the final plants in the pond and did all the fiddly little tasks that normally drove her crazy but suddenly seemed impossibly fun and interesting with Rik next to her interrupting her every thirty seconds to kiss her and tell her how much he loved her.

'Why are most of the tools broken?' he asked, eyeing her pile of shame which included several forks, the notorious watering can and more weeding and de-dandelion-ing implements than she cared to count. 'What have you been *doing* to this place?'

She pulled a guilty face. 'I might have been a bit rough once or twice. Especially if Lucinda was around.' She scowled. 'That watering can in particular took a great deal of Lucinda-related punishment.'

Rik giggled.

'It's not funny,' she said. 'She was constantly drivelling on about your sex life, it was awful.'

'God, really?'

'Not explicitly,' she said. 'Just lots of giggling and vague references to your wild weekends of passion.' She pulled a disgusted face.

'We didn't have any,' he said, putting the watering can down. 'Which with hindsight was a pretty big warning sign even before you showed up again.'

Faith felt weak with relief. 'But she's so beautiful. I just assumed you were swinging from the chandeliers on a nightly basis.'

'We were not,' he said firmly, pulling her into his arms. 'We both just tried to pretend it wasn't an issue, then she decided we should make an effort and stop blaming the fact we were both tired from work but by then,' he sighed. 'I couldn't stop thinking about you soaking wet in your see-through vest and while there were teenage levels of raging hormones going on, none of them were to do with her.' He giggled sheepishly. 'There's no way I would have been too tired from work if it was you I was coming back to.' He kissed her quickly.

'Good,' she said, 'Because we have lots of time to make up for.'

Lots of time, and lots of things. Everything, in fact. Everything they had set in motion all those years ago, everything they should have gone on to do, and to be, everything they had been trying to find with somebody else, they now had all that ahead of them. Together.

She gazed at him wordlessly, filled with happiness to her very core. It's really him, she thought. He's really here. Any time I want I can just reach out to him, and time I want to I can just kiss him and tell him I love him, and tomorrow morning I get to wake up with his arms around me.

Rik was looking around the garden. 'Paul was totally off the mark calling this place a mud-pit. It looks amazing.'

It did. The new pond and rockery had settled perfectly, the lawns were grander and more sweeping than before, and although the newer features and juvenile plants still had plenty of room for growth, Faith could already picture how the plants would all come together and spill out and over into each other, forming a riot of colour, height, scent and texture.

'It turned out OK in the end,' she said.

'I knew you'd do a great job.'

She smiled happily. 'You were right. I really can't go back to my old job after this. I'm going to go to college and study garden design instead.'

'Good,' Rik said. 'Plenty of horticultural colleges in Cornwall.'

Faith's heart leaped. 'I haven't looked. Should I?'

'Yes.' He smiled at her and she thought she would follow him anywhere. 'You did say you wouldn't leave my side and I'm taking that extremely literally. And they want me over in Hamburg full-time for at least six months after Christmas so you'll have to crack on with the studying or transfer and do it out there. Do you speak any German?'

She shook her head. 'Not a jot.'

'We'll get you one of those ghastly audios and you can drive me crazy asking me the way to the supermarket.' He giggled. 'We can learn all the dirty words and bark them dictatorially to one another during no doubt extremely quick sex.'

'Are you sure?' she asked anxiously.

He nodded. 'Very sure.'

'Oh,' she said in wonder. 'I can't think of anything I want more, dictatorial sex included. Can GT come too?'

'Yeah,' he said. 'But we'll have to neuter him and get him a passport and he'll have to have lots of horrid jabs.'

'I'll hold his paw,' she said. 'Where shall we go after that?'

'Wherever you want.'

'Oh, I love you,' she sighed. 'I know I keep saying it but it's only because it's true.'

'You can say it all you like,' he said. 'I'm never going to get bored of hearing it. Are we done here?'

'All done.'

'Good,' he said. 'Because I can think of something else I'm never going to get bored of either.'

'I can't believe you're going tomorrow,' Minel said to Faith a week later. 'It feels like you only just got here.'

The sun was setting over Hollyhocks, bathing it in a warm, dusky glow, and abandoned plates were scattered across the already yellowing grass. GT was methodically working his way around all of them, licking up any remains frantically, his tail wagging. Beside him trailed a tiny, adorably silky Springer Spaniel puppy, its floppy ears drooping into the plates as it copied GT's pillaging.

Paul had gone straight out and found the puppy, a female who Minel flatly refused to name Tacklette, that morning and Minel was already hopelessly besotted.

Sara, who was dangling her feet in the swimming pool, shot Faith a forlorn look. 'All those hot surfer dude types,' she grumbled. 'Wasted on you.'

'Wasted,' Faith agreed happily. 'You'll have to come and work your way through them instead.'

Sara rolled her eyes. 'I suppose that'll give me something to do while you and Rik continue your unstoppable sex binge.'

Faith blushed. She had been trying very hard not to appear too hopelessly besotted with Rik in front of Sara, not wanting to highlight her friend's newly-single status with a nonstop PDA. Sara had told Faith and Minel that Tony had accepted her decision without question. 'He just said he was sorry I wasn't happy, that he thought it was for the best, and that was that.'

'You will still come and visit, won't you?' Faith pressed. 'And I'll come back here much more often, I promise.'

'You had better,' Minel wailed. 'I've got used to having you around again. And Rik, and you two are so madly in love and completely perfect for each other it's beyond adorable. Although,' she grimaced, 'the sex binge is a bit off-putting.'

Faith blushed guiltily again. 'It's not like we're doing it in front of you.'

'No,' Minel said, 'but it's fairly tedious getting halfway through a conversation only for you two to find something completely innocuous to get all wound up about and then slope off to the cottage giggling like teenagers. Or the hay barn.' She looked at Faith suspiciously. 'Did you sleep in there last night?'

'It was a full moon,' Faith said. 'You should always sleep out under a full moon.'

'You sounded like a bunch of foxes, screeching away out there all night,' Minel said reprovingly.

'That actually was foxes,' Faith protested.

Sara cackled. 'Yes, I'll come and visit you,' she said. 'Something tells me I'm going to be making quite a few changes over the next few months.'

'We'll be with you every step of the way,' Minel said.

Faith nodded. She knew the next few months were going to be unbelievably difficult for Sara, as she and Tony went through the heartwrenching minutae of their breakup, from deciding what to do about the house to dividing their property to learning to live without one another.

I know she feels heartbroken now, Faith thought, but some day soon she's going to realise she still has her whole life ahead of her. And with it, a whole new chance at happiness, to find herself outside of her relationship, reaffirm her identity free of Tony, discover herself all over again and, hopefully, have a lot of fun along the way.

Rik came over sat down with them. 'Come and sit on my knee,' he said to Faith, pulling her on to his lap. 'You look like a fairy, sitting here in the flowers. This is for you.' He handed her a blazing orange Californian poppy he must have pulled from the patch growing by the side of the hay barn. Faith put it behind her ear and Rik kissed her on the cheek.

'Stop that,' she said. 'Not in front of this lot.'

'Oh, don't bother on our account,' Sara said. She smiled affectionately at both of them. 'I really am happy for you two.'

Paul wandered over. 'Your dog has just been sick,' he informed Minel. 'And *your* dog,' he turned to Faith, 'is eating it.'

'Dogs are revolting.' Faith grimaced as she watched GT devouring the pile. She tore her eyes away from the repulsive spectacle and admired the summerhouse, the quaintly cottagey structure looking just like it had always been there. She had planted two standard fuschias, one on either side of the door, and they were both bursting with their gaudily clashing blooms that so resembled tiny ballerinas.

'So are you all set?' Paul asked. 'Ready for your big adventure?'

'All set,' Rik affirmed. 'Well, we still need to find somewhere to live. We're going to stay in a hostel until we do.' He kissed the top of Faith's head.

'I pity the other residents,' Paul said. 'And if you're this bad as grown adults I think we can all be grateful we were spared this when we were teenagers.'

'I really can't believe none of us guessed what was going on with you two,' Minel exclaimed.

Paul puffed his chest out proudly. 'Some of us did,' he said.

'It's true,' Faith confirmed.

'How did you know?' Minel demanded.

'Because I've got eyes,' Paul said. 'How did you not know?'

'Because it's disgusting,' Minel wailed. 'My best friend and my brother. It's the biggest cliché going.'

'Everybody loves a cliché,' Rik said.

'And a happy ending,' Faith added. She watched Paul and Minel as they launched into a round of good-natured bickering, and then her eyes moved to Sara, who was chipping in now and again to entertain herself.

'Only this isn't the ending,' Rik said to her softly. 'It's just the beginning.'

The sun blazed its last and slipped gracefully below the horizon, and Hollyhocks was plunged into soft, fragrant darkness. The summerhouse stood, sleeping peacefully, its sand-coloured stones barely lighter than the shadows that surrounded it. The ground sighed, and an earthy kind of magic rose into the air, sent away on the day's last breeze and carried by the departing rays of the sun, on a slightly higher frequency, just out of reach, on its way to who knew where.

Epilogue

Hollyhocks looked distinctly less sleepy this August, despite the blazing mid-afternoon sun, as Rik flung the protesting Land Rover down the gravel drive. It hadn't moved much in the last year, other than for them to collect it from Faith's mother's house and drive it here, and it had clearly decided it was set in for the long haul and was outraged at having to do any actual work again. Faith had been surprised it even started.

They bounced over a pothole, and she winced as her head made contact with the roof once again.

'Sorry,' Rik said, pulling over to the side of the drive so the car could come to a grateful halt. 'Paul needs to sort this drive out.'

Faith got out of the car and put her arm around his shoulders. The faint waft of the sweet peas she had planted against the wall of the summerhouse drifted over in a heady wave. The Virginia creeper had really taken hold, she noted with pleasure, and the dark green foliage was already tinted with that distinctive gaudy crimson. In a few weeks time it would be a blazing carpet of red, slowly but surely obscuring the sand-coloured wall.

GT leaped out of the car too, sniffing at the air and then looking hopefully up at Faith.

'Off you go,' she told him. 'Just don't maul anybody.'

Minel had hung bunting and streamers around the summerhouse and Faith was touched when she noticed she had matched the colours exactly to her borders, which were spilling over with dusky pinks and ivory whites, cornflower blues and vivid scarlet, sunshine yellow and sunset orange, all interspersed with every shade of green. The surface of the pond was broken in places by the boatlike leaves of water lilies and the occasional showy white flower. Cheerful yellow water irises clustered at one end. Faith could see flashes of orange darting and drifting underneath the greenish-brown water. 'Your parents got fish,' she said to Rik.

Throngs of people were milling over the lawn and into the summerhouse, which Minel had also hung with fairy lights ready to put on later when the light faded.

'There you are!' Minel had spotted them and detached herself from the crowd, her faithful Springer Melody tailing at her heels.

Faith hugged her gently, trying to avoid pushing against her friend's vast, straining belly. 'Jesus,' she said. 'Are you sure you're not having twins?'

'I'm sure,' Minel beamed. 'There's definitely only one in there.'

'You must be ready to pop any day now,' Rik said. 'How are you holding up?'

'Exhausted,' Minel said. 'Shambling, emotional, swinging from angry to happy to excited to terrified to exhausted in the blink of an eye. I can't wait for him to arrive,' she said longingly, 'just to put me out of my misery. I have loved every second of being pregnant but I have had enough now.'

'Can I feel?' Faith put her hands on Minel's bump and felt a firm movement beneath the skin. 'Oh,' she said, delighted. 'I felt him kick.'

'I think Mum was really hoping he'd be here by now, so she could show him off to everybody,' Minel said. 'I hope I don't go into labour during the speeches.'

'I hope you do,' Rik said, 'so we don't have to listen to Dad waffling on for hours on end.'

Paul had spotted them and came over too. 'How was Germany?' he demanded.

'Sehr gut,' Faith said.

He rolled his eyes. 'What's that when it's at home?'

'It means very good. Very clean and efficient. Lots of lovely gardens and no chewing gum on the pavements.'

Sara, who was talking to Helena and Ravi, caught sight of them and squeaked. 'We'd better go over,' Rik said. They all began walking across the lawn, and Faith looked around for GT. He was sniffing Melody's backside hopefully.

'You have neutered him?' Minel asked anxiously, and Faith nodded. 'Don't worry. He's firing blankety blanks.'

Sara embraced Faith delightedly. 'How long are you back for? I've got loads to tell you.'

Minel burst into noisy tears.

'Oh, there she goes again,' Paul said. 'Waterworks.' He manoeuvred Minel against his chest protectively.

'I'm just so happy to have us all back together,' Minel sobbed. She looked at Faith imploringly. 'You are sticking around until the baby comes, aren't you? You'll at least meet him before you jet off somewhere else on another adventure?'

'We're sticking around,' Rik confirmed. 'At least until —' he stopped abruptly.

'Until what?' Sara, sensing intrigue, demanded.

'Until the baby comes,' Rik said, but he was shifting from foot to foot in a distinctly agitated manner.

Faith shot him a questioning look. 'What's up, Rikki?' she asked. 'Why are you fidgeting around like you're all excited about something?'

'I'm not,' he insisted. 'I'm just excited about becoming an uncle.'

'Hmm.' She narrowed her eyes.

323

'Rik,' Helena said quickly. 'I have to finish getting ready before the ceremony and I need your help getting something down from the loft. Would you come over to the house with me? You stay here,' she beamed at Faith, 'and catch up with this lot. We'll see you later.'

Faith watched Rik put his arm companionably around his mother's shoulders and steer her off in the direction of the house. He was definitely all worked up about something, bouncing a little on his toes as he walked. He really is sexy when he's excited, she thought dreamily. Maybe he was planning on making a speech for his parents. That would be sweet, she decided, and very thoughtful of him.

Helena and Ravi had been so ecstatic with the summerhouse they'd immediately announced they wanted to throw a party, and that had led to the idea of them renewing their wedding vows. 'Thirty-five years,' Faith said to Sara. 'Can you imagine? That's longer than we've been alive.'

'Just about, in my case,' Sara deadpanned.

'Oof.' Minel grabbed at her stomach and buckled a little.

Paul seized her shoulders anxiously. 'Min!'

'It's OK,' she said weakly, waving her hand. 'Just a kick. Quite a kick. He's strong,' she said to Paul. 'It shakes all my organs when he moves. He's going to be just like you.'

More guests were arriving. Faith saw her mother and father approaching. They were holding hands, she realised with surprise. Judith had seemed quite upbeat and cheerful when Faith had seen her earlier. Maybe she's getting some more help, Faith thought hopefully. Changed her medication, or talked to somebody, or even just opened up a bit more to my father instead of shutting him out. She wasn't going to push and she doubted Judith would tell her, but she smiled warmly at her parents as they came to join the group.

'You left this.' Judith passed Faith a notebook.

It was her and Rik's gift to Helena and Ravi, the new and completed version of their notes and illustrations of all the plant and animal life hosted by Hollyhocks. They had sent it to be copied, bound and laminated to give to his parents on their anniversary. A labour of true love, Faith thought happily, entirely valueless and worth more than gold, to her and Rik and she knew it would be to Helena and Ravi too. They had made several copies, one for Paul and Minel to pass down to their son along with the estate he would one day inherit, and a few for themselves and whoever they might eventually end up passing them, and their share of Hollyhocks, to.

'I hope you don't mind,' Judith said, 'but I couldn't resist having a peek.'

'Of course not,' Faith said. 'I'd have showed it to you if Rik hadn't been in such a tearing rush about something.'

'He did seem a bit distracted,' Judith said. 'Your father and I both had a look and we thought it was absolutely beautiful.' She smiled. 'You and Rik are very talented.'

'That's the second version,' Faith said. 'The new, improved one. The first version was created when we were teenagers, and it had all the features from the original garden at Hollyhocks. I really wish I'd kept it.'

'Is that what you were doing with all that time you spent here?' Judith asked, looking slightly shamefaced. 'I just assumed you were up to no good.'

'There was a fair bit of that too,' Faith admitted and her mother looked startled.

Rik had returned. 'Hi Judith. You've had your hair done, it looks great.'

Judith touched her hair and smiled again.

'Come with me a minute,' he said to Faith, taking her hand. 'I've got something to show you.'

'The ceremony will be starting soon,' she protested.

'Mum's trying to shoehorn herself into her original wedding dress, it'll take hours,' he giggled. 'We've got time. I really want you to see this.'

Rik tugged at Faith's hand and she followed him obediently towards the drive. He must have left something in the car, she thought, but instead he took her to the hay barn, whose gleaming new red doors moved aside easily. He turned on the light, and it flickered a few times then illuminated the empty stalls, the rusting machinery and the stack of bales at the back.

'After the drive,' she said, 'this needs to be our next project. We should clear out all that metal before little Tackle Junior is crawling so he can't come in here and injure himself on it.'

'Minel's adamant they're not calling him Tackle Junior,' Rik said. 'The bales need to go too. I think they're still the same ones from Minel's 18th.'

'And the same ones you and I first did the nasty on,' she said.

'Nothing nasty about that,' he said, drawing her to him and kissing her. 'Not then, not now, not ever.'

'You do seem agitated,' she mused, noting the tension in his body. 'Are you sure you don't want to get not at all nasty right now to calm you down?' She kissed him again.

'I always want to do that,' Rik said. 'But I have something for you first.' He dug around in his pocket, and pulled something out. 'This is for you.'

She took it from him. It was a ring, a vintage rose-gold band with a circular yellow diamond in the centre and clear oval-shaped diamonds arranged around it like petals.

'That's your mum's old engagement ring,' she said in surprise, remembering all the times she'd admired it on Helena's finger and said it reminded her of a daisy.

'It is,' he confirmed. 'Do you like it?'

'I love it,' she said. 'I always loved it. Doesn't she want it any more?'

'Dad got her a new engagement ring and she asked me if I'd like to give this one to you as she knew how much you liked it,' he said. 'See if it fits.'

She moved to slide it onto the ring finger on her right hand, and Rik stopped her.

'The other hand,' he said softly.

His eyes were very black in the dull yet garish light of the hay barn. Faith gulped.

'I love you, Faith,' he said. 'More than ever, every day. I want to spend my life with you, fill this place with rowdy children and grow old and push zimmer frames around the quarry with you.'

'I love you too,' she said, choked.

He smiled. 'Shall we get married?'

He made it sound like an adventure and she thought yes, that's how it should be, an adventure.

That's what he and I do.

'Yes,' she said. 'Let's get married.'

He took the ring from her and put it on the third finger of her left hand. 'I measured your finger while you were asleep,' he giggled, 'actually you woke up and I blamed GT for disturbing you. I asked my mum to get it resized so it should fit.' It slid over her knuckle and rested at the base of her finger like it had been made just for her.

'I love it,' she said, staring down at her hand in wonder. 'And I love you. I can't wait to marry you.'

327

'I can't either,' Rik said. 'Let's not have a long and torturous engagement.'

'Is this what you were all agitated about?' she asked.

He nodded. 'I've been planning on asking you for a while, but considering you famously dumped the last guy that proposed to you, I wanted to make sure I did it right. You obviously didn't go for the identikit engagement ring and the asking your father for your hand and getting down on one knee in front of all your friends.'

Faith's heart melted. 'Rikki, you could have proposed to me via my father with a rusty old curtain ring while we were both face-down in the bottom of that pond surrounded by the entire village and I would have still said yes. It wasn't the circumstances,' she said. 'It was the person. It was always going to be you.'

'I know,' he said cockily and she giggled.

'You didn't,' she countered. 'If you were actually nervous about it.'

She looked down at the ring again. It really did look like a tiny, glimmering daisy, nestled on her finger. I won't be able to wear it for work, she thought. I'll get it covered in mud and filth and general detritus. She had finished her course out in Germany and had already made a few calls locally to prospective clients.

'I thought it should be here,' Rik said. 'Not in the pond, obviously, but somewhere that meant something to both of us.' His eyes were doe-like and soulful, windows to the soul, Faith thought. They really are in his case. 'It wasn't that I was nervous you would say no,' he went on, 'I wasn't nervous at all, actually. Just excited. Excited about spending my life with you.'

'I am too,' she said. 'I still can't believe I get to spend my life with my best friend.'

'Don't let Minel hear you say that,' he said. 'She's still adamant you were her friend first.'

'She's going to want to plan it all for us,' Faith warned. 'And my mother. They'll be unbearable, the pair of them.'

Rik giggled. 'Hopefully Min will be too distracted by the baby. We can keep your mother in line.'

'She'll want us to have it at the church,' Faith sighed.

'It's up to you.'

'Up to us,' she corrected.

He took her hand. 'Come on, let's go and tell everybody.'

'Your parents won't think we're stealing their thunder, will they?' she asked anxiously. 'We can wait a day or two.'

'No need to wait,' Rik said. 'They'll be made up — my mum knows, obviously, because of the ring, and she's over the moon. Although she said that as I wasn't buying you one I should give you something else. What would you like?'

She thought for a moment. 'You can get me a new bike if you like. Mine is falling to pieces.'

'Done. Now let's go and tell everybody before Minel drops that sprog and steals *our* thunder.'

He pulled her into his arms and kissed her.

In the distance, a lawn mower fired. A gust of gentle, high summer breeze drifted in through the open doors, bringing with it some stray dandelion seeds it had picked up on its way. The tarpaulin on the half-covered stack of bales rustled faintly and a few minute dust particles from the hay rose up into the air and joined the dandelion seeds in floating around them, spinning and twirling then, just before they dropped to the floor, hanging suspended around them, iridescent as they caught the glow from the light above, illuminated like tiny specks of stardust.

A NOTE TO THE READER

Dear Reader

If you've made it this far, firstly I want to say a huge thank you for reading! I really hope you enjoyed *Summer At Hollyhock House*. It's been such a pleasure to share with you the adventures of the gang at Hollyhocks and I hope you adored them all as much as I did.

The characters in this book aren't based on real people, but they have been informed and inspired by many I have met along the way while navigating my own journey. In particular I wanted to take a moment to pay tribute to somebody who was part of my inspiration for the character of Rik. Like Faith and the gang I grew up in a small village in the heart of the countryside, where everybody knew everybody. It was overwhelmingly, exceptionally white. Other than one of my friends, a boy I attended primary and then secondary school with.

I met Chris Lowe when we were both five. At that age the fact he was mixed-race was a non-issue. Race remained a non-issue for me, a white girl growing up in a white world. Chris's experience was very different. I can't speak for him, I can only speak for what I witnessed of him. When I was creating the character of Rik, I was thinking about boys I knew during my formative years, and wondering what defined the boys you wanted to cross that line with, to go from friends to something more? And the first person I thought of Chris, because all the girls wanted to cross that line with him. His race was a factor, one of the reasons he stood out, an obvious physical differentiator along with his beauty, and his charisma. But what really defined him wasn't the colour of his skin, it was his ownership of it. He had the courage to wear dreadlocks to school at the age of 13 – a school with a population of 1,000 white kids, and just a handful from any other ethnic origin. For a teenage boy, let alone a teenage boy who is visibly and notably different, he had an incredibly developed sense of self, an unshakeable confidence and knowledge of who he was. He was the leader, the most iconic to all of us, he was the coolest, the edgiest, at times the naughtiest, but he was always the boy we all wanted to be around. He had a wicked – in both senses - personality and a beautiful soul.

I'm writing about Chris in the past tense because he tragically died at the age of nineteen. It's been nearly twenty years since he left. I still remember him, the very essence of who he was, like it was yesterday. Once or twice I have dreamed about him and he's unchanged. He will forever be a teenage boy to me. Part of him is truly frozen in time.

The character of Rik isn't based on Chris and his racial heritage is different, but some of his individuality, his differentiating characteristics, were inspired by the Chris that I knew. As was one particularly entertaining scene between Rik and Faith – but not one that made the final cut. You can thank my wonderful editor Amy Durant for sparing you that.

If you enjoyed Summer At Hollyhock House, I'd love it if you left a review on **Amazon or Goodreads**, so others can find the book and enjoy it too. I'd also love it if you came and chatted with me on **Instagram** or **Twitter** – I'm @CathyBussey on both – or dropped by my website **www.cathybussey.com**. I adore hearing from people who have read my books. You're my greatest inspiration, and I hope to be entertaining you with gorgeous happily-ever-afters set in the magical English countryside for many years to come.

With love, Cathy x

Sapere Books is an exciting new publisher of brilliant fiction and popular history.

To find out more about our latest releases and our monthly bargain books visit our website:
saperebooks.com

35010623R00195

Printed in Great Britain
by Amazon